Molly Hopkins worked as a tour guide on the European coach circuit for over fifteen years. She visited many fabulous destinations, always with no fewer than forty people in tow. She now lives in a picturesque village in Middlesex. *It Happened in Venice* is her second novel.

Also by Molly Hopkins

It Happened in Paris

It happened in
Venice

Molly Hopkins

sphere

SPHERE

First published in Great Britain in 2012 by Sphere

Copyright © Lynnette Hopkins 2012

The moral right of the author has been asserted.

*All characters and events in this publication, other than those
clearly in the public domain, are fictitious and any resemblance
to real persons, living or dead, is purely coincidental.*

A CIP catalogue record for this book
is available from the British Library.

ISBN 978-0-7515-4464-0

Typeset in Bembo by M Rules
Printed and bound in Great Britain by
Clays Ltd, St Ives plc

Papers used by Sphere are from well-managed forests
and other responsible sources.

MIX
Paper from
responsible sources
FSC
www.fsc.org   FSC® C104740

Sphere
An imprint of
Little, Brown Book Group
100 Victoria Embankment
London EC4Y 0DY

An Hachette UK Company
www.hachette.co.uk

www.littlebrown.co.uk

For my dad, Phillip Moffat.
We miss you every day.

Acknowledgements

Thank you to *everyone* at Little, Brown, especially my brilliant editors Rebecca Saunders and Manpreet Grewal, who are both show-offy clever and have *amazing* ideas that I always wish I had thought of myself.

Thank you to my sister, Pauline, and her husband, Graeme, who gave me food, accommodation and lots of white wine while I had the builders at home and was editing this book. And also to my friends Annmarie Gildea, whose knowledge of men is on a global scale, and Sue Besser, my editor/critic/posh lunch companion.

I would also like to thank my daughter Elise, and her friends Holly, Melissa, Heather, Kirsten, Meg, Freya, Alice and Amy, for dumping their boyfriends on a regular basis, and telling me all about it. They are an inspiration, offering me a constant supply of debauchery-fuelled information. And finally a big thank you to my son Jack and his girlfriend Hayley, who out of desperation and the fear of starvation learned to cook, because when I'm writing I can do nothing else.

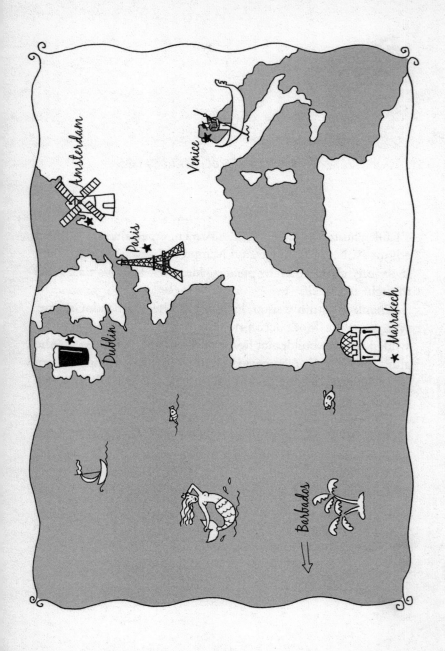

Amsterdam

Venice

Paris

Dublin

Marrakech

Barbados

Chapter One

OK, he cheated on me but he couldn't be sorrier, and it was *only once*.

Sitting beside Rob on the flight from London to Barbados, I pondered the amazing U-turn my life had taken over the past ten days. Rob and I were back together, after a separation of two long months.

I gave him an adoring look and nuzzled my head in the crook of his neck. He smiled, wrapped his ankles around mine and tucked my legs behind his. We've made a pact. We're going to move forward and put the whole sordid episode behind us. I am *not* going to ruin the rest of our lives because of one silly mistake on his part; a mistake that I know will never be repeated. And I won't be rubbing his face in it, because I want this relationship to work. And it *will* work because I love him. So I won't mention his silly little indiscretion, ever. It's in the past. I've forgiven him completely because I'm a forgiving person with a forgiving nature. There is no room for grudges in this relationship. We're engaged and I have a whopping diamond ring to prove it. I rubbed my cheek against his shoulder and snuggled in to enjoy the rest of the flight.

*

The hotel was amazing. It was a fabulous vanilla-coloured wooden affair flanked by palm trees and a kaleidoscope of tropical flowers. I stepped out of the taxi, clasped my hands to my heart and gasped in awe. I stared in silent wonder as a turtle edged its way through the shrubs. I was about to bend down to have a chat with it, when Rob gripped my arm and whizzed me through the oak-floored, lavishly decorated lobby towards the reception desk.

I spotted a glass display cabinet full of handbags.

Rob followed my gaze without breaking his marathon pace. 'You *don't* need any more handbags,' he said stiffly.

'I'm only looking,' I shot back. 'But you're wrong. I don't have a purple bag.'

We halted at the reception desk. He slid a menacing look at my new red Louis Vuitton Monogram Vernis bag, which I'd bought just before Christmas.

'I *cannot* believe how much you paid for that bloody bag,' he said. 'What were you thinking?'

I'm instantly rattled, because this is a *major* sore point.

I clutched the bag protectively to my chest. 'It was cheaper than therapy and better for me than Valium. What was I supposed to do? I was depressed. You'd gone off shagging around behind my back and if it hadn't been for that, I wouldn't have been in the position where I needed to buy the bag, would I? It was *your* fault!'

A crimson stain soaked his cheeks, as well it might.

'I could've ended up a Prozac addict,' I told him bitterly. 'Or a manic-depressive, or addicted to gin or self-help websites. Anything could've happened to me. More to the point, what were *you* thinking?'

He exhaled an infuriated sigh. The cheek of him! I thought. I'm the one with the axe to grind. I'm the one making all the allowances here.

'You promised me that you wouldn't mention that again,' he said, measuring *every single* word.

I spread my arms wide. 'I've hardly mentioned it at all. In the past week, I've only brought it up eleven times,' I told him factually.

'Exactly!'

'Am I just supposed to roll over and accept the fact that you are a harlot and I have a love rival? Am I?'

Quick as a flash, Rob's hand shot out and he grabbed my Lipsy waistcoat. He drew my face towards him and gave me a long, hard, lip-bruising kiss.

The receptionist coughed – *ahem* – into her fist.

He raised me on to my tiptoes by my collar. The kiss lingered for a bit and then he ran his tongue around my lips.

'Evie, if you *ever* mention that singular moment of madness on my part again, for which I am eternally sorry, I'll pin you to the floor and pluck your eyebrows until they're non-existent.'

There was a beat of silence. Blue eyes held my gaze.

'You'd look like an eejit without eyebrows,' he said with a shoulder-shaking chuckle.

'You're choking me.'

'I'm not choking you but I admit I'm sorely tempted. So have we reached an understanding?' he asked, giving me another kiss. 'You agreed to put it behind us and you promised never to throw it in my face.'

I gave a noncommittal shrug, privately regretting having been so amiable.

'A promise is a promise,' he said dolefully, tracing my cheeks with his thumbs.

I gave a congenial nod.

'Truce?' he asked, cupping my face in his palm.

I sighed and blinked a yes.

He kissed my forehead and then turned to the receptionist who pushed the registration card in front of him. I quickly turned and took a picture of the display cabinet on my phone. I would check out the handbags later if I had time.

We've now been blissfully cohabiting in a luxurious beachfront villa on this beautiful island for eight glorious days. In that time Rob and I have encountered only two other human beings. There was a maid who Rob catapulted from the room when her lips quivered suspiciously, as though she might've been about to strike up a conversation, and there's the waiter who delivers our room service meals. Rob said he wanted me all to himself and I'm more than happy to comply with that sentiment.

Robert Harrison is the love of my life, my *raison d'être*. An invisible cord draws me to him, heart and soul. This randy handsome Adonis is my destiny, of that I am absolutely positive. I simply cannot get enough of him. Every nerve ending in my body tingles and jives when he puts his arms around me and a cascading torrent of excitement erupts and percolates in my chest when he kisses me, leaving me breathless. My obsession with him is both physical and psychosomatic. I'm driven by and demented with lust. I've been behaving like a sex-crazed lunatic, even waking in the middle of the night with this fierce ache in my groin that only he can satisfy. My fiancé, Robert Harrison, doesn't have a normal willie like other blokes. Robert Harrison has a bloody magic wand.

This obsession of mine is showing no signs of waning, which frankly has me worried because I'm exhausted and I don't feel very well. I have a vicious throbbing in my tummy as though I've done two hundred sit-ups. OK, I've never actually done a sit-up, so perhaps a more appropriate metaphor would be to say that I feel like I've had my appendix removed.

My lips are bruised and I've ruptured a muscle, which I never knew I had, in my inner thigh, the result being that I now have a limp. I'm dragging my left leg around as though it had a club foot. And as for my hair, I can hardly bear to look at it. Sweat and friction damage have morphed my long shiny brown extensions in to a frizzy matted beehive. In short, I look like a hairy goblin.

This cannot go on, so this morning I showered, straightened my hair, put on my white bikini with a matching sarong and a wraparound top, and accessorised with silver bling. I'm going to wake Rob up and *insist* we go out. I will not be swayed. I'm resolute and determined. I whizzed some Glam Shine around my lips and peered in the mirror. I looked quite normal, not like the haunted, sunken-eyed tart who woke up an hour ago. I've also got a tan because a fair bit of our shagathon has taken place on our stretch of private beach. I stood at the foot of our four-poster canopied bed and nipped Rob's toe.

'Get up.'

He blinked like a drowsy bull and curved an arm above his head. 'Why?'

'Because I want to do something different!'

He sat up slowly. The sheet fell around his waist and he wore nothing but a lazy smile. 'You do?'

His face shone with the promise of possibility, his eyes were pooled and glazed and his smile beatific. He looked like he'd seen an apparition of the Blessed Virgin or the Angel Gabriel. Obviously he thought I was talking about sex.

He Mexican-waved the sheet and looked below for signs of life. His already wide smile grew wider. 'I'm game,' he boasted, 'to do something different.'

I snorted inwardly. 'I want to go out.'

'Out? You mean, out on to our terrace?'

5

I crossed my arms defiantly and jerked my chin at the open window. 'No, I mean out to the hotel pool or the beach bar.'

He lifted his eyebrows. 'Why?'

'I want to meet other people. You know, do that holiday thing where we get chatting to someone and they ask where we're from. I'll say, "London," and they'll say, "Oh, my sister lives in London. Perhaps you know her? Her name is Mary Lewis, she lives in Staines." And I'll scrunch up my face and pretend to think hard, and then say, "No, I don't think I do," and they'll say, "Never mind," and then we'll strike up a conversation and maybe have a drink and—'

'Evie, shut up and get back in this bed.'

I held up the flat of my hand. 'No.'

He threw back the sheet and padded, naked, towards me.

'Rob, a shag is off-limits. Tonight perhaps,' I said, in my ward sister voice, 'but not now!'

He flashed me a manic smile.

'I don't want my holiday filled with raunch and porn and precious little else.'

He loomed above me. 'I do,' he said, lifting a long strand of hair and tucking it behind my ear.

He held my shoulders and bent his blond head to mine. His tongue tickled my forehead, then slowly travelled the length of my cheek. He stopped briefly to nibble the lobe of my ear before exploring my neck and hairline. My groin flashed on super-high alert, my spine stretched and my back arched, pushing my pelvis towards his.

'That's a shame . . .' he whispered, his voice warm on my cheek.

I felt a rush of excitement. He slipped his thumb inside my bikini bottom and did that fantastic little cartwheely thing he does that activates my lust-bubble trip switch.

'Because I was going to spoil you . . .'

My eyes followed the hum of the ceiling fan in contemplative diversion.

'But you might not be interested . . .' he said.

The problem was that my mind and my erogenous zones had completely different principles.

'Really spoil you,' he said, rugby tackling me to the bed.

I wriggled free and pointed a stern finger. 'Right, Rob, I'm telling you and I mean it; a quickie as a favour to you. And then we're out of here,' I said primly.

The view was breathtaking. Turquoise, choppy white-capped waves lapped the beach, stretching as far as the eye could see. In the distance the deep, blue calm of the ocean merged with an azure sky, forming a line of indigo where both met. It wasn't yet nine o'clock, but already the sun was high. I halted, and tilted my face towards a welcoming patchy breeze.

'We should've come here before now,' I told Rob with a wistful sigh.

'Why? This beach is exactly the same as our beach.'

I felt a flicker of irritation; he'd said that without even glancing at the ocean. I trudged past him through the sand towards the beach bar. I could see the sunbed flunkey sleeping on one of the loungers that he was supposed to be distributing to guests, like me.

I gave the flunkey a gentle prod on the arm. 'O-l-a!' I punctuated loudly. 'Ola! Ola!'

'Ola?' Rob echoed. 'What language is that, if you don't mind me asking?'

I tossed him a backward glance. He rocked on his heels and dug his hands into the pockets of his linen shorts.

'Is it the local dialect?' he asked, arching his brows in question.

'I am trying to wake him up. The beds are locked and linked with a chain, it's not as though we can help ourselves. I simply refuse to lie on the sand,' I told Rob. 'It makes me itch.'

'We could go back to our villa, and—'

I cut him off. 'No! We're out and we're staying out.' I turned and gave the beach attendant another jab in the arm. 'Ola!' I tried again.

'Evie, I'm not convinced that this is your man.'

I wheeled round. 'What do you mean, not my man? I don't see anyone else around here, do you?' I asked, gesturing around the beach.

Rob pushed his sunglasses to the top of his head; smiling denim-blue eyes teased mine.

'No, I don't see anyone else either, but still, I'm fairly positive that this is a case of mistaken identity,' he said, rooting at the sand with his big toe.

'Oh really? So in your esteemed view, this person looking after the sunbeds could not possibly be the sunbed attendant?'

'I think it's highly unlikely.'

'Why?'

'This guy is wearing a pair of chinos, a long-sleeved shirt and a black waistcoat. He's also cradling an empty bottle of vodka. I suspect he's drunk and on his way home from a blinding night out. I *don't think* he's the sunbed attendant you're looking for.'

I heaved my beach bag on to my shoulder. OK. He had a point.

'Fine, we'll lie on our towels. It's no big deal.' I said.

I fidgeted miserably on a towel on the sand for over an hour. This was supposed to be a five-star hotel, and I had sand riding uncomfortably up my backside. What was going on? I'd a good mind to complain to the management. In fact, I'm definitely complaining. In fairness, I didn't have to prompt Rob to sort the beds out; he sauntered over to the bar as soon as the beach attendant arrived with a key for the padlock.

I arranged myself on the bed, out of Rob's shadow, and slipped the straps of my bikini over my shoulders. I didn't want white lines. I took my magazine out of my beach bag. This was the life.

'Evie, why must I use the blue bottle of suntan lotion and not the yellow? Is it his and hers?' Rob asked.

I lifted my eyes from my magazine.

'No, it's Superdrug for you and Clarins for me,' I told him, flicking through the pages of *Vogue*.

'Right,' he said with a bewildered nod.

I gave a weary sigh and frisbeed my magazine under my sunbed; I'd seen all the pictures. To be honest, I find sunbathing boring. Well, it is, isn't it? The ocean view was *absolutely* breathtaking. The glimmering reflection of the sun skimming the shifting waves drew me to it; I had to get out there, I had to.

'Shall we take a pedalo out?' I suggested, seized by a flash of adventure.

Rob relaxed back on his elbows and gave me a lazy smile.

'Sure, but you have to do your fair share of the pedalling,' he warned.

'Of course I will,' I told him.

Why did he think I wanted to go on a pedalo if not to pedal? Does he think I'm stupid?

'Pedalling is the *whole point* of going on the boat, everyone knows that,' I said, gripped with enthusiasm.

The thing is, pedalos look much more fun than they actually are. I mean, I'm now pedalling and wondering, *what is the point?* We have no destination, I'm thirsty and now that I think of it, I'm quite hungry. Still, we've only hired the boat for an hour. That's no time at all.

I trundled the pedals; they were quite noisy.

'How long have we been pedalling?' I asked Rob conversationally, not that I was bored or anything, I was merely curious. After all, this had been my idea.

He eyed his watch. 'Four minutes.'

I gave him an incredulous stare. Had it *really* only been four minutes? I put my hands squarely on my knees.

OK, I admit I was surprised. I thought we'd been pedalling for half an hour or so because my thighs were beginning to sting. My legs crunched on. I quickly turned around. The shore was quite far away. In fact, I couldn't see our beds. I stole a glance at Rob; the sun flickered and twinkled on his sunglasses as he titled his head and slowly circled his neck. He had both hands on the steering wheel. Was that necessary? The only direction is straight on, surely! What's to steer? Bloody hell, my legs were going like the clappers. What's the rush? Are we being chased? Are we fleeing from pirates?

'There is *no need* for you to pedal so quickly! I have to keep to the same pace and your legs are longer than mine, and so obviously I'm working much harder than you!' I snapped.

He really was making this quite unpleasant.

'Don't be ridiculous! The length of your legs has nothing to do with how hard you work; you're covering exactly the same rotations as I am.'

I pedalled on.

The same rotations!?

Listen to him talking as though this was some sort of military manoeuvre, some sort of amphibious naval operation. I was beginning to sweat. Actually I was sweating quite a lot. I looked sideways. Rob's arms were now folded across his chest. He looked . . . *relaxed*, even though his legs were pumping. My fingers, which were gripping the plastic seat, were clenched into a white-knuckled knot because my thighs were absolutely blazing and my tummy muscles were beginning to contract. This was like a bloody spinning class. Not that I've ever been to one, but I've watched a spinning DVD. I would take a break, I decided. I lifted my feet off the pedals. You have to listen to your body when you're working out, everyone knows that. I inhaled deeply and breathed out slowly, leaned back and stretched my legs. I was almost horizontal. It felt good, it felt really good.

'HAVE YOU STOPPED PEDALLING!?'

I shot upright in shock, and while my feet scrambled manically for the pedals my backside nearly fell off the seat.

'Of course not!'

'Well, it felt suspiciously like it. The tension shifted down a gear,' Rob said sharply.

I trudged on.

Tension? Gear? *What is he talking about?* This was a plastic dinghy, not a friggin' seaplane or a flying boat! I pushed my damp hair from my forehead. Rob takes things far too seriously; the truth is he can be a real knob sometimes. Like now!

I turned around.

We were so far out that I couldn't even see the beach; we were at sea. Literally at sea! In a crappy little yellow plastic tub. I felt a swoop of misery. Even if we went no further, I would still have to *pedal all the way back*. The thought was depressing. I'm on holiday, I thought. I'm supposed to be enjoying myself.

I racked my brain for a get-out, a way to end this grinding hard labour, because that's exactly what it was. My heart was racing, and there was a buzzing sound in my ears. I was exhausted. The blood in my fingertips was pounding. Even my teeth were sweating! I was on the point of collapse. Surely an engine should be an optional extra on a pedalo?

All of a sudden, I had a flash of inspiration.

'Rob, how about a swim? Shall we stop for a while and ... cool down?' I suggested, breathless. If he didn't agree there was a chance I'd burst into tears. In fact, I *would* burst into tears; it was a certainty.

He stopped pedalling and nodded. He didn't even look tired.

I exhaled with relief, emptying my lungs of whatever air was left.

He stood, steepled his fingers and stretched his arms.

My jellified legs trembled as I edged out of the plastic chair.

'Nice breeze,' Rob said, planting a kiss on my shoulder as he bent to take his shorts off.

Breeze? I hadn't noticed a breeze. There certainly hadn't been a breeze on my side of the boat. I had been slowly cremating!

'I'm quite enjoying this, now that we're here. Are you?'

Was he joking?

I was too tired to reply. My sarong fell in a chiffon puddle at my feet. I stood at the edge of the boat, raised my arms above my head and gave a spirited leap. Although the sea was warm I felt a cold shiver of delight when I hit the water.

'Is it nice?' Rob asked as I broke the surface.

'Fabulous,' I told him. And it was. There was new life in my limbs.

In one stealthy, fluid movement he dived into the water and glided like a shark towards me. To my surprise he was able to stand. I tried, but I couldn't.

'There are advantages to being in shallow water,' he said, smiling and shaking his head like a wet dog.

My legs floated as he pulled me close. He nibbled my ear. At his touch, a warm prickle ran down the length of my neck. He eyed me levelly. I curled my legs around his waist and circled my arms around his neck. His expression clicked from jovial to serious.

'I love you, Evie,' he said solemnly.

'I love you, too.'

'I'm sorry . . . I'm sorry I hurt you. I'm lucky that you've given me a second chance. I'll make you happy, I swear.'

I pressed my lips to the salty hollow of his neck.

'I know you will.'

His knuckles travelled the length of my back.

'So . . . shall I show you?'

'Show me what?'

'The advantage of being in shallow water, of course.'

'Yes, show me,' I said as the waveless sea lapped our shoulders. And he did. Twice.

The hotel restaurant was huge. It was full of potted palm trees, fairy lights and bamboo furniture draped with lemon linen, and it had an enormous aviary with noisy, coloured birds squawking in accompaniment to a calypso band. I couldn't help but do a salsa hip-shuffle as we followed the waiter to our table – no small task considering I'd pedalled a triathlon earlier.

'I love it, just love it,' I told Rob, dropping heavily into my chair.

He reached for my hand across the table and by the shadow of a flickering candle, lifted my palm to his lips and kissed it. But instead of launching in to his usual repertoire of chatty banter, he dropped his gaze and slowly turned my hand in both of his. He appeared preoccupied, meditative. It wasn't like him.

'What's wrong?' I asked.

He looked caught out.

'Nothing,' he said defensively. 'Nothing, I'm just . . . *happy*.'

He folded his palm over my knuckles and gave them a squeeze. 'I'm happy, Evie. Sometimes I just want to take a silent moment to appreciate it,' he said.

This solemn Rob was a bit of a stranger; still, I suppose there's nothing wrong with appreciating happiness. I jerked my head buffetwards.

'Shall we go to the buffet table and choose something delicious to eat?' I asked, lightening the mood.

He pushed back his chair. 'Sure,' he said.

He held out his hand to me. His smile seemed . . . stilted and forced. Inexplicably, I felt a needle of foreboding.

'You would tell me, wouldn't you, if something was bothering you?' I asked.

He slipped his arm around my shoulders, pulled me close and gave me an absent kiss. 'What could possibly be wrong now that we're back together?' he asked.

We're in Bridgetown Hospital. Rob has a vicious oyster allergy. He hadn't realised there were oysters in the fish stew: he ate three mouthfuls and collapsed. The hotel manager called an ambulance, and now Rob's having his stomach pumped. A doctor jammed a long plastic tube into his mouth. On tiptoe, I craned my head around the doctor's shoulder to see how much of the tube disappeared down Rob's throat. It was quite a lot.

Rob was jerking and thrashing violently, as fountain after fountain of projectile liquid spurted from the other end of the tube into a bucket. Fortunately he was on a gurney, with supporting side frames. He would've fallen off a normal bed, I'm sure of it. What a vile procedure. Well, it's certainly a vile procedure from a spectator's perspective. I'm sure Rob thinks the same.

I'd seen enough.

I found a chair in the corner of the room, and quietly opened my handbag and began to give it a spring clean. I may as well make the most of the spare time. I slid a guilty look right and left, and quickly jabbed off my phone. You're not supposed to have phones on in hospitals in the UK, it's likely to be the same in Barbados. I dragged the metal waste-paper bin along the tiled floor and placed it between my legs, and closed my ears to the violent retching noises Rob was making. It was amazing how much clutter I'd collected considering I'd only had my Louis Vuitton a couple of weeks. I decided to be ruthless; tube tickets, out of date Tesco Clubcard coupons and Starbucks' lids were the first to go. I counted eleven torn magazine advertisements but I couldn't throw them out because I hadn't got round to buying any of the things in the adverts yet. And nine lipsticks but I needed those because they were different shades. And four pens, but isn't it always typical that you can never find a pen when you need one, so I decided to keep those, and—

'Would you like to see your husband now?' a friendly voice asked.

Taken aback, I looked up. 'My what?'

'Your husband?'

A nurse with a jolly ebony face looked at me firmly. The room was quiet. The doctor had left, and Rob was asleep on the gurney.

'Yes, yes,' I said prudently. *Husband*. I quite liked the sound of that. I quickly jammed my handbag under my arm and walked over to Rob's bed. He wore a green smock-apron with a sheet lying loosely across his waist. His face was sheened with dampness; he looked ... waxy. He made a sudden unconscious convulsive movement. I took a startled step back.

'He be tired, we keep him here ovanight,' the nurse said, rubbing my back as though winding a baby. 'I think we rid him of his poison, but to be certain we give him a . . . laxative,' she told me brightly, as though this was fabulous news and I should be delighted to hear it.

'Right. OK, thank you, for . . . for that, and . . . for everything.'

Rob's breathing was deep and heavy. I put my bag on his bed, snaked an arm inside for my lip balm, gently coated his cracked lips, and then rested my palm on his cheek. His skin felt chilled and clammy. Poor thing. I felt an overwhelming surge of protectiveness towards him. I smoothed his hair from his forehead. I was here for him, for as long as he needed me.

The nurse gave me an energetic smile. 'You can stay with him if you want, I'm sure we can find something for you to sleep on,' she said kindly. 'I'll leave you. If you need me I be in reception.'

'Thank you,' I replied to her retreating figure.

I didn't like seeing Rob any other way than his strong, domineering, robust self. I wouldn't go back to the villa without him, definitely not! I would stay with him. A fleeting image of me sitting in the villa, clutching his shirt to my face, crying, popped into my head. I couldn't leave him. He wouldn't leave me. My place was *here*, by his side.

But then I remembered the laxative. What if, what if . . . it worked?

I grabbed my bag. I'd go find the nurse and ask her to call me a taxi. Rob would be fine. Of course he would. It's not as though I'm leaving him in the hands of kidnappers. I glanced around. On the contrary, it was very nice here. He'd love it. I could pick him up tomorrow. He was asleep, what difference would it make to him whether I was here or not? None at all. In fact if he were awake he would probably insist that I go back to the luxury of the villa.

So I did.

VENICE

Chapter Two

We're on a pony-trek; I booked it when Rob was convalescing. Thankfully he's fine now. I'm riding a gorgeous white pony called Button, and Rob is riding an enormous black pony called Bluebeard, which appears to be suffering from some sort of an equestrian multiple personality disorder. Bluebeard *will not* let any other pony walk beside him, not even close, not even the guide. Who I noticed is very sexy. Not that I'm particularly interested. I'm, well . . . I'm thinking of my flatmate Lulu – she would like him.

The guide's name is Ronaldo and he's twenty-nine. He has black hair that is tied in a ponytail, and a broad hairless chest. I suspect he has it waxed; he's from Rio de Janeiro. I'm awestruck. Ronaldo rides bareback. He flicks the reins with a practised twist of the wrist, lowers his torso, whispers in the pony's ear and bolts off, hair billowing. I am loving this. Rob, however, hates every single minute of it and when he catches my eye I know he's looking to me for confirmation that he's not alone. Out of loyalty to him, I put on a scowly, sour, *make it stop* face – all the time trying really hard not to smile – but it isn't easy. I'm riding à la posse with three middle-aged French couples who, like me, are making the most of it, and two lovely gay German blokes.

OK, to be fair to Rob he hasn't been able to chitchat while idly trotting along the ocean surf like the rest of us because, as I said, his pony wants to be up front. His pony wants to be up front all the time. It rises on its hind legs, hoof-scrambles mid-air and bolts if anyone comes within a furlong, not that I know what a furlong is exactly, but it sounds like the appropriate term to use. Rob's horse thinks this is some sort of steeplechase as opposed to a leisurely trek. To avoid being thrown Rob has to lie flat and *cuddle* the pony. At one point both his arms and legs were practically around the pony's neck; he'd looked ridiculous, absolutely ridiculous, like an idiot clown in the circus. We're now trotting to a halt to stop for lunch, at a rather grim-looking tumbledown shack on the beach. Still, I'm sure the food will be delicious. Appearances can be deceptive.

Not surprisingly Rob beat the rest of us to the restaurant. He was pouring a bottle of Evian down the crotch of his trousers when we arrived. I thought it a waste, as Evian is quite expensive here.

I dismounted with a jaunty landing hop. 'You won the race,' I said to Rob, trying for joviality. He didn't appreciate my attempt at humour.

'Evie! Tell me there are a fleet of jeeps waiting behind this hovel to take us back to the hotel!'

I smiled at the lapping ocean. I felt a tingling all over my body. The ride, the fresh air, the guide – everything was so perfect and *exhilarating* and—

'Evie!'

'No,' I told him flatly. 'We ride back.'

I tied Button's reins over a wooden post and ran my palm along the length of his neck. He gave me an affectionate snort.

'My balls are killing me!' Rob snapped, squatting and flapping the waistband of his shorts to try to generate a draught.

Bluebeard, tied next to Button, shook his mane, raised his head and eyed Rob distastefully.

'What a handsome animal,' I said, slapping Bluebeard's glistening rump.

'*Don't do that!*' Rob shrieked, shaking me by the elbow. 'If you piss him off, he'll ram-raid the restaurant.'

'He really is a beautiful boy,' I complimented.

'That thing is the Devil's steed . . . I don't care how much it costs; order a taxi to the hotel! I'm not getting back on that horse! I'd be taking my life in my hands!'

I looked at him in disbelief. *His life in his hands?* This was a perfect example of Rob at his most melodramatic. We were talking about a horse here, not a flying dragon!

'But I'm enjoying myself.'

'Well, I'm not!' he snapped, spitting strands of coarse black hair from his mouth. 'And nor would you be if you were riding my horse.'

'Why does everything always have to be your way or no way?' I demanded.

'My way or no way?' he spluttered, incredulous. 'We're here because *you* want to be. If anything, it's the other way around. If I had *my* way, we wouldn't have come in the first place.'

'You take a taxi! I'm *not* coming with you, I'm riding back,' I told him, lifting my chin in defiance. 'I seem to have a natural aptitude for horse riding. I may even take it up when I get home.'

'You *are* coming with me!'

'I'm not!'

'You are!'

'I'm not!'

We're in the taxi on our way to the hotel; we're not talking. Periodically Rob slides a look my way. He wants to say something,

I know it! He's rubbish at not talking. Especially if he knows he's wrong, and he *is* wrong. He threatened to carry me to the taxi if I didn't walk to it by myself and he meant it, so here I am, press-ganged!

He turned his head to the right to look out the window. His left hand crept towards my leg. I slapped it. He winced. The only excursion I'd booked and he had to put the kibosh on the whole day. I watched his hand crawl slowly across the seat. His hand twitched and hovered before inching on to my thigh. I gave his wrist two karate chops. He yelped. The thing is, I'm quite good at not talking. Let's be honest, it's easier than talking – all you have to do is, well, *not talk*. Rob lifted his bum and sat on his hands. I'll teach him, I thought. I folded my arms and scowled at the speeding view. What a waste of money; we hadn't even eaten the included lunch.

In the villa, I tossed my bag onto the dressing table and strode purposefully to the bathroom. I flicked on the bath's taps and watched Rob through a crack in the door. He idly walked to the desk, sank into the chair and flipped open his laptop. It was the first time he'd touched his laptop since we had arrived. I was surprised he'd lasted this long. He's a workaholic. As though feeling my gaze, he raised his chin and looked towards the bathroom. I quickly moved back but managed to keep my eye on him. The Harrison's Coach logo danced on the laptop screen. The sight of the familiar maroon and gold lettering brought on a cardiac flutter. It signified *normality*, it signified going home and going back to work. It meant I'd soon be facing my sister Lexy, and Lulu, with my errant boyfriend in tow. I'd forgiven him, but would they? I wasn't sure they would.

Rob owns a fleet of coaches, eight or nine in total. He charters them to a tour operator that runs a programme of European coach tours. I started working for them last year as a European tour guide and Rob was the driver on my first weekend break to Paris. We had the most amazing summer, working together in Paris every weekend and spending the days in between at my flat in London. All was going well until late autumn, when Rob had worked with another guide on a trip to Austria and she'd walked in on him naked. Not wanting to pass on a free lunch, and being under the influence, he'd strayed. Subsequently we split up. We got back together a couple of weeks ago after Rob followed me to Scotland where I was working on a New Year's break in the Highlands. He asked me to marry him; I said yes. He's *the one*, I'm sure of it. I'd felt only half-alive without him.

I inched towards the bathroom door. Rob was hunched over the desk, head in hands. He looked . . . morose. I felt a spear of guilt. I wasn't really that bothered about the pony-trekking excursion now that I thought of it. And I was bored of not talking. Suddenly he stood up. I lurched back from my lookout post. Six determined strides later and he filled the doorway.

'Evie, we need to talk,' he said softly.

I felt a twinge of apprehension. This was a serious statement coming from him. He flipped down the toilet seat, sat on it and patted his knee.

'Sit,' he said.

I took an idle step towards him and sat on his lap. He folded his arms around my waist.

'We go home in a couple of days,' he said.

I tweaked the soft golden hair on his forearm. 'Mmm.'

'But, Evie, home for you is your flat in London, and home for me is a flat in Birmingham. We're engaged now. We should live together.'

I felt a whoosh of excitement. Of course we should live together. I hadn't thought it through because there had been no time, but he was absolutely right. He should move in with Lulu and me, it would make perfect sense. And OK, I know it's not ideal having a third wheel around all the time, but Lulu's often out, and I love Tooting, and my neighbours, and there are lots of fabulous pubs and restaurants. And I love my part-time job in Bar Thea, which is opposite the flat, and I love my friend Nikki who owns it. I palmed his cheek.

'I don't want to live in your flat with Lulu,' he said, as if he'd read my mind. 'We should be alone. I want a house with a garden, a dog and,' – there was a brief pause – 'and a baby,' he said, eyes bright.

He's still speaking, but I'm not listening. *A baby?* I know people have them, but I'm only twenty-six, and he's only thirty. What's the rush? And a garden? And a dog? Was he serious? I swallowed. How can we have a dog and a baby if we're touring Europe throughout the summer? How? I'm a European tour guide and he's a continental coach driver. Has he forgotten?

He settled me against his chest. I leaned in to him woodenly. A baby? I'd rather give birth to a Prada handbag! I tuned back in to the conversation.

'I want to stop touring,' he announced.

I felt my blood rush to my head. What is he talking about? Stop touring? But I love touring!

'I've made a few changes as far as the infrastructure of the business is concerned. I've sold the yard in Birmingham, most of my charter contracts originate in the south so it makes commercial sense to base the coaches there,' he said conversationally. 'I'm due to take premises in London in four weeks' time at the end of February.'

He's moving the business from Birmingham to London, just like that!

'The relocation of the business will bring expansion opportunities. I should have done this before but I needed an incentive to move south,' he said, leaning back slightly. 'You are the incentive.'

I turned to face him. 'Moving the business to London and expanding doesn't necessarily mean you have to stop touring,' I pointed out.

'I'll be increasing my client base, which for the most part will mean I'll be desk-bound. I don't want to be office-based in London if you're touring Europe. We'll live together and if we travel, it's together or not at all. Occasionally we'll escort the odd trip, but realistically it would be one trip every couple of months.'

I'm taken aback. Actually I'm more than taken aback; I'm sucker-punched.

'It's an antisocial job, Evie. Our relationship comes first. You're the most important thing in the world to me. I don't want us spending any time apart unless it's absolutely necessary. We're going to build a life together and we can't spend half of our time hundreds of miles apart if we're going to make this work.'

OK, hang on a minute! Let me just run a post-mortem on the conversation here. To be together always – wasn't that what I wanted? Thoughts skittered through my head. Yes. Yes, absolutely. I gave a happy sigh. Yes, it is, I thought, it is what I want. I want to build a life with him. We're engaged. I smiled at my diamond ring. I may take a rain check on the garden and the baby and the house and the dog and the move from Tooting, but overall this sounds fabulous.

'I love you, Evie. You're my life,' he said, arranging my weight squarely.

Being together always . . . I couldn't wish for more.

'I love you, too.'

He's right, of course. Things have to change. He's pointed out the obvious. Given time, I'd likely have suggested exactly the same thing myself. We'll live together and we won't tour unless it's together, otherwise we would never see each other. I felt a spasm of happiness. Well, actually, I felt a spasm of a feeling I didn't entirely recognise but I was sure it was happiness.

'So, that's it?' I asked.

His gaze was riveted on mine. 'What do you mean?'

'In the bedroom, you were sitting, head in hands, serious frown. I thought something was wrong.'

'Nothing's wrong,' he said firmly.

'But you looked—'

His face clicked from serious to light-hearted as he cut me off. 'Evie, we only have two days left of our holiday. That's not a very comforting thought, is it? The time has flown by,' he said.

'Er, yes it has,' I agreed.

'Let's not waste what little time we have left. Shall we have a bath?'

And we did – a lovely, long, scented bubble bath.

Chapter Three

The day after Rob and I got back from Barbados, my sister came to visit, her kids in tow. Lexy and I were trying to discuss my engagement but it was impossible because Lexy's phone wouldn't stop ringing. She lifted my hand to admire my ring when her phone rang again. She sighed and tucked her short dark hair behind her ear in a sharp jerky movement.

She eyed her caller display. 'Another mother from the nursery!' she told me, flipping her phone open. 'Will this ever end? I could scream.'

I wheeled to four-year-old Becky.

'Why did you do it!? Why did you tell all the kids in the nursery that Santa has been shot in the eye and kidnapped!? What were you thinking!?'

The eye! Couldn't she at least have said that Santa got shot somewhere less horrifically pictorial, like the big toe?

Becky sat on the edge of the sofa, rolling a slice of ham in the palm of her hand. 'Because he has,' she said flatly.

'He has not!'

'He has, I know it!' Becky said, folding the ham into her mouth and pushing her blonde fringe from her eyes.

Now, here's the truth. I'm not sure how I feel about Becky.

I love her, of course I do. I have to, she's my niece. But I often ponder that she may be possessed by a demon or some form of evil spirit because by nature she's horrid. Sometimes, when I look at her, I feel an icy clutch at my chest. *What exactly is a poltergeist?* In contrast her twin, Lauren, is an adorable dark-haired, green-eyed angel. Thank God. I couldn't cope with two Beckys.

'Auntie Evie, we need to help Santa,' Lauren pleaded tearfully, nervously twisting the toggle of her hoodie. 'Call a policeman. Call, call . . . Superman!' she suggested in desperation.

Becky gave a nonchalant shrug and absorbed herself with the Velcro straps on her sparkly trainers. 'Why should we help? Santa forgot our Barbie cars,' she reminded Lauren.

'He remembered your bikes,' I told Becky.

Lexy snapped her phone shut and tightened her Gucci neckscarf, almost garrotting herself. 'We're leaving!' she announced, exasperated. She turned to Becky. 'We are meeting your friends in Pizza Express with their mummies, and you are going to tell everyone that you made a big mistake and that Santa is safe and living in Lapland.'

Becky's eyes were riveted on her mum; she gave an uncertain frown and twirled a long spiral of blonde hair. 'But—'

'No buts. Tell everyone that you watched the news today and that Santa has been found, and that he's safe,' Lexy said encouragingly. 'We'll discuss it tonight. Perhaps Daddy can phone the elves or, or Mrs Claus, and get to the bottom of this, find out what really happened.'

Becky looked interested. Lexy looked desperate. Lauren looked hopeful.

Lexy came over to me and kissed my cheek. 'I have to go. It's great news that you and Rob are back together. Lulu thinks so too; you were miserable without him. It's worth another try, of course it is.' She bent down to usher the kids off the sofa. 'Tell him I'm sorry I had to leave before he got home. I'll call you,' she said, guiding the twins out the door without looking back.

Becky turned and smiled; it was a terrifying smile. On impulse, I hugged myself.

Rob's key rattled in the lock just before six o'clock. A shadow fell across the room when he appeared in the doorway. He held his arms wide. I took a step towards him and buried my face in the folds of his shirt.

'I've missed you,' he said, although it had only been nine hours since he'd seen me. We hugged and swayed slowly.

'I've missed you too.'

The phone rang. He tightened his hold. 'Leave it,' he said. 'I'm enjoying the cuddle.'

I was enjoying the cuddle too but I wanted to answer the phone. It could be for me! OK, it may be for Lulu or Rob, but still. I didn't like the thought of missing a call, even a call that wasn't for me. I tried to wriggle free.

'Leave it,' he repeated, his breath warm in my ear.

Who was ringing? Who?

The answer machine clicked on. Nikki's voice filled the lounge.

'Evie, you're home! Welcome back! Have you forgotten you work here? Your first shift is on Thursday. You have one more day to laze around. I'll see you at six!'

Rob stiffened. 'Tell him you're not going back to work for him,' he said crisply. 'It's only a part-time waitressing job. You don't need it.'

'What? What do you mean *not going back*?'

Rob held my shoulders; his clear blue eyes pierced mine. 'I'm not sure I like Nikki,' he said flatly and to my astonishment.

For a minute, I was speechless. 'Nikki is my friend and neighbour. What do you mean you don't like him?' I asked sharply.

Rob's face switched from unsmiling to upbeat and he shook his head good-naturedly. 'Evie, I didn't mean I don't like him,' he back-pedalled. 'What I meant was that I don't like you working for him. I'm working more or less nine to five and I come home to you every night. What's the point of me moving from Birmingham to London to be with you, if you're out working in a bar in the evening?'

'It's only three nights a week,' I pointed out defensively.

'It's three nights a week too many.'

'I need the money.'

'You don't!'

'I do.'

'Evie, I'm in a position to be able to cover everything,' he said with a conciliatory smile. 'You know that and that's fine with me. I don't mind. Business is good – we may as well both benefit. You going out to work as I arrive home is hardly ideal. Surely you agree?' He kissed my forehead. 'I thought perhaps we could buy you a shop,' he said, eyes bright and scheming.

'A shop,' I echoed. 'I don't want a shop.'

'Why not? If you're happy to commute, we could buy you a boutique in town. You have a brilliant eye for fashion. Why not open your own shop?'

I felt discomfited. I've always felt sorry for sales assistants, folding jumpers all day just to watch some selfish critter mess them up again; braving the daily torment of special offers and tempting discounts on heaps of stuff they can't afford and can't escape.

I'd spend every penny I earned. It would be the ruin of me.

Rob guided me to the sofa, sat me down and put an arm around my shoulders. 'Evie, I haven't moved a hundred and twenty miles to spend the evenings on my own.'

28

'I want my own money,' I told him.

'Why? What's mine is yours. I would rather we spent more time together than have an extra couple of quid in the bank. It's not always about money; it's about quality of life.' He took my chin between his forefinger and thumb. 'Think about the boutique,' he said with an encouraging smile.

I suppose I could wear the stock in the shop myself. And if I got tired of something, I could stick a price tag on it and sell it. I would have an extended wardrobe . . . I would have an enormous wardrobe.

'What's for dinner?' Rob asked.

'Chicken dippers,' I told him absently. A shop?

'Great,' he said with tepid enthusiasm. 'Let me take you out for dinner, babe,' he suggested brightly.

'What about the chicken dippers?' I asked.

He gave a thoughtful frown. 'I might snack on them later,' he said.

'Oh, OK. I'll get changed.' A shop? Why would a tour guide want a shop?

'I want to spend as much time with you as possible. Surely you feel the same?' he said.

'I do, of course I do,' I told him, slowly standing.

And I did.

The following afternoon I sat on the sofa, twisting the strap of my handbag. I was dreading this. I was letting Nikki down and I knew it. OK, I thought. I will walk calmly over to Bar Thea and tell Nikki I'm not coming back. Simple! It makes perfect sense. Nevertheless my stomach cramped with nerves at the thought of it; Nikki won't be happy at being one staff member down at such short notice. I've been waitressing in his bar part-time for about eight months. I needed something regular and consistent because guiding is sporadic and seasonal. I had been overdrawn too, but my overdraft is all sorted out now. Well, strictly speaking it isn't sorted out at all. It's kind of crept up again but I can only cope with one personal tsunami at a time. I had thought of resigning from the bar by phone but I owed Nik more than that. I owed him a face-to-face explanation. We've been friends and neighbours for over two years and he was a rock when Rob and I split up. I sighed. I haven't seen Nik since Rob and I got back together . . . and that's another thing I don't suppose Nik will be impressed by. In fact, I know that he won't be.

I stood up purposefully. *Pull yourself together*, I told myself. It's a simple matter of furnishing Nikki with the facts, and the fact is, Rob is right for me and he's right about the job too. Here I go!

A few minutes later, I pushed my way through the door of the bar, breathing through contractions of trepidation. Nikki was searching for something in the drawer beside the cash register; he looked up, our eyes locked. He slammed the drawer shut and, arms outstretched, edged around the bar and strode towards me, an enormous grin on his face.

'You're back!'

My pulse did an erratic hop. Despite my growling nerves I was really pleased to see him. *Really* pleased! The muscles in his wide shoulders moved against his shirt as, in one fluid movement, he gripped my waist, lifted me up, and sat me on the bar.

'Evie, you look fabulous, so tanned and healthy. I've missed you. I haven't seen you since . . . ' He broke off, thinking. 'Since Christmas Eve,' he said at last.

He blew my fringe from my eyes. Impulsively, I lurched forward, circled his neck, held him close, and breathed in the scent of his trademark lemon shampoo. There was a drumbeat of silence. I smoothed my palm over his thick black hair, squeezed my eyes shut, and had a mental dress rehearsal. *Hi, Nikki. Great to see you. I'm not coming back to work.* I felt sick. I couldn't say it. Nikki has been brilliant to me. He lifted me from the bar as though I weighed nothing at all and set me on my feet.

'I'm *so* pleased to see you,' he said, cupping my face. 'You are by far my best-looking waitress. Let's have a drink and catch up,' he suggested, underscoring my eyes with his thumbs.

'I'm your only waitress, apart from your mother.'

'OK, you are my favourite person.'

Nikki has such an intense presence. At the moment, his look is passionate and sincere, his dark eyes are searching and pooled, his lips are pressed together and a nerve in his strong olive jaw is twitching. He was genuinely delighted to see me. And much to my surprise, I was delighted to see him.

He kissed my forehead, put an arm round my shoulders and slow-walked me to an alcove table. As we eased into a horse-shoe bench, he barked a drinks order to Costas, one of the waiters, who was sitting at the bar smiling at a copy of the *Racing Post*.

'I heard you're back with him,' Nikki blurted out with a sharp edge to his voice.

Gosh, Nik, I thought. Get straight to the point, why don't you? I was about to shoot back defensively when I realised that although his jaw was firm and his smile fixed, his dark eyes were kind and soft, not challenging. I weaved my fingers together and formed a spire.

'Yes,' I admitted with a nod. 'I'm back with Rob.'

'If you're happy then I'm happy,' he said with a tight half-smile.

The conversation halted as Costas rattled an ice bucket in front of us. Nikki opened a bottle of champagne with the flick of a thumb and poured with practised ease. He handed me a glass.

'Very extravagant,' I said, smiling at my drink. 'What are we celebrating?'

'Nothing . . . You're worth it,' he said. 'We're celebrating you being home and me seeing you for the first time in almost a month.'

There was an uneasy pause. A serious war of emotions was raging in my head. I took a nervous gulp of bubbles and studied Nikki over the rim of my flute. He'd had his hair cut short. It suited him. It highlighted his chiselled jaw and high cheekbones. He looked great.

'You're too good for him,' he said, giving me a hard stare.

I put my glass down with exaggerated care.

Nikki's eyes defied mine.

'I know what you think—' I began.

'You don't. You don't know what I think,' he fired back.

'OK, I can imagine what you think but it's fine between us and I want to give it a go, and so—'

He raised the flat of his hand. 'I admit it; I don't approve but if he's your choice, then fine. But you're too good for him, far too good.' He gave a nonchalant shrug. 'Now, tell me about your holiday in Barbados,' he said in an effort to lighten the atmosphere.

'It was very nice.'

'Just nice?'

I couldn't put it off, I had to tell him. I opened my mouth but closed it again when I couldn't find my voice. Looking him in the eye was out of the question. Nikki leaned towards me, folded my knuckles and squeezed my hands gently.

'What's wrong? You can tell me, you know you can,' he cajoled. 'You're too quiet.'

'Nothing, nothing at all,' I said with force and in a rush.

He shifted closer and slid a strong arm across the back of my chair. Our heads touched. I stole a hooded glance.

'I know you; you have something on your mind. Whatever it is, you can trust me,' he said with a patient smile.

I was trapped.

'I'm not coming back to work in the bar,' I blurted out bravely.

There, I did it. I told him straight.

Nikki lifted my chin. The patient smile slid off his face . . .

I held my breath.

There was a drumming tension before he slapped his palm on the table.

I jumped.

'What?' The buttons of his white shirt strained as his body-builder's chest heaved.

Costas raised his chin at Nik's sharp tone, slid off his stool and quietly disappeared into the kitchen.

'I am busy! I need you! And you are available! What do you mean you're not coming back to work?' he bellowed.

I held the stem of my glass in a cluster of white knuckles. I felt faint. I loathe confrontation, especially with Nik. He's so loud.

Still, I managed a businesslike pose. 'It's not ideal, Nik . . . I would be heading out to work as Rob arrived home,' I reasoned. 'I'm so sorry, it's just—'

'Fine,' he snapped, cutting me off and giving the table another slap.

'Fine?' I echoed in disbelieving relief. I risked a smile. That was it? Fine?

He leaned close. Our noses were almost touching. On impulse, I pulled back.

'Yes, fine! If that's the case, forget working in the evenings. You can work the lunchtime shift instead,' he said.

My smile crumpled.

'Start between ten and eleven, and finish at six,' he said matter-of-factly. 'Problem solved.'

I was thrown and stunned with indecision. I wasn't quite sure what to say. This was certainly a compromise, but I knew it wasn't a compromise Rob would be overly enthused by. Nikki caught my hesitation, and fielded it brilliantly. He palmed my hair in soft, wheedling strokes. I eyed his hand warily. This was Nikki's gentle alter ego. I've seen it before. Not too often, mind you, and only ever when he wants something.

'What's wrong with that?' he asked, his eyes scheming. 'Surely that's the perfect solution? You will continue to work for me because I am your *friend* and I need you, and you can still spend your evenings with Romeo.'

I stared at him in mute hesitancy.

'Well?' he asked, his brow dissected in a frown.

'Yes, fine. I'll work lunchtimes.' I heard myself say assertively.

He gave an energetic smile. 'Good! Now we'll eat. What would you like? Steak?' he asked, rubbing his palms together triumphantly, his mood having jigged up a couple of gears.

Chapter Four

Rob had gone to work. I wasn't entirely sorry. He had been sulking about me accepting Nikki's compromise. No big surprise there. I took a breakfast tray into the lounge for Lulu and me. She was splayed on the sofa, mobile phone to her ear.

'Yes, I'll do it! Absolutely! I welcome the challenge, Andrew. Definitely,' Lulu enthused, dangling an out-of-season tanned leg over the armrest.

I settled the tray on the dining table and gave her a quizzical backward glance.

'You heard that,' a voice boomed from the radio. 'The challenge has been accepted by Lulu from Tooting ... Stay on the line, Lulu; we'll need your contact details ... Before I play Beyoncé's fabulous new single, I'd like to say happy birthday to Chrissie from Ashtead who is one hundred years young today!'

Lulu scrambled off the sofa, turned the volume on the radio down, jammed the phone between shoulder and chin and scribbled a couple of notes on the back of her cigarette packet. Intrigued, I sipped my coffee and listened as she spelled out our address and rattled off her mobile phone number.

She snapped her phone shut and tossed it on the chair. 'I'm going to stop smoking,' she boasted.

'You've said that before.'

She weaved a biro into her thick vanilla ponytail, and edged into the chair opposite me. 'I mean it this time. I have an incentive.'

'You've always had some sort of an incentive.'

'Ah, yes! But this time, the whole of London knows about it. I've accepted the challenge to go head to head with Andrew Blackbourne from *Good Morning, this is the Capital.* So obviously with thousands of people listening, I'll have to stick to it. Andrew has been smoking longer than I've lived so I should beat him hands down,' she said.

I gave her a sceptical glance. She lit a fag and opened the window behind her.

'Being a nurse, I know how bad smoking is for me,' she said, frowning wisely at her cigarette. 'I'm determined to pack it in. In fact, I'm looking forward to it.' She plopped a couple of sugar cubes into her mug.

'Great, good luck,' I said, rallying a supportive smile.

She whizzed a teaspoon around her cup thoughtfully. 'Are you sure Rob doesn't mind me being here? You know, living with you now that you're engaged?' she asked.

'No, of course he doesn't mind,' I said in a hollow voice and with a shimmer of unease.

'Good, because he can fuck off if he does mind because I was here first,' she said, waving her fag randomly. 'He's only your *first* fiancé. You could easily get engaged two or three more times before you settle down. Whereas I am your best friend in the whole wide world and I will be there for you always.'

I tried to look grateful.

'He is only a man,' she added factually.

Lulu's recipe for success with men is quite simple. She can take them or leave them. According to her, no matter how hungry she is, she could never eat a whole one. Vic, her man of

36

the moment, is a marine biologist. She's been seeing him for about six months and hasn't managed to stay faithful even for that short time.

My phone vibrated in my dressing gown pocket. Lulu's brows lifted in question. It was a text from Rob.

Put the flat on the market – do it today. R xx

I felt my cheeks burn. I held my phone under the table and pinged back a reply.

Will do. E xx

'Who was that?' Lulu asked.

'Rob to say he misses me.'

She flicked her cigarette out the window. 'Prat! He only left the house two hours ago. What a knob,' she said, 34Ds jiggling as she buttered a slice of toast. 'Doesn't all that mushy crap get your gander up?'

'No, not really. I think it's quite romantic,' I told her.

'Well, it would irritate me . . . Evie, I've been thinking. We should chip in together and buy a tumble dryer. There's no room for it in the kitchen but we could put one in the shed. What d'you think?'

'Yeah sure,' I said.

'I'm sick of the sight of damp knickers over all the radiators,' she said.

I twisted my wrist and checked my watch, suddenly eager to cut short breakfast and get to work.

But I soon changed my mind. The bar had been heaving. I was exhausted. Seven hours on my feet had nearly killed me.

Lunchtimes are much busier than the evenings. I wasn't convinced that I had made the right decision. Not that it had been a decision offering much in the way of options. Glad to be home, I sat on the sofa massaging my feet.

'Did you put the flat on the market?' Rob asked the minute he got home.

I was ready for this. I had a plan; a master plan that I thought would serve as a stay of execution. I inhaled sharply. He filled the lounge doorway.

'No, because it occurred to me that perhaps we don't need to sell it. It could be wiser to rent it out. You know, keep it as an investment, unless we need the equity to move on,' I told him.

There was a frozen silence.

He put down his briefcase, studying me fixedly, his eyebrows creased in thought. 'Do you know, Evie, perhaps you're right,' he said with a slow, thoughtful nod. 'Yes, we'll see how much we need to spend to buy what we want. And we'll hang on to the flat if we can. Lulu and Vic could rent it from us,' he suggested. He walked slowly towards me, shrugging out of his jacket. 'Are we alone?' he asked with a leer.

I grinned.

He knelt on the floor in front of me.

'Yes, we're alone.'

'Fabulous,' he said, fingers working the buttons of my blouse.

No sooner had I fielded the 'moving house' situation, than the 'guiding Europe' black cloud drifted in the following evening. I was sitting glumly on the bathroom floor, knees to my chest, arms enveloping my legs. Rob was in the bath, his face twisted in annoyance. He snatched the soap and scrubbed his arms.

Tina, my friend and the Operations Manager for Insignia Tours, had called to ask if I would escort a corporate event to

Marrakech next weekend. The client – John Jackson, a zillion-aire I had worked for last year in the South of France – had requested me. I said I'd do it.

The thing is, my Harrods statement came this morning. I feel sick just thinking about it. I had only been in the shop for *six short hours*, and somehow . . . I owed an astonishing £3,200. It's extortion! I've checked every item and double-checked the totting-up. I *cannot* believe hair extensions, an evening dress and a bit of Christmas shopping – oh, and my Louis Vuitton hand-bag – cost that much. I considered admitting the debt to Rob but just as swiftly changed my mind. Rob thinks store cards are a poisonous deadly menace. So there's no way around it. I have to go to Marrakech; I need the money. And, in truth . . . I want to go too!

I licked my lips. I loathe arguing.

'Rob, one weekend. It's only one weekend,' I pleaded.

'Evie! I don't want you to go to Marrakech with a group of businessmen for four days. I don't understand why you would want to do it. You should want to stay here with me!' He squeezed a blob of shampoo on to his palm.

'But I need to work.'

'That's the whole point. You *don't* need to work. Not at the moment. If I need you to work, I'll tell you. Your time would be better spent house hunting. It's what we both want, isn't it?' he said, covering his face in a soapy lather.

I wasn't getting through to him. I stood and reached for the toilet roll, pulled off a strip and blew my nose. 'I'll leave you to finish your bath,' I said, slamming the door behind me.

Lulu was in the kitchen, whizzing the cloth in an irritated, jerky zigzag over the worktops.

'Vic is in the lounge. He needs a bath,' Lulu snapped.

'Does he?'

'Yes, he does. He works with sick fish!'

'If he needs a bath, then I suggest you tell him!'

'I don't need to tell him, he knows he needs a bath.'

I felt a dart of annoyance. 'If Vic knows he needs a bath and he smells of fish and he's not looking to do anything about it, then why the hell are you with him?' I asked.

'Vic can't get in the bath because Rob is in the bath. Make my day and tell me Rob has drowned, because he uses all the hot water every single night.' She tossed the cloth in the kitchen sink. 'If you won't tell him to get out of the bath, I will,' she said.

'He won't be much longer,' I reasoned.

She made for the door. 'He's already been in there for over an hour.'

I tackled her. 'I'll get him out.'

'Well, see that you do because it's not fair.'

I inched busily past her into the hall. She was right. Rob does use all the hot water. He tops up and refills the bath for as long as it takes him to read two newspapers.

A startled Rob, head frothy with shampoo, looked at me big-eyed when I opened the bathroom door.

'Vic wants a bath,' I announced and walked off, leaving the bathroom door ajar.

Two minutes later, Rob stormed into our bedroom, dripping water on the bedroom carpet and tugging a towel around his waist.

'Do you see what I mean? We need to move,' he said, shooting me a sharp glance. 'We need our own space. If I want to spend all night in the bath, then I should be able to do exactly that.'

In spite of his mood, I couldn't help but grin at him.

His skin, still suntanned, glowed, appearing sleek and oily. He looked beautiful, with long toned arms, firm broad shoul-

40

ders and flat rippling tummy muscles. Despite himself he exhaled a smile. He hadn't shaved. I eyed the bristle of dark blond stubble on his cheeks, chin and neck. Reaching up, I cupped his face and circled his eyes with my thumbs. He moved in to my touch and pulled me to him, pressing my face against his chest.

'Evie, I need to go up north for a couple of days. Next weekend would be as good a time as any. If you really want to go to Marrakech, then go. I can make a few sales calls that I've been putting off,' he said softly. 'I'll be back in London to pick you up from the airport.'

I admit I felt a needle of confusion. We had argued for over an hour and now this welcome, if unexpected, U-turn? And he had never mentioned any sales calls up north before. Still, I wasn't complaining.

He lifted my chin with his forefinger. 'We'll work together on the Paris weekend breaks in July and August. Insignia have chartered some dates from me. I'll schedule myself as the driver and you ask Tina to roster you as the guide.'

I nodded.

'I'm not laying down the law, it's just that I don't want us to get in to the habit of spending too much time apart,' he said apologetically.

'Neither do I. I don't want us to be apart either, but I'm not giving up my job completely.'

He held up his hands in defeat. 'We'll work something out,' he said smiling. 'I don't expect you to give up something you love doing, I honestly don't. But our relationship comes first.' He slipped off his towel and wearing nothing but a couple of droplets of bathwater, he walked slowly to the dressing table and picked up a comb. 'Do you fancy a workout, Evie?' he asked casually.

I stared at his bum hypnotically.

'Sounds good to me.'

I woke with a start in the middle of the night. I held my breath. An arm snaked behind my neck and another crossed my chest. I froze. The arms didn't belong to Rob. He was snoring softly on the other side of the bed. I lay on my back, eyes wide and darting.

'Evie, move over,' Lulu said in a dramatic whisper. 'I need you. Vic had to go home.'

'You what?'

She pressed a tear-stained cheek on my shoulder. 'Evie, I can't stop crying,' she said in a wobbly voice. 'Because . . . because I haven't had a fag for thirty-nine hours. I'm having terrible dreams about fags. Evil, talking cigarettes; you have no idea. I think I'm losing my reason. I've cleaned the oven.'

There was a ruffle of quilt.

'What the hell?' Rob demanded.

Lulu strangled me protectively. 'Fuck off you,' she snapped at Rob. 'Evie,' she drew a raspy breath, 'I don't know how I'm going to survive. Having a fag is on my mind *every waking minute*. But I can't have one because I've been bragging on the radio that I've stopped smoking. The nation's eyes are on me. I know how Churchill must have felt, when the whole friggin' country was gathered around the radio, hanging on to his every word. It's the same for me. I'm sure of it. It has to be.'

'Hardly!' Rob thundered. 'What are you doing in our bed? Get out!'

'No! I'm not getting out. Evie, make *him* get out! I need you to help me stop thinking about fags. He doesn't need you. He doesn't even smoke.'

Rob flounced on to his back.

I breathed a sigh. This was so typical her. The last time she stopped smoking, she gained a stone, maxed out her store cards and, as drunk as a lord, bought a barn online in Afghanistan.

'Evie, I'm going to go to a hypnotist. Will you come with me?'

'Do you think the hypnotist could make you forget your address?' Rob asked hopefully in the gloom.

Lulu gasped. 'Did you hear that? The cheek! What have I ever done to him?'

'Can you loosen your hold on my neck?' I asked her.

'Evie, will you come in the lounge with me and have a gin and tonic? I can't sleep. It must be nearly forty hours since I've had a fag. If I had one small gin, perhaps it would take my mind off smoking.'

Two-thirty flashed in neon green on the bedside clock.

I nudged her out of bed. 'Come on then,' I agreed. 'One drink.'

Rob made a loud hmph sound.

'Evie, I'm having hot flushes and I feel light-headed. I feel . . . I feel like I'm kind of floating,' she said in anguish.

Rob punched his pillow to a ball. 'Perhaps you're possessed,' he suggested. 'Have you thought of asking a priest to do an exorcism – of your otherwise empty head?'

She whipped the quilt off the bed. 'You can freeze, you nasty bastard. Evie and I need the quilt to have a cuddle on the sofa.'

Three gin and tonics later and by the shimmering cosy glow of the log fire, we lay head to toe on the chintz sofa.

'Evie, you won't leave me, will you?'

'What do you mean, leave you?'

'Rob's not more important to you than I am, is he?'

'It's a different kind of important.' I hedged tactfully.

'Yes, but obviously he's *less* important, right?' she said with determination. 'The gin has made me quite tired. I'm not think-ing of a fag at the moment, I'm too knackered. Let's go to sleep, shall we?'

I woke with Rob's face hovering inches from mine. I sank back into the sofa cushion and pulled the quilt under my chin.

'You! Are dragging your heels!' he hissed. 'I'm going to regis-ter with estate agents, and have details of what is on the market sent to us.'

Lulu stirred. I inhaled sharply. What if she had heard? I held my breath and watched Lulu push her Zorro mask up her nose (she can't sleep without it). She didn't stir, not at all. Thankfully.

Rob's eyes darted to the slumbering Lulu.

'I'll end up killing her. She would try the patience of a saint, and I'm no saint! Much better for us to move, don't you think, than for me to get arrested for murder?'

He pulled back the quilt.

'Come back into our bed.'

VENICE

Chapter Five

The bar slowly emptied; we'd served eighty covers for lunch. I was sitting on a bar stool gazing at a plate of risotto Nikki's mother, Maria, insisted I eat. Maria was brushing my hair with powerful, sweeping strokes. She'd been talking for a good ten minutes. I have absolutely no idea what she'd been talking about. I don't think she knows what she's talking about most of the time. Usually she's telling me how loving and handsome Nikki is. I've heard it all before. As long as I nod in reply every now and then, she's happy.

Pepi, one of the waiters, had left a newspaper beside the till. I pushed the risotto aside, shook the newspaper open and flicked to the property section. Houses are expensive, four hundred thousand on average, and that's here in sunny Tooting. Hampton, where Rob wants to live, would be much more expensive. I felt a tickle of satisfaction. Surely the price would put him off moving. I don't see why we can't stay where we are for a while. There's nothing wrong with Tooting, and I love my flat.

I felt a whisper on my cheek. Maria's chubby, happy face craned round my shoulder. She twisted her mother-of-pearl hairbrush into the pocket of her nylon apron.

'I have a geeft for you,' she announced proudly.

I forced an appreciative smile, and watched apprehensively as she rummaged in her patent shopper, which was propped on the bar. I'm not ungrateful, of course I'm not. Maria is very kind and I love her to bits, but she's trying to turn me in to a frump. And if I've told her once not to buy me anything, I've told her a hundred times.

She bullied her generous frame in front of me, and teased a canary-yellow cardigan over my shoulders. 'I knit it myself,' she told me, a grin spreading across her face. She pressed her palm on my cheek. 'You are so beautiful, with those ice-blue eyes,' she said. 'I had a dream! A vision! You will marry my Nikki,' she prophesised.

I gave her an agreeable smile and nodded. I've heard this before as well. She lifted a strand of my hair.

On cue, the man himself strode through the door. Maria froze to admire her boy.

'Mother, food!' Nikki demanded. 'I'm starving.'

Maria gave a euphoric smile. She dropped my hair and clutched her hands to her chest and almost burst with happiness. Nikki wanted food! What joy! She would prepare and cook it, and Nikki would eat it, and she would watch! There wasn't a moment to waste. He could die of starvation waiting or, worse, change his mind and decide he wasn't hungry after all. She pivoted on her Hush Puppies and rushed into the kitchen.

I smiled into my newspaper and impulsively tugged my new canary cardigan tight around me. Nikki loomed behind, hands clutching my waist.

'It's not like you to read the newspaper,' he said, chin resting on the crown of my head.

My eyes travelled the page. 'Mmm, I know, but Rob wants to move. He wants to buy a house.'

His hold on my waist tightened. 'Why, what's wrong with your flat? It's bigger than most houses.'

'I know, but he's not keen on this area and he thinks we should live alone.'

'Does he now. Well, make sure you don't move too far. I don't want you being late for work. You're not leaving me in the lurch just because you move from across the street.'

He sidestepped the counter, pinged open the till and with the precision of a Las Vegas croupier, reckoned a thick bundle of notes and credit card receipts.

'About eighty covers for lunch?' he guessed correctly, as always.

That evening, Rob took me to Wimbledon Village and we dined winter al fresco. At first I hadn't wanted to go. It seemed pointless because I'd already cooked fish fingers and I'd buttered the bread for sandwiches and everything, but Rob insisted.

We sat at a linen-draped table, drenched in the rays of a nuclear overhead heater.

'Evie, business is booming, my coaches are working flat out. I reckon I'll buy a couple more within the year,' he said, waving his fork randomly. 'At the end of the summer season, we'll take a whole month out and travel. We could do Thailand. But that's not to say we need to wait until the end of the season. I'll take you to New York for a long weekend; I've never been to New York. Would you like that?'

I sawed at my steak. 'I would, I'd love to go to New York, but do you know what? I think I'd like to visit your parents in Spain. I've never met any of your family.'

His smile buckled to a frown. 'Spain? You'd rather go to Spain when you have the chance to visit New York?'

I shook my head. 'It's not a matter of Spain versus New York.

We spent last year either here in London, among my friends and family, or working in Paris. My parents have been visiting my aunt in Australia; they're due back next month. Their numero uno priority will be to meet you. Your parents live a two-hour flight away. I think we should make the effort to visit them. I am going to be their daughter-in-law, after all.'

He looked away.

'Well?' I prompted.

'Absolutely!' he said firmly. 'You're right. We'll visit my parents.' He reached across the table and stroked my cheek. 'They'll love you,' he said with a definitive nod.

'So when shall we go?' I asked.

He tapped his knife on his plate in an aid to thought. 'Leave it with me. I'll call and see when suits them.'

Lulu was flat on her back on the lounge floor when we arrived home. Her eyes were closed and her breathing was deep and slow. The lights were dimmed, candles burned and the television was on. There was an eerie gloom. I dropped my bag on the floor and knelt beside her. She held a DVD cover in her hand – *Stop Smoking with Self-Hypnotism*. I put my hand on her forehead. She felt clammy. I felt a whoosh of panic. Rob stood, arms crossed, in the doorway. He tilted his head to read the DVD cover.

'Has the crazy bitch hypnotised herself?' he asked.

I lifted my eyes to the television screen. A white-haired old lady sat in a winged chair, hands clasped. 'Relax, relax, follow the light,' the old lady said softly.

I quickly snatched the remote from the coffee table and jabbed the off button. I didn't want the television hypnotising me!

I straddled Lulu, tipped forward and cupped her cheeks.

'What shall we do?' I asked Rob urgently. 'Read the DVD cover; see if there are any instructions on how to wake someone or, or . . . an antidote or something.' I told him.

'No rush,' he said, sinking casually on to the sofa. 'Why not leave her there on the floor for a couple of days?'

I rounded on him. 'I will not!'

'Why? She's a royal pain in the arse.' He gave her leg a nudge with his foot. 'I like her like this, she looks almost friendly. I really like her.'

I pointed to the door. 'If you're not going to help me, get out.'

He shrugged and stood up. 'Before you wake her, tell her to reserve herself a seat on the next space shuttle.'

I scanned her beautiful face and smoothed her hair from her forehead. 'Lulu, can you hear me?' I asked experimentally.

'Yes,' she replied robotically.

She could hear me. I gave an energetic sigh. OK, I can do this. I've watched Paul McKenna loads of times. I frisked my sweaty palms on my thighs.

'Lulu,' I began in a low tone, 'when I click my fingers you are going to wake up. Do you understand?'

'Yes.'

Rob rubbed his hands together fiercely. 'If you're going to wake that hibernating viper, I'd rather not be around. At least plant a seed in her mind to emigrate,' he said, stepping over her.

I shot him an angry glance. Four purposeful strides later and the lounge door slammed behind him.

To business!

'Lulu?'

'Yes?'

'I've changed my mind. I'm actually not very good at clicking my fingers, sometimes I can't even make a noise. I'm going to count to three and clap twice, then you will wake up. Do you understand?' I asked authoritatively.

'Yes.'

I was about to start counting when suddenly I was seized by a flash of inspiration. I could create a two for the price of one situation here. She could stop smoking and perhaps as she's already hypnotised, I could help her in some other way.

She lay still.

I squared my shoulders and arranged my face into a serious expression. 'Lulu, when you wake up, you will have an over-whelming desire to do the ironing,' I told her. 'Not just your own ironing. You will want to do *my* ironing and Rob's iron-ing. Can you hear me?'

'Yes.' She licked her pink lips.

I felt a microsecond of guilt. But it soon vanished. The iron-ing basket is piled a mile high. Something has to be done. This makes perfect sense.

'You will feel this urge every Thursday night,' I told her.

'Every Thursday night,' she parroted.

I felt a flutter of praiseworthiness; my sister is always telling me how uplifted she feels when her ironing lady has been. Hopefully Lulu will experience the same thrill.

'One! Two! Three!' I announced loudly and smacked my hands together twice.

Her eyes pinged open. She looked at me with a wide stare. 'Why are you straddling me?' she asked. 'Get off.'

'That's gratitude for you,' I told her crisply, crawling over to the sofa. 'You hypnotised yourself.'

Her face clouded over. She sat up. 'Did I?' she asked, tossing a wing of blonde hair over her shoulder.

'Did it work?' I asked, peering at her.

'What do you mean?'

'I mean do you want a fag or not?'

She looked at me for a moment with an indecisive eye. 'I'm gagging for a fag,' she blurted, 'and I'm wearing three patches.'

'I'm going to bed.' I slid a glance at the DVD. 'I'd take that DVD back for a refund if I was you.'

'I'll definitely take it back,' she said, padding up the leg of the coffee table with shaky hands. 'I think I'll do the ironing. Perhaps that would take my mind off fags.'

My heart constricted with excitement. I couldn't look at her. I stooped and grabbed my bag. Bloody hell. She would have done the same thing to me. I know it.

'OK, I'll leave you to it,' I said, making a hasty exit.

Lulu's quit smoking challenge with Andrew Blackbourne has the London masses glued to the radio every morning. It's amazing. She's famous! She's taken a month's unpaid leave from her job as a community nurse because she's now a daily guest speaker on *Good Morning, this is the Capital*, offering advice to listeners on how to quit smoking. Nikki, Pepi, Costas, Maria and I were sitting in the horseshoe alcove in Bar Thea listening to Lulu live on the radio.

'OK,' Andrew Blackbourne began loudly, 'we have Pauline from Leatherhead on line two. Pauline, what would you like to ask Lulu?'

There was a slight crackle and something that sounded like the sucking of lips.

'Pauline?' Andrew prompted. 'Are you there?'

'Yes, yes, I'm here,' an assertive voice confirmed. 'I've been trying *really hard* to stop smoking but there are certain times when no matter how hard I try, I buckle, give in and have a cigarette.'

'I understand,' Lulu sympathised.

'I just don't have your willpower, Lulu,' Pauline from Leatherhead bleated.

'Of course you do!' Lulu shot back solidly.

My eyes scanned the table. I can't help but beam with delight; Lulu on the radio! Who would have thought it? A tear of jubilation rolls down my cheek and I wipe it away with a finger. I'm so proud of her! Nikki squeezed my hand gently. Maria didn't miss the gesture. Her eyes flashed and her nostrils flared in animated exhilaration. She stayed Nik's hand over mine.

'Tell me, Pauline, is there something that triggers this situation you're talking about, a pattern in your daily routine perhaps?' Lulu asked professionally.

I was in awe. Lulu sounded like Oprah. I marvelled at her brilliance.

'Yes, actually there is,' Pauline admitted. 'It's my coffee break at work. A few of us meet at the fire exit, and there's nothing else to do but smoke. I just *cannot* sacrifice the coffee break ciggie,' Pauline admitted with a sigh.

'Pauline, have you thought of doing something else in your coffee break?' Lulu suggested. 'Wouldn't that be the ideal time to utilise the office phone lines to make personal calls? Or do some online shopping. Buy your lottery ticket, catch up with friends on Facebook! Check out YouTube! Do the things you don't get the chance to do because work gets in the way.'

There was a pensive hush while Pauline from Leatherhead considered this advice.

'Yes, I suppose, I suppose . . . I could,' she said at last.

I wasn't sure what to make of Lulu's advice, but I quickly reminded myself that she *was* the expert. Nikki gave me a dubious frown. I tore my eyes away from Nik and smiled at the radio in contemplative consideration.

'Fabulous!' Andrew said strongly. 'So Pauline is happy! Let's move swiftly on to Julie from Egham. Julie is holding on line four . . . Julie, what would you like to ask Lulu?'

'Hi, Lulu!' Julie squealed.

'Hi, Julie!' Lulu squealed in reply.

'I can pretty much give up every fag of the day except the one I enjoy the most,' Julie said, loud and clear.

'And what one would that be?' Lulu asked conversationally.

There was a beat of silence.

Julie from Egham cleared her throat. 'Actually it's my post-sex ciggie,' she admitted.

'Ahhhh! Yes!' Lulu boomed with a knowing note of under-standing. 'Julie, dump your boyfriend because obviously if you're not having sex there will be no post-sex,' Lulu said, pausing to let Julie digest this recommendation. 'And use your vibrator! Your vibrator requires much less energy than sex, but offers pretty much the same results. In fact, in my experience, you often get *better* results! Reducing your expended-energy level means less adrenalin floods the system, so you won't get the same overwhelming desire for a nicotine boost.'

I could tell by Lulu's sing-song tone that she was pleased with herself. I turned to Nikki; he was studying his fingernails. I couldn't read his face. Costas was weighing this revelation with piqued male pride and Pepi was grinning into the *Racing Post*. Maria wasn't listening to Lulu. She stabbed blindly at a piece of embroidery, her eyes scheming back and forth between Nikki and me.

'Erm,' Julie hesitated. 'I'll give this some thought.'

'Good luck, Julie,' Lulu said brightly.

There was a music jingle and a round of applause in the background – most likely Lulu congratulating herself on her own performance.

'Lulu, I must say, you certainly seem to know what you're

talking about,' Andrew said crisply. 'And now it's over to Jack Hopkins for the news and weather.'

Nikki slapped his palm on the table.

'She's really something, don't you think? Her medical background certainly shines through,' Nik said, standing. 'OK team . . . to work. And, Evie, do the wine and spirits order today because you're going to Marrakech tomorrow.'

VENICE

Chapter Six

We've arrived at the Kasbah Tamadot hotel, in the heart of the Atlas Mountains. It's amazing. It has rose-petal-filled fountains, fabulous antique furniture and gorgeous landscaped gardens. There's a gym, which, sadly, I won't have time to visit, and a spa, which I'll make every effort to check out.

It was nice to see John Jackson again. John is a handsome media tycoon and a Sean Connery lookalike. He's also Insignia Tours' biggest corporate client. I like him. I like him a lot. He's stern but fair, and as wealthy and important as he is, he patiently listened to my drunken ramblings last year when I found out Rob had cheated on me. Not that he could exactly escape me, mind you; we *had* been sitting side by side on a flight from Nice to London. I cringed at the memory. I hope he's forgotten about that.

I was enjoying a pre-dinner drink in the fabulous hotel bar. It's crammed with colourful rugs and beautiful gold statues and I think the waiter could be clairvoyant, because without being intrusive, he appears the second you think of something you want. I was sitting on a squishy, low-level, red velvet sofa. *This wouldn't suit Maria*, I think to myself; she would need a tug of war team to get her to her feet. In fact, I may need help getting up myself. A waiter, wearing a white lounge suit and a red fez hat with a black tassel, placed a balloon-shaped glass of wine on the marble and gilt table in front of me. He scattered a few rose petals around my glass, smiled, and magically melted away. I sipped my drink and idly flicked through the hotel brochure.

John arrived. He gestured to the seat beside me. 'May I?' he asked, sinking on to the sofa and crossing one leg over the other.

John is tall and broad-shouldered, commanding and charismatic. His voice rings with an effortless, consistent air of authority. I'd fancy him if he weren't also as old as Moses, sixty if he's a day. His charcoal eyes twinkle when he smiles.

'Let's Make it Happen!' he announced, slapping the arm of the sofa.

'Yes,' I nodded enthusiastically. 'Let's!'

'Let's Make it Happen' was the event title.

'I don't recognise any of the guys you have with you,' I told him.

'No, you haven't met any of them before. These guys are in marketing. You've only met my sales chaps. I have four magazine titles on sale globally that no one had ever heard of three years ago. It's all thanks to this bunch.'

I gave him an impressed nod. 'Remarkable,' I said.

His lips curved in to a smile, displaying a row of perfect white teeth. 'So, have your spirits been restored since we last met? Have you made up with your boyfriend?' John asked with a lift of his eyebrows.

I squirmed. He hadn't forgotten. I suppose sitting next to a gin-soaked, sobbing girl on a flight from Nice to London is a fairly memorable experience.

I met his gaze. 'Yes,' I replied at last.

'I sincerely hope the boy behaves himself,' he said, shooting me a warning glance.

I was about to argue in Rob's defence when the lift door hissed opened, and our group spilled into the lobby.

'Party time!' John said, placing a hand under my elbow and raising me to standing.

Later in my room, I sat on my bed cross-legged and flicked through the itinerary. I sometimes wonder why I get paid to tag along on these corporate events. OK, I have to confirm restaurant reservations, act as John's secretary, make sure cars and guides show up on time and generally act as a dogsbody, but to be honest, it's no hardship. Take this evening for instance. I'm pissed and I've eaten a sumptuous meal. I'm not entirely sure what I ate; everything was yellow ... but it was yellow and delicious. Tomorrow we're going on a jeep safari into the heart of the Atlas Mountains, which sounds fantastic. We'll travel in a convoy. I've never been in a convoy; it's all so Indiana Jones. A vision of me, marching up the mountainside wearing a pair of khaki shorts and a wide-brimmed hat tied with a chiffon scarf, popped into my head. I was looking forward to it. John said these guys didn't know each other very well, so it's my job to make them 'gel'. How easy is that? I'll have them giving each other blokey back-slaps and swapping email addresses in no time.

My mobile rang.

'Evie, babe, I'm missing you like mad,' Rob said with an edge to his voice.

'I'm missing you, too.'

And I've just spotted that we have a treasure hunt in the souk on Sunday. Fabulous! I love treasure hunts! Who doesn't?

'This is *not* happening again! We should be together,' Rob said forcefully.

And I love souks! There's even a shopping list drawn up for the treasure hunt; a list of things we have to hunt for. Genius!

57

'Evie, think about it. This is an outrageous situation, you being on your own in Marrakech. If you want to visit Morocco, we hop on a plane together. It's *that* simple.'

And there's a prize for the winner of the treasure hunt.

'I'd love us to come here together,' I said absently.

Do you know what? I bet because I'm working, I won't be allowed to win the bloody treasure hunt prize. I'm going to ask! No point in me running around a dusty souk if I can't be the winner! I may as well take my time, visit a souk pub. Make a few souk friends.

'I've found a couple of houses I like,' Rob said.

He had my ear now.

'Where?'

'Hampton, Teddington.'

'How much?'

'Roughly around the four hundred grand mark. Obviously we won't look at any properties just yet. There's no point until we have the finance in place. I have a meeting with the bank manager next week.'

I suffered a shimmer of panic. Bank manager?

'Wow, this is ... so, so quick,' I said, trying to sound jubilant.

'Evie, the whole process, even if we found a house the day you got back, would take at least twelve weeks.'

I felt a surge of relief. That's three months!

There was an awkward pause.

'Evie, I know what you're thinking; you don't like the idea of change. But, babe, it'll be a change for the better. We won't sell your flat if we don't have to. Lulu can stay there, Vic could move in with her. You can visit her every day if you want, and if that silly job in the bar makes you happy, then fine, work there. I want to provide a home for us. It's what every man wants to do for the woman he loves.'

I felt watery-eyed and nippy-nostrilled. He is so *sweet*. What was I thinking? I should be delighted that he wants us to live together. Suddenly, and to my surprise, a tear brimmed my bottom lashes and travelled slowly down my cheek.

'Are you there, babe?'

'Mmmm.'

'What's wrong?'

'I . . . I miss you,' I managed in a snuffly voice.

A rumbly chuckle sounded down the line. 'You are going to get *the best* welcome home anyone has ever had,' he said.

'Promise?' I asked.

'Promise!'

It wasn't until I was snuggled in my canopied *Arabian Nights* bed that I realised I hadn't bothered to ask Rob how he was getting on in Birmingham. No big deal. I would ask tomorrow.

Five Land Rovers arrived to take us on our mountain safari. I assembled the guys by the main entrance. They milled around, hands deep in the pockets of their uniform chinos, making wooden, if polite, conversation. I'd soon change *that*. A couple of glasses of wine at lunchtime, a few group photographs, and they'll be friends for life. It's what I'm here for!

When John strode through the lobby the guys' mood shifted gear from relaxed to starched. Whether by accident or design, John terrifies the people who work for him. He expects everyone to be as manically obsessed with his businesses as he is. This prompts a pretence of infatuated professionalism, making relaxing enough to be sociable in his company close to impossible. In truth, if John wanted the guys to have the best possible time on these events, he shouldn't come himself. That said, he always seems amiable enough to me.

With my clipboard under my arm and my camera around my

neck, it was obvious who was in charge. I was wearing cream jeans, a pink blouse, and a wide-brimmed hat. I couldn't believe my luck when I spotted the hat in the hotel gift shop. Bon chance, I'd thought, whipping it off the mannequin.

I split the party into five groups of three, and I joined with John and two of his guys, Tom and Simon, in the first jeep. Both driver and guide were about four feet tall, wore white pyjamas, red neckscarves and flip-flops, and had no teeth. Still, they were pleasant enough. I tweaked my hat, and stepped on to the jeep. I was looking forward to this.

We crunched forward in an excited convoy.

'Oh my God, look at that. Isn't it amazing?' I enthused, sweeping my hand at the breathtaking vista of dramatic fertile slopes, dotted with clusters of Berber villages, orange groves, small farms, and picture-postcard clay houses.

John, Tom and Simon smiled non-committally.

What was wrong with them? Were they blind? Could they not see what I saw?

That's the trouble with these businessmen: they become complacent. They become accustomed to being whizzed off to exotic places and wined and dined at the company's expense. I was really quite annoyed at their attitude; they're so ungrateful. I was just about to tell them so when the jeep rumbled over a pile of rocks and my elbow, which was supporting my chin, slid off the armrest and I bit down hard on my tongue.

My eyes pooled with the pain. I glared at Tom in disbelief; he was absorbed with his BlackBerry. He wasn't even looking out the window. What's so interesting about a bloody phone? I shot Simon a dirty look. He was reading a newspaper, and John, rubbing his knuckles on the crease between his eyes, was settling back for a sleep. A sleep! On a fabulous trip like this! They could be anywhere. They might as well be in their kitchen at home.

I was the only one recognising this trip for the thrilling experience it was.

I waved my arm in an extravagant gesture. 'Well! I think this is a beautiful place,' I said with a shaky dip in my voice as we swooped around a hairpin bend. I gripped the armrests. It was quite a choppy ride.

I will *never* stop appreciating the excitement and adventure of foreign travel, I thought gratefully. I drew a deep breath as the driver negotiated a death-defying curve in the road. I wouldn't like to drive here. I eyed the gradient of the drop – actually it was quite steep. In fact, it was probably the deepest drop on a curvy treacherous road that I'd ever seen. I won't look down, I decided, straightening my hat. I'll focus on the road ahead. We took a perilous bend on two wheels. I was thrown across the seat. As I sat back up, the driver crunched the brakes to the floor and did a tailspin around a curve. A mushroom cloud of dust erupted in our wake. This was like being on a trapeze – one wrong move and I'd be dead. Did I say dead? I did! A vision of the jeep rolling down the mountainside flashed in my mind in a series of vivid, terrifying pictures. All of a sudden a fuse blew in my brain and I was seized with irrational terror. I threw my hands up.

'What if we crash? What if this heap of junk leaves the road?' I yelled, demented. 'And we roll down the mountain? And the jeep explodes? And we all die?'

Startled, John sat up quickly. Simon jerked his chin from his newspaper. Tom dropped his BlackBerry. They exchanged desperate glances.

I'm only twenty-six. I'm too young to die.

'And as if it's not bad enough that we're all dead, our bodies will explode in the flames!' I'm totally freaked.

There was a unified burst of urgent assurance.

They thought I was mental. It was obvious.

I'm not.

I crammed a clenched fist in my mouth.

'Evie, don't be silly. No one is going to die or explode,' John said, as though explaining something incredibly simple to someone exceptionally stupid.

What am I thinking? This is a bloody sightseeing trip, not a bomb squad emergency call out. I mustered a smile and checked my watch. We'd been driving for five minutes, so only another ... seven hours and fifty-five minutes to go. Fine, absolutely fine.

'Hypothetically speaking,' I said, jamming my sunglasses on my face and turning back to the view.

My nerves were shot to pieces. I wasn't enjoying this drive at all. A suspicious bubble erupted in my windpipe and the muscles in my tummy coiled. I inhaled sharply. I felt woozy and ... *travel-sick*. I sighed. That's all I needed. A surge of last night's yellow dinner erupted like a tidal wave from my stomach to my tonsils. I pressed my palm on my mouth. The nauseous swell passed, only just. Bloody hell, I was exhausted.

The jeep rolled and pitched around a bend. This drive was purgatory, hell on earth. Did the driver even have a driving licence? Sweating, I sank into my seat and pulled my hat over my eyes. If I blocked out the rolling scenery, perhaps I'd feel more *grounded*. After all, if you've seen one Berber village, you've seen them all. Why am I here?

We stopped at an olive pressing farm. It wasn't on the itinerary, but John expressed an interest so the driver pulled over. I could've done without it. Basically an olive is an olive. What's to see? I stepped tentatively from the jeep and enjoyed a microsecond of fresh air before the pungent smell of compressed olives hit me like a slap in the face. I lurched back into the jeep and slammed the door.

John's torso appeared through the window. 'Evie, are you all right? You look a little pale,' he said, his voice low and cultured.

'I'm fine,' I lied.

Am I all right? Was he serious? First of all, I almost died of fright on a death defying drive! And now I'm afflicted by whatever toxins the hotel fed me last night.

'Take this jeep ahead to the restaurant. Let them know we'll be running late,' he said. 'There's plenty of room for us to travel in one of the other vehicles.'

'OK,' I managed.

I felt like kissing him. At least if I vomited, I wouldn't have an audience. I untied my hat, used it as a fan, sprayed the air with a generous cloud of Flower by Kenzo, and settled back to concentrate on surviving the drive to the lunch stop. The jeep lurched as the driver jigged into first gear. I closed my eyes and wedged the nozzle of my perfume bottle up my nostril. If I shut out sight and smell and took my mind elsewhere, anywhere other than in this jeep on this mountain, I would hopefully keep last night's dinner down.

By the time John and the group arrived at the restaurant I was the colour of leprosy. I was exhausted, tearful and dehydrated, having spent a good hour being sick. John appeared in the doorway of the ladies' toilet, led by the toilet attendant, her eyes bright with importance.

'Come on, Evie,' John soothed, stooping to pick me up off the floor, where I was slumped against the cool tiled wall. 'Let's get you back to the hotel and tucked up in bed,' he said with a faint smile.

I felt a rush of relief at seeing him. I couldn't remember the last time I'd felt so ill.

'But I'm supposed to be looking after you,' I said weakly.

'I think on this occasion I may do a better job of looking after you. I'll have the hotel send for a doctor, although I'm pretty sure all that's wrong with you is an adverse reaction to driving in the Atlas Mountains, after a rich evening meal. Nevertheless I want to be sure,' he said, placing a guiding arm around my shoulders.

I held him tight. 'But—'

'No buts.'

I spent twenty-four hours in bed, with yellow-dinner-itis. It was horrendous. I bet I've lost weight. At one point I suspected poison. But who would want to poison me? John sent flowers. How sweet is that? Flowers to a hotel room! It's not even as though I could take them home. I called Rob to ask how he was getting on in Birmingham.

'It's boring and I miss you, I really, *really* miss you,' he said. 'I'm never letting you out of my sight again.'

Today is our last day in Marrakech; the souk treasure hunt. I gave everyone dirhams to spend and a shopping list. The task is to find and buy the items on the list and get back to the coach as quickly as possible. I don't want to boast but I'm pretty confident I'll be the winner, even though I'm sitting in a stone dungeon, which is cluttered with dusty perfume bottles and baskets of dried flowers, having a henna design painted on my hand.

I did look at the shopping list: saffron, a hubbley-bubbley pipe, a tobacco pouch, black soap, mint tea and a couple of pieces of fruit that I've never even heard of. I decided that the most sensible thing to do would be to employ a personal shopper. So that's what I did. I approached a couple of kids outside the henna artist's with a *proposal* . . . the proposal being that I give them three bags of gummy bears and they ran around the souk gathering everything on the list. Subsequently, I now have my shopping bag on the floor between my legs and I'm idly admiring the beautiful floral vine snaking my wrist. I love it!

My already high spirits soared as I stepped from the henna place into the hubbub of the souk, a labyrinth of clay passage-ways. It's like a scene from *Arabian Nights*. You can't walk two steps without someone throwing a rug at your feet in the hope that you'll buy it, waving a fresh pastry under your nose, or trying to lasso you into their shop. The guys will get hopelessly delayed or, even better, totally lost. I was sure of it. I, on the other hand, knew exactly where I was going because as well as a per-sonal shopper, I had hired two personal guides. They were seven-year-old twin boys who, for the price of a bag of Kola Kubes, were now rushing me back to the coach park. It was simply a matter of initiative.

I wheezed; jogging was giving me a stitch. I wish I'd thought to wear a sports bra. Still, it would be worth it. I was sure the prize would be fabulous, and I was eligible to win. I'd asked John.

As predicted, I was the first to arrive back at the coach. Simon was the second. He handed me his shopping bag for inspection. I tipped the contents on to the dashboard.

'No hubbley-bubbley pipe or black soap?' I gave a withering sigh. 'You're disqualified,' I told him sharply.

He wiped a hand across his sweaty brow. 'I couldn't find them,' he admitted miserably.

'You shouldn't have come back until you had. Where's your fighting spirit?'

John, straight-backed and legs crossed, browsed the *Financial Times*.

'Evie is right, Simon,' John said from his comfortable, air-conditioned front seat. 'It's a matter of determination and drive.'

Simon looked wounded, as though John's disapproval had been a physical blow. I slid John a cynical look. He had a nerve. It was easy for him to say that; he'd been to a business meeting in a luxury five-star hotel. He hadn't been running around a baking souk, breathing in choking red dust like the rest of us.

It was one sorry tale after another. Elliott bleated that he'd lost his shopping bag, and Tom had bumped in to someone he knew from home and spent the entire time in a bar. The guys were hot and exhausted, with deflated spirits; no one, with the exception of my good self, had completed the task. I wasn't entirely surprised. Everyone slept on the drive back to the hotel, except John, who studied his newspaper.

OK, now I feel guilty. We've just finished dinner in a private room in the hotel. John made a speech thanking the guys for all their hard work. It got boring at one point when he babbled about performance, sales drives and world markets, but it picked up at the end when he announced the winner of the treasure hunt. It was me! I'm now turning an envelope over in my hand. It's the prize. It's a weekend for four in Disneyland Paris. The reason I feel guilty is because now that I have this prize, I don't want it. These men have wives and kids. What do I want with a weekend in Disneyland?

'Guys,' I announced, inspired and jumping to my feet. 'I'll surrender this prize to the best belly dancer as voted for by the two waitresses who've just served us.'

It was hilarious; Tom won. He deserved it. He fell in the lily pond. With an elaborate sweeping gesture and a gushing speech, I presented the prize to a grinning, dripping wet Tom. He was elated.

John, arms folded, had watched in silent amusement. He placed his hand in the small of my back and steered me towards the bar.

'Evie, did you cheat?' he asked in a confidential whisper.

'Cheat?' I echoed, affronted.

'Did you?'

'Don't be ridiculous. How can you cheat at shopping?'

He lifted my hand and stabbed a finger at my henna flower.

'Did you cheat?' he demanded.

I felt a shimmer of guilt. 'Yes!' I confessed.

He nodded knowingly.

'I didn't actually cheat,' I rallied, 'because there were no rules as such and—'

'You cheated! It's *not* in the spirit of the game. That said, I'd like to know how you managed it.' He signalled to the barman. 'Would you like a glass of champagne?' he asked.

'I'd prefer a gin and tonic.' As I reached into my bag for my lip gloss, I caught John's sideways look. 'What is it?' I asked.

'I have an event next month in Dublin; I'm taking a group to the Six Nations. Would you like to come?'

I gave him an appreciative smile. 'Yes,' I said. 'I'd love to come to Dublin.'

'Now, tell me – how did you manage to win the treasure hunt and have a henna tattoo painted at the same time?'

Chapter Seven

Rob and I had been in bed for twenty-eight hours. We've had three picnics! Rob rolled towards me and rubbed his stubbly cheek in the hollow of my neck. A slither of early-morning sunshine nudged through a slit in the blinds highlighting the strawberry tint in his blond hair.

'I have something for you,' he said, throwing off the quilt.

Naked, he padded to the chest of drawers and flipped opened his briefcase. I leaned on my elbows and studied his firm bum, the long channel of his spine and his broad, toned back. The muscles of his shoulder blades moved smoothly as he closed the lid of his case. He turned to me with a triumphant smile.

'Here it is,' he said, brandishing a colourful A4 folder.

The mattress shifted as he climbed back into bed.

'Houses!' he announced, closing his hand over mine.

I felt a wave of discomfort.

A smile lit up his face.

'You do want us to buy a house, don't you?' he asked, his eyes bright and energetic.

'I do! Of course!'

'Good.' He gathered me to him and kissed my cheek. 'Babe,

look what we could have,' he said eagerly, handing me a glossy Trackson Estate Agents portfolio.

I was impressed. Words like 'newly refurbished', 'beautifully presented', 'period features' and 'stunning breakfast room' piqued my interest. But when I read 'close to boutiques', 'adjoining en suite' and 'fully appointed dressing room', frankly, I was excited. I had a vision of me throwing open the doors and walking into a floor-to-ceiling shoe cupboard. Of course, I'd have to go shopping. What's the point of having a three-bedroom house if you don't bother to fill all three wardrobes?

'These are three bedrooms but, Evie, I think I can stretch to four.'

Four?

I would learn to make pancakes; I'd have to. Why would you want an Aga stove otherwise?

We fell silent leafing through the description sheets, both of us lost in thought. I stole a glance at Rob and felt a surge of affection. He wanted this so badly and he wanted it for *us*. He wanted to do this for me.

'Once I meet with the bank, I'll have a better idea of how much we can afford,' he said keenly. 'I'd prefer to push myself; I have a couple of policies I can surrender to give us a more sub-stantial deposit. Ideally I'd like us to hold on to the flat.'

Policies? He has policies? If I can't eat it, wear it or drink it, I don't buy it!

He tossed the papers aside and cupped my face. I stroked his cheek.

'You and I have the rest of our lives to look forward to,' he said.

He pulled me hard against him and put his mouth over mine. I felt a shattering burst of happiness. I wanted him. I wanted to be with him always and I wanted to live with him in our own home. It was the right thing to do. I knew it, I was certain.

Rob went to work. Lulu and I were sitting in the lounge with cups of coffee. My mind worked frantically. I had to tell Lulu that Rob and I were buying a house. I licked my lips. Basically, I reasoned, it was a simple matter of evolution. You can't live with your best girlfriend for ever; and she *has* been seeing Vic for over seven months – a record for her. She was probably thinking along the same lines herself . . . kind of . . . *eventually*. Head bent, she was gnawing at her nails and sorting out her fan mail. I know, can you believe it? Fan mail! I gave the letters on the table a hard look. That anyone would seek advice from her is unbelievable.

My head was bubbling trying to arrange my words.

She gave me a flighty glance. 'What up?' she asked.

I tried for a smile. 'Guest-speaking on the radio certainly seems to be a serious demand on your time,' I said conversationally.

'Mmm, it is,' she agreed. 'I love it. Talking about smoking is far better for me than smoking itself.'

'Absolutely,' I said. 'So . . . how are you and Vic getting on?'

'It's finished,' she said casually.

My thoughts were in free fall. 'Finished?'

'Yes, finished. I couldn't stop smoking and police a relationship at the same time. You have no idea how time-consuming stopping smoking is. I have no time to do anything else.'

'But you adored him.'

'Did . . . past tense!'

'But . . . but what will you do about sex?' I prompted.

She gave a dismissive wave. 'I'll shop for that as and when the mood strikes.' She tossed a sheet of blonde hair over her shoulder and clutched my hand. 'Men come and go but friend-ships are for life. I have you and that's the main thing. The most important thing is that we have each other. Isn't it?'

'Yes,' I agreed with a gulp.

I won't mention the house just yet, I decided. I may tell her next week, or the week after that.

Rob and I were in bed having a post-sex cuddle. I watched the shifting yellow light that was thrown into the room by the lamp post outside. I now had two pressing issues:

1. I must tell Lulu I'm planning on moving in with Rob and leaving her on her own;
2. I must tell Rob I'm going to Dublin with John Jackson.

There is absolutely no point doing anything about either one right now. I have been putting it off for a whole fortnight, and in fact both would wait for anything up to a month. Now was not the time to tell Rob about Dublin, because last night we had to get out of bed at midnight to rescue Lulu who had run out of diesel on the A3. She had been sitting cross-legged on the hard shoulder crying when we found her.

'I can't concentrate on simple everyday tasks, like filling the car, painting my nails, checking Facebook or straightening my hair, because I'm too busy trying to stop smoking. It's exhaust-ing,' she'd wailed. 'There's no time for anything else,' she had added, smudging damp mascara around her eye socket with the heel of her hand.

I'd given her a tissue, put my hand under her elbow and coaxed her to standing.

Rob, bent to the task of opening a canister of diesel, had shot me a murderous look.

'Ask me what I'm doing this weekend,' she'd challenged. 'Go on! Ask me!'

'What are you doing this weekend?'

'I'm not smoking all weekend. That's what I'm doing!' she had told me, and burst into tears.

'That's a good thing to be doing,' I'd told her, trying to sound supportive.

I had driven Lulu's car home, while she'd rocked in the passenger seat chanting, 'I want a fag, I want a fag,' for the entire journey.

Rob, enraged, had followed in his car.

And tonight we had to help her again. She rang to say she had a flat tyre. We found her leaning against a bus stop, arms folded, staring hypnotically at the traffic circling the Wandsworth one-way system. Her eyes had brimmed when she saw me. She'd lurched towards me, arms outstretched. I'd gathered her to me.

'Evie, I lost control of my car. I could've died. My tyre blew.'

Rob, hands in the pockets of his leather jacket, had walked around her car kicking each tyre experimentally in turn.

'She doesn't have a flat tyre,' he'd said emphatically.

She'd turned on him. 'I do! My hearing went all funny and tinny, there was a hollow echo in my head, like my car was driving on . . . on steel wheels. And my car turned left all by itself. I do have a flat tyre!' she'd insisted. 'I almost ended up across two lanes and on the wrong side of the road.'

Rob had given her an unblinking stare. 'You don't!' he'd told her.

'I do!'

'You don't!'

She'd wheeled to face me, eyes wild. 'Tell that fucking idiot that I have a flat tyre!' she'd shrieked, jabbing a finger at Rob.

Rob had pressed his palm on the bonnet and had shook his head from side to side. 'She doesn't have a flat tyre,' he'd repeated.

I didn't doubt him.

'Murder! That's it! He wants me dead because he's jealous. He wants you to himself. It's obvious. And he thinks me driving a death trap is the answer. It wouldn't surprise me if he's cut my brakes or something.'

'D'you know what?' I'd begun diplomatically, 'I think nicotine withdrawal causes a rumbly noise in your ears.'

Her eyes had grown wide. 'Would it?' she'd asked, jamming a finger in her ear and giving it a wiggle. She'd chewed her bottom lip, her eyes brimming with tears. 'Evie, I think I might join the AA because—'

'I sincerely hope you're referring to the Automobile Association?' Rob had interrupted coldly.

'No, Alcoholics Anonymous,' she'd said. 'I think it's time I met with other addicts . . . like me.'

I'd put Lulu to bed with a hot water bottle and a plastic cigarette.

No! Now was definitely not the time to tell Rob I was going to Dublin. I laid my arm across his chest, pulled the quilt over my shoulder and blew my fringe from my forehead.

'I have an appointment with the bank tomorrow,' he said.

My eyes roved the darkened room.

'Fabulous,' I managed with a silent gulp, and realising with nerve-stiffening certainty that I had to tell Lulu about the house and the sooner the better.

The following afternoon Nikki took me to Wimbledon Village. He's negotiating the purchase of a property with a view to converting it into flats. When I saw the building I seriously doubted his sanity. We were standing in the gravelled courtyard. It looked like something from a Hammer horror movie. It was totally dilapidated, with boarded windows emblazoned with gothic graffiti, flaking paintwork and the guttering was literally swinging from the eaves. I was racking my brains for something nice to say. I must be able to think of something, surely!

'It's big,' I said at last, startled as a flock of pigeons flew out of the roof.

Nikki smiled at the façade fondly. He held the garden gate in his hand; the gate had fallen off its hinges when Nik opened it to let us in. He tossed the gate on top of a pyramid of rancid-smelling black bin bags.

'I want it, I want it badly,' he said with an urgent smile. He gave me a drill-like gaze. 'It's perfect,' he said, and meant it. 'There's only one other interested buyer, so only two of us are in the running.'

I pulled my jacket around me and wondered who the other madman was. There was a sudden flurry of motion from the direction of the pyramid of bin bags. I turned to the sound. Nik put his hand under my hair and massaged my neck absently.

'I'll be disappointed if I lose out on this,' he said, 'bitterly disappointed.'

The bin bags shifted. I pointed a shaky finger.

'Did you see that?' I asked in a rush. 'Those bags moved.'

Nik gave a casual shrug. 'Oh, it's only rats.'

'Rats!?' I shrieked, barrelling past him. 'Nik, get me out of here,' I yelled, marching down the path without looking back.

We had over a hundred covers for lunch. A hundred! Nikki must be raking it in. No wonder he has spare change to buy buildings in Wimbledon with. I trailed a cloth over the counter in a slow, sweeping figure of eight and watched Nik, his dark head bowed as he counted the money in the till, faint lines at the corner of his chocolate eyes creasing as he smiled. He caught my eye and blew me a kiss. The front door opened with a whoosh and rattled against the wall.

'Evie!'

Startled, Nik and I turned to the voice. I gaped. Rob filled the doorway. His face was flushed, and a vein pulsed in his jaw. He was livid. There was a weighty silence. Stunned, I took a couple of brave steps forward.

'Out!' he snapped with a jerk of his chin.

My terrified mind searched for a reason for this display of fury. I looked at my watch; I couldn't leave work an hour early. I thought of telling Rob this but swiftly changed my mind when he took a step towards me.

'Out!' Rob repeated, enraged.

Bloody hell, he was fuming!

Nikki took my jacket from the peg beside the till and without shifting his dark gaze from Rob, walked round the bar and tugged my jacket over my shoulder. I shot Nikki an apologetic glance.

'Call me if you need me,' Nik said crisply.

It was awful. Rob grabbed my elbow and hurried us across the road. He didn't speak, not a word, not until we got into the flat. Even then he paced the lounge in contemplative rage. My insides churned with nerves. He was still wearing his dark blue business suit – he'd obviously come straight from the bank. He turned and glared at me with a scary expression.

'What, what is it?' I asked in a voice that didn't sound like my own.

He slammed a fist in the palm of his hand. 'You've got a county court judgment against you!' he yelled.

I shook my head mechanically. A county court judgment? I ransacked my mind. Where did I get one of those? Where?

'Don't you *dare* deny it, Evie, because it's a fact!'

'I'm not, I'm—'

'Do you have *any* idea how angry I am?' he roared.

I did. It was glaringly obvious how angry he was.

'We can't get a mortgage until I sort this out. And to be told by the bank that you have a zero credit rating . . . ' He broke off and exhaled deeply. 'Evie, I've never been so embarrassed in my life. There will be *no* house until this mess is cleared up and it's all your fault!'

I felt a reflexive twitch at the corner of my mouth and my nostrils stung with the effort of trying not to cry. I suddenly desperately wanted the Aga and the en suite bathroom, and it had all been taken away from me because of a county court judgment, which, now that I thought of it, I ended up with because I hadn't had a postage stamp when I needed one.

One blond brow flicked up. Rob took a giant closing step; I shrank back.

'So what's it all about? Last year we paid your store cards. We got rid of your credit cards and we cleared your overdraft.'

I nodded.

He rocked on his heels, hands jammed in his pockets. 'So who the hell do you owe money to?' he bellowed.

My throat was tight. 'Parking tickets,' I confessed.

'Parking tickets!' he roared. 'Parking tickets! How many parking tickets does a person collect before the financial establishment takes an interest?' he asked acidly, eyes shining with rage.

'I'm not sure, they, they're in the parking ticket drawer.'

Red blotches stained his cheeks. 'You have a parking ticket drawer?' he roared.

'Some are Lulu's,' I shot back defensively, 'and there are a couple of speeding fines but they're Spanish so they don't really count. And there's a congestion charge but I don't remember driving into central London, I was going to dispute that. And I was sorting them all out but Lulu used a whole stamp book, entering competitions—'

He held up the flat of his hand. 'Evie, shut up!'

I felt weak and fluey. I felt as though I was melting.

His eyes narrowed. He took a couple of deep breaths to steady his voice before he spoke. 'OK . . . now . . . listen.'

I was all ears.

'This would be a good time to tell me if there's anything else I should know.'

I silently doubted it.

'The house will eat the lion's share of my savings, and the mortgage will be as much as I can afford. I don't want to be faced with a situation where something comes up and I can't cover it. Your debts are *my* debts. Tell me now, is there anything else? I want the truth, Evie. We agreed – no secrets.'

I lifted my eyes from the hollow of his throat and raised my chin for combat.

'My overdraft yo-yoes around the one thousand mark but I can pay that easily. I got a Harrods card at Christmas but the minimum payment is nothing. It's reasonable, it's—'

'Get the parking tickets, the Harrods bill and Harrods card,' Rob demanded. 'And get me your last bank statement.'

It was horrendous. He didn't care that I was upset. I cried, thinking he might feel guilty about shouting, but he didn't – he ranted for over an hour. And when Lulu rang to say she was pissed and needed a lift home from Clapham he told her to sober up and get a cab.

But as unpleasant as the evening had been, it didn't compare to the following morning.

Rob left for work. To be honest I was happy to see him go. We'd slept back to back all night. I'd just wriggled under the quilt to dream about something nice and enjoy having the bed to myself before getting up for work, when Rob ram-raided the bedroom door.

'Keys!' he bellowed.

I sat bolt upright. 'You what?' I asked, startled.

'Give me your car key. My car has been stolen.'

'Go away, it has not,' I said, pulling the quilt over my chest.

He grabbed my handbag from the dressing table and tossed it at me. 'Keys, now!' He stood at the bottom of the bed. 'Evie, we are *not* staying here. I'm renting a house. You and I are moving out, the sooner the better.'

He snatched my car keys from my outstretched hand and strode from the room, jacket tail flapping.

And the day got steadily worse.

My paperwork arrived for Dublin, reminding me that I still hadn't mentioned the trip to Rob, and Lulu lost her job at the surgery. The surgery gave her an ultimatum: come back to work or else. She opted for the 'or else'.

Lulu, Nikki and I sat down for a coffee in the bar after the lunchtime rush.

'Evie, I can't go back to work at the surgery. I love my radio slot.'

'Well' I began. 'It's not actually a slot as such, is more of an . . . appearance and . . . '

She gripped my arm and reached across the table for Nikki's hand. 'I'll be skint for a while, but at least I know I've got bed and board, because you'll keep me, Evie, won't you?' she asked, eyeing me feverishly. 'And you'll feed me, Nik, won't you?' She gave us an appreciative smile.

I chewed my lips, digesting this whole nightmare.com situation. I couldn't leave her in the flat jobless and penniless. Could I?

'What's wrong?' she asked. 'You look worried.'

'Rob's car was stolen this morning.'

'Was he in it?' Lulu asked, her already wide smile widening. 'Tell me he was.'

Nikki fired her a warning glance.

'I'm only joking,' she said. 'Who would want to steal him? Kidnappers would pay you to take him back.' She stood, whizzed the strap of her bag up her arm, and swooped to kiss us in turn. 'I have to go to the surgery to pick up my P45. I'll see you at home,' she said, departing in a cloud of Flowerbomb.

There was a meditative hush. I fingered the rim of my cup.

'Evie, do you have something on your mind?' Nikki asked in a low voice.

'Rob wants to move from Tooting now, he wants to rent somewhere. His car being stolen was the last straw.'

Nikki placed his hand over mine and leaned forward, causing his shadow to fall on the table. His eyes swam with thoughts.

'Renting doesn't make financial sense, not when you already have somewhere to live and you're paying a mortgage on it. It's money down the drain. He's a businessman. Point that out.'

I smiled. Nik is so sensible. He was absolutely right.

The following morning, Rob left for work. Two minutes later he was back. Lulu and I were having breakfast in the lounge.

'I can't believe it. My car has been returned,' he said, placing my car keys on the coffee table. 'I won't need your car today.'

'Are you sure it was stolen in the first place, you big dramatic tit?' Lulu asked, eyeing him sceptically.

Rob worked the knot of his tie tighter to his collar. 'I didn't see your broomstick parked in the drive. How did you get home last night?' he asked Lulu.

'Very droll,' she replied, waving a slice of toast.

When I walked into the bar later, the first thing I did was challenge Nikki.

'Did you have anything to do with Rob's car being returned?'

'I may have done,' Nik admitted evasively.

I angled myself in front of him, hands on hips. 'Did you have anything to do with the car being stolen?'

He smoothed a palm over his thick black hair. 'Definitely not!' he insisted, affronted. 'I simply mentioned down the gym that if anyone had taken it, or knew who had taken it, I'd appreciate them returning it.'

'Thank you.'

His face clicked from indifferent to serious. 'For you, I'd do anything.'

The bar was quiet – it was the lull after the storm. Maria and I were alone. I closed my eyes to the pain as she twisted sponge rollers in my hair. Nikki and Pepi were at the betting shop and Costas had gone home with a girl he'd chatted up at lunchtime.

I called Rob.

Maria angled my head to the side, humming as she worked. I cradled the phone between my shoulder and ear.

'Rob, I've been thinking. It doesn't make financial sense to rent,' I said wisely. 'We would pay over a thousand pounds a month and get nothing in return. And likely we would have to commit to a rental agreement for a minimum term of at least six months and—'

'You're absolutely right.'

I was thrown because I was never usually absolutely right.

'So?' I hedged.

'So we stay in Tooting until we find a house to buy,' he said swiftly.

Now for my little bombshell. I felt a pink flush rise in my cheeks and my stomach dipped.

'Right. And, Rob, er, the thing is, a job to Dublin has come up. It's for John Jackson, which as you know is a breeze. He's a treasure and he pays well. I really enjoy working for him, and—'

'When?'

'This weekend. I was going to mention it sooner but—'

'Fine, I need to go up north for a couple of days. The timing is perfect.'

'Right,' I said, over-slowly.

'Anything else?' he asked stiffly.

'No, you're obviously busy,' I said catching his sharp tone.

He exhaled loudly. 'I'm sorry, babe, really I am. Yes, I am busy but I should never be too busy to speak to you. Are you all right?'

'Yes,' I gave Maria a warm smile. 'I'm having my hair done.'

'Well I'll have to take you out for dinner then, won't I?'

'That would be lovely.'

He gave a lazy chuckle. 'Leave the reservations to me. Wear something sexy and expensive.'

I smiled into the phone.

'Oooo I like the sound of that . . . wear something sexy and expensive.'

Maria gave my hair a tug and thumped the heel of her hand on my forehead.

I flinched.

'I love you,' he said.

'Ditto,' I said, giving Maria a wary smile. I couldn't tell Rob I loved him in front of Maria. I couldn't!

'Evie, the argument about money, forget it, we'll work something out. I'll pay your Harrods card today. And before we move, we'll discuss a budget. We'll start with a clean slate and there will be nothing to argue about. I'll see you tonight. Remember . . . sexy and expensive,' he repeated.

'I'll remember,' I said, gazing out the window at the rumbling double-decker buses and the bumper to bumper late afternoon traffic.

I put my phone in my bag and tugged my cardigan around me. Rob has something on his mind, something more important than complaining about me touring, moving house or my spending.

'Beautiful, beautiful hair. These rollers you can keep. I can buy more,' Maria offered, edging around me and admiring her handiwork.

'Thank you,' I replied woodenly.

It can only be work. I made a conscious decision to show more interest.

'I give you a green scarf for over the rollers to go home,' Maria said.

'Fabulous.'

I never ask him anything about his business, I should be more supportive. He works so hard and pays for everything.

'I have a beautiful necklace I give you because I know one day you will be my daughter,' Maria told me, nodding gravely.

What is she talking about?

Chapter Eight

John Jackson is an evil fiend. I'm worth every penny the skin-flint pays me! I am shattered after one of the worst mornings of my entire life.

At Heathrow, a client arrived who John was positive had declined, which meant we were one flight ticket short. I begged British Airways to do a name change on my ticket, so at least the client was on the flight, but that meant I was on standby. John was furious. He rang his *own pilot* only to be told that *his* plane was being refurbished as per *his own* instructions and wouldn't be ready for another three days. He threw his BlackBerry into his briefcase in a rage.

John has his own plane! He's not just any old man; he's a man with a plane!

'I am not escorting this group alone,' John snapped. 'Sort it, Evie. Get yourself on a flight! Get to Dublin!'

I ran a marathon around the airport before *finally* securing a seat on the same flight as the group.

On arrival into Dublin airport the coach was nowhere to be seen. When I eventually found the driver, he had his three kids on board because his wife was on a hen weekend in

Ibiza, which meant I didn't have enough seats for my twenty Armani-suited gents. Honestly, what was the driver thinking? I'm running a corporate event, not a crèche. I swiftly ejected the kids into a taxi and instructed it to follow our coach. Only then did the coach driver casually admit he'd never been to Dublin before. He was from Cork and had been drafted to Dublin to help cope with the influx of rugby supporters in the city for the match. He imparted this news as though this was really exciting stuff and I should be delighted to hear it. I was frantic. I had to log into the GPS on my phone and direct the eejit all the way into town. Me! It beggars belief. I can't even find central London from Tooting, and I've lived there for years. I have nada sense of direction, everyone knows that.

We're now in the hotel lobby, one room short due to our unexpected client, and Dublin is packed to the gunnels – there's not even a spare closet to be had. And I mean absolutely zilch! It's the Six Nations Final, England versus Ireland, and every bed and sofa for miles is taken. The upshot is . . . John and I will have to share a room. He's livid and frankly I'm not exactly delighted myself.

The group sauntered towards the elevator and up to their rooms.

'Evie,' John stormed once we were alone. 'There must be some other way.'

'There is.'

'What?'

'I'm on the streets . . . If I don't share with you, I have nowhere to sleep.'

His salt and pepper brows were drawn in annoyance, and he pressed his lips together. Charcoal eyes scanned the carpeted foyer of the luxurious Fitzwilliam Hotel.

'Penthouse suite,' the receptionist announced brightly, sliding a key card across the desk.

'Thank you,' I replied with a smile.

John gripped my elbow, bent his head to mine and guided me purposefully towards the elevator.

'Evie, you will *not* answer the telephone in our room. My wife would *not* understand, and no amount of explaining the situation would change that. And I do *not* want my clients to know we are sharing,' he said in a warning tone. 'Do I make myself clear?'

'Crystal clear.'

A thought occurred to me.

'You can't answer the phone in the room either,' I told him, stepping into the lift.

Dark eyes held mine. The door whispered shut.

'Why ever not?'

'My fiancé won't be overly enthused at the thought of me sharing a room with you.'

His broad chest rose indignantly. 'I can assure you, you are safe with me!' he boomed, affronted.

'And I can assure you, you are safe with me!' I echoed.

'Evie, I think it's fair to say that my wife would have a valid reason for being enraged if she were to find out that I was sharing a room with a girl thirty years my junior.'

'That may be true, but Rob can be ... *unreasonable* — very unreasonable.'

The lift door pinged open. We collided in the rush to leave. He breezed past me. I skittered in his wake.

'There's only one solution; neither of us will answer the telephone in the room,' he said, marshalling his thoughts. 'I'll instruct the butler to do it,' he added, deadpan.

I halted. 'Did you say the butler?' I asked in soprano, arms pumping to catch up with him.

We have the most luxurious *penthouse* apartment. It's bigger than my flat. It has a lounge and three bedrooms. We could take in lodgers and a family of refugees and you wouldn't know they were there. And we have our own bar. And a butler – his name is Sidney. I was sitting on a spongy leather high stool at the bar, chatting to Sid, sipping champagne. I only accepted the drink to give Sid something to do. And we have a massive grand piano. I wouldn't be surprised if piano lessons were included in the room rate. Perhaps I'll ask.

John slow-walked into the room, straightening his tie.

'D'you want a drink?' I asked him.

'No, thank you,' he said dismissively. 'I have a meeting in five minutes in the lounge downstairs. I'll meet you for dinner.' He snaked his arm into the sleeve of his jacket and tugged it over his broad shoulders.

'This room is much bigger than the lounge downstairs,' I said into my glass. 'I'd stay here if I were you.'

'What are you doing this afternoon with your free time?' he asked.

'I don't have anything to wear to bed. I thought I might go shopping.'

He eyes widened and his forehead creased. 'Nor do I. I don't have anything to wear to bed either.'

'Shall I buy you pyjamas?'

'Yes . . . yes please,' he said, evading eye contact.

He ferreted in his pocket for his wallet, flipped it open and pulled out a wad of notes. He handed me about five hundred euros.

'Will that be enough?' he asked.

Was he serious?

'It should be,' I told him. 'I'll do my best to shop around,' I couldn't resist adding.

He spun on his heel. 'I'll see you later,' he said, with a backward glance, closing the door firmly behind him.

I tried to talk Sid in to having a drink with me but he wouldn't hear of it.

The phone rang – I lurched for it.

'Hello,' I said brightly.

'Evie, I knew you would answer the phone ... Don't do it again! The butler will do it!' John bellowed.

I gulped and slammed the handset down. Bloody hell, he's a monster sometimes.

The phone rang again.

My stomach clenched and my fingers itched, but I didn't answer it. Sid did. It was John.

Dublin is amazing and so are the Irish. They're a nation of party animals who can sing and tell great jokes. And the shops are fabulous, if a bit of a rip-off. I bought John a pair of navy pyjamas festooned with green leprechauns for ten euros from a stall in the middle of the shopping centre, and I bought myself a pair of black silk pyjamas in a posh shop in Stephen's Green shopping centre. It was a glorious, bitter but sunny day, spring was definitely on its way, tulips and daffodils nodded and swayed in the sunshine beneath an azure sky. I decided to take a horse-drawn carriage ride through the park. Why not? After all, this was God's own country according to our coach driver. I ran an admiring hand over the plush, red velvet upholstery of the gleaming white carriage, and snuggled under a thick wool blanket. A young couple wearing matching puffa jackets waved. I nearly fell off the seat waving back. The horses clip-clopped slowly past a row of leafy trees that were reaching for the heavens. I felt an enormous flush of happiness, like I belonged. I wanted to be Irish. I loved it. I was in this fair city and savouring every minute. I settled back to enjoy the ride.

John didn't like his pyjamas.

'What's wrong with them?' I asked with a lofty sniff. My nose was frozen and running. The carriage driver had insisted on giving me two rides for the price of one. Why he thought I would want to plod round the park in sub-zero temperatures more than once I don't know. Never again! My face was numb! If you've seen one leafy tree, you've seen them all!

'They have dragons on them,' John complained drily.

'No they don't, they're leprechauns.' I gave him an eager smile. 'They're a hundred per cent cotton, and you have four hundred euros in change.'

He took the pyjamas from me with a sigh. He wasn't impressed. Sid and I stared after him; we jumped as he slammed his bedroom door. Well, that's gratitude for you, I thought.

I had one of the best nights of my life in a bar in Capel Street. The karaoke singers were amazing; every one of them could've won *The X Factor*. Usually when I'm drunk, I stagger up and belt out a fairly good 'Maggie May' but I didn't dare this time. I'd have looked like an idiot. And the food was delicious. I ate a pie the size of a car roof. To be sociable, I tried a pint of Guinness, which made me feel sick. I had to have three fruity Bacardi cocktails, two glasses of champagne and a glass of red wine to take the taste away.

When we got back to the hotel, John went to bed early (no change there then) and I refereed a drinking competition in the bar downstairs. We needed one of those long, slim yardstick glasses, so I called Sid and, lo, one very long yardstick glass appeared as if by magic. At first I thought this group a rather staid bunch; turns out, I couldn't have been more wrong. They were great fun. It was past two o'clock when I finally got to bed. I didn't see John in the room. I wasn't surprised.

The atmosphere on the transfer coach to Lansdowne Road for the match the following day was electric. I got quite excited myself until I remembered I didn't have a ticket for the game because I'd given it to our unexpected guest. Still, I was going back to the hotel to have a massage and get my hair trimmed. And I thought I might tinkle the ivories on the grand piano, just to see if I could still play 'Three Blind Mice'.

'Evie, I'm sorry we don't have a ticket for you,' John said grimly, as he stepped off the coach. He looked smart in an impeccably cut navy suit, with a white shirt and pink tie, all of which complimented his dark eyes.

'Oh, I'll be fine,' I insisted.

'We'll meet you in town after the match. I'll call you to tell you where we are.'

The coach driver gave me a lift back to the hotel. We blasted Westlife on the sound system. I was Irish again.

Back at the hotel, I have my hair trimmed, and get a massage, a manicure and a pedicure. The thing is, Sid wants to arrange all these things for me. In fact, I was struggling to keep up with him. He's so full of ideas. Apparently full service is included so I may as well take advantage. Sid is amazing, I thought. He can do anything. Honestly, if for instance I said, 'Sid, can you get me a chimpanzee, an elephant and arrange for me to have sex with Louis Walsh?' he'd sort it. Not that I want any of those things. But anything I've asked him for has just appeared.

I was in a hurry to get ready because I had to meet the group in a bar on Grafton Street. I wore a long-sleeved black chiffon mini dress with a sweetheart neckline from Karen Millen, a pair

89

of jewelled killer heels that I paid a fortune for when I was in mourning over Rob, and a pair of black hoop earrings.

The pub was rocking. I felt a surge of exhilaration the minute I opened the door. A Riverdance troupe were hammering the hell out of the floorboards – the sound of it made my heart do a loop-de-loop. I felt patriotically Irish. I'd love to be able to dance. I pogoed in the doorway in search of my group. I spotted them hugging the bar.

'Police!' I yelled, elbow-barging my way through the throng. A path cleared. It never fails.

The guys cheered when they saw me. England had won the rugby so spirits were high. I wondered if the Irish knew the score because their spirits seemed to be soaring even higher. We stayed in the bar for ages and forgot to eat.

John was shooting pining glances at his watch. 'Evie, call Sidney and ask him to arrange a couple of steaks. I don't think we're needed here, do you?' John said. 'We'll eat in the room.'

I had to agree. A couple of our guys sported green tinsel wigs and another two wore enormous green foam hats. All were totally trashed and one had joined the dance troupe. They didn't need to be entertained by me or John so we slunk away unseen.

Dinner in the room was formal and red-carpeted. The table was dressed with white linen and dominated by an imposing crystal candelabra. Sid wore a wing-collared shirt, a tailed dinner jacket, and a serious frown. I looked on as Sid and John communicated in silence with a series of shifty eye manoeuvres. Napkins were laid on our laps, champagne was poured, the silver domes were spirited from our plates, and then Sid magically disappeared.

The steak was delicious. John didn't say much during dinner. In fact, he hardly said anything at all. I told him about my day.

He managed to maintain an air of interest, offering sporadic nods and a knowing smile. After the meal he folded his napkin and placed it on the table. The flickering candle picked up a flash of steely slate as he blinked.

'Would you like a brandy, Evie?' he asked.

And, like a genie from a bottle, Sid appeared and with exaggerated ceremony he placed two crystal-cut brandy globes in front of us. John sipped from his glass, held the brandy in his mouth, and gave Sid a blink of approval. I prefer to drink brandy with diet Coke but I didn't want to say so now. I'm sure this was one of those excellent brands that it would be criminal to dilute. John stared deep in to the amber liquid, idly tipping his glass, his dark lashes hiding his eyes. He had *tuned out*. It occurred to me that perhaps I bored him. There was an uncomfortable quiet. I placed my palms on the table and stood to leave.

'You're tired. I'll say good night.'

He reached over and stayed my hand. 'No, Evie, I'm sorry. I was miles away but no, I'm not tired. I'd very much like you to stay and chat for a while. We've found ourselves thrown together so we may as well make the best of it.'

Me, stay and chat?

He stood and picked up his glass and walked to the sofa. 'Come here,' he said, taking his seat slowly.

I plucked my glass from the table.

'Sit down,' he said, patting the cushion next to his.

Charcoal eyes with a serious intensity searched mine as I took the seat next to him. For some reason I felt as though I was under the microscope. A flush rose in my cheeks. He patted my hand.

'Sidney has gone to bed. How about another brandy?' he asked, taking my almost empty glass from my hand. The brandy wasn't too bad at all. I may ditch the diet Coke in future.

I watched John walk to the bar at the far side of the lounge. He took off his jacket and tossed it on to a bar stool. He hunched his shoulders and, easing his shirt from his waistband, he reached for the decanter.

My eyes scanned the soundless, luxuriously furnished room, resting on the window, which reflected the twinkling lamplights bordering St Stephen's Green. This really was a beautiful suite, large but cosy, imposing but—

There was a sudden crash. I lifted my chin.

John was on the floor!

I leaped to my feet and rushed across the room. He lay still on his side. I dropped to my knees and eased him on to his back. His lips were pressed in a seam, his eyes were closed and his chest heaved slowly. I cupped his face. He was clammy. I scrambled to standing, lurched over a bar stool and snatched the phone from the bar.

'An ambulance!' I shrieked to a telephone operator who to her credit managed to extricate a semblance of coherent sense from me, enough sense for me to tell her what had happened.

I crumpled to the floor and crawled alongside him. I tugged off his tie, unbuttoned his collar and massaged his shoulders ineffectively. Nothing was happening. Nothing. But . . . what should happen? I held his hand tightly to my chest and burst into a torrent of tears.

'Don't you dare die, John . . . Don't,' I sobbed.

His face was white. I lifted his unreceptive arm and felt his slack wrist for a pulse. But I don't know how to look for pulses. Why don't I know how to look for pulses? This is important! My heart hammered against my ribcage.

'John!'

My eyes roved the room. It looked the same as before but how could that be? Nothing was the same. Where was the ambulance?

He was so still.

Strong hands gripped my elbows and brought me to standing. Sid's reassuring eyes fielded mine. A woman wearing a black suit and pearls dropped to her knees, busy over John.

'Evie, the ambulance is on the way. This lady is a doctor. Mr Jackson will be fine,' Sid assured me in low tones.

I leaned against Sid, eyes fixed on John, tears streaming down my face.

The paramedics let me travel in the ambulance with John. I'm sure they regretted it – I made more noise than the siren. He had to be all right.

He had to.

When the doctor finally allowed me into John's room, I felt weak with nervousness but oddly calm. John was asleep. He'd had a heart attack. Not an off-the-Richter-scale attack, something the doctor called 'a warning'. The worst was over. Gingerly in my killer heels, I pulled a chair alongside his bed and watched as he slept. John was sallow and ashen. He wore a green hospital tunic, a drip was attached to his hand, and he was wired to a monitor. He was *stable*. The gentle rise and fall of his chest was a comfort to watch, hypnotic even. I placed my hand over his and lay my head beside his arm. And for the first time in my life I said a proper prayer. Not a robotic recital that you learn in school, but a prayer where I made the words up. A prayer where I wasn't asking for anything for myself, a prayer that made me cry.

Morning came as a surprise.

Slowly pacing up and down the hospital corridor, I called the hotel. Sid said that he would explain what had happened to our group and organise everyone's transfers to Dublin airport. He was also going to pack overnight bags for me and John to be delivered to the hospital. I updated Tina from Insignia Tours who was in bed with a Sunday-morning hangover. I had no contact details for John's family; Tina said she would deal with that. John had been ferreted directly from the hotel to a private hospital and, of course, he had private medical insurance, so I had nothing to worry about on that count. And I spoke briefly to Rob who was only really interested in when I would be home.

I edged quietly into John's room.

An afternoon sunbeam danced on his face, highlighting a smattering of silver and black stubble. My eyelids felt heavy and prickly, as though lined with sand. I pulled my chair close to the bed and laid my head on bowed elbows.

Drained, I slept.

When I woke, John's hand, relaxed in sleep, rested on the crown of my head. I sat up slowly. His pallid face was silhouetted by the dim glow of the overhead lamp above his bed. The room was lending to darkness and a gentle wind beat the branch of a rose bush against the window. There was a faint rustle of starched sheets. John, eyes wide, struggled on one elbow to force himself upright. He turned to face me and grappled for my hand.

'Evie, are you all right?' he asked.

'Me? Am I all right? You, you fell, and I . . .'

He reached for the jug of water. I stood and rushed to help him. He watched me, eyelids blinking heavily, as he sipped from the beaker I held to his lips. Upright against the pillow, he tried for a smile. I placed the empty beaker on the bedside cabinet and fought for control of my facial muscles. I didn't want to cry. I plucked at the bedclothes with nervous fingers. When our eyes locked, John's face clouded over. He extended an arm, placed a

94

hand behind my head and drew me to him, pressing my cheek into the hollow of his shoulder. I circled his neck and very loudly fell to pieces.

He held me tight.

'Shh, come on now. Everything is going to be fine,' he said softly, palming a length of my hair.

'I know,' I managed, dropping into the bedside seat. 'I know.'

John turned my hand over in his. I still wore my black minidress and heels. It had been almost twenty-four hours since I'd run a brush through my hair, and I still wore what hadn't dissolved of last night's make-up. Exhausted with relief, I closed my eyes to the comforting sounds of the busy hospital corridor, tipped forward in my seat and cuddled John's arm. He was right, of course he was right, everything was going to be fine. I felt a glow of reassurance. I felt safe although I hadn't been in danger in the first place. Everything would be OK. I wiped my damp cheeks with the heel of my hand.

'I'm hungry,' John said flatly.

I lifted my chin. His eyes were dark and weary.

'Me too,' I said with a sniff.

'The doctor was here earlier, I spoke to him while you slept. There is a room for you next door to freshen up, we'll have something to eat and then you can go back to the hotel. I'll be fine here,' he said.

'I don't want to go to the hotel. Can't I sleep next door?'

'I suppose you can. It hadn't occurred to me that you'd want to.'

I jerked my chin to the corner of the room where our luggage stood. Sid had sent everything.

'Sid packed our bags.'

'He's a great chap, your Sid,' John said, smiling weakly.

*

My room was modern but clinical, with a high, bouncy, metal-framed bed, two bedside cabinets, a dressing table, and a couple of winged chairs in the window alcove. I sat on the bed for a couple of minutes collecting my thoughts. I felt a twist of fear. It occurred to me that I didn't know any dead people, none at all. I had never met my grandparents so, although they were dead, technically they didn't count. I'd never come face to face with a dead anything, not even a mouse. I shut my eyes. Everything was fine and John was fine. In protest, my tummy rumbled. I pulled off my heels and slid off the bed. I'd organise something to eat, and then shower.

I called Tina. She had contacted John's PA so I expect his family will be arriving tomorrow. I rang Rob. He was still in Birmingham.

'I have no desire to break bread with Lulu the Wicked Fairy. I'll drive back to London tomorrow night. I don't want to arrive at the flat before you,' he said. Why wasn't I surprised?

I tiptoed quietly into John's room in case he was asleep – he wasn't. Three large flower arrangements had been delivered. They filled the room with a heavy scent of lilies.

'What time is it? And what have you ordered for dinner?' John asked as I closed the door gently.

'It's seven-thirty and I've ordered omelette with salad.'

'Omelette? That is *not* a meal,' he said crisply.

'It *is* a meal,' I shot back, matching his tone.

'It's a snack.'

'Well, it's what the nurse suggested . . . and so it's what we're having.'

He removed his stare.

'Are you sulking over an omelette?' I asked, plucking the television remote from the bedside table.

'I do not *sulk*.'

'Good.'

I jabbed the remote at the wall–mounted television.

'Would you like to watch *Friends*?' I asked him.

'Never heard of it,' he said gruffly.

I gasped, disbelieving. 'Rachel, Monica, Phoebe, Joey, Chandler and Ross!' I rattled. I watched him closely. There wasn't even a flicker of recognition. 'Have you been living underground?' I asked.

Central Perk's sofas filled the screen. He relaxed against the pillows. He didn't lift his eyes to the television once, not even at the funny bits. Instead, he sat idly flicking through yesterday's newspaper.

The omelettes arrived. I angled my plate on the edge of John's lap table. We ate with the chatter of *Frasier* in the background. (John hadn't heard of *Frasier* either.)

'Delicious, I admit,' John said, placing his cutlery on an empty plate. He managed a lopsided smile.

'Tired?' I asked him.

He gave a sleepy nod.

A stout lady wearing a white trouser suit barrelled into the room, gathered the plates on to a tray, offered us a wide smile and left wordlessly.

'I'm tired. Exhausted actually,' I said, yawning.

He lifted my hand. The glow of the lamp behind him cast a shadow on the bed. There was a charged hush. We didn't speak, but each knew what the other was thinking. What would have happened if he had been alone? He circled my wrist with his thumb, eyes brimming with thoughts. I bore back into my seat. His hold on my wrist tightened. With my free hand I palmed his forearm.

'Go to bed,' he said softly.

*

I slept like a log, waking just before noon the following day. I showered and pulled on a pair of jeans and a pale-blue cashmere crew neck and straightened my hair. I expect John's wife will be arriving today. I was curious to meet her. OK, I was *gagging* to meet her. I'd be disappointed if she was one of those skinny, horsey types, with a ferret face, who doesn't wear any make-up. I shook the skinny, horsey image from my head. Instead, I imagined an Ivana Trump lookalike. I was sure I was right. As ancient a relic as John is, he's attractive and absolutely minted. What would he be doing with a ferret-faced wife? As soon as he was safely in the bosom of his loved one, I'd book a flight to London. I should be romping with Rob before *News At Ten*. My loins were a-tingle at the thought.

I edged gingerly into John's room.

'And how's our patient today?'

Listen to me, sounding for all the world like Pollyanna.

John was secreted behind the *Financial Times*. He closed the newspaper and laid it on his lap. He looked much better. He still had the drip in his hand, but the tube which had connected his chest up to the bleeping machine beside his bed had been removed. There was the flicker of a smile at his lips and his complexion, although not the healthy, rugged glow he usually sported, was a good few shades brighter and less ashen than when I had last seen him.

'I've ordered lunch.' He eyed his watch. 'It should be here in fifteen minutes.' He folded the newspaper and set it on the bed-side cabinet. 'Did you sleep well?' he asked.

'I did, thank you.' I settled into the chair beside his bed. 'You look much better.'

'I feel better.'

'Brilliant,' I said, tapping my manicured hands on the bed.

'So, what time is your wife expected?' I asked nonchalantly. I didn't want to appear nosy.

'My wife?'

With all the fuss, I'd forgotten I'd had my nails done a couple of days ago. They looked pretty amazing, shiny black with glitter tips.

'Yes, your wife.'

'My wife is *not* expected.'

I tore my eyes from my shiny, black, glittery nails. 'Not expected?'

I stared at him in disbelief. What kind of woman wouldn't hurry to the bedside of her ailing husband, who'd recently faced death? No matter where she is, or what she's doing, her place is here, by his side. I had to deal with this tactfully. I didn't want to upset him. I felt a needle of sympathy. I ordered my words.

'Not expected . . . until what time?' I ventured.

There, that was a stroke of genius. I could be a counsellor. How tactful was that?

'Not expected at all,' he replied flatly.

I was thrown. 'Er,' I began, 'have you called her and explained what's happened?' I hedged.

'No.' he said, his gaze sliding from mine.

'No? John, she will want to know! What are you thinking?'

'My office will have informed her.'

I was stunned. 'Your office? You've left something as important as this for your office to deal with?'

He squared his shoulders and spired his fingers in his lap.

My chin firmed. 'It's your turn to speak, John,' I told him sharply.

He gave a deep sigh. 'My wife and I are in the final stages of divorce. We communicate when needs must, we haven't come face to face in six months. I think it highly unlikely she'll hop on a plane from Los Angeles to Dublin to ask me how I'm feeling.'

I felt a twang of disappointment. No Ivana? My head flooded with questions.

'But then, if you're divorcing, why would she care if you shared a room with me? Why did it matter who answered the phone?'

'Oh that,' he said dismissively. 'I didn't want to provide her with ammunition.'

I tilted my head in understanding. OK, right, I suppose that makes sense.

The reason they're divorcing is *none of my business*. People do. Don't they? I sighed. It happens all the time. I'll change the subject. This is way too personal, and to be honest, I'm not really interested. Why should I be? I teased the sleeve of my jumper over my watch.

'So who's divorcing who?' I blurted out.

He folded his arms across his chest, mindful of the needle in his hand. 'She is divorcing me.'

'Why?'

'I had an affair.'

I leaped up. 'You told me last year you were faithful to your wife! And you had the nerve to have a dig about Rob behaving himself. The cheek of you!'

He raised the flat of his hand. 'Evie, enough! Sit down.'

I sat slowly, with overstated purpose, and ran a challenging eye over his face. 'You lied to me,' I said frostily.

'Yes, I did,' he admitted, not looking at all fazed. 'I did lie to you.'

'Why?'

'I have no idea,' he said with a regretful sigh. 'Actually, that's not strictly true. I do know why I lied.'

'Why?'

100

'You were upset because your boyfriend had cheated on you. I didn't want you to think you'd confided in someone no better than the man who'd caused all the upset. I thought it the right course of action at the time.'

I felt mildly appeased. 'I feel sorry for your wife,' I said firmly.

'Don't. She's had three affairs that I know of.'

I stared at him in horror. 'Three? *You* should be divorcing *her*.'

He gave a casual shrug. 'It makes no difference; the end result will be the same. I can tell you that from experience.'

'Have you divorced before?'

'This is my fourth shot at it.'

My jaw dropped. 'Four wives?'

'Evie, that's over a period of thirty years. I've lived a lot longer than you.'

'But still.'

A white tunic-clad figure barged a serving trolley into the room. I digested John's news. Four wives. He's had *four* wives! I gave him a mystified glance. And affairs. No wonder his heart gave out, I thought as I plucked a glass of water from the trolley. The white tunic-clad figure left in a flurry of panic as a beeper announced she was needed elsewhere. I studied John over the rim of my drink.

'Do you have children?' I asked.

'No, I don't have any children,' he said with a tint of sadness. Charcoal eyes held mine.

Am I nosy enough to ask why? No, I'm not. Well, perhaps—

We turned to the sound of rapid footsteps in the corridor. The footsteps halted outside John's room. The door burst open. A tall, broad man with saffron eyes, a shock of black hair and a high forehead filled the doorframe, flanked by a nervous triangle of medical students. Three purposeful strides and he towered over my chair.

'Doctor Keating,' he introduced, extending his hand to John.

Doctor Keating looked down at me.

'Can I ask you to step outside for a moment while I have a chat with your father?' he said with a professional smile.

Chapter Nine

John was going to be discharged the day after tomorrow, and I decided to stay with him. Beyond the call of duty I know, but I don't want to leave him on his own. Ridiculous, because he's a grown man and a multi-millionaire and he can look after himself, and if he can't look after himself, he can afford an entourage to do it for him, but I would feel bad. I was on my hands and knees in the television lounge raking through the games cupboard. I fancied a game of Monopoly and John was up for it. My phone was leaning against a lamp on top of the cupboard; Rob was on loudspeaker.

'Evie, this is outrageous! I don't want to be alone in the flat for two nights with Cruella De Vil!' Rob said irately.

I found Frustration but it's impossible to cheat at that game, unless the other person goes to the toilet and you get the chance to move your counters. The dice being in the plastic bubble makes the game practically cheat-proof.

'This isn't working. Be fair, it's not normal. I want you home!'

Trivial Pursuit, but sod that because John is smart, and while I'm not thick, I know nothing about sport, and I'm crap at general knowledge.

'Any more than two more nights and I'm warning you, Evie – I'm coming over to bring you back. I can be in Dublin in an hour. I mean it!'

Chess. I don't even know where the pieces go on the board. I drew my head from the cupboard and sneezed. Someone needs to get in here with a duster and a tin of Mr Sheen. The cupboard was bloody filthy.

'Rob, I miss you like mad but I want to stay here. I can't explain why. I'll be home in forty-eight hours. It's no time at all. Can't you stay in Birmingham? Don't you have any more sales calls you could make?'

There was a hum of quiet. I sneezed again. My knees were beginning to burn. I eyed my phone waiting for a reply.

'Well, yes, yes,' he said at last. 'I suppose I could, I—'

'Do that then. Stay in Birmingham and I'll see you on Wednesday.'

'Er, OK, babe. Well, I'll speak to you before then, but yeah, see you Wednesday.'

'I can't wait,' I told him.

That was simple. Must I always do the thinking? I dived back in the cupboard. Ah, found it. Monopoly!

My phone buzzed, it was a text from Tina.

What r u doing. Why did his heart give out? Are u shagging him? He is our biggest client, be careful. We need him alive!

I didn't reply. As if!

John won both games of Monopoly. I was frothing with rage; he looked smug. I hate a show-off. He finished with more cash than the bank, and loads of houses and hotels, and he didn't go to jail once. I had a tenner and I lost all my property. I was worm-ridden with envy. I was glad when dinner arrived and we had to tidy the game away.

We ate risotto. I had a glass of wine, my first drink in two days – it was delicious. John fell asleep early. I didn't mind because I'd been waiting for a chance to read the gift cards on the flower arrangements. I tiptoed to the table. They were from Amanda, Ava and Catherine, all with love and kisses.

'Satisfying your curiosity?' John asked, startling me.

I swivelled. 'I suppose you'd have needed name tags and a turnstile on the door for loved ones had you invited all of them,' I shot back frostily.

He opened his mouth to say something, thought better of it, and snapped it shut again. 'Am I right?' I challenged.

'Something like that,' he admitted.

'Shall we watch television?' I asked, taking the seat beside his bed.

His checked his watch. 'Put on the news.'

I gave a snort. I'd been thinking more along the lines of *America's Next Top Model.* I stabbed the remote at the television. A balding RTE newsreader filled the screen, droning on about a volcanic dust cloud drifting from Iceland to England. I hoped Lulu didn't have any washing hanging out.

I eyed John's comfortable prime seat, propped against the pillows, facing the television. In contrast, I was in an uncomfortable, low-level, right-angled, neck-twisting position, and I thought if he budged over I could sit next to him. I'd sit on his left because his drip was on the right. I kicked off my shoes and climbed on the bed. He moved over wordlessly.

We watched *The Devil Wears Prada* and *Mamma Mia!* on DVD because Meryl Streep was the only living actress John could name. Side by side we shared a club sandwich.

'Evie, I want you to promise me something,' John said in a low, serious tone.

I twisted to face him. 'Depends what it is.'

There was a skirmish of emotions going on on his face. 'I want you to promise me that you will come to me if you're ever in trouble. I want you to promise that you will call me if you need help . . . of any kind.'

My sandwich hovered en route to my mouth.

His brows lifted expectantly. 'Do I have your word?' he asked.

I gave him a baffled glance. 'Like what? I don't get in to trouble.'

He took the sandwich from my hand and set it on the plate on his lap. 'You never know what's around the corner.'

I felt a bit caught out, as though I'd been doing something I shouldn't.

His gaze sharpened. 'Promise me.'

'I promise,' I said.

'Good,' he replied with a sharp nod. 'Let's finish this and have an early night.'

The following morning I edged slowly into John's room. To my astonishment, he stood beside the bed, resplendent in an immaculately tailored light-grey suit, white shirt and navy tie. He flicked through the contents of his briefcase, phone wedged between shoulder and ear.

'Meet me in London, don't come to Dublin. I'll be home before you arrive,' John said, before flicking his phone shut. He eyed me levelly.

'You're not working already, are you?' I asked. 'Who was that?'

'My brother. He's on his way from New York. There's no point in him coming to Dublin – we're leaving.'

'Leaving?'

'Pack your bag. A car will be here in twenty minutes to take us to the airport. My plane is waiting.'

I gave him a challenging glare. 'Have you been discharged?'

He closed his briefcase with a click. 'Yes! Now hurry, we don't want to keep the driver waiting.'

'But this is too quick. Do you have medication? You almost died.'

He walked round the bed and gave me a light hug. 'Yes, an aspirin a day.'

'An aspirin!' I echoed.

He held me at arm's length. 'Yes, an aspirin . . . to thin the blood. And I did *not* almost die,' he said, spinning me round and urging me gently towards the door. 'You have twenty minutes.'

I tailed after John up the steps of his plane. My heart curled with excitement; there was no queue of passengers and no arguing over seats. We had the *whole* plane to ourselves. At the top step I stopped to look around. We were in some sort of private plane parking lot. I couldn't resist waving to the crowds and the paparazzi. OK, so there weren't actually any crowds or paparazzi, but in my mind's eye there was a barrage of them. I gave a vigorous wave.

Someone gripped my elbow and firmly yanked me backwards through the aircraft door.

'Will you hurry up?' John snapped, giving me a cool gaze. 'Who were you waving to? There's no one out there!'

My eyes skimmed a circle as John prodded me down the central aisle past two flight attendants standing like a couple of stiff poles. I was impressed. Who wouldn't be? There was a low-level cream sofa along one wall, which nestled against a coffee table at the end. Opposite the sofa was a wall-mounted television

107

screen, and in the far corner two winged armchairs flanked another table with a decorative fan of magazines and newspapers. I was speechless.

'What's in there?' I asked, pointing at two doors in between which hung a caricature of a man with one eye.

'Bedrooms,' John replied. He relaxed into one of the armchairs and motioned for me to do the same. 'Sit down and put your seat belt on or we'll never get going,' he said, shaking open the *Wall Street Journal*.

I sat down mechanically and clipped the seat belt on. 'This is very nice,' I complimented inadequately.

John flicked an eye at the magazines on the table. 'For you, I ordered a selection of the garbage you read,' he said, crossing one leg over the other.

'Thanks.'

And it was very nice, much more than very nice. It was like a flying caravan.

Once we were airborne, I wandered round the plushly carpeted cabin. There was a dining table and a bar discreetly tucked behind a rosewood-panelled wall, and a bathroom stuffed with Harrods products. I trailed a finger over the soft leather upholstery of one of the bar stools. It felt like silk.

'Would you like to eat something?' John asked.

I turned.

He patted the cushion on the sofa next to him.

'Is it too early for a gin and tonic?' I asked, sitting down with him.

'Well, it is for me. It's only eleven-thirty.'

'I want to sit at the bar,' I said.

I spotted a discreet gold handle under the coffee table and pulled it.

'We can have breakfast at the bar,' he suggested.

'Fine,' I agreed, head bent, picking through the contents of the padded drawer.

The flight attendant materialised beside me. I slammed the drawer shut. I didn't want her to think I was nosy. She wore an elegant navy suit, her hair was scooped in to a tight blonde croissant, and a delicate string of pearls decorated her slim, alabaster neck. But her lipstick was a touch on the scarlet side and her foundation was as thick as the Earth's inner crust.

'Breakfast for two, Mr Jackson?' she asked professionally.

'Yes, please,' John replied. 'We'll eat at the bar, Sadie.'

Sadie bobbed her head, swivelled on her Pradas and disappeared.

John folded his newspaper, set it on the table and moved to the bar. I joined him. I stole a concerned sideways glance. His trademark healthy glow had almost returned. Still, an aspirin a day? I wasn't convinced. Long lashes hid his eyes. As I edged on to the bar stool next to him he caught me staring. He leaned towards me solemnly and gave me a long look.

'What?' I asked, eyeing him dubiously.

He didn't reply for a minute. 'Evie, I want to thank you for keeping me company. You could have flown home when I was admitted to hospital. I'm sure you would rather have spent your time with your handsome boyfriend, as opposed to playing nursemaid to an old man,' he said in a low voice. 'But you chose to stay. I enjoyed your company, I can't tell you how much.'

He was big and broad and close, and smelled of something spicy. He lifted my hand from the bar, turned it over and circled my palm with his thumb.

We were quiet for a bit.

'Let's keep in touch,' he suggested, breaking the silence.

'Of course we will,' I said through a smile.

'We'll meet every couple of weeks for dinner. Would you like that?' he asked.

'I'd love it.'

'And remember, if you ever need anything, call me,' he said with an insistent nod.

'There is one thing.'

He sat up purposefully. 'You've got it! What is it?'

My eyes scanned the cabin. I felt a lurch of excitement. 'Could we fly around for a while, spin the flight out to more than just an hour?'

He let my hand drop. 'No!'

I pulled my jacket around me. 'You said anything,' I reminded him.

'I said anything you need. You do not need to waste my time drifting in European airspace. Can you think of something else?'

'Not at this moment in time, no.'

'Well, when you do, let me know.'

John arranged for a chauffeured limousine to drive me home. It was amazing. It had a drinks cabinet. I was almost sorry when it pulled up outside the flat. I sided into the lounge, wheeling my suitcase. Smiling, Lulu leaped up from the sofa. I dropped the handle of my suitcase.

'Evie! Guess what? Fabulous news! Andrew Blackbourne from *Good Morning, this is the Capital* has been charged with possession of cannabis,' she burst out excitedly. She wove her fingers through mine and clutched my hands to her chest.

'Why is that fabulous news?'

Her eyes were big and darting. 'Because . . . he's been fired. Isn't it brilliant?'

I gave a confused shrug. 'And why is it brilliant that Andrew Blackbourne has been fired?' I asked.

She dropped my hands, gripped my shoulders and held me at arm's length. 'Because, silly goose, I've been offered his job. Well, I've been offered his job temporarily.'

Silly goose? This wasn't normal Lulu speak.

I was pleased, but stunned. When I'd left home last week, Lulu had been an unemployed nurse.

'You've been offered his job as a radio presenter?' I asked, bewildered.

She tugged me by the hand to the sofa. 'Sit down. I'll open a bottle of wine. Let's celebrate,' she said, and disappeared out of the lounge and down the hallway.

I sank into the cushion. At least she was earning again, I thought, but a radio presenter? What was going on?

She barrelled into the lounge, cradling an ice bucket and picked her way through the magazine-littered room. She placed the bucket on the coffee table.

'I've been trawling iTunes for the past three days. I'm studying really hard so that when a *listener* asks if I can play, er, something like . . . a real oldie, like, mmmm, let me think—' She pendulummed the wine bottle absently, eyes searching for inspiration. 'Ah! Like Wham! You know, the group George Michael was in? Did you know he used to be in a group? Likely you didn't, you're not in the business. I now know about six Wham! songs off the top of my head,' she boasted. 'All I have to do is key the artist in to a keyboard–laptop thingy and the artist's playlist pops up and I ask the listener who requested the *number*, the *number* is technical speak for *song*, I say, "Ah! You want *blah blah* by *blah blah*?" Like I knew the song all along and then I play it. But, Evie, the songs are the boring bit. It's the interviews I like best. Interviewing is my *strength*,' she told me, flushed with happiness.

I tilted my head in question. 'Interviews?' I asked numbly, accepting a glass of wine from her outstretched hand.

Eyes twinkling, she rushed on. 'Yes, interviews with listeners or celebs. You know, anyone promoting a book or denying they've had a facelift or swearing to God they're not bankrupt when all the newspapers say they are.' She sat next to me and took a couple of hurried gulps of wine.

'So, how did a community nurse with no previous experience get offered a job as a radio presenter?'

'It was luck really,' she told me cheerily. 'Andrew's house was raided at eight o'clock on Friday morning. He was taken in to custody, and so didn't turn up to present the show, which started at ten. And there I was, sitting patiently, flicking through *Heat*, headphones on, waiting for the Quit Smoking Challenge phone-in to begin. Evie, it was like a friggin' cabinet level incident. The production team was demented. There was no one to present the show. "Let's deploy the marines or similar, someone with amphibious capabilities, to rise from the Thames and save the day," I'd suggested, joking. And then in a flash of brilliance, I thought of myself. I shot to my feet and shouted, "I'll do it. I'll present the show." And that was that. A star was born,' she told me triumphantly. 'And, Evie, the phones didn't stop ringing after the show with listeners calling in to say how refreshing I had been.'

'But doesn't Andrew have a contract or anything?'

She gave me an incredulous stare. 'I don't know and I don't care,' she said.

'Right, well then, that's great news . . . Congratulations!'

Beaming, she clinked her glass against mine. 'To Andrew!' she said.

'To Andrew!' I parroted. I put my glass on the table, snaked my hand in my handbag and pulled out my phone.

'Who are you calling?' she asked suspiciously.

'Rob. He's not expecting me home until tomorrow. He'll come back from Birmingham if he knows I'm here.'

She stayed my hand. 'Evie, can't we have a night, just you and me, without Mr Warty Nose?' she pouted.

'Rob does *not* have a warty nose,' I punctuated.

'OK, without Mr Know-All Knows Bugger All.'

I gave an exasperated sigh. 'Why don't you like Rob? You liked him last year. You were the one who said, "the guy is a fanny magnet, stick to him."'

'I know, but that was before you got engaged,' she said, her chin tight.

'What difference does that make?'

'I thought you would shag him out of your system and be done with him. Just like all the others.'

Listen to her. All the others, as if I had a football team of exes.

'I miss . . . ' She broke off and bum-shuffled closer. 'I miss just us,' she said with a sad smile.

My phone rang. Reading the caller display, Lulu snorted and downed her drink in one. It was Rob.

'Evie, babe! I'm bursting to see you. I can't wait. I've missed you *so* much. Twenty-four hours and—'

'I'm home,' I interrupted, holding my glass out to Lulu for a refill.

'Oh!'

'Yes, I just got back. John was discharged a day early. I called to tell you but your phone was switched off and your voicemail didn't kick in.'

'Sorry, I was in a meeting. I've only just noticed the missed call.'

I watched Lulu slosh yummy ice-cold wine into my glass. 'So, what time will you be home?' I asked him.

Lulu's face went stiff.

'Babe, I have two more meetings set up and the second isn't until seven o'clock this evening,' he said, apologetically.

I felt a plunge of disappointment. 'Right, well—' I began.

'I'll cancel!' he offered swiftly.

Bless him.

'No, no, don't do that.'

Lulu gave a questioning frown and took a swallow from her glass.

'Well, if you're sure, staying would save me having to come back up here for a while,' he explained. 'And I've already paid for my hotel.'

'Stay there tonight. It makes sense,' I said firmly. 'Get the sales calls out of the way.'

'OK, I'll see you tomorrow.'

'Only twenty-four short hours,' I told him, smiling in to the phone.

'Bye, babe.'

I tossed my phone in my bag.

'Hip hip hooray, Mr Warty Nose isn't coming home. Let's have dinner with Nikki at the bar,' Lulu said brightly.

Bar Thea was heaving. I almost didn't walk through the door. In fact, I was reversing when Lulu gave me a mighty push forward, sending me tottering into the hat stand. I turned on her.

'Nikki will ask me to work,' I hissed. 'It's packed in here. You know what he's like.'

She put her arm around my shoulder. 'No, he won't. Look at you, you're pissed,' she said, smiling sweetly at a table of guys. 'And I'll tell him to bugger off.'

Nikki was working the bar. He tore an order from the board and lurched to the fridge for a bottle of wine while simultaneously flicking the lager tap on with his elbow. His dark eyes roved the room, stopping briefly at each table. His handsome face split with a smile when his gaze fell on mine.

'Evie, can you work?' he asked, hopeful.

I clutched Lulu's arm. 'I told you,' I said in a dramatic whisper.

Pepi whizzed past, balancing a pyramid of plates on a tray.

'No, she cannot work. We're pissed and starving. Two steaks and a bottle of Shiraz,' Lulu said, hitching her leg on to a bar stool.

Nikki leaned over the bar, curved his arm around her neck and kissed her. I took the stool beside her.

'You have such a way with words,' he said. 'Have you considered writing poetry?'

'Very funny. We're having a girls' night out so we expect you to look after us,' she told him.

The muscles of Nik's toned arm shifted as he clutched my elbows and inched me across the bar towards him. 'I'll look after you with pleasure,' he said, giving me a noisy kiss on the cheek. 'Always!'

'Oh right, Nik! Will you look after her in an "if I take you out to dinner as a friend will you shag me as a friend kind of way?"' Lulu asked, and burst into fits of laughter at her own sharp wit.

Nik shot her a sub-zero look. He always bites when she rattles his cage about his promiscuity. I'm surprised he cares.

Nik is a player. Never have I known a man to attract female glorification as regularly and with such devotion as Nikki. As a rational consequence, I've never looked on him as anything other than friend, boss, neighbour and gigolo. That said, now that I think of it, I haven't seen him with a girl for a while.

Lulu's phone rang. She flicked it open. 'Listen, I don't really care what you're doing tomorrow night. I just want to know if I need to shave or not,' she said to the caller.

I reached for the wine bottle Nik had left on the bar. My eyes

115

slid a quick left and right. It was nice to be a customer for a change. And it was nice to have a night out with Lulu on our own. Not that I wasn't missing Rob. Of course I was, I couldn't wait to see him.

VENICE

Chapter Ten

Rob arrived home at seven-thirty the following morning. I hadn't expected him until lunchtime. He crawled into bed and gathered me against him, his belly to my bum. He rubbed his chilly cheek against my jaw, and sank his teeth playfully into my neck. I stretched my hand back and slapped the cold leg wrapped round mine.

'You're freezing.'

'And horny,' he said. 'Horny as a bloody stoat.'

'Unless you can cure my hangover with your penis, I'm not really interested how horny you are,' I told him.

'Hangover? I take it you were out with the poison troll.'

'I was, and you smell like a bacon sandwich,' I complained. 'It's a turn-off.'

'I needed fuel.'

'You needed fuel for what?'

He flipped me on to my back, buried his hands in my hair and lowered his head slowly, pressing his lips on mine.

'Fuel to service your every need,' he whispered through a smile. 'I'm not sure that I can cure your hangover with my penis but I'm happy to give it my best shot.'

*

Rob works so hard. The poor thing had to be in the office for ten-thirty. Nikki, the slave driver, must have seen Rob's car leave because two minutes after he pulled out of the driveway Nikki rang to ask me to work.

'It's been manic in here and you've had over a week off,' he said sharply.

'I'm casual labour, you pay me cash. I can have as much time off as I like.'

'Not if I need you. Get over here or I'll come and get you,' he threatened.

I got up. My hangover had miraculously disappeared.

Nikki, Maria and I sat around the window table listening to Lulu's show. Uncle Spiros, chef and fearsome family patriarch, who treats me like his little princess, was listening in the kitchen maintaining that, unlike us, he was too busy to sit down. I just can't believe Lulu has her own radio show! I felt ready to burst with pride. She even has her own jingle, the Lulu signature tune. Maria was painting my fingernails, Nikki was reading the newspaper and I was eyeing the radio with the eagerness of a citizen waiting to hear Churchill's next broadcast to the nation.

'Good morning, London!' Lulu sing-songed.

I felt a surge of excitement. 'Good morning, Lulu!' I blurted, slapping the table with my free hand.

Nikki blew out a tiresome sigh and gave his newspaper a studious shake.

'Today in the studio we have Sherry Coil, wife of the Liverpool goalkeeper, Anton Coil!' Lulu boomed.

There was a round of applause and a distant echoey cheer.

I elbowed Nikki. 'Sherry Coil,' I mouthed in starstruck wonder.

He raised a lazy brow in mock interest and smiled into his newspaper. He didn't care. It was obvious. Lulu was interviewing an A-lister and Nikki didn't give a toss. He's a right bore sometimes.

'Sherry, today you are here to set the record straight,' Lulu stated authoritatively.

'I am, Lulu,' Sherry replied, matching Lulu's serious tone.

Set the record straight! The genius of her! My God, she sounded like . . . like, the prime minister.

'Sherry, four of today's national newspapers allege that you were unfaithful to Anton, your footballer husband, and that you had an affair with your children's riding instructor,' Lulu said with an apologetic accent.

'Yes, I've read those reports,' Sherry confirmed with a sigh.

'In fact, the story has made the front page of today's *Daily Globe*,' Lulu pointed out with a grim lilt.

The *Daily Globe*. That's the newspaper Nik reads.

I lurched towards Nikki and, careful of my damp fingernails, peeled back the sheets of his paper until I found the front page. Sure enough there was a picture of Sherry picking her way out of a stable, blonde hair matted with straw and her lipstick smudged. She had a bottle of champagne tucked in the crook of her arm and a very nice pair of turquoise Jimmy Choos dangling from her index finger. Nikki slapped my hand. I yelped. He snatched his newspaper. Maria's jaw dropped and her eyes narrowed. She stretched across me and smacked Nikki a cracker on the ear and then lifted my hand to her lips and blew on it gently.

'So, Sherry,' Lulu continued, measuring her words, 'these are pretty serious allegations.' There was a meditative hush as London digested this. 'What would you like to say to the alligators?'

I exchanged a doubtful glance with Nik. I wasn't sure if someone who makes an allegation was an alligator. Obviously Nik wasn't sure either – his expression was blank.

'Well,' Sherry began, 'I'd like to say that they should get their facts straight.'

'Absolutely!' Lulu said fervently. 'So, did you have an affair with the riding instructor?'

'Yes, Lulu, yes I did!' Sherry stated forcefully.

'Fabulous, this is fabulous news. Congratulations, Sherry,' Lulu shot back with a festive ring to her voice. 'And tell me, was he any good?'

'Yes, yes, he was good. Or should I say he *is* good,' Sherry replied with a knowing chuckle. 'Very good!'

'Sherry, you are a true inspiration. Footballers' wives should take a leaf out of your book. Go for it, girls. Riding instructors, piano teachers, gardeners, you can have them all. How opportune,' Lulu counselled. 'Why should the men have all the fun?'

Nikki gave me a puzzled frown. I felt my face flush pink and I frowned in reply. Still, I'm sure Lulu knows what she's talking about. Maria, indifferent, unscrewed a bottle of topcoat, eyes scheming between Nikki and me.

'And now, Sherry, I believe Fiona from Batchworth Heath is on line three and would like to ask you a question,' Lulu announced. 'Hi, Fiona. What would you like to ask Sherry?'

'Hi, Sherry. Hi, Lulu. I would like to know if Anton was any good?' Fiona asked.

'Anton? Good at what?' Sherry asked in a bewildered tone. 'I'm told he's not a bad goalkeeper if that's what you mean?'

Nikki stabbed the remote at the radio, switching it off.

I elbowed him in the ribs. 'Put that back on.'

'No! Next it'll be Lulu telling us how many days, hours and

120

minutes it's been since she's had a fag. I can't be bothered to listen to her,' Nikki said, standing. 'Come on, get to work.'

Rob and I ordered pizza for dinner, and we ate it in bed. Lulu was out with Sherry Coil. Sherry had wanted to go out tomorrow but Lulu stays in on a Thursday to do the ironing.

Rob placed the empty pizza box on the floor and rolled to face me. 'You, madam, are now in the black. The parking ticket nightmare has been sorted and the county court judgment settled. You are no longer blacklisted for credit and we can apply for a mortgage.'

I gave a stiff nod and a muted thanks.

'So this weekend we'll start looking for houses. I think it's safe to say you don't have to worry about the Evil Elf. She's on cloud nine over her new job, she'll be fine. If she's here on her own, she can pay the same rent she's always paid. We'll make up the difference. You can't be joined at the hip for ever. Things change,' he told me.

'I know.'

He rolled me on to my back. 'I don't mind sharing you but not every day. Turn out the light,' he said.

We've been house hunting for a couple of weeks now. I'm now absolutely positive a house with Rob is what I want. House hunting is such a romantic thing to do together, I love touring people's homes with Rob's guiding hand in the small of my back. Rob is *so right* about everything, about us having our own space and a garden. I can't wait. Frankly I marvel that I've been able to live without a view of Bushy Park, an enormous kitchen diner, and under-floor heating for so long. Rob said obviously I can't have everything and that I should draft a list of my preferred requirements, which I've done. The trouble is my list of preferred requirements has now spread over three sheets of lined A4. I was sitting at my dressing table deliberating on what to sacrifice. I had to be ruthless. Rob was losing patience.

I chewed my pen meditatively. I suppose I could live without the integrated floor-to-ceiling fish tank. I scribbled it out. And the remote-controlled curtains – I scribbled those out as well. And then I thought, Why should I get off the sofa to close the curtains when there's no need? I quickly reinstated the remote-controlled curtains to the bottom of the list and sighed because my list looked longer than it had before I started shortening it. I scribbled out 'A study'. I only read one book a year and that was on holiday. I didn't really need a study to read *OK!* and *Hello!* magazines.

'Evie, get dressed! As gorgeous as you look in your bra and knickers I'd rather see you ready to go out. I don't want to be late and make a bad first impression,' Rob said, bending over me.

I tossed my pen on the dressing table and cupped his face. Rob was meeting my parents tonight for the first time. He'd been stressing out about it all day. He'd even had his hair cut.

His face clouded. 'I'm nervous,' he admitted, planting a soft kiss on the tip of my nose.

'Don't be nervous, Mum and Dad are great. There's nothing to be nervous about. They're looking forward to meeting you,' I told him in earnest.

He took a step back and sat on the edge of the bed and pulled my chair between his open thighs.

'I'm looking forward to meeting your parents but perhaps after, you know, what happened, they may think I'm not ideal son-in-law material,' he said sheepishly. His finger traced my collarbone, rimmed my bra and travelled to my belly button. He gave a shy smile.

A love bubble burst in my tummy.

'That's all in the past and it's not as though the evening will be intense. My sister, brother-in-law and the twins will be there,' I said, eyeing his finger now looping inside the leg of my knickers. 'That'll make it easier.'

He pressed his mouth on mine.

I felt a whoosh of desire as his arm curved my neck.

'Thinking about it, as your parents have been travelling for over ten months, perhaps we should give them time to bond with their grandchildren before we arrive,' he said, doing that 180-degree wiggly thing he does with his thumb.

'I agree,' I said, straddling him shamelessly.

When we arrived at Lexy's, the hallway was booming with music from a mini tape deck sound system and shrieks of delight from the twins, as they ram-raided scooters against the skirting boards. I led Rob by the hand, following my brother-in-law, Graeme, who navigated past a wigwam, a family of koala bears and a blow-up canoe. In the lounge, Lexy, resplendent in a backless knee-length sheath and multi-storey jewelled sandals, edged around the coffee table tilting champagne into crystal flutes. I smoothed the front of my cream mini dress and smiled at my platform courts, glad that I'd made an extra effort. Mum shot from her chair and, arms outstretched, rushed towards me, enveloping me in a cloud of freesia.

'It's been so long,' she said, giving me a fierce hug.

Mum didn't look like Mum.

I darted a glance over Mum's shoulder at my sister. She wouldn't meet my eye. Lexy twirled as much as she could of her very short fringe round her finger, while studying a spot on the carpet. I slanted my gaze to Graeme who gave a deadpan shrug.

'Let me look at you,' Mum said, holding me at arm's length.

I pressed my lips in a line.

Mum was wearing a low-cut, long-sleeved, sapphire maxi dress with fraying cuffs, and what looked suspiciously like a pair of black, gutted snake's heads as shoes. An enormous yellowing tooth dangled from a silver chain around her neck, a collection of wooden bangles rattled on her arm, and draped over her shoulder was a knitted handbag in the shape of a kangaroo's head. What she didn't have was a placard stating, Ban the Bomb and Save the Whale, which was a pity because a placard would have looked lovely with her outfit.

'Look at her, Allister,' Mum said, swivelling to Dad who walked nonchalantly towards us dressed in a flowery Hawaiian shirt and a pair of khaki shorts.

Dad gave me a hug to match Mum's.

My mother, Mrs Isobel Dexter, captain of the ladies' bowls team of Canterbury, until this moment in time, has been a Jackie Onassis clone. Kitten heels, twin sets and pastel-coloured suits have been her *only* wardrobe. And as for Dad, I don't think I've seen his legs since our last family holiday at Butlins about fifteen years ago.

I gave them a pop-eyed smile. 'You both look . . . amazing,' I managed politely, eyes busy between them.

Mum spread her arms wide and gave a twirl.

Lexy snorted suspiciously.

'Travelling is so enlightening,' Mum said, swinging her tooth on a chain. 'You discover your inner self. You realise what matters in life and what doesn't.'

Dad nodded in agreement. His eyes drifted behind me. 'And this must be your young man,' he said.

I swivelled and clutched Rob's hand, tugging him alongside me. 'This is my *fiancé*, Rob,' I announced, prodding him forward.

There was an approving glint of astonished surprise in Mum's eyes as she gazed at Rob. I know I don't stop harping on about how handsome Rob is, but honestly he *is* Abercrombie & Fitch naked-torso-model material. Mum's pencilled brows lifted. She stepped forward offering the proverbial cheek for a welcoming kiss. Rob bent his head to hers and obliged.

Dad's hand shot out. 'Allister!' Dad introduced himself, pumping Rob's hand and giving him a vigorous punch on the arm.

Mum's face switched from hardcore admiration to welcoming. 'Shall we go through to the dining room?' she suggested, looping her arm through Rob's, who looked overwhelmed, flanked as he was by the Odd Couple.

Graeme, Lexy and I stood in a calculating triangle. My sister threw back her head and downed her champagne in one gulp.

'What *is* she wearing?' Lexy asked, belching softly. 'D'you remember she told me I looked like a Victorian miner's wife when I wore that gorgeous black shawl I bought in Fenwick's?'

'Who cares?' Graeme said, tucking the ice bucket under his arm. 'They're happy and they've had a good time.'

'Do you think it's a one-off outfit?' I asked.

'No,' Lexy said, topping up her glass. 'There's a yellow maxi cape and matching skirt hanging in the spare room. They're staying the night here so they can both have a drink and not have to drive back to Kent.'

'Both have a drink!?' I echoed, agog. 'They never *both have a drink.*'

Lexy gave a certified nod. 'They do now.'

Lexy's soufflé was a disaster. It looked like a burst football but we made the requisite compliments. Entrée was spiced, grilled salmon with seasoned couscous, which I'm sure Marks and Spencer advertised last week on their Dine in for a Tenner promotion. Dessert was tiramisu, which I know for a fact Lexy didn't make herself, although she insisted with a deadpan lying face that she *did* make it. But in fairness, it was a very nice meal and in no time the plates were cleared and Dad was pouring brandy.

Mum, sitting opposite, looked at me expectantly. She gave me an encouraging nod and splashed what was left of the bottle of Chardonnay she'd drunk by herself into her glass.

'What is it?' I asked her.

Her smile was wide and her stare rheumy.

I smiled inwardly. I had never seen her drink more than two sweet sherries. I was impressed that she was still vertical.

'Have you set a wedding date?' she asked, hugging her tooth pendant.

Rob cut in. 'There's no rush,' he said politely.

I gave Rob a conspiring smile. Set a date indeed. I haven't even bought a *Brides* magazine yet. I was most definitely *not* ready to set a date.

I nodded in agreement.

'There's no time like the present,' Mum said, doing a magician's sweep with her glass.

She was tipsy, very tipsy.

Rob lifted his chin and gave a no-can-do head shake.

'We're not ready, not just yet. It's not exactly a pressing issue at the moment,' he said in an assertive tone.

I eyed my engagement ring. 'Not a pressing issue,' I whispered into my glass. I felt the hairs on the back of my neck rise. I swivelled to face him.

'So why are we *not ready*?' I interrupted, rattled. Suddenly, I wanted to know *why* the man I was engaged to was in no rush to marry me. It was a matter of principle. I whipped my hair over my shoulder.

'Babe, I thought, let's move house first, and—'

'Yes, Evie, you should be settled first,' Lexy refereed. 'Most definitely.'

Having articulated one question, Mum felt confident enough to steam ahead and ask another.

'Is the other trouble sorted? Is she gone?' Mum asked sweetly. 'You know, the other woman?' she felt compelled to add, lest we not be absolutely certain exactly who she was referring to.

There was a mortified hush.

Lexy and Graeme absorbed themselves in silent napkin folding at each end of the table. Dad, opposite Rob, sloshed a shaky measure of brandy into his glass. And Mum, realising her faux pas, dived into her Chardonnay.

Jaw tight, Rob scanned the room. I followed his gaze. He was staring at the cat stretched comfortably in front of the crackling open fire.

The room was still. Dad gave Mum a scornful look.

Rob leaned forward, elbows on the table, fingers in a spire. He jerked his head towards the cat lying on the floor under the radiator, its chest rumbling with contentment.

'I wish I could do that all day,' Rob said in an effort to break the tension.

By the time Mum, Dad, Lexy and Graeme turned to the cat, it was busy licking its balls. Everybody exchanged uncertain glances. I twisted the end of the tablecloth into a taut tube. Rob pressed his hand over mine and gave a rallying sigh. He met Mum's eye.

'Yes, it is, it is all sorted,' Rob announced, scanning the table boldly. 'I made a mistake and I'm sorry. I've been lucky. Evie has taken me back and I promise I'll spend the rest of my life proving she was right to give me a second chance. I love her more than anything. I'll make her happy, I'll—'

Mum held up her hands in apology. 'I'm sure you will,' she said. 'I shouldn't have mentioned—'

Lexy slapped her palms on the table and leaped to her feet. 'Champagne?' she suggested loudly.

'I'll help,' Mum offered, hurrying in her wake.

'More brandy?' Dad asked, his tone grave.

'Let me,' Graeme said, lurching for the bottle.

Rob stared into the middle distance.

I gripped his chin and forced his gaze. 'You do make me happy,' I told him, smoothing my thumb along his jaw.

He curved an arm round my neck and pulled me to him. 'If you want to set a date for the wedding, then we'll do it,' he said firmly.

A bubble of excitement bounced inside me. 'Christmas?' I blurted.

'Christmas it is,' he shot back swiftly.

'A Christmas wedding!' Dad said, toasting his brandy randomly.

'Fabulous!' Mum chimed, siding into the room, handling a tray of champagne flutes with the exaggerated care of the inebriated.

I was fit to burst with excitement; I was getting married at Christmas. Dad beamed, so did Graeme. And Lexy, the idiot, started crying, which made me cry. It was the topic of conversation for the rest of the evening.

Rob drove us home; he'd only had one glass of wine and a small lager. Now that I thought of it I had only had two drinks myself. As Rob pulled his BMW into the driveway his phone rang.

'Go inside, babe. Warm up the bed. I'll be right behind you,' he said, cutting the engine and flicking his phone open.

I was giddy with disbelieving happiness. I, Evie Dexter, was to be married at Christmas. I switched on the lounge lights. The sight of Lulu's magazines and home waxing kit (with used strips) on the floor, and a plate of congealed baked beans on the dining table, did nothing to dampen my spirits. Tonight had been brilliant. OK, Mum had been a rent-a-mouth, but we'd all got on famously in the end.

Rob strode into the lounge, phone wedged between his ear and shoulder. He slammed his briefcase on the dining table and flicked it open. I studied myself in the wall-mounted mirror. I didn't look any different. But then what does someone getting married at Christmas look like? Rob barked a series of instructions and orders into the phone while rustling through the contents of a leather folder. I put on some lipstick. I still didn't look like I was getting married. Maybe if I pinned my hair up?

'Evie, I've got to go out.'

I swivelled from the mirror, lipstick aloft. 'Now?' I asked, giving him a perplexed stare. 'But . . . it's almost midnight.'

'One of my coaches has broken down. The driver has a full load of passengers. He can't drive the relief coach because he's over his driving hours. Thankfully he's not too far away, he's only at Gatwick. I'll have to drive his group into town. I'll take your car,' he said, plucking my keys from the coffee table. 'I don't have time to fill mine. I've been running on empty.' He clutched my forearms and closed his mouth over mine. 'Don't wait up. I'll be a good couple of hours.'

And with that, in a whirl, he was gone.

Rob's papers littered the table, and twinned with Lulu's rubbish there wasn't a square inch of polished pine to be seen. I put the leather folder back in his briefcase, pulled back my hair, looped it into a knot and set about gathering Rob's paperwork. I turned an envelope over in my hand. The addressee in bold black italics was Mr and Mrs Robert Harrison. My eyes shifted to the postmark; it was dated last week and had been mailed to an address in Birmingham. Rob's parents! He's obviously forwarding their mail to Spain. My back stiffened. But Rob's dad's name was Harold, not Robert . . .

My throat went tight. I fingered the envelope. It was open. Why would Rob open his dad's mail before sending it on? Foreboding and panic hissed like rising steam inside me. I whipped out the contents. It was a Visa statement, addressed to Mr Robert and Mrs Cassandra Harrison. My legs turned to jelly. Robert Harrison? Cassandra Harrison? I pulled a chair from the dining table and sank into it. I moved forward and rested my forehead just left of the plate of beans. I felt sick and dizzy. Robert and Cassandra. OK, I should look, I told myself. I should check this mail. Of course I should. This cannot be Rob, not *my* Rob. I sat up slowly, clutched the statement with shaky hands and scanned the transactions:

Boots	£18.90
Debenhams	£99.99
Superdrug	£23.99
Tesco	£80.47
River Island	£8.50

I could hear the blood pumping in my ears. My hands tore frantically at the envelopes littering the table. There was a gas bill, a council tax statement, an invoice from a plumber and heaps of other stuff, all addressed to Mr and Mrs Harrison. My face flamed and my vision blurred. I felt breathless.

Rob, married? My Rob, married? To Cassandra?

My eyes raced over the paperwork, fanned like a dark cloud across the table. My face went numb. I couldn't take this in. It was a mistake. I'd call Rob and he'd explain.

Rob with a wife in Birmingham.

No way. I shook the thought from my head and twisted my arm in my bag for my phone. Rob picked up on the second ring.

'Hi, babe! Are you ringing to say good night?'

I felt a scalpel-sharp spike of fear. 'Do you have a . . . a . . . ' I took a ragged breath before exhaling the word, 'wife?'

I couldn't believe I was actually asking this.

There was an excruciating silence.

Say no, I prayed silently, clutching the phone with clammy hands.

'Babe, I can explain. It's not what you think, it's—'

My heart took a cardiac plunge. 'Are you married?' I shrieked. 'I need a simple yes or no answer.'

'Evie, listen to me!' he yelled. 'I can explain, I—'

'I don't think you can,' I yelled.

'I'm sorting it out, Ev—'

I snapped my phone shut and threw it in my bag. I felt a rush of conflicting emotions that literally knocked the breath out of me. I stood, ignored my ringing phone and stumbled blindly from the lounge, down the hallway, tears streaming down my face.

Lulu's bedroom was cold and the bed was empty. She was out. I closed her door with trembling hands and walked back to the lounge.

I sank into the sofa. What do you do when you discover your fiancé has a wife? Rob *is* married. It's true. I stared at the letters. Tears rolled down my cheeks. My world had collapsed. I felt angry. I felt sad. I felt . . . confused. Thoughts fought for attention in my mind. A wife. A house.

In a jolt of awareness I sat upright. A vapour of fear spread in my chest. Rob could come back here. I had to get out, out of

131

the flat. I didn't want to see him. I leaped to my feet and lurched to the table for Rob's car keys. I swiped my running nose with the heel of my hand, gnawed at my bottom lip and listened to the silence. A wife? I had to see for myself, I had to. I would go to Birmingham. I snatched the Visa bill, scrunched it in my handbag and left the flat. I would go there now.

Chapter Eleven

I filled Rob's car, punched the Birmingham postcode into the satnav and without paying much attention to where I was going, headed out of London. I drove robotically, conscious of nothing. My brain worked in spasms. For a while my mind was numb and then suddenly, my head would jam with thoughts. I preferred the numbness, but that made me drowsy. So despite intermittent hysteria I concentrated on following a train of thought. I asked myself why I hadn't suspected. How could I have been so ... so stupid, blind and trusting? And why hadn't Rob said anything? And more to the point, why had he married? Well, I worked that one out pretty swiftly for myself; he'd married because he'd loved her. This unwelcome realisation sent my already plummeting mental state in to a spiralling high-speed decline. Hot tears spilled down my cheeks and my knuckles, gripping the steering wheel, turned white. I felt like I was having an out-of-body experience, like this wasn't happening to me. Inside I was cold and although the heating in the car was like a nuclear blast, I shivered. The amber glow of my phone ringing on silent lit the car interior. My eyes slipped from the road ahead to the hands-free cradle.

It was Rob. Again. My jaw tensed. I couldn't talk to him. I'd collapse with grief. I gave a loud sniff and wiped my damp cheeks with a clenched fist. As the car spliced through the empty darkness of the motorway, my thoughts drifted to Mum and Dad, and to Lexy and Graeme. What would I tell them? The memory of the Christmas wedding announcement brought on a wave of nausea, and for a minute I thought I was actually going to vomit. I had tried to call Lulu four times but her phone was switched off, as was Tina's. I needed to talk to someone. I pulled up my phone's contacts list, found John's number and on impulse, hit dial.

'Evie, do you know what time it is?' John scolded in a deep, serious tone.

At the sound of his voice my heart raced. My eyes found my watch. It was one o'clock.

'Evie!'

I swerved on to the hard shoulder, cut the engine, draped my arms around the steering wheel, gulped a lump of misery and rested my head in the curve of my elbow.

'Evie!'

'Rob's married,' I blurted quietly into the darkness. 'He has a wife . . . A wife.' I pressed my forehead on the steering wheel and very loudly broke my heart.

John's voice exploded in the car. 'Evie! Where are you?'

Huge, salty tears splashed down my face.

'Answer me!'

My head throbbed and my eyes stung. And I felt lonely, so lonely and frightened.

'OK, Evie. Sit straight and try to breathe in . . . and slowly out. Come on, Evie. In and out, breathe in . . . and out.'

I raised my chin, closed my eyes and concentrated on this breathing in and out business. After a couple of shaky starts, it began to work.

'Come on, sweetheart, in . . . and out. You're doing well, that's it.'

I stared into space as my pulse normalised.

'OK, you're doing fine.'

I cast my eyes around. The road was comfortingly silent apart from the whirr of the sporadic, speeding, late-night driver. With a clenched fist I wiped a tear from my cheek then lifted my phone from the hands-free cradle and pressed it to my ear.

'Now come on, that's it, good girl.'

'I'm, I'm fine,' I said faintly, holding the phone with rigid fingers.

'Good,' John said with a sigh.

My throat was dry and tight and my eyelids heavy.

'Now,' he began in a clipped tone, 'where are you?'

'In Rob's car.'

'Are you alone?'

'Yes.'

'Tell me exactly where you are and I'll have you picked up.'

I peered into the darkness. I had no idea where I was.

'I'm on the motorway,' I told him.

'Which motorway?'

'I don't know,' I admitted and tears brimmed because I should have known which motorway I was on. 'The, the, B . . . Birmingham motorway. I'm going to meet his wife,' I said, my voice quivering.

'You are *not* going anywhere. Give me your car registration number.'

I gnawed at my thumbnail. 'I don't know it. It's, it's a BMW. Shall I get out and look?'

'No!' he shouted, making me jump. 'Are you en route from London to Birmingham?'

'Yes.'

'Can you remember passing any signs?'

I squeezed my eyes, thinking hard. 'Oxford, I, I think.'

'Stay where you are. I'll have you and the car picked up within the hour.'

I sniffed. 'Am I allowed, to, to wait on the hard shoulder?'

'Not really but don't worry about that. It's safer than losing control of your car. Wait there, do *not* drive. Do you hear me, Evie?'

I nodded miserably.

'Do you hear me?'

'Yes.'

The tawny glow from my phone flickered and diminished as the line went dead. I tossed the phone in my bag, reclined the driving seat and folded my arms across my chest. I was tired. No, I was exhausted. I'd wait for John. Fat drops of rain splashed and wriggled on the windscreen. I let my heavy lids drop to embrace unconsciousness and I felt a drowsy calmness. Perhaps I would feel better if I slept for a while. And John was right, I shouldn't be driving. I would rest.

My eyes pinged open. The Visa statement was emblazoned in my mind like a floodlight on the Alcatraz perimeter. River Island! That'll be clothes, shoes and accessories. Debenhams! I bet there's a Topshop concession in the Birmingham branch. Boots and Superdrug! That'll be perfume and make-up, no doubt. And let's not forget Tesco, which is obviously her wine and gin supply. Although I was sitting down, I felt as though the ground below me shifted. I came over woozy and light-headed because in a flash of understanding it occurred to me that *she*, the other woman, had a credit card, whereas I didn't. Because Rob, the two-timing skinflint, had confiscated all my credit cards last year and made me promise not to replace them. A promise I've kept. I've been going without, economising, living on a shoestring, and for what? For him to finance a wife?

I sat up, switched on the engine and throttled from nought to seventy in less than a minute.

We'll soon see about that, I decided, knuckles gripping the steering wheel.

Arriving in Birmingham my bravado deserted me. Like, totally. The weather was fittingly dismal with the sky moving in shades of grey, and sheets of rain being carried by a biting wind. The clock on the dashboard flashed three a.m. I unclipped my seat belt and glanced up at the front of *their* house, and let out a whimper. It was a cosy Victorian semi with magnolia painted walls and a terracotta roof. A pelmet of wisteria hung over the front porch and underscored the bedroom windows. It looked . . . homely. Obviously I couldn't knock on the door at this time in the morning. I'd have to wait, wait until, until, at least seven-thirty. I nestled into the driving seat. I'd try to sleep.

But I couldn't sleep without a blanket. Rob would have something I could use in the boot, I hoped. As I edged out of the car, the wind picked up my hair. I curved an arm over my head to keep the rain from my face and hurried, as much as cream platform courts would allow, to the back of the car. I tugged a quilted jacket from the boot, shrugged it across my shoulders and pulled the hood down over my forehead. As I leaned in to the wind, fumbling with the handle on the driver's door, a light hand pressed my shoulder. I whizzed round.

A slim, attractive girl with long blonde hair stood in front of me. She had deep-set brown eyes and a heart-shaped face. She wore a pink dressing gown, over which she'd draped a green Barbour jacket. Chin high, she skipped a hand over her eyes to catch the splatters of rain dripping from her hood.

'Evie?' she asked, pitting her voice against the rising wind.

I gave a surprised nod.

'I'm Cassie. I've been expecting you.'

Expecting me?

Pivoting, she hurried to the house, gesturing for me to do the same. I delved into the car, grabbed my bag from the passenger seat, tugged Rob's jacket around me and quickly followed her.

'You came, I thought you might,' she whispered, closing the front door with overstated quiet. 'Come into the kitchen,' she said, tossing her jacket over the banister and leading me down a mosaic-tiled hallway.

Wet, tired and miserable, I followed her into the kitchen, where I sank into a leather-padded chair at a scrubbed pine table. Gingerly, Cassie took the chair opposite. Her skin was tight on her cheekbones, her complexion almost transparent. She looked as tired as I felt, with a shadow of sleeplessness and lines of fatigue around her eyes. A gust of wind rattled the kitchen door.

'What am I thinking? You're soaked. your coat is dripping water on the floor. Let me take it from you,' she said, stepping round the table.

I wriggled Rob's jacket from my shoulder and watched her move with a nervous grace as she hung the jacket on a hook by the door and moved to the sink to fill the kettle. As she turned, a feeble smile hovered on her lips.

'I can see what the attraction is,' she said in a measured voice.

She relaxed against the worktop, arms folded, watchful, while the kettle boiled. I tucked a strand of damp hair behind my ear. We looked at each other for what seemed like a long time.

'What did you mean, you've been expecting me?' I asked.

She gave me an unblinking stare. 'Rob called – he's frantic. He's phoned three times. He said if you arrived I was to ring him straight away . . . I won't, of course.'

She turned and reached into the cupboard for cups. The

kitchen was large and square and airy. Polished pine cupboards lined the walls, a dark-blue stove nestled in a fluted alcove, and thick cream voile curtains dressed the windows.

Cassie watched me closely as she placed two cups of coffee, milk and sugar on the table, and edged into the seat opposite. The room was quiet but for the rhythmic ticking of a wall clock. Her clock, Rob's clock. Their clock. The realisation hit me that she wasn't the other woman; I was. My fingers tightened around my cup.

'We meet at last,' she said.

Flames of burning red crept up my neck.

'How is it that I am absolutely stunned to find out about you, but you don't seem surprised to find out about me?' I asked, finding my voice at last.

She cast my cream cocktail dress a glance.

'It looks like you've only just found out, whereas I've known since last summer that Rob had met someone else.'

'Last summer?'

'I'm guessing that's when he met you, because that's when everything went wrong between us,' she told me, her eyes glazed and distant.

My stomach clenched. 'Cassie,' I said, 'how about you tell me your story and I tell you mine?' I suggested.

She nodded and leaned forward conspiratorially.

My mind swam with pictures and dates. I was trying very hard to come up with something to blow the story Cassie had just told me out of the water. I watched entranced as she made toast and more coffee. This was real, I wasn't dreaming, it was really happening. Marshalling the facts, I knew there was no other way to do this than to face it head-on. Rob was a faithless bastard. Cassie's story confirmed it.

139

Rob and I had met last July in Paris. He split with Cassie in August and moved out of their house and into a flat about three miles from here. He spent four months with me, dividing his time between Paris, where he and I worked, and my flat in London, popping back to Birmingham once a week to oversee the business. When he and I split up at the end of October, he returned to Birmingham. At New Year, Rob and I got back together. He moved to London to be with me and asked Cassie for a divorce. Oh, and his parents live around the corner, not in Spain.

I massaged my collarbone. I could feel tension rising in my neck. This was too much to take in.

Cassie rattled a plate of toast on the table. 'It all figures,' she said nonchalantly, turning to the worktop for the mugs of coffee. 'But if it's any consolation, it's you Rob wants. He has driven me mad over this divorce. He'll agree to anything to speed it through.' Her eyes scanned the room. 'He's prepared to give me this house.'

I eyed the toast and tried to work up the wherewithall to eat it.

'And shares in the business,' she added, sinking into her chair. 'But I don't want a divorce, and I told him that.'

'You told him you don't want a divorce?' I asked, staring at her levelly.

She gave a sad nod.

I was stunned. If Rob knew Cassie didn't want a divorce, then he knew he was in no position to marry me at Christmas, unless his intention was to have two wives.

'Cassie, he treats you like a game of ping-pong, and you still want him?'

Her chin was tight. There was a defiant edge to her stare. She had a secret, I sensed it. A pang of foreboding rocked my chest as my heartbeat slowed to a juddering rhythm.

'You don't know about Marcus, do you?' Her brown eyes locked with mine. 'Our three-year-old son,' she added flatly.

I slumped against the seat back.

Cassie caught my tortured expression; her hands flew to her mouth. I stood and walked shakily to the sink. I felt an enormous spasm of grief. I felt wounded. Betrayed by Rob, my best friend and lover, and I felt wretched and confused. I had been convinced that this girl was to blame for bursting the bubble of my perfect life. Of course, it wasn't like that. Trying to be objective – and I *was*; I was trying my very best – I had to admit that she was as much a victim as I was, if not more . . . a *son*?

I took a look around the kitchen. I couldn't see any little boy stuff. No bike, no fishing rod. But then I spotted a door in the far corner with a 'Playroom' sign, and I supposed the mayhem and carnage lived in there. I gave a sniff and wiped my nose with the back of my hand. Rob's visits to Birmingham had been purposeful and regular now that I thought of it. A fresh wave of despair washed over me and I closed my eyes and shivered as I took the full, devastating force of the blow.

I hated him.

'You can have him,' I told Cassie.

She gave me a sad smile. Instead of hating this girl, I felt a flip of compassion towards her. This wasn't what I'd expected at all.

'I thought I'd hate you, but I don't,' she said, her thoughts mirroring my own. 'But then we do have something in common, don't we?'

'Do we?'

'We love the same man.'

'We don't!' I shot back with calculated venom.

Her brows lifted in question. She moved her coffee cup in a pensive, aimless oblong on the tabletop, her brown eyes never leaving mine.

We turned to the sound of a sudden knock at the door.

'Someone's at the door!' Cassie said quickly. Her already wide eyes widened. 'Who could it be?' she asked.

I looked at her vacantly. 'It's your door. It's hardly likely to be someone for me,' I pointed out.

Our eyes flew to the wall clock.

'Four o'clock,' we chorused.

'Rob?' I voiced, feeling feverish with nerves.

She shook her head fiercely. 'He wouldn't have made the journey this quickly, and he wouldn't have come here just on the off chance,' she said sensibly. 'He thought it more likely you would still be in London.'

A second tempered knock jolted her to standing.

'They'll wake Marcus,' she snapped. 'Who is it?'

'We'll answer it . . . together,' I said.

She hurried from the kitchen, dressing gown flapping, and I clip-clopped behind, resplendent in last night's evening dress and tear-streaked make-up.

She opened the door to two men in black suits.

'Evie Dexter?' one asked, his eyes switching between me and Cassie.

I flinched back, not sure whether to identify myself or not. I mean, who were these people? They looked ominous, they looked *menacing*. Cassie shot me a wary glance and then stood bravely in front of me. She pulled on the cord of her dressing gown and squared her slim shoulders.

'What do you want?' she asked boldly. 'Who are you?'

'Mr Jackson sent us, he—'

'Oh, right,' I interrupted. 'Sorry, but I don't need a lift any more,'

'I'm sorry, Miss, but we're to take you to him,' one of the men said, taking a purposeful step forward.

In reply, Cassie and I took a cautious step back.

The man flipped his phone open, punched a couple of digits and then handed it to me.

'I suggest you speak with Mr Jackson. His instructions were very clear.'

Cassie looped her arm in mine. I took the phone obediently, pressing it to my ear.

'John?' I hedged.

'Evie! What the hell do you think you're playing at? When I tell you to stay where you are, that's exactly what you do. I'm furious. Now get in my car. We'll discuss this when I see you.'

'The thing is . . .' I began, but snapped my mouth shut when I realised I was speaking to a dialling tone.

Cassie stared at me in mute alarm. I put a reassuring hand on her arm.

'Who was that?' she asked.

'Er . . . A friend. I have to go. We'll talk again, I'm sure.'

'Can I have your car keys, Miss?' the man asked, giving an awkward bow. 'I'll drive your car to London. You'll be travelling in Mr Jackson's car with my colleague,' he explained, gesturing to the man behind him.

Cassie lowered her voice confidentially. 'Leave Rob's car here. Why deliver it back to him when making him come to pick it up is far more inconvenient?' she said, her pale skin pink with mischief.

I smiled, dropped Rob's keys in to her palm and left.

John's driver took me to East Midlands airport, where Sadie and the crew were waiting. They informed me I was going to Amsterdam. As one does. Fortunately, as all organsied tour guides do, I had my passport with me.

On arrival at Schiphol airport, I was driven in a car with darkened windows through the cobbled streets of the Dutch capital, to the Hotel Pulitzer, where I was met and escorted through the silent lobby to an elevator and up to the top floor.

John's figure filled the doorway of the penthouse suite. He wore black trousers and a pink, long-sleeved, open neck shirt. He stood with his legs apart, hands deep in his trouser pockets. He gave me a cordial nod. When I saw his eyes soften and a smile curve his lips, I quickened my pace, literally running the length of the hallway towards him. He stepped forward, closing the distance between us, and enveloped me tightly. I was so pleased to see him.

'Evie, I'm exhausted. I've been awake all night sorting you out.'

'He has a wife and son,' I wailed.

John gripped my forearms, held me at arm's length and shook me gently. 'Your fiancé does not deserve you.'

'But I love him.'

He curved an arm around my shoulder. 'Come in, tell me everything,' he said, brows drawn in concern.

'How did your driver find the house in Birmingham? Have you spoken to Rob? Did he give you the address?' I asked, so eagerly it came out sounding more like a list of demands.

'No, I have not spoken to Rob, nor do I intend to. When my driver couldn't find you, I had your phone signal traced and a dammed complicated nuisance it was too,' he grumbled. 'I owe a few favours to a quite few people after tonight, I don't mind telling you.'

This was a bit too clever for me. Phone signal traced? I couldn't be bothered to ask what that meant. Instead, I started crying. John led me to a sofa in the window alcove. He didn't sit next to me. He pulled up a footstool and sat opposite. My eyes skimmed the room. There were huge vases of fresh flowers everywhere. Gold velvet swags and tails draped the windows and a haphazard arrangement of velvet winged chairs surrounded an enormous low-level coffee table.

John leaned forward, elbows on knees. 'OK, from the beginning, and take your time, we have all day,' he said slowly, eyes narrowed.

I looked down at my hands clenched in my lap and, surprising myself, told him everything, leaving nothing out.

John had listened in silence while I finished my story, shaking his head in supportive bewilderment. I clutched a cushion to my chest. I was drained.

'The man – the *boy* – is a fool,' he said.

I nodded, not trusting myself to speak. John moved from the footstool to sit on the sofa next to me and pulled me to him. We sat still in independent thought.

He raised my chin with an index finger. 'Have a bath, I'll order breakfast, and then you're going to bed. You look exhausted.' He stood and reached for my hand. 'Come on,' he said.

An hour later, wrapped in a fluffy hotel dressing gown, I sat miserably at the dining table opposite John, inhaling the steam from my coffee. I couldn't eat a thing.

John eyed me shrewdly. 'Does anyone know you're here?' he asked.

'No.'

'Give me your phone.'

I rattled my cup on the saucer and under John's watchful gaze, crossed the room and took my phone from my bag. Not surprisingly, it was out of battery. He heard me sigh.

'Give the phone to me,' he said.

I sank into my seat, handed him my phone and rubbed

furiously at my eyes. I was shattered. It had been twenty-four hours since I'd slept.

He turned my phone over in his hands. 'Write a list,' he said.

'A list of what?'

'A list of what you'll need over the next couple of days. Toiletries, clothes—'

'Couple of days?'

He leaned forward. 'Are you in any rush to go back to London?'

'No,' I admitted, pulling the dressing gown tighter around me.

'Take my phone. Call home now, let everyone know you're safe and well, then off to bed with you. By the time you wake I'll have your phone charged and a change of clothes. And we'll go out for an early dinner.'

I was seized by a rush of panic. I couldn't possibly go out for dinner. I wasn't hungry. And I didn't want to face people. And who should I call? I didn't want to speak to anyone.

John pressed his phone in my hand. 'Make the call,' he repeated.

The problem over who to speak to was quickly resolved by the fact that the only number I knew off by heart, other than my own flat, was the landline in Bar Thea. Calling the flat was not an option. What if Rob answered? So under John's steely gaze, I rang Nikki.

Nik's voice detonated down the line after he realised it was me calling.

'Evie, this better be good! That boyfriend of yours called me at three o'clock this morning. Where are you? I don't care what lovers' tiff you've had, but God help you if you don't make it in here for the lunchtime shift. We have a party of twenty, and . . .'

I opened my mouth to say something but no sound

emerged. I pressed my lips together and breathed through my nose. John gave me an encouraging go-on-then nod. Nikki barked on.

'Have you smashed his car? Is that it? Your car is in the drive-way, but his is gone. Evie, a car is only a car, now listen to me—'

'Nikki, Rob's married and he has a son,' I interrupted.

I pressed the phone to my ear. There was an awed silence.

'I'll kill him!' Nikki blurted.

'You won't!'

'I will!'

'Can you call Lulu and Lexy? Tell Lexy not to mention this to Mum and Dad. I'll speak to them myself at some point,' I said in a voice that sounded hollow and surreal.

I was doing well. Having managed a couple of sentences, I felt encouraged to push on. I felt like a presenter on *Crimewatch*, updating the public on the latest developments in the 'Murder on the Railways Killer.' Grim-faced and jaw tight.

I tossed back a wing of damp hair. 'I'm in Amsterdam,' I ploughed on. 'In Holland.' I added, as if there might be some doubt as to which Amsterdam I was talking about.

'Did you drive there?' Nik asked.

That was a normal enough question but I halted, because momentarily I couldn't remember how I got here. My nostrils stung and my eyes pooled. I scanned the room. How did I get here? How? Buckling under the pressure of being a *Crimewatch* presenter, I burst into tears and handed the phone to John.

John stood and, head bent, walked towards the window and finished the call with Nikki in hushed, rushed tones.

I wrote a list. Cleanser, toner, moisturiser, knickers. I couldn't think of anything else. John took the list wordlessly and led me to my bedroom. He pressed a kiss on my head and gently closed the door behind me.

The room was deadly silent.

I took off the dressing gown, slid between the cool sheets, and cried myself to sleep.

I slept all day, waking at four-thirty. I made a toga of the quilt and with determined strength, opened the heavy, powder-blue, velvet drapes. Unlike London, Amsterdam was bathed in sunshine. I opened the window slightly and gazed down at the street below. Tall blossoming trees lined the cobbled pathways and window boxes spilling with spring flowers decorated the façades of imposing, terracotta-gabled buildings. The canal, busy with brightly coloured barges, shifted like liquid silver. There was a polite knock at the door.

'I heard movement,' John said, coming into the room. 'I guessed you were awake.'

'It's beautiful, isn't it?' I said, tucking a stray lock of hair behind my ear.

'What is?' he asked.

'The city, of course,' I said, gesturing to the window.

'Er, yes, I suppose it is,' he replied absently, and rushed on. 'I'm hungry. Can you be ready at six o'clock? I've reserved a table downstairs.'

I felt a prickle of anxiety. 'I'm not hungry, and I don't want to—'

He raised the flat of his hand for quiet.

'We are eating,' he said, 'at six, so be ready.' He placed three boxed white bags on the bed. 'You'll find something to wear in here.'

I gave a grateful nod. My heart pounded and my eyes stung. I didn't want to cry, not again, not yet, my head was banging.

'And your phone is charged,' he said, placing my phone beside the bags. 'Don't keep me waiting, I skipped lunch.'

As a whoosh of misery hit me, I quickly bent my chin to my chest and pinched my nose between forefinger and thumb.

John exhaled patiently.

'Why would he keep such a secret from me? Why?' I wailed, giving in to another flurry of tears.

John held his arms wide. I tightened the toga and stumbled towards him. He drew me to him.

'You'll get the answer to that question from him,' he said.

'I hate him!'

He gave a weary sigh. 'I wish you did. It would certainly make life easier.' He held me tight, which was what I wanted.

'I do hate him,' I repeated with a mighty sniff.

A chilly spring breeze drifted through the room, making me shiver.

'You're freezing. Come on, get washed and dressed,' John said, rubbing his palms on my shoulders. He raised my chin. 'I want to see you dressed and pouring me a drink in an hour and a half. Understood?'

I gave a sad nod.

'You'll feel better after a meal and a few gin and tonics.'

I managed a watery smile. 'I'll be ready,' I said, wiping my eyes with the heel of my hand.

'Good,' he said, walking towards the door. 'Get straight in the shower.'

'I will,' I told him, chin high. 'Right this minute.'

I paced the room like a demon. I really should give Rob a chance to explain. I mean, there's obviously an explanation. You don't ask someone to marry you, knowing you're already married, without some sort of game plan. So I should quietly and calmly call him, and ask him to make sense of all this mess, and sort everything out. I grabbed my phone and sank into an armchair next to the bed. But then, I thought, I've met the wife, haven't I? What's left to explain? The faithless bastard!

First, I'll listen to my messages, and then, then . . .

I will call him. There is no harm in listening to what he has to say.

But what can he possibly say that will change anything?

No, I won't call him. I sniffed.

My voicemails began.

LULU (sounding totally enraged): 'What's going on!? That fucking boyfriend of yours has every light in the house on! Every single one! He's gone through your address book, and mine . . . And the cheeky bastard called me Cruella to my face! To my bloody face! The nerve of him! Have you stolen his car? Is that it? I'm getting *no* sleep and you know I need to be up early. Get back here and sort him out. Shag him or something, anything to stop him walking the floorboards . . . Oh! And on your way back, could you buy a pint of milk?'

LEXY: 'I don't know what you're up to. Graeme thinks our whole family needs therapy. After you left, Mum set the bathroom curtains on fire; she's started smoking roll-ups. Can you credit it? At her age! This is ridiculous. Rob is frantic and I don't blame him. He pops out to aid an emergency and you go missing. And don't forget you're looking after the twins tomorrow while I have my legs waxed.'

TINA (in a confidential whisper): 'Rob called looking for you. Thinking on my toes I said you were in the shower, and then he said he was coming over. So I freaked out and admitted you weren't here. But I didn't know you were supposed to be here, did I? You should've told me. I

assume you're shagging someone else, which, hey, I'm not
pointing the finger or anything because I know you'd
alibi me, but you should've tipped me off.'
ROB (in a sorry for himself voice): 'Evie, I love you, I've
always loved you, I always will. That's all you need to
know, that's all that matters. We can work this out.
Where are you, babe? Call me please.'

My chest tightened at the sound of his voice. I leaped to my feet
and resumed my pacing, swishing the tail of my toga behind me.

ROB: 'Call me please.'
ROB: 'Just let me know you're safe.'
ROB: 'Call me.'
NIKKI (in a businesslike tone): 'I've spoken to Lulu and
Lexy. I can be in Amsterdam within a couple of hours if
you want me to pick you up. Costas and Pepi will cover
for me. Let me know.'
LULU: 'The bastard! Nik told me everything! I'm ringing
Lexy right now to tell her.'
LEXY (with punctuating sniffs): 'Mum and Dad are still
here. I haven't breathed a word. This is so hard. I feel
weighed down with the knowledge. I had to speak to
someone so I told a couple of girls at the playgroup,
when I dropped the kids off. Apart from them and the
lady in the newsagents I haven't told a soul. I'll take it
to the grave. I'm so upset. Call me ... Don't do anything
stupid. I've cancelled my appointment; I can have my
waxing done next week. I don't want you to worry about
my waxing.'
MUM (with a skip in her voice): 'Darling, what a lovely
young man Rob is. Your dad and I are thrilled for you.

151

We've decided to climb Kilimanjaro. We'll be back for
the big day, so exciting.'

Climb Kilimanjaro? She doesn't even walk to Weight
Watchers. And that's only ten minutes from her house.

ROB: 'I tried to tell you so many times, but there was never
the right moment. It's not important.'

I slid down the side of the bedpost and landed with a thud on
the floor. Not important? He has a wife and son, and it's not
important? I felt feverish. I pressed the phone to my ear. Not
important!

ALICE: 'Rob rang looking for you, he thought you may've
been here. He told me everything. I'm very disappointed
in him. Duncan gave him a stern talking to. Take care of
yourself, love.'

Rob and I had met Alice and her husband Duncan last year
in Paris. Although twenty years older than me, Alice and I had
become friends and we still kept in touch. Rob really had been
through my address book. I felt a pang of guilt. Now that I
thought of it, I owed Alice a couple of calls.

There was a sharp knock on the door. 'Evie, you've got fifteen minutes,' John said in a deep, hollow tone.

Fifteen minutes?

I scrambled up the bedpost. 'OK, give me twenty.'

I threw off the toga. Not important? He has a wife and son.
In what way is that not important? We'll pretty much have to
agree to disagree on that front. No reason to call him. I hate him.

*

I wore a crimson knee-length wraparound cocktail dress to dinner. It was a bit wide on the shoulder and too swishy around the knees for my liking. I accessorised with crimson sandals that had a silver heel, and a matching clutch bag.

'I look like a hooker,' I whispered to John as he guided me through the busy dining room.

'You look lovely,' he said. 'In fact, you look better than you usually do.'

'What's that supposed to mean?' I snapped, rattled.

'You look like a lady.'

I turned on him. 'Don't I always?'

'Frankly, no, especially when you wear those silly thick tights without feet,' he said with a grimace.

'Those are leggings.'

He pulled out my chair.

I gave him a swift look up and down. 'You could be twelve years old or ninety-four in that outfit,' I told him.

In fairness, as always, he looked very smart but he'd insulted my leggings! A girl has to give as good as she gets.

'This is a lounge suit,' he shot back, affronted, smoothing a hand over his silk tie.

'Exactly. You never wear anything else.'

He edged into the chair opposite. 'I do.'

'Yes, chinos and pastels,' I conceded stiffly.

He gave me a baffled look. 'What else *is* there?' he asked, before turning his attention to his menu. 'I recommend the lamb,' he said, looking officious.

Wife and son. Sod Rob, I thought, I'm in Holland. On holiday. I closed my menu with a jaunty slap. 'Lamb it is,' I replied.

A bottle of Châteauneuf-du-Pape later, and I was sinking into a quicksand of depression. I buried a piece of lamb under a potato. I couldn't eat; my appetite was purely for liquids. Tears clouded my vision.

'Don't!' John warned.

'Don't what?' I asked.

'Don't cry.'

My fingers tightened round my glass. I felt a spasm of misery. I wiped a tear from my cheek, which was instantly replaced by another. John closed his hand over mine, pressing my fingers round the stem of my glass.

'I wasn't going to cry until you said, don't cry,' I blurted out quickly.

'You were. Now stop it . . . Take a sip of wine.'

I drained the glass. 'There's no need to be so draconian,' I told him with a sniff.

He smiled broadly and gestured to the waiter for a bottle of water. I sat poker-straight and gave him a watery stare.

'I've been called many things but never draconian – not to my face anyway,' he said, his shoulders lifting in laughter. 'Although I'm sure almost my entire staff think it.'

I was about to nod my agreement but stopped myself by fishing in my bag for my lip gloss. I happened to suspect his entire staff *did* think it. I can't see it myself, but according to Tina he is half-man, half-werewolf.

'I'd appreciate it if you didn't laugh at my expense,' I said, whizzing pink frost round my lips.

'I'm not,' he said, mouth curving suspiciously.

I cast an eye over the exquisite opulence of the Restaurant Keizersgracht. Ice cubes and glassware rattled, accompanied by the animated hum of a room full of smartly dressed diners.

'So why are we here?' I asked, toasting my glass towards the window and the breathtaking canal view.

'In Amsterdam?' John asked.

154

'Yes.'

'I have an office here. I come at least once a month.'

'Very nice,' I said in a chalky voice, tears temporarily at bay.

His dark eyes were steady on my face. 'Evie, this boy Rob,' he said, frowning in earnest.

My tummy did a flippy thing at the mention of Rob's name. I felt my whole body stiffen.

'I don't like him,' John said bitterly.

'What do you mean you don't like him? You don't even know him, and he's not a boy, he's a man,' I snapped loyally.

There was a beat of silence.

'OK, perhaps a better way to phrase what I'm trying to say is that I don't like him for you,' he said, giving a consenting nod to the waiter to pour.

'We were good together.'

'No, you thought you were good together.'

'We were!'

He emptied his lungs with a sigh. 'Evie, it's different for a man.'

'What's different?'

His eyes shifted as he arranged his thoughts into words. 'We seem to be better liars, more apt at locking things in the margins of our thoughts when we don't want to address them. We are experts at dismissing our own faults. I've done it myself many times. Rob will have two sets of rules in his mind's eye, one for you and one for him.'

I rubbed my knuckle on my chin. This was too much to take in. I couldn't fathom it out, I was too tired.

'The lies and deceit aside, are you prepared to assume the responsibilities of a stepmother?' John asked, giving me a solemn glare.

Stepmother?

I was silenced. I glanced around the restaurant, feeling

disorientated. All the lively noise and chatter seemed to become muffled. John's face swam in and out in a haze. I blinked furiously. The word 'stepmother' had the same effect on me that 'man the lifeboats' may have had under different circumstances. I clutched the side of the table with one hand and gripped my glass with the other. The only stepmothers I knew were the evil crones from *Cinderella* and *Snow White*. I didn't want to be twinned with *them*. Definitely not. I took a healthy gulp of wine.

John gave a knowing smile. 'You *will be* stepmother to his son if you decide to marry him,' John pointed out animatedly, as though this was fabulous news and I should be thrilled at the prospect.

I dropped my eyes to my glass.

Stepmother?

'Evie, you are a beautiful twenty-six-year-old girl. You have your whole life in front of you. Forget him.'

Ah, a piece of good news – I was twenty-six. But I felt eighty-six. A vision of Rob's handsome face popped into my head.

'But I love him,' I said.

'You'll love others,' he shot back.

I shook my head from side to side. 'Not like I love him.'

John relaxed back, arms crossed, chin on his chest. 'If that's the case, call him now and tell him you forgive him.'

I sat up. 'I don't forgive him,' I said.

'Nor should you, and I'm not even referring to the wife and son. I'm referring to the incident last year. You should never have taken him back in the first place.'

I felt a wave of self-righteousness. 'I was miserable without him.'

'You didn't give yourself a chance to get over him,' he said in a condescending tone.

'Listen to you: four divorces and three girlfriends. You're hardly an authority on lasting relationships,' I counter-attacked.

He leaned forward menacingly.

My heart gave a panicked hop.

'I have considerably more experience on relationships than you,' he said in a cool voice. 'That is all you need to know.' He closed his hand over mine. 'I have not met the right person yet. When I do, she will be the only woman in my life,' he said tonelessly.

Privately I thought that he'd better get a move on; he was no Peter Pan.

'Still, three girlfriends,' I reminded him.

'One,' he defended.

'One? So you've dumped two? And is she by any chance The One?'

'No, she's not, but . . . ' he broke off, words hanging mid-air.

'But what?'

His brows met in consternation.

'But what?' I pressed.

'Would you like dessert? he asked.

'Dessert? No thank you. I want to know what you were about to say.'

There was an awkward pause. His eyes drifted behind me.

'You've met someone, haven't you?' I challenged in a flash of understanding.

He sipped his wine, avoiding eye contact.

'Tell me about her, who is she? What's she like, where did you meet?'

'Evie, those are very intrusive questions.'

'Intrusive questions? I've told you everything about me, but I know practically nothing about you.' I gave him a glance of wild amusement. 'Tell me.'

He took a larger than usual sip of wine. 'When the time is right, I will tell you. For now, the subject is closed,' he said, thumping his glass on the table signalling that, for now, the subject was indeed closed. 'Let's move to the bar for brandy,' he said, pushing back his chair.

Chapter Twelve

I woke at nine-thirty, cried for an hour, and felt absolutely no better. John was out but he had left a note on the coffee table in the lounge to say he'd be back at eleven. I phoned Lulu; she was at the radio station.

'Evie! You need *me*. I want to look after you. Come home; you should be with me at a time like this,' she said urgently.

'Have you seen him?' I asked.

She exhaled heavily. 'No I haven't, but I heard him banging around this morning, the bastard,' she snapped. 'I tell you, I'll—'

'I want him out of the flat before I get back,' I interrupted.

'Before you get back? He'll be out of the flat before the kettle boils when I get home. I've been waiting for the nod from you. What are you playing at jetting off to Holland? And what is it with you and that millionaire?'

I grimaced.

'Oh! And guess what?' she asked brightly.

'What?'

'I won the challenge! Andrew Blackbourne was photographed having a fag walking out of the police station.'

'That's brilliant,' I told her.

'Not that there's a prize or anything, but still. It's nice to be the winner.'

There was an uncomfortable dip in the conversation.

'Evie, I wasn't Rob's biggest fan but I didn't want this. I wanted—'

'I know you didn't want this,' I said sadly.

There was another quiet beat, hitherto unknown in a conversation between me and Lulu.

'I'll call to let you know when I'm coming home,' I said.

'OK. Take care of yourself,' she said in an assertive tone that made her sound like her mother.

I called Lexy. I didn't speak. I didn't get the chance. It was like a Punch and Judy sketch, with her playing both characters.

'How are you?' she asked.

'Terrible, I'll bet,' she replied.

'How could he? What was he thinking?'

'A double life – can you believe it?'

'Well, I can't.'

'I know, I know, likely you still love him.'

'But you'll be fine. You have lots of people who love you.'

And so it went on. She even said goodbye for both of us.

I phoned Tina.

'Evie, You're upset. It's all very raw. You're disillusioned and probably not thinking straight. But listen to me. *Do not return the ring!* You'll regret it if you do, when you're back to your normal, spirited, spiteful self.'

I told her I was with John Jackson in Amsterdam.

'He's a monster! Aren't you scared? His demands are endless. He reduces our MD to a snivelling bag of nerves,' Tina warned. There was a pause. 'Why, why him?' she asked at last. 'Evie, be careful.'

I teased Rob's ring off my finger, and put it in my purse.

Nikki spoke in a sombre, throaty tone. He told me to take as much time off work as I needed, which must have nearly choked him to say. I could imagine him gnawing his knuckles to the bone as he said it. Maria fought the receiver from him; I heard the struggle. Crying, she told me love was all around me.

Now it was Rob's turn.

I held my phone in a white-knuckled grip and took a couple of short sharp breaths. My heartbeat quickened to a gallop at the sight of Rob's name in my contact list. I wavered, tears simmering.

The swish of John's key card in the door made me jump.

'Evie! What are you doing skulking around at this time of day in your dressing gown?' he scolded. He looked pointedly at his watch.

I was sitting on the sofa, legs crossed, hugging a cushion to my chest, phone in hand. As his eyes challenged mine, my bottom lip trembled. I couldn't stop it. I buried my face in the cushion as the tears streamed from my eyes. I heard John sigh and felt the welcome pressure as he sank on to the sofa next to me. Instinctively I lurched towards him, circled his neck, and squeezed my eyes in reflex. He held me tight. His throat moved against my forehead.

'Evie, I'm going to suggest something to you I've never suggested to a woman in my life,' he said, lifting his shoulders as if his jacket was too tight.

'What's that?' I managed.

'That we go shopping. I believe it cures a multitude of female ailments. I thought we could give it a go. I'm attending a charity ball tonight. If I'm taking you with me you'll need an evening dress,' he said thoughtfully.

Head resting on his chest, I sniffed loudly and worked my thumb round the cuff of his sleeve.

'Shopping doesn't get rid of wives and kids,' I pointed out.

161

'Does that mean you don't want to go?'

I sat up. 'I'll be ready in fifteen minutes.'

'You've got ten. I'm regretting my offer already.'

'I was about to call Rob.'

'Call him when we get back. Don't give me time to change my mind. As I said, I'm having second thoughts. Third, in fact.'

Now, I hate to sound ungrateful, but the clothes in the three boxed bags are horsey, conservative, expensive, and I am sure they would look marvellous on Princess Anne. I *need* this shopping trip. I put on a pair of jeans (the best of a bad bunch) and one of John's crew-neck sweaters, which was way too big for me. But it was cashmere and so I didn't care what size it was and John said I could keep it. As for the rest of the clothes, John arranged for the concierge to pick them up and return them whence they came.

'It's a waste of money,' I explained, tugging my fingers through my hair as we left the room.

'I agree, if you don't like them,' John said.

'It's fabulous that you can send someone else to line up in the returns queue.'

John nodded absently.

'Surprisingly the lingerie is lovely and a perfect fit. I've kept that,' I told him.

'Good,' he said.

A thought crossed my mind.

'Who guessed the sizes?'

'I did,' he said, guiding me towards the elevator.

He did?

John was hilarious. In the first boutique, one of the assistants enquired politely if she could help him. He asked for a news-paper and an espresso and to be directed to the seating area. There was no seating area, let alone espresso and a newspaper.

When he handed over his credit card, he told the assistant we were staying at the Pulitzer and to send our bags there. Leading him by the arm from the shop, with my bags looped over his shoulder, I explained the process of purchase and carry.

'If the boutiques won't deliver our bags, the hotel will pick them up. I'll make damn sure they do,' he said with a scowl.

Dam Square, with the backdrop of the Royal Palace, was heaving. Tourists, with chins held high, marvelled at the beauty of the lofty Renaissance buildings and shoppers fought for space on the busy pavements.

'Amsterdam's signature is its sound,' I told John as we made a hot chocolate stop.

'What sound?'

'The rhythmic hum of the trams and the tinkle of bicycle bells,' I told him.

'Really?' he said, lifting an uninterested brow.

'Have you ever been on a canal cruise?' I asked him.

He tilted his head, as though thinking hard. 'No!'

'Would you like to?'

'No, not really.' He gave me an arctic stare. 'Why am I standing on a street corner, drinking from a Styrofoam cup, when I could be sitting in the relative comfort of a coffee shop?' he asked sharply.

I licked the froth from my chocolate. 'You can buy hashish and marijuana in some coffee shops in Amsterdam. Cannabis cafés they're called,' I told him, ignoring his mood.

He narrowed his eyes. 'Is that so?'

A fast-moving snake of school children happened past, separating us and pinning him into the doorway of a shop.

He tossed his cup in a bin. 'Let's get on with it,' he said. 'Now that I'm out I'd rather keep on the move.'

*

I was back in my room, surrounded by bags – fourteen bags to be precise. John was right about the hotel picking them up. Amazing! We had stopped in the bar downstairs for a drink and, like magic, the bags had beaten us to the room. I have never spent so much money in one day, or even in a month. I've said thank you a zillion times. John says he'll send the whole bloody lot back if I say thank you one more time. I have an entire new wardrobe. And the weird thing is that John cajoled me into buying almost every item. He did! I expected him to make me run a marathon for an evening dress and then to hot-foot it back to the hotel as quick as he could, but the opposite was the case. He had stood lazily in each boutique, reading a newspaper and insisting I took as much time as I needed. I don't even know how much my evening dress cost; he wouldn't tell me. 'This charity ball is a high profile event. I'm not taking you looking anything less than your best,' is all he would say.

There was a tap at my bedroom door.

'Come in!'

'The concierge rang. The hairdresser is on her way up,' John said.

'I didn't ask for a hairdresser.'

'No, but I did. I thought you could do with some help with that long flowing mop of yours,' he said, grinning widely. He walked into my room, arm outstretched. 'Give me your phone.'

'My phone?'

He gave a sharp nod with his eyes. 'We've had a whole day without tears. I don't want you brooding over messages. You can do that tomorrow.'

I cast my eyes over my handbag, where my phone was tucked up safe. I'd been planning to call Rob.

'The phone,' he repeated softly, but with a demanding click of his fingers.

I took it from my bag and handed it to him.

'Thank you,' he said, and left the room.

My hair was piled high into a pineapple and decorated with a glittery tiara, with a couple of long, springy tendrils strategically pulled around my face. I wore a chiffon, off-the-shoulder, black dress with a discreet slash to the thigh, which hugged my bust and hips, and swirled to a trailing fish tail. A white faux fur wrap was draped around tanned shoulders. Yes, tanned! The hairdresser gave me a St Tropez tan treatment and while she was at it, she glued on false eyelashes. I was looking rather lean too – the recent discovery that my fiancé has a wife and child having rather put paid to my appetite.

John was in the dimly lit lounge, sitting in an armchair, one leg crossed elegantly over the other, resplendent in black tie, studying the *Financial Times*.

'I'm ready,' I said, feeling an inexplicable crawling sensation of nerves.

He folded his newspaper and gazed up at me as though I was a crystal ball. What the crystal ball told him must have been good because an enormous smile licked his face. He stood and walked slowly towards me.

'You, my darling girl, are a beauty.'

A bubble of happiness bounced in my tummy.

'There's one thing missing,' he said, reaching for a blue velvet box on the bar. He opened the box.

I held my breath.

A sapphire pendant on a white gold chain with matching earrings nestled on a cushion of cream satin.

'Are they real?' I asked, face burning with pleasure and amazement.

His lips twitched, hiding a smile. 'Of course they're real!' he said, clipping the chain round my neck. He took a step back and dusted his palms. 'Perfect match!'

'Match to what?' I asked.

'Your eyes, of course.'

I felt a warm glow.

'Put the earrings on,' he said.

I removed my boring crystal studs. 'We've been together all day. When did you have time to go to a jeweller?' I asked.

'I had the jeweller come to my office. I bought them this morning.'

'You bought them?'

'Yes.'

'They're not borrowed?'

His brows shot up in surprise. 'Borrowed? How could I make a gift of something borrowed?'

'You mean these are mine . . . to keep?' I asked.

'Of course they're yours to keep!'

Tears welled. He placed his hands on each side of my tiara as if in benediction. His touch felt . . . warm and safe and nice.

'Don't cry!' he warned, wearing a scowl I knew for a fake.

My wrap slipped down my arm. I pulled it round my shoulders in a sharp jerky movement.

'It's not what you think; it's happy crying—'

'I don't want to see *any* crying.'

On impulse, I hugged him. He felt strong and broad. I swallowed hard. He rubbed my back gently.

'Come on. Let's go,' he said, looping my arm through his. 'We're late.'

The charity ball was being held at the Dutch Stock Exchange, a four-centuries-old constitution. As our limousine purred to a halt I edged from the car, extending a St Tropezed leg. My heart took a cardiac leap when I stepped on to a red carpet. *A real red carpet!* To the left a spotlighted man held an enormous furry microphone while a young girl powdered his face and a camera man danced around him. I swivelled to John.

'Who's he?' I asked, pointing my bag at the man.

'I have no idea,' John said, tweaking his perfectly straight bow tie.

'Let's go find out,' I suggested eagerly, eyes flirting everywhere.

He clutched my arm and propelled me into the glittering crowd of guests milling near the entrance.

'We'll do no such thing,' he said sharply.

I trotted forward while looking back. If I got in range of the camera perhaps I'd be on television. John clamped my elbow.

'Evie, look where you're going. You're tripping over my feet!' he snapped. 'Be careful.'

I chewed my bottom lip in irritation, but quickly broke into a smile for a flurry of popping flashbulbs. My gaze landed on a triangle of photographers, cameras slung lazily over their shoulders, chatting among themselves. My jaw flexed. Shouldn't they be . . . taking pictures?

The outward plainness of the building belied the magnificent interior. An enormous room was decorated in white and gold, with spotlights targeting floor-to-ceiling pictures of dancing Renaissance couples. A broad set of stairs, garlanded with lilies, led to a balcony where guests gathered in animated groups, while white-jacketed waiters bearing trays of champagne meandered smoothly between them. It was fabulous. A sense of giddy recklessness gripped me. I stroked my faux fur wrap fondly. I'm going to have a blast. Depression be dammed. Rob? Rob who?

John took two glasses from the tray of a passing waiter and handed one to me.

'Would you have come here on your own?' I asked over the rim of my glass, casting an awed glance around.

'I have three tables of ten.'

'You have twenty-nine friends here?'

'No, I have twenty-nine members of staff.'

'Are we sitting with them?'

'No,' he said without further explanation.

It was positively coma-inducing. I kid you not. I had an Austrian banker on my left, whose opening gambit was to ask my views on the UK Government's policies on Inheritance Tax. As I had no views whatsoever, the conversation was rather one-sided, insomuch as I pretended to listen to his views instead. He also had a lengthy and (he seemed to think) hilarious story about interest rates. I wanted to kill him. John, on my right, spent the evening chatting to a short woman with a fiery complexion, dressed like Little Bo Peep.

Alone but for a bottle of Chablis, thoughts and memories of Rob ran through my mind. Watching a lovey dovey young couple at an adjacent table, I felt a spear of envy. I hugged John's arm. I wondered if he had my phone on him. I could sit in the ladies' toilet and ring Rob.

'I'm bored. Do you have my phone?' I asked.

'No, I don't and I wouldn't give it to you if I did. The auction starts soon,' he told me, patting my hand.

'The action! Are you serious? There's no action here!' I was certain.

'The *auction*,' he said with a sigh.

'The auction,' I confirmed, my interest tweaked.

'Yes,' he said, his voice low and level. He raised my chin with an index finger. His gaze was wide and his smile eager. He bent his head to mine conspiratorially. 'The lady on my right is the representative for International Trade and Investment for the Netherlands.'

'Not your fairy godmother?' I asked, eyeing her dress discreetly.

His shoulders shook in a silent chuckle. Grinning, he plucked a glossy brochure from the centre of the table and handed it to me.

'Take a look, see if there is anything you want to bid for in the auction. Give me a few more minutes and I'm all yours,' he said, planting a kiss just shy of my tiara, before turning to the representative for International Trade and Investment for the Netherlands.

I hid behind the brochure. I may as well show willing.

When I reached page five, I did a double-take. I couldn't believe my eyes. Lot twelve was a Prada Saffiano-print tote bag in baby blue, dove grey and white.

I had to have it. I had to!

My eyes did a circle of the page. No price! Do you have prices at auctions? I didn't know. I'd never been to one. If I got that bag, I would never need to buy another bag ever; that bag would go with everything! Think of the money I'd save in the long run. I gave John a dig in the ribs. He fobbed me off with a backward wave. I gave him a bigger dig. He placed his hand over mine and gave it a warning squeeze. In desperation I turned to the Austrian banker – maybe he would know if auctioned items had prices. His seat was empty! Marvellous! I'd been wanting him to vanish all night but the minute I actually need him he's nowhere to be seen. I pinched John's hand. He turned quickly.

'What is it?'

I waved the brochure. 'Where are the prices?' I asked, one word tripping over the next.

'The auctioneer determines the opening bid. There are no prices,' he said, swivelling back to his lady friend.

No prices! OK, fine! It didn't really matter, did it? I often buy things from Topshop without checking to see how much they cost. I twisted John's watch and checked the time. Ten minutes before the auction began. I would quickly go and have a pee and then scooter back. I didn't want to miss anything – it's for charity after all. I pushed my seat back, scooped up my fish tail and beetled out of the dining room.

The evening had taken a turn for the better.

There was a hush in the room, but for the tinkling of ice cubes in glasses. Bidding started on the bag. I thought I was going to faint with excitement.

I must've been an angel in a past life – the founder of the Red Cross or Florence Nightingale's assistant or someone equally kindly – because once I started bidding for charity, I couldn't stop. This charity would do well. I would see to it personally. My heart raced, my palms sweated and my thigh muscles ached. I was up and down like a yo-yo. I leaped to my feet, my hand shot up, and I shouted 'here, here' just to make sure the auctioneer was in no doubt as to the seriousness of my interest. I was demented with desire at the sight of the Prada Saffiano-print tote displayed on the stage under a spotlight. I had no idea whatsoever what the auctioneer was saying; I had no idea how much the bidding was up to now. All I knew was that I had to have that bag! John clamped my wrist. I slapped him off. It was the third time he'd interrupted me. What was he playing at?

'Here, here!' I yelled, on my feet and flapping my arm madly. I sank into my chair and swivelled to John. 'I'll pay for it myself,' I snapped, 'if that's what you're driving me mad about.'

'That's not the point!' he said.

The auctioneer called.

I leaped to my feet. So did John. He got me in an elbow stronghold and pulled me back.

'Here, here!' I hollered, chin held high.

John fought me into my seat. I craned round his shoulder. My bid was accepted. Thank God.

The auctioneer called again.

I moved to stand.

John locked both wrists behind my back with one large hand and with the other hand he pressured my pineapple hairdo, forcing my face into the crook of his neck. I struggled like a fiend to shake him off. I couldn't stand, raise my arm or shout.

'Evie! Be quiet!'

I had to have that bag! The auctioneer called. I tried for 'here, here' but with my lips pressed to John's collar it came out as a muffled 'nneer, nnneer.'

The auctioneer hit the hammer.

'Sold!'

I felt a whoosh of panic. With a grunt, John released me. I searched his face with frantic eyes. Who got the bag? Who?

'The bag is yours,' John said flatly. 'The bag has been yours all along. You were the only damn person bidding for the bloody thing. No one else in the room wants it. You've been pushing the price up yourself. I've been trying to tell you but you refused to listen. Physical intervention seemed the only option,' he said, shrugging his shoulders to settle the folds of his jacket.

I straightened my tiara, which had wobbled to the side in the struggle. 'But . . . *he* kept putting the price up,' I argued, pointing at the auctioneer.

'That's his job and each time he did you matched the bid, making his job a damn sight easier.'

My face clicked in understanding. 'So I could've got the bag cheaper?'

'You probably could have got the bloody thing for the opening bid,' he said, persuading the cuff of his jacket over his shirt sleeve.

'Do you mean to tell me I've been *mugged off* by a charity?' I asked, affronted. 'So, er, how much was the bag . . . in the end?'

'Two thousand euros,' he said with a sideways glance.

I felt a bit sick. But, I reasoned – sensibly – that since I don't have any credit cards any more I can afford more of an overdraft.

A man with a stoaty head tapped John on the shoulder, gave him a numbered plastic disc and asked for his credit card.

'I'll pay for it myself,' I insisted, burrowing in my clutch bag.

'Don't be ridiculous,' John said, giving his credit card to Stoaty Head.

'Thank you, but I *really* can pay for it.'

'I'm sure you can, but you're not embarrassing me by getting your credit card out when you're with me.' John placed the numbered disc on the table.

'Where's the bag?' I asked.

'I'll have it sent to the hotel.'

'Sent to the hotel? I want it now. I can't wait until we get back to the hotel. It's a Prada Saffiano-print tote bag,' I reminded him, though the idea that he could have forgotten was frankly boggling.

'Why do you need it now?'

'To have, hold and admire,' I told him.

He gave an indulgent sigh and raised an arm. A flunkey waiter appeared. John pressed the numbered disc and some notes into his hand and whispered an instruction.

'Brandy?' he asked.

'Not here.' I curved his neck and drew him to me. 'Let's go somewhere more *lively*,' I suggested discreetly.

He slid me a quizzical glance. 'Shall I ask my fairy godmother for a recommendation?' he joked.

I smiled into his neck. 'Leave it to me. I have somewhere in mind,' I said. 'And thank you for the bag and for every—'

'What did I tell you? One more thank you and it will all go back. I don't make idle threats.'

As we edged out of John's car, he shot me a withering look. I felt a happy flutter as I stared up at the tall, thin, gabled buildings shadowed by the welcoming fluorescent lilac and red glow of Amsterdam's erotic entertainment district.

John's expression was grim.

'Evie, the Red Light District? Why don't we have a drink in the hotel bar?'

I slammed the car door. 'Stop moaning. It's a tourist hot spot.'

It was beautiful and busy and noisy, with gorgeous girls of all nationalities wearing eye-popping underwear, sitting invitingly in shop windows. I tugged a reluctant John by the sleeve along the cobbled canal past a gay bar, a coffee shop and a sex museum.

'Let's take a look in one of the shops,' I suggested.

He replied with a grunt.

I pulled an orange sweatshirt over my evening dress. *Treat Yourself, Take Me Home* was festooned on the front. John squinted at the logo and numbly handed twenty euros to the shop assistant.

'I'm freezing,' I told him.

'You wouldn't be freezing if we'd gone back to the hotel,' he pointed out glumly.

I ignored his tone and tucked my white fur wrap and my evening bag in my Prada tote and proudly slung the tote over my shoulder.

'I love my new bag,' I said to John, stroking it fondly.

'Do you indeed?'

Revellers tumbled from clubs on to the street, music spilled from bars, and men in business suits sidestepped the throng in a hurry to head back to the anonymity of the suburbs. I linked my arm through John's and smiled up at him.

'Prostitution is one of the oldest professions in the world,' I told him as we fell in slow step with the crowd on the cobbled pavement.

'I don't doubt it.'

I flapped my hand at the neon window display of a sex shop. 'Have you not visited this part of the city before?'

'Of course not!' he said forcefully.

'I suppose if you wanted a prostitute, you'd have her sent to your hotel, rather than picking one up yourself. You have everything else sent to your hotel,' I said brightly.

John halted, gripped my wrist, spun me round and delivered a slap on my backside. He gave me a hard look. I rubbed a hand briskly on my bottom.

'You deserved that,' he said, grabbing my arm and looping it in his.

'I was only joking.'

'I didn't think it was funny.'

'Of course you'd choose your own prostitute. You could end up with a right battleaxe otherwise,' I said, diving into a doorway, out of his reach.

We stopped at a bar. I sank gratefully into a chair. The effect of stiletto heels on cobbles was beginning to tell on my feet. John wore a sour expression. His wide gaze scanned the chipped blue walls that were decorated with a collection of car number plates, the wooden floor and rickety jukebox. He took the seat opposite. Two elderly gentlemen wearing cardigans and bow ties were the only other customers. They toasted their glasses to us and smiled in welcome. John, broad and imposing, gave a polite nod in return.

'What can I get you?' the waitress asked, throwing out her pelvis.

She bent over John, showing a fair bit of cleavage and a lot of teeth as she smiled. John coughed into his fist.

'Two beers,' I answered for him, before he showed me up by asking for something ridiculous like hand distilled brandy and a dish of caviar.

She jammed her biro into a heavily lacquered blonde beehive. 'Coming right up, handsome,' she said to John directly, ignoring me.

I palmed peanuts into my mouth and raised my eyes to the sound of a door being slammed and footsteps on a staircase. John inched back, crossed his arms, and gave me a perplexed stare.

'Evie, you're wearing a tiara and a sweatshirt,' he said with a disapproving shake of his head. 'I'm not sure I like it.'

'I'm warm and comfortable.'

'The hotel bar would be warm and comfortable,' he said.

The waitress rattled two beers in front of us. Overhead a toilet flushed and a clanking noise sounded, followed by the whoosh of water rushing through pipes. John's eyes followed the sound. His lips spread into an amused curve. The toilet flushed again.

'What are you sniggering at?' I asked him.

'Nothing. It's just been a while since I've been anywhere like this,' he said, eyeing his bottle of beer dubiously.

'What's wrong with it?' I asked.

'Nothing, nothing at all,' he said, eyes soft and warm. 'Did you enjoy the ball?' he asked.

'Yes, I did . . . sort of . . . but I was happy to leave.'

'Me too!'

'Would you like to go on a candlelit canal cruise?' I asked.

'If we must,' he said.

'I'd like to,' I told him.

'Drink up then,' he said, toasting his beer.

'You're on,' I said, raising the bottle to my lips.

I lifted my chiffon fishtail to better negotiate the wooden steps leading from the quayside into the glass-roofed canal boat. As we walked down the narrow aisle, a Japanese lady wiggled a discreet finger at John. 'James Bond,' she whispered to her friend. I cast John a backward glance. Not a bad simile, I thought, edging into a wooden bench seat and shuffling over to the window. John sat next to me, spread his arm over the back of my seat, crossed one long leg over the other, and stared into the middle distance, oblivious of his admirers.

Flickering streetlights lent a cosy, yellow glow to the narrow barge as it sliced the canal, flanked by the imposing gabled houses of old Amsterdam.

'Why have you never taken a boat trip before? You come here once a month,' I asked John.

'I don't know,' he said in a tone so low I almost missed it.

I put my tote bag on my lap, all the better to admire it.

We gazed up through the glass roof of the barge at a dark blue sky sprinkled with stars.

'Thanks, John.'

He turned to me. 'For what?'

'For everything. For bringing me here and spending time

with me. For buying me so many nice things and for, for everything. I—'

He pressed a finger to my lips. 'You've given me so much more,' he said.

'I've given you nothing.'

He frowned at that and pulled me close. 'You have.'

'What? What have I given you?'

The overhead speakers on the boat spluttered into life.

'Be quiet,' he whispered into my hair. 'The guide is beginning the tour.'

Back on the quayside John breathed deep and shivered. He pulled my fur wrap from my bag and tugged it over my sweatshirt.

'Now, clever clogs, as you sent the driver away, we'll have to walk back to the hotel,' he said, placing a piloting hand on my back.

'I don't mind walking,' I told him truthfully. 'Did you enjoy the cruise?' I asked, looking up at him.

'I did actually,' he admitted, guiding me artfully around a chap swaying from one side of the pavement to the other, obviously a schooner of sweet sherry the worse for wear.

'You know, John, you work too hard. Last year in Nice you divided your time between the Acropolis Convention Centre and the hotel. Apart from that you didn't so much as taste fresh air. In Marrakech you missed the souk because of a meeting. You never sightsee or take advantage of any of the fabulous places you visit. Why?'

He shrugged. 'I have businesses to run. Many issues can only be addressed by me,' he said, his voice firm.

'Is that so?'

'Yes, it is.'

'So you can't be done without?'

'No, I can't.'

'Graveyards are full of indispensible men, did you know that?' I said with a casual lilt. 'You have more money than you'll ever be able to spend. Why do you need to push yourself to make more? Are you determined to be the richest corpse in the mortuary?' I asked.

He froze, breaking our step. Halted by his arm draped lazily round my shoulder, I lost my footing and stumbled back. He gripped my elbows and spun me to face him.

'What did you say?' he asked.

'I said graveyards are full of indispensible men and that . . .' I began but trailed to silence when I caught his haunted expression.

He stood very still.

Dark eyes held mine but his gaze seemed inward. He was thinking, not seeing me. He stood as though awake but in the throes of a dream. The blinking fluorescent light from the window of a brothel lent a lavender glow to his looming silhouette. I rubbed my forearm over my brow to smooth back some hair that had escaped from my tiara.

'Are you all right?' I asked.

His focus changed. The ghost of a smile creased his face. 'You're right, Evie. You're so right,' he said. 'Graveyards *are* full of indispensible men, I'm going to bear that in mind.' He nodded towards the darkened canal ahead and linked my arm through his. 'Let's get you back to the hotel and dressed in something warmer than a paper thin evening gown and a cheap sweatshirt.'

We walked back in silence.

Back in the suite, John placed my phone on the coffee table. I unpinned my hair, and pulled the sweatshirt over my head.

'Go to your room and call Rob,' John said his voice taut. 'We leave for London at lunchtime tomorrow.'

'Tomorrow? But I thought, well, I don't know what I thought . . . I didn't think we were going back so soon.'

He jammed his hands in his pockets, and rocked on his heels.

I felt a rush of nerves. I'd been on the verge of making this call for two days, rewinding and rehearsing the conversation in my head over and over, and now it was time to make it, I couldn't think of a thing to say.

I felt John's watchful stare.

'I don't know what to say to him,' I admitted, eyeing my phone as if it were radioactive.

He gave me a lazy smile.

'Let him lead the conversation, he's the one with all the explaining to do,' John said, his tone low and even.

'But, it's past midnight,' I argued.

'I doubt the lad has had much in the way of sleep; I expect he'll be ready and waiting to hear from you no matter what time you call,' he said sagely. 'What are you frightened of?' he asked.

I bristled.

'Frightened? I'm not frightened! I'll call him.'

There was a hum of quiet. John raised his chin and loosened his bow tie.

'Well then, go on, get on with it,' he said.

'Right, I will,' I told him with a nod of bravado.

'And Evie, compose yourself, and don't tell him how upset you've been.'

My eyes widened.

'What do you take me for? I am composed.'

I lurched towards the table, grabbed the phone, and swished from the room in a cloud of black chiffon. Compose myself indeed.

I sat on the edge of the bed, waiting for the roaring sound of blood rushing in my ears to tone down, no point ringing Rob if I couldn't hear him. I felt sick, and found I was holding my breath. My heart froze. I squeezed my eyes shut. My mind must be playing tricks because I thought I could smell Rob – actually smell his Dolce and Gabbana aftershave – and feel his arms closing tight around me. I could see his clear blue eyes smiling at me, picture his strong chiselled jaw. A warm flame spread across my chest at the thought of him. Maybe, just maybe, there was a way to work around this mess. But then a vision of the cosy house in Birmingham popped into my head, causing a geyser of fury to extinguish all my hopes. I swallowed hard and called his number.

It rang once. Nerves were gathering in my tummy.

'Babe! Where are you? I've left you so many voicemails, and I must've texted you twenty times and . . .' he blurted.

I cut him short.

' . . . I'm in Amsterdam, I've listened to some of your voicemails but not all of them, and I haven't bothered with your texts.'

'Amsterdam? What are you doing there?'

'Didn't anyone tell you?'

'Like who? Who would tell me?'

He had a point, my friends and family are masters at hating at a distance.

'I'm with John,' I told him.

I was doing a great job. I sounded almost brash, like I hadn't a care in the world. I tossed a wing of hair over my shoulder; this was easier than I thought it would be.

'Oh! Right!' He said, surprised.

'Rob . . .'

' . . . Evie, come home babe, let me explain. I know I should have told you, but there never seemed to be the right moment. I was a coward; once I got you back I'd have done anything to keep you, anything! My plan was to buy a house; set up a home together, to show you how happy we could be, and then . . . then I would explain,' he said, words tumbling out one after the other.

'Didn't you think I'd rather have known you had a wife and child *before* we set up a home together?' I asked acidly.

The nerve of him!

He caught my tone.

'Yes, I know, I'm sorry, but, as time passed it got harder to tell you. Evie, we can get through this, we can. I'm heart sick, I need you. I think of you every minute of the day.'

'But I'm not the only one you have to think about, am I? What about Cassie?'

'Cassie will meet someone else, there's nothing to worry about on that front,' he replied, in a toneless ultra-logical voice. 'She's a good-looking girl,' he said.

'And Marcus?' I asked, my voice raising an octave.

'He's a great kid, you'll love him,' he said proudly. 'You two will get on brilliantly.'

My heart squeezed tightly with a feeling I wasn't familiar with. It wasn't resentment or jealousy exactly – I would not expect any man to be anything less than proud of his son. I just wasn't sure I really wanted to 'get on brilliantly' with Marcus.

I pressed the phone to my ear.

'Rob, you're married; you have a wife and son. My first child will not be your first child. My wedding day will be your second shot at it. You're also a liar . . . ' I said sharply.

' . . . I've never lied to you.'

I felt a stab of fury.

'That's a lie for a start. You told me your parents lived in Spain.'

'OK, but I panicked; I wasn't ready for family days out to Birmingham, and . . .'

' . . . You told me you were making sales calls up north.'

'I did make sales calls; I swear to you, every trip I made was multi-purpose.'

'You said we should be *honest* with each other. You don't think hiding something as monumental as a secret family constitutes lying, by default?'

'Evie, I know, I know, you're right, and I'm sorry, so sorry, but babe, now it's all out in the open we can deal with it. In a strange way I feel . . . relieved. I've carried the weight of the guilt for so long, but Evie, I've looked after you, haven't I? I've been all that a man could be. This has been eating me up . . .'

' . . . and so it should've,' I said, my voice trembling.

Rob masters the art of self-absolution to perfection. He's never completely in the wrong; he justifies his vices by highlighting his virtues. Despite knowing this, I was buckling.

'Evie, don't cry . . . we'll be fine, I want you home, we need to talk this through face to face. When will you be back?' he asked. 'Shall I come for you? I'll catch the first flight.'

'No!' I snapped.

I rubbed a knuckle nervously across my lips.

'OK, babe fine, it was only a suggestion, don't get upset . . . so, when are you back?'

Sod him.

'Friday,' I heard myself say; despite it being Tuesday tomorrow.

'I'm sleeping at the garage in Feltham.'

He's sleeping in a garage. I almost felt a jolt of pity.

'I'll come to see you on Friday night.'

'That's too soon, I need more time.' I said. Bloody hell. Friday. I couldn't, I just couldn't.

'I'll be there Friday. I need to see you; I can't work, eat or sleep. We've got to sort this out, and we will.'

'Rob, I don't think this is going to work, I think . . .'

' . . . Friday.' he repeated. 'Please Evie, meet me. I love you. This has been a shock, but once that's passed, you'll realise we can live with this. People do.'

'Did you sleep with Cassie last year when we split up?' I shot back.

Where had that come from? I hadn't thought of it until now.

'NO! No Evie! I didn't . . . We can't discuss this on the phone. I'll see you on Friday,' he said, and hung up.

I stared at the silent phone in my hand. Shouldn't I have been the one to ring off? But then, Rob always finishes a conversation quickly if he thinks it's not heading in his favour.

I exhaled noisily; I was exhausted. Never had I run the gamut of emotions in such a short time. Was I any better off for having spoken to him? I didn't think so. I stared numbly at my hands clenched in my lap. My heart was banging like a bongo drum. He thinks everything will be fine, that we'll push forward as we were before, that this situation is a mere cloud on the horizon of eternal happiness. *A great kid!* I'm sure Marcus is a great kid, but I felt cheated, I wanted Rob's children to be *my* children, when the time came. And OK, perhaps I hadn't been initially overly enthused in Barbados when Rob mentioned the house, baby and dog. But I certainly preferred to be the central focus in that image, as opposed to sharing the stage with a whole cast of characters as I found myself doing at the moment. I hadn't shouted or sworn at him, which was odd, because that's what I thought I'd do. Equally strange was the fact that I wasn't crying now. I was sitting on the edge of the bed, staring at my hands, thinking how my tiara was beginning to itch.

There was a knock on the door.

'Come in,' I said, tossing the tiara on the bedside cabinet.

'Did you call him?' John asked, walking slowly into the room.

'I did,' I replied with a martyred air.

He sat down, dwarfing the small velvet barrel armchair chair next to the bed. His bow tie hung loose and the buttons of his waistcoat were open. He leaned forward, elbows on knees, fingers locked.

'And?' he asked, iron-grey eyes searching mine.

'He said, we can work it out, that in a way he feels a sense of relief now it's all out in the open . . . and that . . . he loves me.'

'Indeed?'

Johns granite jawline tensed. He was making a masterful effort not to voice his opinion, so I put him out of his misery and asked him for it.

'What do you think?'

'I think you should finish it! No more chances!' He said sharply. 'I don't accept that there has not been a window of opportunity since last July for him to tell you he had fathered a son, and that he had a wife.'

He placed his hands gently on my elbows; I let him lift me to my feet.

'A nightcap and then bed,' he said.

VENICE

Chapter Thirteen

Since I arrived in Amsterdam with nothing more than a hand-bag, and was leaving with a whole new wardrobe, John called De Bijenkorf – a department store in the city centre – and had them deliver a Louis Vuitton suitcase to the hotel (casually mentioning it was mine to keep). He then left for a meeting and said I should be packed and ready when he returned. So now I was packing – OK, not me personally. *Housekeeping* was packing and I was standing idly watching two maids lasagne my clothes in layer after layer of tissue paper. There was a mile of it at least. I wasn't looking forward to squashing all the paper into the wheelie bin when I got home.

I texted Lulu and told her I was flying home and asked her to keep it quiet; I wasn't ready for Lexy's melodrama, or Nikki's pitying stares.

My initial cool acceptance of Rob's take on the whole situation had swiftly been erased by a fit of hysteria the minute John had said *you should finish it* and handed me a gin and tonic.

This morning I had felt a jolt of terror at the thought of going home to the flat, having to open my wardrobes and find a gap where Rob's clothes should be – because if I know Lulu, there won't be so much of a hair from his head left to show he was ever there.

I stood facing the mirror, teasing my hair into a ponytail.

A door slammed, heralding John's arrival.

'Evie, are you ready?' he shouted, marching through the lounge and bursting into my room.

'Almost,' I told him.

'Good, let's have brunch downstairs, before the drive to the airport . . . You look lovely,' he said, admiring my new indigo minidress and matching coat.

I hadn't been sure about the outfit when I bought it. But looking at it now – accessorised with pretty heels, lilac eye-shadow and a purple dress ring that I bought in the hotel gift shop to replace my engagement ring – I loved it.

'Come on,' he said, ushering me out the door.

We'd been airborne for about fifteen minutes. I surreptitiously slid an admiring glance around the cabin, soaking up the opulence and wealth that John takes for granted. It occurred to me that since boarding I hadn't seen any members of the crew. No Sadie, no barman, no sizzling percolator. I placed my *OK!* magazine on the coffee table, shrugged off my coat, kicked off my heels, and looked at John. Head bent, he leafed studiously through an official-looking manila folder.

'Where is everyone?' I asked.

'I asked for us to be left alone,' he said, gathering his paperwork into a tight bundle.

'Why?'

'Because I want to talk to you.'

He searched my face.

'What about?' I asked.

He slapped the folder on to the coffee table.

'What are you going to do about this boy?' he asked, leaning forward.

I swallowed hard, looking everywhere except at him.

He levered my chin.

'I don't know?' I said, 'I need time to . . . to think.'

He fired a scathing look.

'You've had time, plenty of time.'

'I know what you think I should do, but it's not easy to just stop loving someone,' I said, my voice rising in justification, 'just like that,' I said, snapping my fingers to illustrate my point.

He gave a withering sigh, and relaxed back into the sofa.

'Come and sit beside me,' he said, patting the cushion.

I shuffled from the armchair at the head of the coffee table to sit on the sofa next to him.

'Rob made me feel . . . beautiful,' I told him. 'Always.'

John put his arm round my shoulder.

'You *are* beautiful.'

I folded into him.

'I miss him. One minute I'm furious, the next I'm forgiving.'

'You miss what you thought you had, but the goalpost has moved now. If you take him back, you'll have a ready-made family. And, albeit indirectly, you'll take on the maintenance of a wife.'

'You maintain four ex-wives,' I pointed out.

'I don't have children. Therefore no reason to sustain contact. A child makes a big difference. And we are talking about Rob here, not me. Rob does not have an *ex-wife*. If I remember correctly his wife doesn't want a divorce. Are you going to force that upon her? That won't be a pleasant business at all, not in the least.'

'You're right, I know.'

He pulled me close.

'Whether you take my advice or not, I'll support your decision.'

I raised my gaze to his.

'And what about you, will you take my advice? To relax more and work less.'

'I will,' he said, eyes crinkling into a smile. 'I'm glad you came to me, we're a tonic for each other.'

'I'm glad too.'

There was a comfortable silence. I *was* glad I'd called him. Really glad.

'Just don't ever put me in the company of the boy and expect me to keep a civil tongue in my head. Because I have a thing or two to say to him that won't keep,' John said sharply.

Twenty minutes later, we landed in London.

John insisted on escorting me home in his car. Immediately, I texted Lulu to tell her to make sure the lounge was clear of all vestiges of leg-waxing, all bras, knickers, plates of congealed curry – and that if she had a man in the house, for god's sake to make sure he was dressed. She texted me back to say she was knackered but working through the list. I was outwardly composed, staring at the passing London traffic. Inwardly I was panic stricken. *John in our flat!* He may just drop me at the door and whizz off, I could be fretting over nothing, but for form's sake I suppose I should ask him if he wants to come in for coffee. And there's always the chance he could accept.

The large black limo whispered to a halt.

I clambered from the car and slung my new Prada over my shoulder. It felt weird being home, and that hollow dread I'd felt in Amsterdam opened up inside me. The hubbub of the Broadway was at its afternoon peak. School kids poured noisily on to the pavement from a convoy of double-decker buses lined at the bus stop outside our flat, and shoppers fought for elbow space on the pavement. A woman at the front of the bus queue lit a cigarette and eyed John appraisingly as he angled out of the car, before sliding her eyes across to the limo's uniformed driver who stood like a statue holding my suitcase.

'Do you want to come in for a coffee?' I asked John.

He gave the overflowing wheelie bin a dubious glance, and patted my arm absently.

'No I must push on.'

I nearly swooned with relief. He took my bag from his driver, and placed a guiding hand on my back.

'I'll see you safely inside, though.'

I could've done without that, but John pushed ahead, opened the squeaky garden gate and then stepped aside to let me pass.

'I know it's stupid, but I feel scared to be home,' I told John.

He squeezed my shoulder reassuringly.

'You'll be fine.'

'My flatmate Lulu's a good listener, and tonight it's just the two of us, so I can work at preparing to face everyone else,' I told him with a noble sniff. 'We'll have a few drinks and an early night.'

I pressed my key in the lock.

'Sounds perfect,' he said.

The door flew open, taking my arm with it. Lulu's brown eyes were darting and moist; she gazed at me warily, and then threw her arms around me.

'The bastard,' she said, stroking my hair.

We hugged fiercely.

'I couldn't agree more,' John piped up.

I'd missed her, she has always been my rock, and I'm hers.

I was so glad to see her. Behind her the hallway shifted as tears clouded my vision. I untangled her arms from my neck and brushed an escaped tear from my cheek. Lulu peered round my shoulder; her heart-shaped face broke into a smile.

'You must be Evie's . . . *friend*,' Lulu said with emphasis and hesitation. Come in, come in, this is a surprise, I wasn't expecting Evie to bring anyone with her,' she lied. 'The place is a mess,' she told him, with a phoney laugh.

She grabbed my limp wrist and led me in through the door. John followed dutifully.

'Evie, I've missed you like mad, we all have, I feel as though I haven't seen you for ages,' she said. Turning, she slammed the door with a kick. 'Still you're home now and that's the main thing, because we . . . '

She froze, her eyes widened and her lips parted. The cheery smile slid from her face. She gave a startled gasp, and smoothed a palm down my arm. Her eyes were like big Frisbees.

'Is that . . . a lovely new coat?' she asked reverentially.

I blinked a *yes*.

She slipped her hand inside my coat and ran her hand from bust to hip.

'With, with . . . a dress to match?'

I glanced at my watch pointedly, four o'clock. *Rob would've been coming home from work in two hours' time*. I swallowed back tears.

I went to move, Lulu blocked my path.

'Are those new shoes?' she challenged, her voice rising.

John stood beside me, she caught his polite gaze.

'I'm only asking because we both take a size four,' she explained to him. 'We share shoes.'

If everything had been as normal, I'd have been cuddling up to Rob in two short hours.

190

Lulu lifted my sapphire pendant.

'Evie, *is this real*?' she punctuated, slack-jawed.

'Yes,' I said sidestepping, and overtaking her. Bloody hell, did she expect me to spend all day in the hallway?

There was a vicious tug on the strap of my handbag which caught the collar of my dress, choking me. I staggered in a circle. John lurched for my elbow to steady me.

'Evie! Is this a Prada Saffiano-print tote bag,' she asked with a hysterical edge to her voice, 'because it looks like one to me!'

'Yes it is.'

She clasped her hands to her heart.

I edged past her.

'What joy!' she exclaimed, addressing the ceiling. 'What joy!' she repeated, and gave a round of applause. '*We* have a Prada Saffiano tote.'

I pushed the door of the flat open and walked into the lounge.

My jaw dropped.

Lexy and Tina, their faces creased in misery, stood beside the fireplace. Nikki, head hung low and beefy arms folded, relaxed against the dining table. Alice and Duncan, grimly side by side, sat on the sofa. Everyone lurched towards me.

Lulu sided past me and staved them off, showing the flat of her hand, in a crowd control way.

'Everyone, this is John Jackson, Evie's friend,' Lulu announced brightly, sweeping an arm in John's direction.

Everyone froze.

John filled the doorway, commanding and dashing in a navy suit, white shirt and mauve tie. He took a step forward and placed my suitcase beside the sofa.

'Evie and John have been having a *marvellous time* in Amsterdam. Haven't you, Evie?' Lulu said in a rushed shrill voice. 'They've just flown home in *John's plane*,' she felt compelled to tell everyone.

I groaned. Lexy, lips curved in welcome, stepped forward and took John's hand. He kissed her cheek lightly. She beamed. And then like a light going out, she fixed me an austere solemn look, and pressed her palm on my jaw.

'Be strong,' Lexy said.

'I'm Alice,' Alice told John, offering her cheek for a kiss.

She took a step back, tweaking the skirt of her Miss Moneypenny straight black dress, and gave me a brittle smile.

'Hello love,' she mouthed, tucking her short black shiny bob behind her ears nervously.

Duncan, a red-haired mountain of a man, gave John a curt, white-knuckled handshake.

'Delighted,' Duncan said in his deep gravelly Highland brogue.

'Lass,' he said, giving me a kiss without eye contact.

A purposeful stride forward from each, and Nikki and John clasped hands.

'We spoke,' Nikki said to John, before resuming his stance by the dining table.

Tina stood like a sculpture; she raised her hand stiffly and gave John a tight wave, her face frozen in terror. You'd have thought I'd brought Lucifer himself home. She gave me a sad smile and chewed her bottom lip.

I scanned the room; the lounge was clean and tidy. Lulu gave me a knowing wink.

'What can I get you to drink?' Lulu asked John.

'Nothing, thank you,' John said politely, coughing into his fist. 'I really must go; I just wanted to see Evie safely home.'

Six dour faces stared at me earnestly.

I stood twisting my fingers into knots.

'I'll see you out,' I said to John.

At the front door, John placed his hands on my shoulders and held me at arm's length.

I sighed. 'I can't believe Lulu has a house full. Have you seen the faces on them, you'd think I had died.'

He smiled thoughtfully. 'Maybe it's not such a bad thing; it gets facing them out of the way.'

There was an easy silence.

'Thank you again,' I said.

He shook his head dismissively, took out a handkerchief and dabbed below my eyes.

'I'll call you in a couple of days. In the meantime if you need anything, you have my number.'

I jerked my chin towards the lounge window. 'I suppose I'd better go and face my mourners.'

He nodded. 'Off you go then,' he said, turning me towards the hallway.

When I went back into the lounge, my suitcase lay open, the contents strewn. There was a sea of fabric all over the place with a frothy wave of tissue paper lapping against the fireplace.

Alice was holding my black chiffon evening dress against her body.

'Duncan, what d'you think?' she asked. 'Maybe I need to let it out at the side seams!'

Duncan snorted in reply.

Lexy was in the armchair with my Prada bag cradled in her arms, stroking it lovingly, like Goldfinger with his fluffy white pussy cat. An adoring smile was painted on her face.

Lulu's eyes jumped with excitement; she pulled a pair of Versace jeans on under her skirt.

'You're a dark horse!' Lulu said tossing me a grin. 'Here we all were, worrying about you, when all the while you'd landed on your feet.'

Tina's smile was radiant; she stuffed her arm inside the sleeve my new white coat.

'What am I thinking?' Tina asked no one in particular. 'I can't borrow this; I can't wear white to a wedding.' She gave me a hard look. 'Let me try on the lilac coat. I'll borrow that instead. That coat you're wearing is the same, isn't it?' Tina asked, tugging my sleeves down my arms. 'My cousin is getting married in three weeks time and I have nothing to wear.'

Lulu pulled her jumper over her head; her 34D-cups confined in black lace, jiggled on release. Duncan and Nikki tactfully averted their eyes and gazed at their feet. Breathing hard, hair messy and tousled, she sank to her knees. 'I saw a red dress here somewhere,' she said, brows creased in deliberation. She frisbeed a couple of items out of her way. 'Ah! Here it is.'

Alice on all fours crawled over to Lulu; she pushed a hand through her hair. Eyes flashing, she shot Tina an appraising glance.

'Lilac suits you,' Alice complimented. 'How about you mix and match the white dress with the lilac coat?' Alice suggested, lassoing the white dress in Tina's face. 'That would be a nice ensemble for a wedding.'

'Gosh yes,' Tina said, giving Alice a grateful laser-stare.

'Wow!' Lulu boomed. 'A pair of Louboutins.'

Lexy clapped her hands in delight.

'I don't know what you're so pleased about,' Lulu said to Lexy, frowning. 'You're an enormous size six, it's a ship builder you need, not Louboutin, these are a four.'

'Shut your mouth, it's the matching bag I've got my eye on,' Lexy snapped.

'I'm a four!' Alice announced, clapping.

Lulu eyed me animatedly.

'I'm so proud of you,' she said, pulling the red dress over her head. 'Amazing . . . bagging a millionaire.'

'I didn't *bag* anyone,' I told her, my voice sharp with underlying principle.

She tucked a red clutch bag under her arm, to match her dress.

'You mean . . . you didn't shag him?' she punctuated, eyes like dinner plates.

Duncan interrupted.

'Dinny confirm that, if the answer is yes. That man is my age, if he's a day. I dinny want to know. Yer but a baby.'

There was an electric silence.

'No!' I said. 'I didn't.'

'*She didn't shag him,*' Lulu mouthed from her crouched position, and looked to see if anyone was as incredulous as her. They all were.

Alice stood and moved to the sofa. Lexy and Tina dropped their booty, and sank into the cushions beside Alice. No one spoke.

Lulu gestured at the explosion of clothes over the floor.

'Let's get this straight! You are telling me . . . that man bought you all of this, and you . . . *didn't even shag him*?'

Alice, Tina and Lexy gazed at me, lips parted, expectant.

'I'd have shagged him just for the Prada bag,' Lulu said, disbelieving. 'Are you mad?'

Alice opened her mouth to speak.

'Alice I'd think verra carefully if I were you, before ye offer any advice on the matter,' Duncan warned.

Alice pressed her lips together.

Duncan slid me a sympathetic glance.

'Lass, any man would give you the world if he had it, unconditionally.'

I caught Nikki's eye. He stood by the dining table, silent and studious. My lip trembled. He held his arms wide, *come here*, he mouthed. I picked my way over the clothes on the floor. Lurched towards him, circled his waist, pressed my cheek to his chest and burst into tears.

There was a scramble of activity behind me. My peripheral eye saw Alice hastily folding clothes and putting them back in the suitcase, while gesturing wildly to Tina to gather the tissue paper and stuff it behind the sofa. Lexy and Lulu silently bickered and blamed each other for upsetting me. Duncan signalled by means of vigorous jerky-head movements to Alice to take my new shoes off.

'Let's go for an early dinner,' Nikki whispered into my hair.

I felt his throat move against my forehead as he spoke.

'I'll close the bar; it'll just be the seven of us.'

'I don't feel like going for dinner,' I told him, with a lofty sniff.

'I'm offering to close the bar for the evening; I'd like just a bit of appreciation,' he said, rubbing my back. 'I wouldn't do that for king or country. But I'd do it for you.'

Despite myself, I smiled into his neck.

'Is that a smile I can feel?' he said, palming my hair.

I straightened and rallied a calm tone.

'I do appreciate it, and yes, let's do that,' I said with a noble gulp.

Nikki, bless him, set a table in the middle of the restaurant, hung a PRIVATE PARTY sign on the door and sent Pepi and Costas home. We served ourselves from trays of moussaka and salad that Spiros had prepared for us. A rosy glow from the red shaded wall-lamps threw a subdued light on the animated faces around the table, and soft Greek music drifted from the over-head speakers, creating a warm, intimate mood. I thought of Rob and zoned out. I *could not* believe he was married. Several times, a string of unanswerable questions winged through my mind; but I didn't want to spoil the evening and so I made a Herculean effort to focus on the here and now.

By the time I tuned back in, Lulu, Lexy, Tina and Alice were distinctly *merry*. No surprises there! Duncan and Nikki were discussing the forthcoming summer World Cup over a bottle of cognac; but whereas Nikki had barely even sipped his — excellent though I'm sure it was — Duncan had stuck his nose into his brandy goblet and inhaled deeply before, in one fluid motion, he tossed back his thick red mane, downed his drink in one and signalled Nikki for a refill.

Alice leaned towards me with a jingle-jangle of bracelets.

'Love, you're miles away,' she said, propping her elbows on the table.

'I'm sorry.'

'Don't be,' Lulu chimed in.

'You'll get through this,' Tina said gravely.

'Of course you will,' Lexy added, sporting my new indigo coat.

I gave them a wintry smile.

'So tell me, how old is John Jackson?' Alice asked with forced nonchalance.

'Fifty-nine or sixty, I think,' I told her.

'I thought he was about fifty-four at most,' Alice said with an astonished lilt. 'He is striking,' she added, eyes shining.

'Fifty-something . . . So he's not too old for you,' Lulu reasoned. 'Because if he looks fifty-four and you're twenty-seven next month, that's only a twenty-seven-year gap. And when you're hungover you look at least forty. And if he wore a wig, he could easily pass for fifty. And so really there's nothing in it . . . ten years tops,' she calculated, draining her glass. 'In fact if you stopped using moisturiser, and took out your hair extensions you could be twins!' she reasoned.

Tina, with a glassy stare, nodded in agreement. She pulled her long platinum hair into a ponytail. 'Age doesn't matter. Look at Hugh Hefner,' she said, toasting her glass high in the air.

'I for one wouldn't mind a brother-in-law with his own jet. Frankly I don't care if he's eighty-four,' Lexy announced. 'If you love him, you love him. And that's all that matters. Nothing in life should obstruct the course of true love,' she said wisely. 'And let me just add, I agree with Alice, he's very . . . *charismatic.*'

Love him? Just hold on a minute, I thought, and held up my hand.

'Did you say "love him"? Are you mad? I've just found out my fiancé has a wife, and you already have me happily-ever-after in love with another man.'

Lexy squared her shoulders.

'OK, maybe that was a bit presumptive, but what I mean is – he gets my vote.'

'And mine,' chimed Lulu.

'And mine,' Alice added.

'And mine,' Tina agreed, 'although he still scares the hell out of me.'

'Well he's no gettin' my vote,' Duncan said, thumping his glass on the table in forceful endorsement. 'Ye need a lad yer own age,' he added, tipping a tot or two – make that three – of brandy into his glass.

Alice gave Duncan a cynical glance.

'There's no need to get *personal*, Duncan. If I didn't know better I'd think you were jealous of Evie's millionaire,' Alice said.

'Me?' Duncan boomed, affronted. 'Jealous?'

'You're very handsome,' Lulu told Duncan. 'No need to be jealous of John.'

'Yes, you are handsome,' Lexy agreed. 'You are quite macho. You look like you should be riding a horse and swinging a sword and fighting alongside Mel Gibson in *Braveheart*.'

Alice giggled into her glass.

'Actually, he does have a sword,' Alice confessed with a prim smile. 'We play this game, he has this outfit ... '

' ... QUIET, ALICE!' Duncan warned, his face scarlet.

Lulu's glass stopped mid-air; she wiggled a questioning finger in my face.

'If you don't fancy him, and there's nothing going on between you, why did you call him when you were on your way to Birmingham? And why would he spoil you so much?'

I sloshed wine into my glass, and cast my eyes round the table. The music had stopped; there was an expectant hush, the only sound being the rhythmic patter of large pre-storm raindrops on the window.

'I don't know why I called John, I just did,' I said, with a shrug. 'We're friends, I like him, but in a strange, different kind of way – I can talk to him, tell him anything.'

Nikki cradled his brandy glass in his cupped hands, mulling over what I'd just said. He lifted his gaze to mine; his eyes were as dark as coal in the reduced light. He placed his palm gently on my wrist.

'It's not John I want to hear about,' he said. 'It's the other one. What are you going to do about *him*?'

Suddenly the room was too hot. My heart began to race.

Lulu gave a snort of laughter. 'She's going to tell him to

bugger off, of course,' she said with certainty. 'Aren't you Evie?'

Nikki ignored Lulu, and with a gesture of his glass encouraged me to speak.

'I have to think,' I said.

'What is there to think about!?' Lulu exploded. 'You could be a granny before you're forty, have you thought of that? Huh? Have you? And what if you need something like, I don't know . . . something really important like, like . . . an Ascot outfit. Who is priority numero uno financially? Eh! You or the wife?' she spat.

I flinched at the word *wife*. My voice froze up. Duncan gave Lulu a silencing tap on the arm.

My eyes fell on Nik. The creases round his eyes deepened in thought. He lifted his brandy, drained it, placed his glass on the table, and then poured another. He shook his head with measured impatience and exhaled. I felt a spasm of nerves. Nik can be blunt; I wasn't in the mood for his opinionated directness. The second brandy must've had some curative effect because Nikki turned to Lulu with a tight smile and told her to open a couple of bottles of Champagne. Lulu shot from her seat, and Tina and Lexy raced to help. Duncan stepped outside for a cigar and Alice went to the Ladies. Nik and I were alone.

A shadow fell across his face, the irises of his eyes, caught by the light, paled from chocolate to amber. He inched closer and worked his knuckles the length of my spine; on impulse I leaned into his touch.

He levered my chin towards him with an index finger.

'Can't you forget him?' he said, less a question, more a request.

I tore my gaze away from his. Lightning streaked from a cloud outside. The shop signs and streetlights glimmered in the

200

nighttime pavement like the moon on a lake. We sat and listened to the thunder rumble and rain splashing against the window.

'I'm trying,' I told him.

'Try harder,' he said.

Chapter Fourteen

Tina went home to north London on the tube and Lexy jumped in a cab back to Hampton. Duncan and Alice had driven from Epping, and they had both been drinking, so they stayed the night, which I could've done without. I had to surrender my bed and I'd been looking forward to a private cry.

Lulu and I sat cross-legged on her bed, sipping the champagne that Nikki had given us to take home. Alice was sitting at the dressing table, rifling through Lulu's make-up bag. Duncan had gone to bed.

My phone buzzed, it was a text from Lulu. I frowned at her, bewildered as to why she was texting me when she was right beside me. She pressed a finger to her lips gesturing discretion. I read the text.

Can we trust Alice with u know what?

I looked at Alice.
Yes, I mouthed to Lulu, behind my hand.
Are you sure? Lulu mimed, with a shifting glance.
I nodded and buried my nose in my champagne. Lulu

whipped a curtain of blonde hair off her face and chewed her bottom lip indecisively. She quickly tapped out another text.

My phone buzzed.

I jumped.

This is so secret u sure she's safe?

Alice was smiling at the mirror vacantly.

'Yes!' I hissed, rattled.

'What did you say, love?' Alice asked, turning to my voice.

'Nothing, Alice. Nothing.'

I gave Lulu an encouraging smile. Simultaneously Lulu and I scrambled from the bed and with practised ease pulled the bed away from the wall. Lulu crawled over the quilt and, bending over, disappeared behind the headboard. She lifted the edge of the carpet away from the floor and reappeared with a packet of Marlborough Lights. She held the little box reverentially.

I opened the window, whizzed the curtains shut, and stood against the window ledge guardedly. I sipped my champagne, eyes calculating between Lulu's guilty smile and Alice's dropped jaw.

Alice clutched her chest and gasped.

'You still *smoke*?' Alice asked Lulu.

Lulu jammed a cigarette in her mouth and flicked her lighter and settled on the bed, her back to the wall, ankles crossed.

'No. Not really,' Lulu said, taking a deep drag on her fag.

'But! But you have a cigarette between your lips ... and you're smoking it!' Alice pointed out. The woman's a genius. You can't fault her logic.

Lulu took a second drag. Her eyelids drooped, smoke billowed from her mouth, and a beatific smile spread across her face.

Alice leaned forward and wormed a cigarette from Lulu's packet.

'You're the nation's non-smoking darling! You have a radio show! You won . . . *the Challenge!* Your face is on billboards! You have a music jingle!' Alice reasoned in a rush.

Lulu inhaled sharply on her cigarette. Her head swayed, and then lolled backwards, hitting the wall. She blinked at the ceiling. Five lazy smoke rings travelled heavenwards.

She dropped her chin on her chest.

'I . . . am an inspiration!' Lulu said with a sigh. 'I need . . . an occasional break from the pressures of . . . *inspiring* people.'

Alice fumbled to light her cigarette.

'Yes, yes I can understand that,' Alice said, over-brightly.

'I didn't know you smoked,' I said to Alice.

'I . . . I don't . . . not normally, but seeing Lulu smoking and enjoying it so much, I thought I'd give it a go.'

'I see,' I said, a smile fixed to my face. Alice had obviously had a lot more to drink than I thought.

'So how long *did* you stop smoking for?' Alice asked, staring at her now lit cigarette reverentially.

She doesn't know what to do with it, I thought.

'Two hundred and three hours,' Lulu boasted proudly, her eyes rolling in my direction for confirmation.

I gave an energetic nod.

'Yes it must've easily been that long,' I said, 'perhaps . . . even longer.'

I rubbed my arms as a light breeze, fresh after the thunderstorm, lifted the curtain.

Lulu shifted; her silk dressing gown fell open, displaying her trademark orangey leg. She took a sip of champagne and held her ciggie aloft.

Alice took an apprehensive puff.

'This is great. I feel like a black and white movie star,' Alice said with a cheeky grin. 'Do I look like something from the silver screen? Champagne, cigarettes and dressing gowns,' she asked.

What was she talking about?

Lulu tilted her head and smiled in reply.

Alice's eyes were alive with interest.

'Do you feel . . . *guilty*?' Alice asked.

'What about?' Lulu said.

'Lying to, well, lying to the whole of London really?'

'No!' Lulu said with a dismissive wave. 'There's a spectrum of acceptance as far as lies are concerned. At one end of the spectrum we have untruths,' Lulu explained, endorsing this statement with a jab of her cigarette. 'For instance, if Evie was going out, and in a hurry, and wearing her black jeans, and asked me if she looked fat in them, I would say, "Don't be silly, of course not," because I would know that, a) she wouldn't have time to change, and b) she really wanted to wear her black jeans. And so I would lie, to avoid upsetting her. Or, if my mum were to ask me if I had paid my car insurance and I hadn't, I would say, "yes of course I've paid my car insurance," because she would worry otherwise. These lies are acceptable. They are *not really* lies, because you don't benefit personally from telling them, you tell them for the benefit of others, out of the kindness of your heart. So they don't count.'

'Yes, yes, I can see that,' Alice agreed with a nod of understanding. Encouraged Lulu pushed on.

'I have helped thousands of people to give up smoking. They will *not* benefit by the knowledge that I haven't actually given up smoking myself. Will they?' she asked Alice.

'No, no, of course they won't,' Alice agreed, 'you're so right.'

Lulu gave a martyred sigh.

'I carry an enormous responsibility.'

'You do. Yes, I can see that,' Alice said in her most under-standing voice.

'Do I look fat in my black jeans?' I asked, niggled.

'Sometimes, you do, yes,' Lulu said nonchalantly, taking a drag from her ciggie.

Discomfited, I examined my thighs.

Lulu inched along the bed, pressed her palm on Alice's knee, and gave her a slow penetrating look.

'This is *our* little secret,' she said, her face bright.

Heavy footsteps made their way along the hallway towards us. Alice and Lulu leaped up and forced their cigarettes in to my hand. Panicked and wide-eyed they stood up straight like a couple of meerkats. I wheeled, whipped the curtain open and threw the butt ends out the window.

Duncan burst into the room wearing boxers and a white vest.

'I canna sleep, the walls in this flat are like paper. Will the three of ye be quiet. Alice, yer coming wi' me. And as for you two,' a pointed finger shifted between Lulu and me, 'if I hear another word, I'll put yees outside. Ye willnay enjoy sleepin' on the doormat.'

Alice flashed a naked shoulder.

'You want your wicked way with me, don't you?' she asked.

'No, I don't, I want some sleep,' Duncan said, taking Alice by the hand. 'Good night girls,' he said, slamming the bedroom door behind him.

Lulu and I lay in bed, staring at the ceiling.

'What are you going to do about Rob?' Lulu whispered in the gloom.

'I don't know. I thought how nice it would have been tonight if Rob had been there. And if things had been the way they were before I found out about . . .'

She cut me off.

'If Rob had been here, the evening wouldn't have happened.'

'What d'you mean?'

'You and Rob never socialised with anyone else. You only went out as a couple. For whatever reason Rob wasn't fond of Nikki, and, well, me and him weren't exactly best buddies. I admit that was as much my fault as his, but even so. And now, of course, we know why he never introduced you to any of his friends or family. It's glaringly obvious.'

I felt uneasy. She was right – apart from Alice and Duncan, Rob and I had no mutual friends. Why hadn't I noticed?

'I haven't looked in his half of the wardrobe yet. Is . . . is all of his stuff gone?'

She gave a little chuckle.

'Half? He had about a tenth of the space in your wardrobe, but yeah, everything of his is gone. You couldn't find a fibre to match his DNA profile in this flat if your life depended on it.'

I pulled the quilt up under my chin.

'I'm tired,' I said.

'I'm sure you are.'

Lulu left early for work. The sound of rain pelting against the bedroom window, and the scent of burnt toast, woke me up. Duncan's broad frame practically filled our eight-by-six-foot kitchen. He fielded the cooker like a goalkeeper facing a penalty shot. Forehead dissected in a frown of concentration, he slapped a flame on the oven with a spatula with one hand and reached over for the toaster, which had a cloud of black smoke rising above it, with the other.

'Lass! Yer up. I was thinkin' maybe ye'd gone into hibernation. Alice is setting the table, so go sit down.'

He jumped back as a shower of sparks and spots of oil flew up from the frying pan.

'I have everythin' under control in here!' he said.

I hadn't eaten much at dinner, or eaten much at all in the last couple of days, for fear that I'd not manage to keep anything down. I tightened the cord of my dressing gown.

'Go on!' he said, batting a nuclear haze from the grill with the chopping board.

'OK,' I said, leaving him to it.

Alice sat slumped over the table, head in her hands.

'Evie, I feel sick.' She dropped her voice to a whisper. 'It was the cigarette,' she admitted with a sigh. 'Duncan's been out and bought enough bacon and eggs for an army, I'm not sure I can face it.'

I edged into the seat next to her.

'Nor can I.'

'He won't be happy,' she said, swallowing painfully.

As it turned out he was delighted, because the greedy giant got to eat the whole lot himself. By the time we cleared up and Alice had showered it was noon. Finally they left. I went back to bed. The phone rang, I knocked the clock off the bedside cabinet reaching for it.

'Evie, it's Wednesday.' Nikki announced.

'I know it's Wednesday, so what?'

'You're an hour late.'

'I'm not.'

'You are.'

'Nik, I'm not here at your beck and call, we really need to sort this out!'

'Sort what out? You work on a Wednesday. Nothing has changed as far as I'm concerned.'

I felt a slither of despair, *everything* had changed. The fact that

Nikki was right made me feel worse; I *did* work Wednesday, except if I was on tour.

I could hear him impatiently clicking the end of a pen.

'You tell me when you're touring and we work round those dates, apart from that you're pretty much Monday to Friday, so what are you talking about?'

'I don't feel well.'

He cleared his throat.

'There's nothing wrong with you; *get in here*, we're busy. Don't you have any sense of obligation?'

'Of course I do, I'm just, not up to it today.'

'EVIE!'

'DON'T SHOUT!'

There was a long silence. I held the phone to my ear in a rigid grip, and gave a series of heaves, biting down on a trembling lip.

The pen clicking stopped.

The silence stretched.

'Evie, come to work,' Nik said softly, at last. 'I've given my mum the day off, if you're not coming in, I'll have to tell her to cancel whatever plans she has for today.'

He had me. I was pinned at the thought of Maria sacrificing her day off. Conscience pierced through my depression.

I gave a miserable sigh, and sat up against the pillows.

'OK, I agreed, 'I'll be in by two o'clock.'

'Thank you,' he said, and clicked off.

The phone rang again. I picked it up robotically.

'Evie, hi, it's Tina. We need to pencil your schedule for the next couple of months.' She said officiously.

Months?

I felt a rush of anxiety at the thought of planning anything further ahead than today. I jammed the phone between shoulder and cheek and laced my fingers nervously.

'Could we . . . could we . . . do it next week?' I asked.

'No, it's in your best interests to sort this out now. I spoke to Lydia in Transportation, who tells me Rob's fleet are chartered through to the end of July on Switzerland and Germany: if he drives, that's where he will be.

'I'm assuming you don't want to run the risk of finding yourself working with him,' she said, matter-of-factly, 'so you have two options. Either, you work our Dutch bulbfield weekend breaks, which are by coach from London; or escort our Paris fly-tours. Thinking out loud, I suggest the fly-tours. Take the Dutch trip, and it wouldn't surprise me if Rob tried to wangle himself a driving job with whichever coach operator services the bulb-fields – you know how these coach guys help each other out; he could show up any Friday morning, and you'd be stuck with him for four days. Whereas he's highly unlikely to be able to stalk you by air, is he? This way you'll fly to Paris and hook up with a *Parisian* coach operator.'

'Fine,' I said.

'Fine what?'

'Fine I'll do Paris.'

'Good, your first one is on Friday.'

I'm taken aback.

'But it's Wednesday today.'

'I know.'

'You mean to tell me you didn't have anyone lined up already?' I asked.

'I did, but she cancelled. I'll drop the paperwork in our overnight bag; you'll have it by lunchtime tomorrow. You've got to keep busy, Evie.'

As I threw back the quilt and got out of bed I couldn't help but think there was a conspiracy going on to keep me on the move.

*

I dragged myself through the door of the bar an hour later. I did only what I had to: took orders, served drinks, cleared tables and tended the bar when Nikki went to the bank. I didn't go as far as speaking to or smiling at the customers. Costas and Pepi had seen it all before, me with a face like a wet weekend. For the most part they ignored me and put up with my morose behaviour, which I really appreciated, although in fairness it's no less than I deserve: they are a pair of lazy psychopathic nymphomaniacs, and nine times out of ten it's *me* who has to put up with *their* behaviour. At the end of my shift I sat on a bar stool rolling a cold glass on my forehead. A headache which had started as a stabbing pain above my left eye had grown to a hammering thump in the epicentre of my skull.

'You look nice, Evie,' Nikki said.

I was wearing regulation black trousers, a white blouse and a long bistro apron. There was nothing nice about it, but it was kind of him to say so.

'You OK?' Nikki asked, impinging on my depression.

I felt a coldness in my chest: guilt. I knew Nikki was being patient with me, making an effort to draw me out of myself – and Nik was not renowned for his patience. Even so he had skirted delicately around me all afternoon. And here I was, wishing he'd leave me to wallow.

I glanced at him. He stood behind the cash register, tall and dark, sliding a pen end over end through his fingers.

'I'm fine.'

'Good!' he said with an assertive nod, stepping up the pace on the pen rolling.

My phone buzzed. I lifted my bottom and twisted my phone from my back pocket. My heart gave a swoop when I saw Rob's name on my message display.

I'm looking forward to Friday night. R. xxx

I felt a flutter of excitement, which instantly died when I realised that I couldn't make it on Friday. I was going to Paris.

'Are you hungry? Shall we eat? It looks like the rush is over,' Nikki said.

'OK,' I replied, deadpan.

Head bent, I quickly keyed a reply.

Sorry can't make it, am working. E (I didn't send a kiss.)

His reply pinged back immediately.

Where are you working? R xxx

'What would you like to eat?' Nikki asked.

'Anything!' I shot back.

I'm working in Paris. E

There, that'll show him I'm not sitting at home sobbing into a glass of Pinot.

'Steak or salmon?' Nikki asked.

'Sounds good!' I agreed swiftly.

I'll meet you in Paris. R xxx

I felt a tickle of lust. I crossed my legs in defiance, the nerve of him, inviting himself to Paris.

'Steak *or* salmon means one *or* the other!' Nikki said, sharply.

I chewed my thumbnail. I wasn't sure I wanted to meet Rob

at all, let alone meet him in Paris. What should I say to that? I would have to think.

I twirled a lock of hair round my finger pensively. I've got a good mind to ask if he's bringing the family, I thought.

Nikki slapped him palm hard on the bar surface. I jumped. Bloody hell, he scared the life out of me.

'Put that phone down!' he yelled, 'I'm trying to order our dinner.'

He placed two hands wide on the bar, and bent his head to mine, I squared my shoulders and fielded his gaze.

'I can text *and* have a conversation at the same time. It's called multitasking. Women do it all the time; men don't seem to be able to master the art!' I yelled back '*You* certainly can't.'

His lips twitched; a smile threatened.

I crammed my phone in my back pocket, sat on it to muffle the beeps, raised my chin and gave him a solid stare.

'OK, what do you want, ogre?' I asked.

'That's better,' he said. 'Now, would you like steak, or salmon?'

I folded my arms across my chest.

'Salmon please.'

My phone beeped again. Nikki glared at me. I wanted to reach it out of my pocket but I didn't dare.

'I'll have steak,' he said. He pointed in the direction of the kitchen. 'You go and tell Spiros what we want to eat and I'll open a bottle of wine.'

I clambered off the stool, and picked my way through the restaurant to the kitchen, sensing Nikki craning in my direction. After quickly ordering our meal, I edged outdoors through the fire exit, my back up against the wall – a good distance away from the air conditioning unit that belched steam and kitchen smells out into the courtyard – and then I took my phone out of my pocket to read a string of four messages:

Babe I want to see you so much, don't cancel me. R xxx

I'll meet you anywhere. R xxx

Can u talk. R xxx

My heart skipped an excited beat.

Where are you? R xxx
I'm at work. E (Still no kisses, he'll notice, I know he will).

The fire exit door ricocheted and bounced against the wall. Jesus! It sounded like a machine gun. Startled, I jumped.

'WHAT THE HELL ARE YOU DOING OUT HERE?' Nik shouted.

I inhaled sharply. Nik can be a right pain in the arse sometimes. I rounded on him.

'IT'S NONE OF YOUR BUSINESS.'

'IT IS MY BUSINESS, WE'RE SUPPOSED TO BE HAVING DINNER, GET IN HERE.'

'I'M COMING.'

Nik arched his arm in the doorway for me to pass. I jammed my phone in my pocket, it beeped.

'If that thing goes off while I'm eating, I won't be happy,' Nikki warned.

'You? Not happy? Why does that not surprise me?' I fired back, striding past him.

Nikki and I shared a table in the window alcove. I gave the clock above the bar a wistful glance; it was six o'clock – usually at this time I would be rushing home to Rob. I contemplated my glass, torn between savouring the delicious Chablis and sinking into a self-indulgent, pensive decline.

Nikki poured more wine.

'When are you next going on tour?' he asked.

'Friday.'

His fork stopped mid-air.

'Good!'

'Good?'

He looked at me from beneath dark lashes.

'It'll keep you busy,' he said with the ghost of a smile.

'D'you mind if I have tomorrow off?' I asked.

'Yes I do mind, thanks for asking,' he said, with a glance of cool reserve.

I gave an impatient sigh.

'I'm going to Paris on Friday, I'd like at least *one day* to myself.'

He rested his fork on his plate, and leaned forward, fingers tented. The bar had taken on a charcoal hue in the early evening; shadows of headlights outside flashed intermittently across his face.

'When do you get back from Paris?'

'Monday.'

'You can have Tuesday to yourself. And while we're on the subject of your shifts, there's no reason now why you can't work the odd evening, is there?'

'Apart from the fact that I don't want to.'

'It's not always about what *you want*; I'd like to be able to give Costas and Pepi a couple of nights off. I can't ask my mum to cover for them, she's too slow. It's not fair on her and you could help out. It worked well in the past.'

'Actually at least if I work in the evenings I can have a couple of days when I can sleep late,' I said, weighing the possibilities. 'So yes, fine.'

His stern tone didn't waver, but I heard a note of relieved satisfaction in his voice.

'Good, that's settled then,' he said.

Chapter Fifteen

I lay awake in a tangle of quilt watching the sky turn from black to grey and eventually to pale blue. Somewhere between grey and blue, I heard Lulu leave for work. I stroked the empty pillow beside me, and looked out of the window; a slice of light pierced the clouds and fell on to the bed. For once it wasn't raining. I missed Rob every waking moment in lesser or greater degrees depending on whether I was fixating on Cassie and Marcus, or pretending they didn't exist. Sometimes, like now, I felt as though I was underwater. I'd hardly slept a wink thinking about him. The truth is that with Rob I had not had any sexual inhibitions, *none whatsoever*.

In bed Rob had never asked me what I wanted, he would simply do whatever *he* wanted to do, and if I showed the slightest hesitation or decorous reluctance, he would redouble his efforts, overpower me and do it anyway. Not in an aggressive or forceful way, I hasten to add; definitely not, more as a result of gentle, cajoling insistence. His eyes would pierce mine, to such an extent that it often felt as if he could read my mind. He would tell me in a thick, sexy voice to be still. He'd tell me to trust him and that I would enjoy it. And I did, always. This astute yet selfish resolve of his became his great appeal for me, because

217

it allowed me to experience things I might not have admitted I wanted to try – or ever even known about. Rob was the first man to do so many things to me. At times I was both disgusted and thrilled with myself, because having learnt there was no point being coy I became shamelessly wanton. In short, Robert Harrison brought out the slut in me. And to be honest, I was sorely missing her. I sadly suspect that I won't be seeing her for a while, because I wasn't sure I would be able to introduce her to just anyone. This was the reason I couldn't get Rob out of my head. I missed Evie the trollop, as much as I missed Rob the man.

I hitched myself up on the pillow, reached for my handbag on the bedside table, and pulled out my phone.

I had to speak to Rob. I had to.

'Babe, thanks for ringing,' he said, over-quickly.

Desire tore through me at the sound of his voice.

'OK, I understand why you don't want me to come to Paris. Of course I do, you have a group to look after. So let me come to the flat when you get back,' he said. 'Or tonight. I could come around to see you tonight.'

I cringed at the thought of Rob and Lulu barrelling through the garden gate at the same time.

'Evie, I know this is hard,' he went on. 'I know I've messed up, but the sooner we meet, the sooner we can sort things out.'

He exhaled a drawn out breath. I could visualise him, eyes lusting, pleading, loving and apologetic.

'Do you miss me Evie? I can't begin to tell you how much I miss you.'

He'd have his choirboy face on.

'Evie . . .'

'Of course I miss you.' I said. My voice was taut.

There was a sigh of relief on the end of the line.

'That's a start!' he said with a smile I swear I could hear.

'But I miss the clear-cut relationship we had . . . '

'Evie, *we still have* what we had before. We can work through this. Let me come to the flat tonight.'

'No, I don't think coming here is a good idea,' I said forcefully 'But I . . . I do want to meet,' I confessed.

There, I said it, I admitted I wanted to meet him, and I do. You can't just stop loving someone, can you?

'Right OK, I'll pick you up at seven and take you for dinner, I won't come in. I'm not particularity enthused at the prospect of swapping stories with Cruella.'

'Don't call Lulu that,' I snapped loyally.

'OK, OK! Sorry!'

'No! I don't finish in the bar until six tonight, and I'm going to Paris in the morning. I want an early night. Let's make it dinner on Tuesday,' I said dictatorially.

After all who, is calling the shots here?

There was a beat of silence.

'But, Evie . . . ' he pleaded.

'But what?' I challenged.

'Nothing, nothing,' he stammered, backing down. 'Tuesday is fine, absolutely fine. Have a great time in Paris. I'll pick you up at seven on Tuesday, if that's what you want; I'll spend the weekend looking forward to it. I'll take you somewhere nice.'

'OK, see you Tuesday,' I said and rang off.

I'd done it. I'd called him. I was glad. But the call had drained me. I felt exhilarated and excited but at the same time nervous, jittery and bloody exhausted. My heart thumped. I fell back on the pillows. OK, I told myself assertively. There is *no way*, after all Rob and I have been through, that we can let our relationship end without meeting to discuss things. We need closure if nothing else. Meeting is the sensible thing to do. Of course it is.

219

It's the adult thing to do, I said to the ceiling. I felt my cheeks burn at the thought of him. The thought of him lying beside me, of him bending his head slowly and taking my earlobe between his teeth, I shivered. Yes I wanted to see him, definitely. My heart-beat slowed steadily as I dreamt on, I wanted to sort this out one way or the other, I had to. I closed my eyes, clenched a handful of quilt and snuggled into the pillow.

The phone ringing woke me.

'Evie, if I don't see you walking through the door of this bar within the next twenty minutes, I'll . . .'

My eyes flew to the clock, quarter past eleven.

'Nik, I'm coming, I'll be there,' I said, tumbling out of bed.

Nikki filled the doorway of the bar. Feet spread; arms crossed. I pushed past him.

He marched in my wake. I held up a silencing hand.

'OK, don't start, I'm late, but only by half an hour, and I'm *very sorry*, but I slept in. And yes, as always, you're right! That's no excuse! But, it's *my* excuse, because that's what happened. And you're thinking how can someone who starts work at eleven o'clock possibly sleep in? Because you wake up at six with the burglars and postmen, and leap out of bed and do a triathlon and a marathon at the gym, and play in a charity football match, all before breakfast. And, bully for you, because . . .'

Two strong arms curved my waist and spun me round.

'Shut up! I'm in a good mood; I've completed the purchase on the building in Wimbledon. It's mine, the architect starts tomorrow,' he said, giving me an echoing kiss in my ear.

He set me on my feet and turned me to face him.

A smile split his handsome face. I felt an almighty rush of happiness. I was absolutely elated, and *proud*. Yes that's the word, *proud*. And confused, because, why should I feel proud of Nikki?

220

He's my boss, and he drives me bloody mad, and we're constantly arguing. Expectant eyes pierced mine. He was waiting for me to say something, but all I could manage was a couple of short sharp breaths. He clamped my shoulders and gave an encouraging nod as suddenly, and to my horrified surprise, I burst into tears.

He pulled me to him.

'What's wrong?' He asked, his chin resting on my head. 'Evie, sweetheart, what is it?'

'I'm happy for you,' I sobbed with impeccable logic.

'You're happy for me?'

I nodded into his shoulder.

'I, I am, I really am, that's, that's brilliant,' I wailed. 'It's great news, and I, I couldn't be happier.'

I held him tight.

'In that case, what are the tears for?' he asked.

'I, I, don't know . . . I, I have no idea.'

He rubbed my back.

'You're upsetting yourself for nothing.'

'I'm not upset, I'm fine.'

He clamped my elbows and held me at arm's length. His amused eyes crossed my face.

'I'm going to need your help, Evie, I'll have to spend a lot of time away from the bar. You know how to cash up and do the banking, you know what stock we need and who supplies it. And if needs be you're only across the road; so you can open up in the morning. You handle the Chef better than anyone, he never attacks you,' he said, not entirely joking. 'My mum adores you and Costas and Pepi know they can't take advantage if I leave you in charge. I'll be here at weekends, it's midweek I'll struggle. Obviously I know you need time to yourself, and your priority is your tour work, but . . . '

221

'I'll help, of course I will. I can't work Fridays because I'll be in Paris, but Monday to Thursday I'll cover for you.'

What was I saying? Was I mad? Nik would work me to the bone.

He lifted a long strand of hair and tucked it behind my ear.

'And Evie, I know you've got a lot on your mind, and maybe I've not been as sympathetic as I should have been, but I'll try harder to listen, and I'm here for you, and . . . '

I pressed a finger to his lips.

'I know you are.'

'So,' he said with a relieved sigh, 'you'll help?'

'Definitely, of course I'll help!'

'Brilliant! I can't wait to get cracking on the building,' he said excitedly.

A sudden flashback to that rat-infested building in Wimbledon made me shiver and come to my senses. He'd just bought the House of the Damned. What on earth was I congratulating him for? Privately, I questioned his sanity, but outwardly I smiled sweetly – I truly was delighted by his excitement.

I just hope to god he knows what he is getting himself in to.

VENICE

Chapter Sixteen

Paris was bathed in sunshine, glorious sunshine. I sat alone on a wall, nibbling a cheese baguette, staring up at the west pillar of the Eiffel Tower.

This is the second day of the tour, and I'm ashamed to admit, I haven't made one friend among my group, or bothered to remember anyone's name. That said, I've proved willing, making idle conversation, and taking photographs, waiting patiently while smiley, happy tourists pose in front of every bloody historical monument in the city, most of which are featured on postcards. If they want a decent picture of Notre Dame or the Opera House, they can just buy one; it's themselves they want pictures of. What's the point of having a picture taken with your boyfriend? There's every chance he's shagging someone else, or even secretly married.

I glanced up at the magnificence of La Tour Eiffel, which I personally think should be one of the Wonders of the World. In fact the whole of Paris, not just the tower. I love everything about it yet I felt none of the usual sparkle of glee. OK, the weather is fabulous – unseasonably so – but all I'm thinking is, why are people sunbathing on the grass? What's the point of getting a suntan, if we all turn grey when we die? I eyed a girl in a lemon dress, arms outstretched, spinning on her heel, blonde hair billowing while her boyfriend filmed her. She hugged herself and pouted for the camera. How irritating was that? I hate a show-off!

My eye drifted over to a white-shirted traffic warden. As a group of nuns approached him, he smiled pleasantly and tore up the parking ticket he'd been about to leave on their windscreen. He glowed in their praise and thanks, then promptly issued an officious ticket to an irate pot-bellied man. Behind the traffic warden, my French coach driver did some chubby-armed semaphore and pointed to his watch. *Vingt minutes*, he mouthed. Well I knew that. It was me who had told everyone what time to be back on the bus. I stood, tossed my half-eaten baguette in the bin, tucked my clipboard under my arm and picked my way around a horseshoe of children sitting on the grass, destroying a picnic.

Back in my hotel room, I dumped my bag on the floor and sat elbows on the desk, chin in my palms, in front of the window. I drummed my fingers on my cheekbones. I missed Rob like mad. Paris was *our* city; we had spent a whole summer here last year. His ghost was everywhere, haunting me.

My phone rang. I snaked my hand in my bag, and answered it with a sigh.

'Evie, where are you?' John asked.

'Paris,' I said, flicking the window shutter idly against the wall.

'Fabulous, so you're not sitting at home brooding?'

'No I'm sitting in Paris brooding.'

'Stop it! How long are you in Paris for?'

'One more night, I'm flying home tomorrow,' I said.

'Let's have dinner on Tuesday.'

'I'm having dinner with Rob on Tuesday,' I said automatically, and then clamped my hand over my mouth. 'I mean ... I might ... '

'You will do no such thing,' he said sharply.

'I need to speak to him,' I quickly pitched.

'Use the telephone, if you feel the need to speak with him.'

'Some things can't be discussed properly on the phone,' I said primly.

'In this instance a phone call will suffice.'

'I want to see him to, well, to talk properly,' I said, and swallowed.

'Then do so in a couple of weeks,' he fired back in a sharp tone. 'Evie, the boy will say whatever he thinks you want to hear, trust me. Take it from one that knows. It's too soon. His story won't improve with the urgent telling of it, it'll keep. Give yourself more time.'

'Time for what?' I asked, rattled.

'Time to think things through properly.'

'I've done nothing but think, and—'

'Evie! You have not; you haven't thought things through at all. I suggest you call your estranged boyfriend, tell him you are committed to a prior engagement which had slipped your mind, and that unfortunately you have to cancel. I'll send Alistair to pick you up. Be ready at six o'clock.'

'Who is Alistair?'

'My Chauffeur. Evie, keep the boy waiting, keep him on his toes. I'm giving you insider information on the workings of the male mind. Take advantage of my experience. There are some advantages to growing old, wisdom being chief among them.'

'Ah yes, and going to bed early every night being another.'

He gave a throaty chuckle.

'Cheeky little minx.'

There was a hum of silence.

His tone changed to chatty conversational.

'Evie, trust me, wait a while longer. I don't want you to make a mistake because you've rushed in to this. You should be ignoring his calls, deleting text messages and returning any flowers and gifts. You should not be rushing out on dinner dates.'

Flowers and gifts? What flowers and gifts?!

I sighed. John was right, I was too keen, far too keen. I should be proving a point. That point being: wives will not be tolerated. Right now I was more upset than angry. I should wait until I was in the right frame of mind – absolutely fuming and not vulnerable. That way I will be able to put my case forward forcefully, clearly. Venomously.

'Yes, OK, I'll wait,' I determined, resolute, and feeling very mature. 'You're right of course, I would be starting from a position of weakness, wouldn't I?'

'Absolutely.'

'That's settled then,' I said firmly, congratulating my tenacity.

'Good girl.' John replied with a note of triumph. 'I'll see you on Tuesday. Try not to be late.'

'Late, me? I'm never late!'

Perhaps I could meet Rob on Wednesday, that'll keep him on his toes for a whole extra day.

I stared fixedly off into the middle distance after John's call. OK, if not Wednesday, maybe Thursday. The underlying problem is that it isn't easy to put someone out of your mind. Rob's face constantly materialises when I least expect it. Perhaps if I meet up with him, my righteous anger for the lies he spun will override this constant nagging feeling of desire I have for him. That's a very strong possibility. Obviously a very good reason why we *should* meet. I slipped off my shoes and reached for the room service menu. I didn't want to join the clients in the bar.

It would not be fair on them – no one wants someone as miserable as me for company.

I spent the evening alone sitting on the balcony, entranced by the herby aroma of French cuisine and the sound of a strumming guitar drifting up from the restaurant below, and comforted by every gin, brandy and Bacardi miniature in my mini-bar.

Sunday morning was sunny but crisp. I sat in the crew seat staring morosely at the view as our coach rumbled along the cobbles of the Champs-Élyseés. Leafy trees nodded over the heads of al fresco diners, and tall balconied buildings sunbathed and stretched upwards into the cloudless blue sky. I smiled to hear the gasps of admiration from my group, as we lumbered slowly around the L'Arc de Triomphe, the fifty-metre high monument commemorating the battles and victories of the Emperor Napoleon. Each of the twelve avenues radiating from the arch are named after French military leaders. On every trip last year, I made Rob circle the arch until I had done with showing off my narrative on what I referred to as 'the symbol of French national spirit'. My mind drifted back to the weekend Rob and I climbed up L'Arc. I had persuaded him there was an elevator up to the top. I honestly thought there was one! There isn't. Instead, you hoof it up 284 steps; I thought I was going to die of exhaustion. I kept up the pace and soldiered on as far as I could, but he'd had to drag me up the last 234 steps. I'd hated him in the moment but felt fabulous when we reached the top. I'd been ecstatic, exhilarated at having survived . . . The memory made my eyes sting.

I craned my neck and peered down the aisle of the coach. Forty-two faces stared back expectantly; these people deserve a good tour, I decided, feeling a rush of remorse. Rob or no Rob! Shamed into action, I told the driver to slowly circle the Étoile.

'*Bien sur,*' he replied, with a smile.

I stood, and with a theatrical flourish held the microphone to my chin, and gestured to Avenue Foch with a Grecian sweep.

'To your left is Avenue Foch, named after . . .' and once I started showing off, I simply couldn't stop. I didn't stop talking until we pulled alongside the gates of Château Malmaison, the former country residence of the beautiful Empress Josephine, wife of Napoleon, some thirty minutes later.

This was my first visit to Malmaison. I had read a bit about Josephine last year, but not much. After a two hour guided audio tour of the Château, which I loved, I determined Josephine and I should get to know each other better and so I sat cross-legged in the gardens, head bent to my guidebook and a light breeze wisping my hair.

Josephine and I were kindred spirits. Her first husband had a son by his mistress. My fiancé turned out to have had a son by his wife. It's a clear case of history repeating itself. I raised my eyebrows and nodded in consideration. Yes, we were definitely kindred spirits. Josephine had been furious, and so was I! Her husband took his mistress on a trip to the Caribbean and had the cheek to ask Josephine to pop in now and again while they were away, to keep an eye on his son. Alarms sounded in my head. I dropped the book. What if Cassie went to Majorca or somewhere with her friends – could she foist Rob's legitimate son on me? I picked up the book and flicked forward a chapter. How had Josephine dealt with this? My eyes travelled the page. I can speed read when needs must. Ah! She told him to get lost, and treated him *coldly*. Good for her! Right, I'll text Rob, and treat him *coldly*.

Can't make dinner Tuesday, previous engagement, sorry! E

Cancelled him *coldly*, that'll teach him.

Babe, I've been looking forward to it. When can u make it?
Rx

I decided to read a couple of more chapters on Josephine before replying.

Josephine went on to have two children by her husband – obviously that was because she was married to him already, which doesn't apply to me. Josephine's husband denied paternity of her second child; I was starting to really dislike this guy. Josephine moved into a convent for a while on her husband's insistence. I hated him now. Moving to a convent hadn't been Josephine's idea and I wasn't going to follow suit. During the French Revolution Josephine and her husband found themselves in prison together, where they became friends. I sat up and sighed. Perhaps Josephine thought life was too short to bear grudges. Perhaps she wished they had sorted things out sooner, and had regretted the way they had ended up together again, under such dreadful circumstances, before rekindling their friendship.

I text Rob.

Will let u know when I get back. E

Love you babe, try for Wednesday. Rx

Like Josephine, I extended the hand of friendship. I picked up the book and read on. Josephine's husband had his head chopped off – well I wasn't overly surprised by that, and not entirely sorry to hear it either. Still, it was a bit drastic to wish that on Rob, even for someone as pissed-off as I felt. Now she was a widow, Josephine took lovers. That was more like it!

I tucked the book in my bag and got to my feet. It was time to gather my group and head back into the city. I would read more about Josephine, my friend and soul mate, later. I raised my chin to the sun and decided that Josephine was my new mentor.

On Tuesday, Alistair, John's driver, arrived at six o'clock sharp; it wouldn't have surprised me if he had been lurking somewhere down the road, in order to stage his arrival to precision. Much to Alistair's astonishment and, I suspect, discomfort, I asked him if I could sit in the front with him.

He opened the car door, tipping forward from the waist to stand in a ski position. He didn't look comfortable so I quickly scrambled into the car.

'I don't want to be tempted by the drinks' cabinet in the back,' I explained, sinking into my seat.

'I see, ma'am,' he said, doffing his navy cap.

'Call me Evie?'

'Yes, ma'am,' he repeated, closing the door gently.

I eyed him with fascination. Ramrod-straight he strode round to the driver's side.

Did the guy ever slouch?

I stared ahead.

There was a vicious banging on the side window.

I bolted upright and swivelled; it was Lulu.

My face crumpled. What the hell did she want?

She whipped the door open.

'Give me a lift,' she begged.

'Where to?' I asked.

'Anywhere, take me anywhere you like. I don't care, just don't leave me behind!' she said, lurching towards the back door.

I gave Alistair a tight smile, feeling myself blush.

'I think I'll sit in the back with my friend,' I told him primly, one foot already on the pavement.

'Yes ma'am.'

Lulu palmed the soft-stitched leather interior, awestruck. She found the drinks cabinet and turned on the television.

'Champagne, Evie?' she asked, on all fours beside the fridge.

The large black car slowly divided the gawping crowd standing at the bus stop outside our flat.

'If you're having one. But only one – I don't want to be pissed before I get there.'

She gave me a solemn stare.

'Evie, do you think turning up sober is wise? Perhaps you need some Dutch courage, I mean this is your chance to, well to put right your wrong,' she said, champagne bottle dangling in her hand.

'What wrong?'

'Not shagging John in Amsterdam of course.'

'Shut up, I'm not shagging him anywhere.'

She looked cynically unconvinced.

'Where do you want to be dropped off?' I asked her.

'Back home, if that's all right with you,' she said, sloshing fizz into a glass.

'You want us to turn around now, two minutes into the journey? And . . . '

'No, take me to central London, you get out of the car at John's house, and I can ride back with Jeeves here!' she said, toasting the bottle at the driver.

'I can't let you treat John's car and driver like your own personal mobile wine bar,' I told her, outraged.

'Why not?'

I floundered for words, the nerve of her!

'John is taking me out to dinner, likely we'll need the car.'

'Take a taxi.' she suggested, flatly.

'You want *us* to take a taxi so you can keep the chauffeur?' I asked, my voice swelling with indignation.

231

'Likely you'll have a few cocktails in the drawing room before you go out, the limo will have whizzoed back to you by then.'

'It's not *my* car to give you.'

She handed me a champagne flute and toasted her glass against mine. Fiendish inspiration lit her eyes, she reeled forward and tapped rat-a-tat-tat on the driver's dividing window.

It opened with a purr.

'Excuse me,' she said, edging her nose in the expanding gap. 'Evie and I have some business to discuss, I wonder if it would be possible for you to drop me home after our meeting.'

My cheeks blushed crimson. I pushed in front of her.

'No Alistair, I'm sure John will need you.' I piped up, waving my hand dismissively. 'She's not—'

'That will be fine ma'am. Mr Jackson has three drivers,' Alistair said, interrupting me pleasantly.

'Thank you, thank you so much,' Lulu said in a stiff polite voice I hadn't heard before.

The window hissed shut.

We dropped into our seats in sync; her gaze met mine square on.

'Don't you have anything better to do, than idly drive around London?' I asked.

'No, I don't,' she said, twirling her glass. 'Evie, aren't you impressed? This car is *fantastic*. It must have cost a stack.'

'Of course I'm impressed, who wouldn't be?'

'You're not very quick on the uptake, are you?' she said, placing her glass on the mahogany armrest with care.

'What d'you mean?'

She crossed her arms in a businesslike manner.

'Look at you. You're wearing jeans, a lilac River Island blouse and purple heels, and your hair is in a ponytail. You should be wearing stockings, a minidress, have your hair loose and tousled, legs coated in fake tan and cleavage squashed and elevated.' She leaned back, her eyes sparkled with thoughts. 'I know what you're up to,' she said, sitting straight. 'You're playing coy, aren't you? Good for you. You're playing hard to get.'

'I am *not* playing coy and please don't keep suggesting I'm about to sleep with John. Don't you know what it's like to love someone? You can't just switch off; I don't want anyone else but Rob. Not now.'

The smile faded from her face, and her cleavage reared with indignation.

'Of course I know what it's like to love someone; I've loved every man I've ever slept with,' she said, and meant it. 'OK, perhaps not every single one,' she reluctantly admitted, 'but not far off.'

'I'm surprised your memory recall stretches to half of the men you've slept with, never mind all of them.'

She rolled a lazy eye under a canopy of hair.

'Seriously Evie, the last time you split with Rob you were so glum, and I was so pissed off, and I can't go through that again . . .'

'It won't be like that,' I insisted with shaky conviction. 'I can deal with this.'

'Good!' she said, looking unconvinced.

'I can!' I insisted, with a sub-zero stare.

She started to giggle.

'Evie, imagine the kind of life you could have if you got it together with this John bloke.'

'I won't, he's just a friend.'

'A friend? Let me point out the benefits of him being more than a friend,' she said, flashing a sparkle of straight teeth, and taking a greedy drink from her glass. 'You would have your own private jet, and three chauffeurs, and a mansion off Park Lane, and ...' she swivelled to face me. 'Where else does he have homes?'

'I don't know.'

'Obviously there'll be a New York apartment and a pad in the sun.'

She gave an aspiring sigh, and started to rhyme off points on her fingers.

'Hair extensions every couple of months, obviously, for both of us – you wouldn't want to sit in the hairdressers for five hours on your own. An account at Jimmy Choo – how fortunate we both take a size four! A personal gym at home – I'd chum you in the gym to keep you motivated; and a personal trainer, of course – so many personal trainers are doing two-for-one offers at the moment. Not that John needs to worry about that.'

Her D–cups wobbled as she wriggled in her chair excitedly.

'A stonking allowance for you and, obviously, for your best friend, because what's the point of being minted if you have no one to play with when he's working?'

I settled back against the soft leather and smiled at the traffic. I would love a gym at home, because obviously there would be no excuse for not using it. I'd have biceps and triceps all over my body.

She rushed on.

'A cellulite-zapping machine, the one all the stars are coughing up over thirty grand for? I think we would have to use it one at a time, but still, no matter, I don't mind waiting my turn. A private box at the O2 so we can go to any concerts we wanted. A yacht? I know I'm not the best sailor, but I could get hypnotised again because I nearly stopped smoking, didn't I? A personal assistant, a walk-in wardrobe, shoes, diamonds, bags a-plenty ... Oh! Oh! He could arrange for Topshop to open exclusively for us – I bet he could! I bet he knows Philip Green, I bet they're *best mates* ...'

She was all out of fingers but continued regardless.

'A maid to pick all your clothes up off the floor, an ironing lady, a cleaner . . . '

The list was bloody endless.

Her brows were sliced in thought, her cheeks flushed and her eyes darting, searching for ideas. She became quite breathless at one point.

I held up a silencing hand.

'I don't love him,' I said.

She ground her teeth in frustration.

'But you *will*, you will, Evie, *just try*. I'll help you. He's big and handsome and smells nice and looks at you dreamily and . . . '

'He does *not* look at me dreamily.'

'He does, Evie,' she said with certainty. 'He does,' she assured me.

'Shut up and pour me another drink.'

'Evie, you could go to Relate,' she suggested eagerly.

'Relate? That's marriage guidance!'

'That's what you'll need,' she said, nodding her head vigorously, 'guidance on how to make a multi-millionaire marry you. Now listen to me, I have a plan . . . '

I tuned out; it was the only way to survive the drive. I sank into my seat and let my mind drift back to the holiday in Barbados. I'd loved it so much. Rob could have told me about Cassie and Marcus then, because we had been alone and relaxed, surely that would've made sense? What had he been thinking?

Lulu, still talking, tugged on my arm. As the car circled Hyde Park Corner, she pointed at the Queen Elizabeth Gate, with its imposing forged white unicorn and red lion.

'You could have a memorial gate of your own if you married John, decorated with a jumble of wrought iron lipsticks and handbags,' she said cheerfully. 'Or perhaps just handbags or I

235

suppose you could have one of each,' she added, chewing her lip in deliberation. 'And a vodka Slush Puppy machine! And a wine fountain!'

'I don't drink vodka,' I reminded her.

'Oh fuck off, you know what I mean.'

Slowing, we curved around behind the Dorchester Hotel and drove through a set of lofty stone pillars into a hidden courtyard.

Lulu's nose was pressed to the window.

'Palm trees, in London,' she gasped, toasting her empty glass at an immaculately landscaped garden with a pebbled driveway.

The car stopped. Lulu and I gaped at each other.

'It's enormous,' Lulu said, eyeing a tall white house with a huge shiny red door, decorated with antique brass furniture. We stared up at the façade in wonder. I counted fifteen windows, each underscored with a window box brimming with an array of various spring flowers.

'Do you want to come in with me?' I asked tensely.

'No! No, I must be getting off,' she said robotically, tugging her beaded Benetton cardigan around her. 'You go,' she said, scanning the courtyard.

Alistair resumed his ski position and opened the door.

'Go, go, go!' Lulu said. 'What're you waiting for?'

'Nothing, I'm not waiting for anything.'

'Get out then,' she said, prodding me in the back.

'I am getting out! I have one foot on the gravel.'

'Good luck,' she said.

I tuned to face her.

'Good luck with what?'

'Shagging him of course!' she said, leaning forward to close the door behind me. 'And Evie, remember he has a bad heart, no fancy stuff.'

She is disgusting.

I stood at the bottom of a wide set of speckled marble steps, feeling like Alice in Wonderland. As Alistair turned the car in a horseshoe, an identical car crunched slowly into the courtyard, pulling up behind him.

John stepped out, immaculate in a black suit, white shirt and red tie.

'Evie! Perfect timing!' John said, marching towards me purposefully.

He held my shoulders lightly, smiling grey eyes searched mine.

'Are you well?' he asked.

'I am,' I said, feeling a rush of warmth.

I realised, to my surprise, that I'd missed him. He put a comforting arm around my shoulder and slowly walked me up the steps to the door.

The house was amazing. Impressive from the outside, it was absolutely out of this world on the inside. The marble-floored hallway, dominated by an oval stone fountain with four cascading tiers, was the size of a tennis court, well almost. I leaned over the banister, craned my neck, and marvelled at a sweeping spiral staircase which disappeared into a glass domed ceiling. I counted six floors. *Six!*

'This way, Evie,' John said.

I trotted to catch up and followed him into the kitchen. An enormous light room with a flagstone floor, high ceilings and ornate cornice, deep bay windows, and a pair of French doors leading to a spotlighted quadrangle soaked with an explosion of rioting wisteria.

John stood at a granite-topped island unit.

'It's been a while since I've been in here. Marion, my housekeeper, has the day off, but I think I can rustle a couple of drinks,' he said, giving me a warm smile. 'So you took my advice and cancelled your date. Good girl, well done.'

I slapped my handbag down on to the granite worktop.

'You're kind of insistent with your advice,' I told him, edging on to one of the tall kitchen stools surrounding the work island.

He gave a conceding nod.

'Well yes, granted, I'll give you that; I'm not in the habit of being challenged. Sorry.'

He walked over to a floor-to-ceiling built-in dresser with glass fronted cupboards.

'What would you like to drink?'

'A glass of wine, please.'

'Wine it is,' he said, reaching into the cabinet for glasses.

I leaned over on my stool perilously for a second look at the fountain in the hallway.

'How many bedrooms do you have?' I asked, straightening as he turned.

He tilted his head in thought.

'Nine, I believe,' he said, wine glasses in one hand, bottle in the other.

Listen to him! We have two and that's a certainty.

I slumped over the work island in wonder ... *nine*, I mouthed.

'Will you give me a tour of the house?' I asked.

'No.'

'No?' I echoed, deflated.

'No, I won't give you a tour, but you can take a look around while I make a couple of calls,' he said, teasing his phone from his inside jacket pocket.

I jumped off my stool as if it were on fire and discreetly took the stairs two at a time.

The house at a glance:

238

Drawing Room – Window seat overlooking Park Lane, gigantic fireplace with a carved marble mantle, double doors leading to an ornate balcony. (I wasn't going to admit this, but I stepped on to the balcony and sang 'The Sound of Music'.)

Dining room – No one needs a dining table that size, not even at Christmas.

Library – Parquet flooring, seven occasional tables, and three walls stuffed with expensive leather-bound books.

Study – Looked like a NASA nerve-centre. I know I'm prone to exaggerate, but I swear I'm telling the gospel truth.

Cinema – Honest!

Gym – Who cares?

Bathrooms – Eight in total, all space-age, three had fish tanks. All had bidets. (I'm not sure what I think about that, do you really need to be able to wash your bum wherever you are in the house?)

Bedrooms – To die for walk-in wardrobes, most of which were empty (I checked!). I've never seen anything like it in my life.

Roof Terrace – Swimming pool housed in a glass roofed atrium, with floor-to-ceiling doors leading to a decked patio with a sun terrace. Open plan seating and dining area with double-height barrelled ceilings, marbled flooring and enormous potted palm trees, fully stocked bar with feature Eurocave fridge full of champagne and luxury titbits. I popped a grape in to my mouth, only to discover it was an olive – and I *hate* olives, except when I'm pissed, and happy to eat anything. I spat it out, half-eaten, and hid it under the jacuzzi. (Just to keep the housekeeper on her toes. I'll check to see if it is still there the next time I'm over.)

A self-contained basement flat – Likely the housekeeper's quarters, but I wasn't a hundred per cent certain as it was locked. I gave the door a kick and the handle a good rattle. (Why would she lock it? What does she have to hide?)
A split level underground car park – Five cars, I haven't a clue what models but I know they were not Peugeots or Renaults. (I can recognise a Renault because I drive one, and a Peugeot because I want one.)

I loved the house! Who wouldn't?

John stood, hands placed wide apart on the island worktop, head bent, reading the *Financial Times*.

'Curiosity satisfied?' he asked, lifting his chin.

I pulled a tiny face.

'You have a lot of space for one person,' I said.

'I won't disagree with you there,' he said, palming his silk tie.

I climbed on a kitchen stool, cupped my glass and sipped my wine.

'What would you like to eat? Is there anywhere in particular you would like to go for dinner?' He asked kindly.

My eyes roved in a circle.

'I'd like to stay here.'

His eyebrows lifted.

'Stay here? In the house for dinner? Definitely not! There's no one to cook, and I'm starving. We'll walk around the corner to the Dorchester, that's as close to staying here as you'll get me to agree to.'

'The Dorchester it is. I suppose one of London's finest hotels will have to do,' I said, spinning on my stool.

As John guided me through the glass doors of the Dorchester

I felt knotted with excitement. *The Dorchester! On a weekday! And it's not even a special occasion!* When the concierge greeted John by name, as did one of the receptionists, I wasn't surprised. I looped my arm through his and matched his step through the golden lobby past an array of illuminated glass cabinets brimming with precious stones and expensive watches.

In the restaurant as John studied the wine list, I scanned a prying eye around the room. Certain there was no one famous I needed to concern myself with, I picked up my menu, and nibbled a breadstick thoughtfully. The choices were mouth-watering. How do you decide what to eat in of the most amazing restaurants in London? I was smiling so hard my jaw ached. I *so* belonged here. Nothing could burst my happy bubble. My phone beeped – it seemed unusually loud – I slid a guilty look at my handbag on my lap. It was a text from Lulu.

A condom wrapper is jamming the printer, is it yours?

My mouth twitched into a snarl, Lulu really gets on my nerves sometimes. I am in the bloody Dorchester for god's sake; I *cannot* be concerning myself with printers jammed with condom wrappers.

'Is everything all right?' John asked kindly.

I switched my phone off and dropped my handbag under my chair.

'Perfectly all right,' I told him, tidying the salt and pepper dishes behind a crystal candlestick.

As a sharp-eyed waiter cleared the last of our plates, John stared at me with a challenging frown. I took a huge swig of wine. I felt quite pinned under the microscope. I knew what was coming.

'This young man,' John began, in a businesslike manner. 'Why do you feel the need to meet with him? What's this dinner date nonsense?'

I felt instantly tense.

'I need,' I began, 'I need to sort things out. Surely you agree.'

'No! I don't agree. I don't agree in the slightest.' He gave a relaxed shrug. 'All you have to do is tell him that your relationship has come to an end,' he waved a hand blithely. 'Send him a text. There's no need to meet him, and even less need to have dinner with him.'

I slid my eyes from his.

'I can't do that,' I said, removing a speck from my wine with my fingertip.

'Why not? It is over . . . *isn't it?*'

I sighed.

'Well—' I began.

He cut me off.

'Well what? Evie, you are too young to take on a readymade family. And why should you? Twinned with that, the boy does not even have a track record of fidelity,' he said, his voice dripping with acrimony. 'Quite honestly, I fail to grasp what remains to be said between you. The boy has burnt his boats, and that's all there is to it.'

His shoulders lifted inside his jacket, as he arranged his elbows on the table.

'Frankly I'm at a loss to understand what all the tears were about! You don't see it, but from where I'm sitting, you have the upper hand.'

I tried for foundation.

'He has . . . a hold over me; there's a sort of chemistry between us that I've never shared with anyone else. I think about him all the time.'

John drew his eyes from mine and gave a grunt of disapproval.

'I'll never feel for anyone else what I feel for him. I know it. I miss him like mad. And at night, well . . . ' I trailed off.

A hot flush travelled my neck.

'I can't, I can't get him out of my head.'

John gave me a challenging glare.

'You could have a damn good try, because the boy is nowhere near good enough for you!'

'I think I need him, I need him in my life,' I admitted.

'Don't be ridiculous! You don't need him at all!' he said sharply.

Our eyes locked. There was an awkward silence.

'You can't decide who to fall for, you know,' I told him defensively.

'No, but your heart could sit back and let your head make a couple of decisions, which certainly doesn't seem to be the case at the moment.'

OK, now I felt I had to claw back some ground.

'I'm not totally besotted,' I snapped. 'As much as I miss him, a part of me wants a raging showdown, where I tell him what a shit he is, and tell him that I never want to see him again or have anything more to do with him.'

He tipped forward.

'That, my darling girl, is more like it. That's what I want to hear, that's exactly what I want to hear.'

He exhaled a smile, causing a warm draught on the side of my face. He was close, very close, and his aftershave was spicy and fresh. I felt an excited pop in my chest. I inched to the edge of my seat, his cheek skimmed mine. My impulse was to kiss him. *Kiss him? Kiss John?* I tilted my head to the side and closed my eyes to erase the tape playing in my head, but his appeal seemed to be engraved on the inside of my eyelids. What was I thinking? *What was I thinking*?

'That is *exactly* what I want to hear,' he repeated, in that authoritative tone of his.

Rationality pierced my alcohol-soaked brain. I shuffled back and sat tall. John's face was blank. He pressed his hand over mine, warming my skin to his touch.

'So, you'll tell that young man when he next contacts you that you have nothing more to say to him.'

I looked at his strong hand placed firmly over mine. How much had I had to drink? Is this just normal wine?

'Evie! Are you listening?'

I felt weirdly hollow and . . . oddly thwarted but—

'Evie!'

I dragged my focus back.

'Yes, I heard you, I know what you're saying is right. I'm not stupid.' I said, sliding my hand from his. It still felt warm.

'I have never implied that you are stupid,' he said icily.

I decided on a change of direction.

'Enough about me, what about you?' I asked officiously.

He looked bewildered.

'Me? What about me?'

'Like why are you here with me, when you probably have a black book full of names and addresses of glamorous women?'

He gave a throaty chuckle.

'I'm here with you, because unlike most other people I come into contact with, you want nothing from me.'

I rolled my glass between my palms, and withered at the thought of Lulu's list of things she wanted from him; I don't think she left anything out, from memorial gates to a vodka Slush Puppy machine.

244

He pushed back his chair and stood.

'Let's move to the bar for brandy.'

Amid the splendours of the Dorchester bar I decided my momentary lustful contemplation had been a side effect of temporary amnesia. I had literally forgotten who I was with and what I was doing. There's no other explanation. None!

Alistair dropped me home just before midnight. John had offered to ride with me, but I didn't see the point, it would've been a waste of his time, riding out of town only to turn around and drive back again. I tiptoed into the flat and slid under a cold quilt, and for the first time in two weeks, with the exception of the night we went out for dinner with Alice and Duncan, I fell asleep without crying.

A heavy battering at the front door in the middle of the night woke me. Lulu heard it too. She flicked on the light and, dressing gown flapping, barrelled into my room with an anxious expression slashed across her face.

'Who can that be!?' she asked, eyes wide and frantic. 'Have you been dealing weed or something? It can only be the police at this time of the night and with a knock like that.'

I pulled back the quilt.

'Of course not!' I said sharply.

'Well what have you been up to?' she asked.

'Nothing! Have you been up to anything?'

'No,'

She tossed my dressing gown at me. I whipped it across my shoulder.

'Do you think it's that lunatic boyfriend of yours?' she asked.

'No! No! Rob wouldn't turn up in the middle of the night,' I said with certainty. 'And it's the flat door, not the main entrance. Whoever it is . . . '

'. . . is already in the building,' she interrupted, sounding like a police chief inspector.

The battering intensified. We rushed into the hall and gawked at the closed door.

'Who goes there?' I shouted in a nervous jumpy voice.

Lulu tossed me a scornful glance. '*Who goes there?*' she hissed, brows drawn. 'Idiot! You sound like Sherlock Holmes.'

I knotted my dressing gown belt.

'Miranda!' Came the muffled reply.

Lulu and I exchanged bewildered glances.

'Who?' we chimed.

'Miranda!'

'Who the fuck is Miranda?' Lulu asked me in a dramatic whisper, throwing the door open.

A slim girl with an oval face, framed with long brown hair and huge dark eyes, stood smiling in the doorway.

'I wondered if I could borrow a camera. I'm going on holiday for a week and I don't have time to unpack, and I . . .' she trailed off catching our wide-eyed, open-mouthed expressions. 'Oh! I'm Miranda, I've moved in upstairs,' she explained brightly.

Smiling, she extended her hand.

I shook it robotically.

'Do – you – know – what – time – it – is?' Lulu asked, her voice dripping poison.

'It's *four* o'clock in the morning,' I told Miranda stiffly.

Miranda's hand flew to her mouth.

'Is it really? I have to be at Gatwick by five-thirty! I'll have to get a move on, won't I?' she said conversationally.

Lulu's eyes were screwed up with fury. She pivoted and strode into the lounge, returning with her old digital camera.

I peered at Miranda from under my fringe. She had a nerve!

Lulu slapped the camera in Miranda's palm.

'Thank you so much,' Miranda said.

'Have a nice time,' Lulu replied slamming the door in Miranda's face.

Lulu and I eyed each other in astonishment.

'The cheek of her, the barefaced bloody cheek of her!' Lulu said.

'Well you couldn't have thought it that much of a cheek, you gave her your camera.'

'That camera is as old as the hills; I don't care if I never see it again.'

There was a sudden volley of knocks on the door. Lulu gave me an incredulous look and pulled the door open.

'Any chance of borrowing the charger?' Miranda asked, cool as you please.

Lulu didn't know quite how to reply to this. Her face darkened. She turned on her heel and walked back into the lounge. Returning with the charger.

'Anything else?' Lulu asked, her voice sodden with venom.

'No thanks,' Miranda said. 'We should get together as soon as I get back.'

'No rush,' Lulu said, giving her an icy stare.

A flicker of recognition danced in Miranda's eyes. She clicked her fingers, and tilted her head in thought.

'Hey, that voice, I know it, don't I? You're not Lulu from *Good Morning, this is the Capital*, are you?' Miranda asked, with a beaming smile of adoration.

Lulu's hand clutching the doorframe slid up a notch, she pouted with pride and her eyes shone with gratification.

'Yes, yes, I am actually,' Lulu said.

I rolled my eyes.

'I love your show; I listen to you *every* day. I'm your biggest fan. I haven't smoked for three weeks,' Miranda boasted.

247

'Well done! I love to hear a success story. Let's get together for a couple of drinks when you get back from your holiday ... And welcome to the building.' Lulu said enthusiastically.

Miranda beamed.

'Where are you going? Anywhere nice?' Lulu asked chummily.

'Lanzarote,' Miranda told us, eyes shifting between Lulu and me.

'I've been there, you'll love it,' Lulu said, with a warm smile.

Miranda glanced at her watch pointedly.

'I'm sure I will,' she said, backing off.

'Anytime you want anything, just pop down,' Lulu told her.

'Thank you,' Miranda replied, edging towards the stairs.

'Bye then,' Lulu said, craning down the lobby.

She closed the door with a slow gentle click, and turned to me.

'It makes such a difference having a friendly face around. The doctors who lived upstairs were miserable bastards ... I'm wide awake now, shall we have a hot chocolate and you can tell me how good a shag John Jackson was?'

Chapter Seventeen

I switched on the radio. Lulu's voice rumbled around the bar. I loaded wine glasses into the dishwater absently. Whoever had worked the bar last night hadn't done a very good job of cleaning up.

'And it's over to Suzie from Bracknell on line three,' Lulu announced. 'Hello Suzie!'

Suzie from Bracknell gave a windy sigh.

'I haven't had a cigarette for eleven days,' Suzie said loudly, as if yelling the words added significance.

There was a round of applause in the studio and the 'congratulations' jingle.

'Well done Suzie!' Lulu boomed.

'I'm finding it hard. I'm not myself. I stopped my car to let a pine cone cross the road, it looked like a hedgehog,' Suzie confessed.

'Suzie . . . totally understandable, you were hallucinating as a result of nicotine withdrawal,' Lulu told her.

'I'm drinking too much,' Suzie said bluntly. 'Last night on the way home from the pub I took my tights off and gave them to a homeless drunk. My tights, in public! I've never done anything like that before.'

'Well first of all drinking too much is the logical thing to do,' Lulu said wisely, 'because if you pass out you won't be tempted to smoke. And Suzie, you obviously have a kind heart to be giving your tights away. This generous nature manifests itself when you've had a drink. I wouldn't worry about that. I'm exactly the same,' Lulu said in a gussied voice.

I stopped loading the dishwasher to ponder Lulu's claim to a generous nature. I'd never seen it.

'My mood swings are terrible,' Suzi said in a rush. 'I finished with my boyfriend because he wouldn't give me the last of his pizza, and, OK, he had asked me if I'd wanted one when he bought his, I hadn't, but I changed my mind.'

'Women's prerogative,' Lulu interrupted. 'Tell me Suzie, this boyfriend you finished with. Did the ratio of sex you got from him compensate for the aggravation of putting up with him?'

There was a charged hush. I eyed the radio in anticipation.

'No, actually,' Suzie admitted at last. 'It didn't.'

'So, in brief, you haven't had a cigarette in eleven days. And as a result you have become an astute and cautious driver, a more benevolent and charitable person and you've got rid of a man who didn't appreciate you.'

Suzie made an interested 'mmmmm' sound, as she pondered this revelation.

'Well done Suzie! You are an inspiration!' Lulu boomed.

'Oh! Do you think so?' Suzie from Bracknell asked.

'Yes! Yes I do! And now it's time for the news and weather.'

I closed the dishwasher as the first customer of the day ricocheted the door against the wall.

I was exhausted. I had never worked a full shift without Nikki before. He makes tending the bar appear effortless. It's anything but. I was on the point of collapse.

250

Going to Paris on Friday would be a welcome break from the purgatory of running this place. I couldn't wait.

Lunch and the afternoon rush were mercifully over, and there was still an hour left before Happy Hour began. I sat on a stool, slumped across the counter, hair sticking to my face with sweat and my chin resting in the crook of my bent elbow. I was too tired to eat, and couldn't be bothered to pour myself a drink.

The front door rattled, and I turned to see Nikki, his hand flat against the glass door, pushing his way into the bar. His finely chiselled features and high cheekbones were brought to life by his broad smile, and his brown eyes shone with excitement. He looked giddy with happiness, and stylish and sophisticated in a navy suit, white shirt and maroon tie.

I jumped off the stool and rushed towards him, as if he'd been on manoeuvres in Afghanistan for the past eighteen months, and this was the moment I'd been waiting for, our reunion! His heavy step collided with my urgent dash. I bashed my forehead on the line of his collarbone. He clamped my elbows and held me at arm's length; as I tilted my head back, our eyes locked.

'I can't do this,' I wailed. 'How come you can open a bottle of wine while the Guinness tap is running, but when I tried to do that, Guinness frothed all over my feet. And how do you pour two bottles of lager at the same time? I can't, my hands are too small. And I *constantly* have to look up recipes for cocktails. You don't because you know them by heart. It takes me ages! I get pissed off, and the customers get pissed off!' He nodded slowly while he followed my argument. '*And* we need a new corkscrew,' I said, grabbing his forearms and physically shaking this piece of information into him. 'And the phone doesn't ever bloody stop; and there is *definitely* a knack to working the cap-puccino machine, and—'

He pressed a silencing finger to my lips, and drew a deep breath.

'One thing at a time,' he said, slowly.

He put his arm round my shoulders and guided me to the alcove table.

'Have you cashed up?' he asked.

'Yes,' I said, 'but . . .'

'Have you phoned in the wines and spirits order?'

'Yes.'

'Have you been to the bank?'

'Yes.'

'Did everyone do what you told them?'

'Yes, but that's not the point! I'm rubbish at this, I'm exhausted and I hate it, and I feel like crying at the thought of ever doing it again.'

He sat down and pulled me on to his lap, he palmed his thick hair.

'I can't do it, Nik. I'll work longer hours if you like, I'll take on more tables if that helps, but don't ask me to work behind the bar. I'm a waitress, not a barman.'

His brows flicked upwards, he gave an indulgent sigh, and folded his arms around me.

I felt heat flood my cheeks.

'I'm NOT doing it,' I told him, resolute.

He gave a couple of lazy blinks.

'Evie, tomorrow is a big day for me. I'm meeting the building control officer and the bank manager. I need to raise more finance to renovate,' he said, slow and serious.

I sat straight.

'What time are your meetings? How long will you be gone? That doesn't sound too complicated. Two meetings, could you dash out and dash back?'

I would do an hour or so behind the bar, if press-ganged, no more than that. Definitely not!

He rubbed his chin thoughtfully, then the back of his neck.

'I'll be out most of the day,' he said his tone apologetic.

I gave a distraught gulp.

'Nik I'm not cut out for this!' I held my breath.

What was I doing sitting on his lap?

The lines round his eyes creased as he smiled.

'Evie, you'll be fine,' he said softly.

Nikki's hand slid under my hair, a warm tickle travelled my spine. He dropped his head and pressed his lips to my forehead, my back stretched into his touch. He took hold of my arms and gently placed them round his neck, and then circled my waist and pulled me to him. I felt his mouth curve into a grin against my hairline. We sat still. I closed my eyes, it felt nice . . . and . . . I felt safe and whoosy, because I was so tired, and sooooo comfortable, and . . .

'Evie,' he whispered.

'Mmm.'

'I'm meeting with a team of builders on Friday, is there any chance you could ask Tina to cover for you in Paris, just this once, because I really need you?'

I gave a gasp of outrage. I pulled my arms from around his neck, lost my balance slid off his lap and landed on the floor with a thud.

'No! No way!' I insisted, shaking my head.

He bent down and picked me up.

I slapped his grip from my elbows. He loomed above me.

'I am *not* cancelling Paris.'

He spread his arms wide.

'I'll pay whatever you would have earned over the weekend.'

A scowl settled over my face.

'Money has got nothing to do with it.'

'I need you, Evie.'

'Oddly I don't need you,' I said, backing away from him.

He walked menacingly forward.

'What do I ever ask of you?' he said loudly.

I mustered my most spirited expression.

'In the last couple of minutes, you've asked for quite a lot actually,' I told him defiantly.

'Evie, that's what friends are for.'

'You don't want a friend, you want a slave. And I don't ask you for anything,' I snapped.

I turned on my heel with a determined pivot, and marched towards the bar to reach for my coat. Nik moved faster, he spun me round and clamped my waist. I found myself dangling six inches from the floor. He deposited me with a thump on the counter, next to the cash register.

His brows creased together sharply, he gripped my wrists and pressed my hands on my thighs. My heart raced. He bent his dark head to mine so we were almost nose to nose.

'One, I broke into your flat when you locked yourself out. It was four o'clock in the morning when you called. I wanted to kill you, but I didn't . . . And I slept the night on your sofa, it was freezing, but I didn't want to leave you alone with a broken window. And I replaced the smashed window the next day.'

I gave an embarrassed cough.

'OK, so, one thing, one thing you did for me, big deal.'

'Two, I drove to Wimbledon to pick you up when you fainted after having your belly button pierced. You threw up all over yourself in my new car on the way home. It was revolting, you were a disgrace, and I didn't complain.'

Actually he had *complained. Loudly.*

'Right, two things.' I admitted.

254

'Three, I came to get you when your car got locked overnight in Bentall's car park in Kingston, because you hadn't the brains to move it before closing time. And I took you back the following day to retrieve it. And I managed to get you off with the overnight parking charges because the attendant was Greek.'

In fairness, anyone could have made the same mistake. I thought all car parks were twenty-four hours. They should be.

'OK, three things. So what?'

'Four, the last time you got speed trapped, I took your points, which means I now have three points on my licence, and you have nine on yours. As opposed to the twelve points you deserve, along with an instant ban.'

Fair enough.

His breath became ragged, and his eyes glinted like match flames.

'And five – five – I *need* you . . . and . . .' his voice trailed.

He dropped his chin on his chest.

'And what?' I shot back. Although to be fair I knew at this point that I wasn't going to Paris.

His gaze sharpened.

'And I've remortgaged the bar, so this property deal has to work,' he said, as though to himself. 'I've mortgaged the bar much more than I should have,' he admitted.

I felt a flash of panic. His whole family depended on their jobs here.

He took a step back and folded strong arms across his chest. His mind worked behind his steely gaze.

'So what's it to be, Evie? Will you do it?' he asked, raising a questioning brow.

I was captured.

'Put like that I suppose I have no choice, do I?'

255

He held my elbows as I slid off the counter.

'And, Evie?'

'What?'

'I would do anything for you.'

He shrugged out of his suit jacket, and tossed it on to a coat hook; it landed with precision.

'I know,' I reluctantly admitted. 'But still, Nik, you're asking a lot.'

He lifted his chin, to unfasten the knot of his tie.

'I know I am. Now call Tina. Tell her you can't go to Paris,' he said jerking his head at the phone. 'And I'll run through what I need you to do over the next couple of days,' he said officiously.

I reached for the phone with grim acceptance. Nikki had rehearsed that speech, reminding me of the inconsequential things any friend would do for another. I was sure of it!

Tina was a lifesaver. I was now scheduled to go to Paris every second weekend, which meant I could help Nikki in the bar, keep my finger on the pulse of the travel circuit and still have the evenings to myself. And on the bright side, suffering from mental and physical exhaustion is marginally better than suffering from depression. Working behind the bar had kept me so busy that I hadn't thought of Rob all day.

I left when Nikki's dad arrived for the evening shift.

A lamp spilled light on to the wet pavement outside the bar. I put up my umbrella, and made a dash across the road to the flat, fresh air rushing in my face. As I edged through the front door, the land line was ringing. I rushed into the lounge and lurched for the handset.

'When am I going to see you Evie? I can't wait any longer,' Rob said.

Instantly I felt the hair on my neck rise.

'I'm busy.'

'Don't I know it?'

'What do you expect?'

'I expect more than this, I expect you to return calls, read texts and keep to arrangements if we make them. I'm coming to see you tomorrow night whether you like it or not. If you're working in that bloody bar, then I'll meet you there.'

'Rob!'

'What?'

'Don't come to the flat or the bar; let's have dinner somewhere on Monday,' I said urgently.

'Monday? . . . Evie, it's only Wednesday now. I'm not waiting the best part of a week. You're obviously not suffering in the same way I am. I think of you every waking minute. I need to see you, we need to talk.'

I felt a clench of nerves and a feverish rush of blood to my head.

'EVIE!'

'Yes, OK, Saturday afternoon?' I conceded.

'Fine, where?'

'The pub on the river in Putney, the Kings Arms.'

No Lulu, Lexy, Nikki, Tina or John there.

'Brilliant, meet me at one o'clock,' he said.

'See you then.'

'No cancellations?'

'No cancellations.'

'I love you, Evie.'

I had no answer to that.

VENICE

Chapter Eighteen

I spent the next two days slipping in and out of consciousness, although at a casual glance it might have appeared I was simply overtired due to masquerading as a barmaid and restaurant manager. Nikki never once showed his face, not once! But although I didn't see him, I certainly heard from him – he called several times a day. He kept me going by means of a fine balance of threats and soothing pep talks. Both were lies. Saturday could not have arrived soon enough.

I dressed for my lunch with Rob in a state of excited anxiety. I tried on the lilac dress ensemble John had bought me, but thought I looked too 'prime minister's wife' for a pub lunch, so I put on my white coat with white trousers and a black top. Then I decided that was too *Sex & the City* for Putney. I soon decided against the white coat, and instead twinned the lilac coat with jeans, and loved it! I tousled my hair, grabbed my Prada bag, slipped my purple ring on to my finger and took one last look in the mirror.

Lulu appeared in the doorway of my bedroom, coffee cup in hand.

'Wow! You look great; that coat looks amazing dressed down,' she said, nibbling a Hobnob. 'Where are you going?'

Damn. I'd wanted to slip out unnoticed.

'Putney,' I swiftly replied.

Her chin disappeared into her neck.

'Putney? Are you joking? No one under eighty shops in Putney. What are you buying, a hamster and a bicycle chain?'

I couldn't meet her eye.

'I suppose I might look at bikes,' I said, which wasn't entirely a lie. I could, you never know.

She pulled another Hobnob from her dressing gown pocket and waved it thoughtfully.

'Right, well, I've got a fold-up mountain bike in the cupboard under the stairs, if you buy a bike; we could go cycling together. Couldn't we?' she said.

There really was no point telling her I was meeting Rob. I mean, it really isn't necessary that she knows all of my business.

'I shagged Vic last night,' she said, deadpan, looking intently at her fingernails.

'That's nice,' I said, trying to edge past her.

She lifted her ribcage and we jammed – C cup to D cup – against each other in the doorway.

'You *could* show a bit more interest,' she grumbled.

I gave her a rigid glare.

'I'm pleased for you, really I am. A shag's fabulous!'

Appeased, she exhaled, releasing me, and smiled. I inched past her.

'I'm seeing him again tonight; he recorded all of my shows. Can you believe it?' she said, following me down the communal hallway.

I squinted at my watch. Quarter to one, I had fifteen minutes. I better get a move on!

'Now that I'm more stable, mentally, I feel able to cope with the pressures of a relationship as well as a thriving career,' she said.

'Now that you're smoking again, you mean,' I said, hand on the front door knob.

She gave a startled gasp, gripped my elbow and whirled me round. Her eyes darted a quick left and right.

'Don't mention that in public, you don't know who could be listening!' she hissed.

I gave an impatient sigh.

'We're not in public; we're standing in the doorway of our building,' I reminded her, stepping into a blue-skied sunny spring day.

'That's public enough,' she said, taking a step back and slamming the door in my face.

I had to stop for diesel which I could have done without – I was running late already. I scrambled out of the car, fought with the petrol cap, rammed the nozzle in the hole and waited aeons and light years until the pump registered ten quid. I can't bring myself to spend more than that on diesel, Lulu feels exactly the same. I screwed on the fuel cap and dashed into the garage, slapped down a tenner in front of the guy in the kiosk, and checked the clock on the wall; it was five minutes to one. Head bent, I hurried out, slowing in the doorway to angle past a woman wearing a squishy puffa jacket browsing the newsstand.

'You're looking good, Evie!'

I froze. A chill swooped from my toes to my eyelashes; I looked up with a jolt.

It was Rob.

I took a half-step back. I had the ridiculous impulse to apologise, the way you do when you bump into someone or tread on their toe.

My mouth went dry.

A smile flicked his lips as his eyes swept over my face. He stood tall, blond and handsome, wearing a white shirt, jeans and a black leather jacket. He lowered his head to mine and planted a soft kiss at the edge of my mouth. I felt a flush rise in my cheeks, and a friction of tiny nerves in my stomach.

He looked amazing.

Like a moron I stared up at him wide-eyed, chewing the imprint of his kiss from my lips.

He peered at me anxiously.

'Are you all right? You look a little peaky.'

I gave a couple of sharp blinks and whizzed the strap of my bag up my arm and on to my shoulder.

'Fine thanks,' I said, trying for a light tone.

He looked at me long and hard.

'I can't tell you how much I've missed you,' he said.

I let his words hang mid-air, tore my gaze from his and fumbled in my bag with rubber fingers for my car keys.

'Shouldn't you be waiting for me in Putney?' I asked, conscious the light tone wasn't working.

I raised my chin, surveying his flushed face. His breathing was faster than usual and a quick pulse beat in his neck. I realised that as calm as he was trying to appear on the outside, he was just as jumpy and rattled as me.

'I watched you leave the flat. I wasn't sure you would come. I wasn't letting you cancel me again. If you hadn't left home when you did, I would have knocked on the door,' he said conversationally.

And Lulu would have answered the door, with a mug of coffee in her hand. The perfect missile, my innards jived at the thought.

'As you'll know if you've been watching me, I've been rushing to keep our appointment,' I told him.

Hands in his pockets, he rocked on his heels.

'Yes, I was glad to see it,' he said, nodding sagely. 'Move your car off the pump, park up, and we'll go for lunch in my car?'

He moved to take my arm.

'No thanks, I'd rather drive,' I said, leaning out of his reach.

He spread his arms wide.

'Evie, why take two cars to the pub?'

As I turned from him my hand grazed his hip, igniting a familiar flame in my chest. I hugged my arms and quickly marched off, heels echoing on the forecourt. I didn't want to soften to him.

He fell in step beside me.

'Surely it's better to go together? Why don't we take my car?'

'I prefer to drive, because . . . because I'm not sure how long I can stay,' I said, arm outstretched, thumb pumping my key fob.

The car door didn't open.

Typical!

I breathed out through my nose, and gave my key a torrent of stabs. It wouldn't budge. My hair fell across my face as I rattled the handle. The door was jammed.

'Evie!'

I threw back my head, searching the heavens for patience. This was simply a matter of pressing a key fob and a door pinging open. Why was it not working? With one hand on the roof and a foot on the edge of the wheel I leaned back, putting a bit of body weight behind the handle rattling. This was hard work.

'Evie, I think . . .'

'I don't care what you think, I'm driving!' I said, cutting him off. 'And that's final!'

A bead of sweat trickled down my cleavage.

'Evie, the thing is . . .'

Bloody hell, my arm was aching.

'THE THING IS, I AM VERY BUSY TODAY, SO . . .'

'EVIE!'

I wheeled and pushed my damp hair from my face.

'What?' I snapped.

He put a calming hand on my shoulder, and spoke over-slowly.

'You drive a white Clio which is sitting on Pump 4. We are standing at Pump 9 and you are trying to open this white Honda with your key, which is highly unlikely to do the trick,' he explained reasonably, 'because this is not your car.'

I unclenched my hand from the handle and scanned the fore-court; my white Clio sat two rows to the left.

Fists on hips I glared at him, anyone could've made the same mistake.

A tiny smile lifted the corner of his mouth.

'What are you laughing at?' I asked crisply, wiping a bead of moisture from my forehead.

'Nothing babe, nothing at all, you take your own car if that's what you want, and meet me there,' he said. 'In fact I'll follow you.'

'Fine!' I said.

I watched him from the sanctuary of my Clio. He laughed all right. In fact at one point he bent over double, forehead on the steering wheel. He soon made a swift recovery when he caught my piercing stare in my rear view mirror.

As I parked outside the pub an overwhelming rush of nerves exploded inside me, what the hell was I doing? I seemed to be suffering from some sort of respiratory delay. I patted a bit of air into my chest and got out the car. I was here now; I may as well listen to what Mr Harrison has to say for himself.

Rob's car pulled up behind mine.

My breath caught in my throat as Rob, hand resting in the hollow of my back, guided me through the pub. He pulled out my chair with a gallant gesture at a table by the window, over-looking Putney Bridge, and took the seat opposite, tipping forward so close that I could see the reflection of my face in his eyes. Nettled, I busied myself napkin folding, as the waiter unloaded a basket of bread, cutlery and menus. Rob ordered a bottle of red wine and we both decided on peppered steak.

'New coat, babe?' he asked, giving me an admiring glance.

'Yes, John bought it for me in Holland.'

His eyebrow shot up.

'That was kind of him,' he said.

'Yes it was.'

There was a reflective pause. Chin on spired fingers, he gave a weary sigh.

'I owe you an explanation,' he said at last.

'You do,' I agreed, shrugging my coat off.

I was nervous. I felt like a froth of Coke bubbles had erupted in my windpipe. I hated myself for it. I had wanted to be aggressive and in control, this was all wrong somehow.

Get a grip Evie, I thought, swallowing a lump of rising panic.

I fixed an attentive scowl on my face, and relaxed back in my seat, one hand wide on the table.

'Evie, you and I, well, it happened so quickly. We met and nine hours later we were in bed,' he said, voice neutral.

I lifted an eyebrow in agreement. I couldn't fault his observation on that point.

'The first long weekend we spent in Paris was the happiest four days of my life. For me it was love at first sight, as clichéd as that sounds.' He spread his arms, in a gesture of surrender. 'I didn't mean it to happen the way it did between us, and I'm sure it took you by surprise. How could I sit you down and say, "Oh by the way, I'm married",' he asked, shaking his head. 'I knew Cassie and I had come to the end of the line, it was simply a matter of me moving out of the house. And I did move out! Within two weeks of meeting you.' He drew a massive sigh.

'And then, every time I tried to tell you, somehow I couldn't find the words.'

A bottle of wine and two glasses were placed on the table. Rob gave the waiter an absent thank you and lifted the bottle to pour.

'Then, babe, there was your fight with a motorcycle in Paris.' He closed his eyes at the memory.

I shivered at the recollection. A motorcyclist had tried to snatch my handbag. With martyred principle I'd clung on to my bag, and as a result I had collided at high speed with a concrete pillar.

'To this day I feel a wrench in my guts when I think of the state you were in. There was *no way* I could have risked hurting you. I would rather have been shot . . . I put my life on hold to look after you, you know I did,' he said.

There was a wordless pause. I think this was to give me the opportunity to suffer an attack of gratified nostalgia: I didn't. Although it was true, he had looked after me. I watched thirstily as the wine bottle dangled mid-air. Was he ever going to pour it?

I decided to move the story on a pace.

'And then of course while I was recovering you met Helen, and had a bit of rumpy pumpy when you found yourself with a vacancy in your bed,' I said.

He flinched. And blushed.

'Slut!' I snapped.

'Once!' he protested. 'It happened once,' he said.

At least that got him pouring the wine. I reached for my glass and took a greedy gulp, quickly followed by another. The potent firey liquid, aided by an empty stomach, fast-tracked my blood-stream, causing a welcome wooziness.

'Once too often,' I volleyed, taking another couple of swift sips.

'OK, I was wrong, and I apologised, and you made me suffer, cutting me out of your life for months. And we agreed to move forward and to put it behind us,' he said.

I gave an indignant sniff.

'Your one night stand with Helen hardly seems important now, does it? In view of the recent Robert Harrison revelations. What was your game plan? When were you going to tell me you had a wife?' I asked. 'This year? Next year?' I pressed on, tilting a palm side over side.

He opened his mouth to say something, thought better of it and clamped his lips together. I took three greedy sips of wine, enjoying his discomfort.

Elbows on the table, hands clasped, he gave me a challenging stare.

I wasn't sure I liked his expression. I reached for the bottle and tipped a generous amount of wine into my glass.

He bowed his chin to his chest.

'I wanted us settled in our own home; I wanted to prove my commitment to you, to get you everything you wanted. I did what I thought was best for us. So much was happening. Me expanding the business, us not having the flat to ourselves, and . . .'

He lifted his head slowly.

'And you having to scooter up and down the M40 to visit your family.' I added, helpfully.

His eyes narrowed with hidden thoughts.

'Were you planning on committing bigamy, Rob? Because let's not forget you asked me to marry you.'

'I'll be divorced by September,' he said with a smile in his voice, as if this was brilliant news and I should be delighted to hear it.

I tossed the remainder of my drink down my throat and

poured another – my third glass, which conferred on me the feeling of enhanced wits (alcohol sharpens our perception before it sends it blindly walking into walls).

'So, are you having Cassie assassinated at the end of August? Because unless I misunderstood her, she has no plans to divorce you.'

There was a deafening silence. His already pale face grew paler. I had vowed to take this calmly, and if I say so myself I was doing a champion job of it.

A thought pierced my mind, I eyed him hawkishly.

'Did you actually stay in hotels when you went to Birmingham? Or did you stay at . . . at *your house*?'

He sat straight; he held his glass in a white knuckled knot.

'Evie, I have *never* lied to you.'

'Liar.'

I tipped the neck of what was now an empty bottle into my glass. Had I drank it all? I must have! I swung the empty bottle like a ticking pendulum. The waiter got the hint. Rob lifted a disapproving brow, but made no comment. Thoughts scuttled madly across his face. He was rattled, very rattled. I was winning here, it was obvious. I looked around the bar to see if anyone else looked as triumphant as me. No one came close.

My elbow slid off the edge of the table. How did that happen?

On impulse Rob's hand shot out to steady me.

'OK, I didn't tell you everything and I clearly should have,' he conceded.

I eyed the food placed in front of us with something less than enthusiasm. Rob on the other hand dived straight in.

'Evie, eat something,' he said, slicing his steak.

'I'm not hungry,' I told him, sipping my replenished drink.

He cast narrowed eyes.

'You look as though you've lost weight babe, in fact; maybe you've lost too much.'

I was revving myself up to mention Marcus, the thought of him made my heart thud. I took a generous swallow from my glass. The wine was beginning to make me feel a little sick, I thought of ordering a gin and tonic to settle my stomach.

Rob laid down his cutlery and watched me closely, blue eyes hooded in thought.

'What?' I snapped, filling my glass.

'Evie, you're drunk.'

'I'm not,' I counter-attacked, shooting him a look like a blow torch.

'You are.'

'OK, so maybe a little.'

'Take it easy,' he said.

'Take it easy! You have a wife and . . . *a son*, and you're telling *me* to take it easy. It's almost April, Rob. You've had since last July to tell me. I can't accept there was never an opportunity to—'

'I tried, Evie. I tried when we were in Barbados. It played on my mind every minute of the day.'

'No it didn't, *shagging* played on your mind every minute of the day,' I reminded him. 'This married man scenario isn't the deal I signed up for. I thought I was going out with a single guy, without a care in the world. Someone I could share first experiences with, not someone who's been there and done it all. Not someone with more baggage than British Airways. '

Pwew! I was doing great, I sounded harsh and sober.

He gave a despair-soaked sigh.

'I love you, Evie. I'll do whatever I have to, to get us back on track.'

'If you had been honest from the start we could've dealt with this!' I said in an airy voice.

268

'Then deal with it now! Evie, I want to take care of you for the rest of my life. Let me.'

He tipped forward and gripped my chin between forefinger and thumb, forcing my gaze on his.

There was a charged hush.

'Tell me you don't love me,' he challenged.

I couldn't.

My heart beat like a drum. The draught of his breath was on my face, and his eyes, deep blue, were no more than three inches from mine. The familiar tingle at the base of my spinal cord took me by surprise; my body, if not my mind, still wanted him, badly.

His gaze sharpened.

'If you don't want me to maintain contact with them, I won't. If that's what I have to do to get you back, then fair enough. I won't see them again!' he said officiously, his tone even.

The impact of what he said knocked me sideways. Blood throbbed in my temples, and a coil of repugnance unwound inside me. I moved back from his reach and gave him a look of horrified disgust. Because with sickening clarity I knew that he meant it. I also knew there was every possibility the heartless spear he was tossing around at the moment could be directed at me one day.

I shot to my feet, grabbed my coat and bag, and made a determined effort for a straight line to the door.

'Evie! Where are you going?'

Striding in my wake he was hindered fielding three elderly ladies, which gave me the split second I needed to march through the swing doors on to the high street and hail a taxi.

I dropped into the cab's leather upholstery and hugged my bag to my chest. Did I still love him? The truth was, yes, I did. He was like a drug, a drug that I craved. What a horrid thing to suggest, that I would prefer him not to see his little boy. I felt a shimmer of loathing as a thought occurred to me: if I had a child, he could turn his back on us one day, just like he was proposing doing to Cassie and Marcus. I swallowed. What was wrong with me? I had to forget him. I had to. A one night stand, a wife and a son, and I've only known him eighteen months! Who knows what would be next.

Chapter Nineteen

At home, Nikki and Lulu paced the lounge like a couple of BBC bonnet drama protagonists. I sat slumped in the sofa, drunk and drained. I tipped forward and hugged my knees.

There was a sharp silence.

They exchanged stiff glances. Lulu looked like a fifties wife: dressing gown, bed socks and big rollers in her hair. With her brow set in an irritated crease, she gestured her arms at the ceiling.

'What were you thinking, meeting Rob? What was the point?' she asked with tortured patience.

'I had to see him,' I said, pulling a tissue out of my bag.

'To what end?' she asked, baffled.

I sat straight and blew my nose briskly.

'Closure!'

Her eyes were wide.

'And did you get it? Eh? Did you?'

I sighed, deflated.

My three-second hesitation was all it took to send her internal thermometer rocketing.

'You've got to be joking!' she exploded, rollers bouncing. 'All right he's one shag-a-licious bastard, I'll grant you that, but there are loads of shag-a-licious bastards out there,' she yelled, stabbing a finger over towards the window.

I looked out at the queue at the bus stop. There were definitely no shag-a-licious bastards waiting for the 220 to Shepherd's Bush.

'I don't tell you how to live your love life,' I counter-attacked.

'No you don't, but that's because my love life is straightforward and I'm not going out with a faithless lying good-for-nothing toad.'

Nikki leaned against the fireplace, face set in stone, arms folded, vigilant.

My face crumpled.

Nikki caught my haunted expression; he fired Lulu a warning glance.

'You've said enough,' he warned her.

Lulu jammed her hands in her dressing gown pocket and set her lips in a tight line.

'Why don't you go and put the kettle on,' Nik asked her.

She whirled to face him.

'The kettle?'

'Yes, the kettle.'

She exhaled heavily and trudged out the lounge and down the hallway.

Nikki crossed the room. He dropped into the sofa next to me.

I waved my hanky.

'I know . . . I suppose you think I'm mad and you're going to tell me I'm pathetic, and, and . . . ' my words came tumbling from my lips in an awkward rush. 'I felt that after all the time Rob and I had spent together, that we couldn't end the relationship by text,' I said with a powerful sniff.

Dark slanted eyes went out in my direction. I held Nik's gaze.

'Could we?' I pitched in earnest.

'Why not? That's exactly what he deserves,' Nikki said in a razor tone. 'And no, I don't think you're mad, but I do think there's truth in what Lulu says. I can hardly believe I'm saying this, but I think you should listen to her.'

He surveyed me for a minute or so. The room was still. I sensed he had something to say, something I would not want to hear. I didn't like where this was heading, so I decided to change the direction of conversation.

'I'm pleased to see you Nik, but if you don't mind me asking, why are you here?' I asked. 'You don't usually visit in the afternoon.'

'I came to drop your money in, I thought as you weren't going to Paris you might need it.'

I squeezed his forearm in thanks.

'Evie.'

'What?' I asked.

'Listen to Lulu,' he said, as though thinking out loud.

'I will.'

A movement caught at the side of my eye.

'Drinkies,' Lulu announced, siding through the door, balancing a wobbly tray of sliding gin martinis.

I sat up slowly.

'Evie, I thought that since you're pissed already, we may as well have a schooner or two,' she said, handing Nikki and I a glass. 'You'll slip into unconsciousness within the next hour, and I'll be wired and charged, ready to rock, and as horny as a stoat and looking forward to my date with Vic.'

I nodded and sipped my drink; slipping into unconsciousness sounded good to me.

Mindful of her brimming glass, she sank slowly into the arm-chair.

'Look at you. You're all that a man could want,' she said, giving me an admiring glance. 'You need to get Rob out of your head.'

'I agree,' Nikki chimed. 'Listen to her,' he told me.

'Just keep reminding yourself he could be a grandfather soon.'

I gave a distant shrug.

She gulped her gin thoughtfully.

'Or even better, ask yourself why his wife was allowed to keep her credit cards and he confiscated yours.'

I'd forgotten about that. Although I think I'd worked out the answer to that for myself. Cassie spent £8.50 in River Island. What did she buy, a bar of chocolate? Even on a bad day, when you're hungover, or too fat, you can always spend a swift fifty quid in River Island. Always.

'What you need is a girls' night out,' Lulu announced gaily.

'Listen to her,' Nikki repeated energetically.

I sighed. That was the third time he's said that.

'You need to pick up a bloke, take him home, and have a good ride. Because the way to get over one man is to get under another,' she said with a wise frown.

Nikki thumped his glass on the table.

'Do not listen to her! Have an early night,' he said, 'by the looks of things you need it,' he added, prising my drink from my hand.

I was working in the bar. I wiped a cloth over the counter in a dreamy figure eight. It's been two whole weeks since my lunch with Rob, and without fail he has sent at least three texts a day. He's stalking me via cyberspace. I considered changing my phone number, because ignoring him was becoming increasingly difficult. I sent a message to tell him to leave me alone, and I meant it. Hand on heart, I did – or at least I *thought* I did, but it was so hard. I still wanted him, but I couldn't confess that to anyone, not on pain of death. Hands up anyone brave enough to admit that pure sexual desire has won out over common sense at some time in their life.

Just the thought of Rob is enough to ignite an eruption of desire so strong it's like a sucker-punch, leaving me breathless, wanting, and occasionally light-headed. I was addicted to him; there was no two ways about it. *I, Evie Dexter, am addicted to Robert Harrison.* In the same way Lulu is addicted to fags.

My eye drifted to the door, a fierce gust of wind quickened the step of two busty ladies, our first customers of the day. I gave them a smile as they bustled into the bar in a flurry of shopping bags and umbrellas.

'I'll be back by three o'clock,' Nikki said, marching past at a formal pace, immaculate in a navy suit and lemon shirt.

I felt a jolt of panic; I whipped the cloth into the sink.

'Just a minute,' I shouted, sidestepping the bar.

I hurried in his wake, lurched forward and grabbed his arm. He whirled round.

'You told me you would be here all day today. Where are you going?'

'Something has cropped up, I have to go out,' he said, casually tightening his watch strap.

'What? What has cropped up?' I asked, eyeing him urgently.

He sighed with forced patience, took a step forward and pressed his palms down on my shoulders.

'Evie, I'm paying a team of eleven blokes to renovate my building,' he said slowly. 'I have to make sure they keep to speed. I don't have to spend all day there, but I *do* need to pop in and out.' He gave my cheek an affectionate tweak. 'And sweetheart, you can *guarantee* that whatever time it is I show up, they're having a tea break.'

'Can't you just call? And ask them what they're doing, perhaps you could—'

He cut me off.

'You cope brilliantly. Just look at this place,' he said, waving his arm in a gallant sweep. 'You have blackboard wine lists and jugs of the most popular cocktails prepared and chilled.' His eyes grew wide in admiration. 'That was a fantastic idea,' he said with overstated enthusiasm. 'You have new 50ml wine carafes, another stroke of genius because hardly anyone orders wine by the glass any more. I should have put you behind the bar months ago. Honestly sweetheart, if you carry on the way you are, I'll be redundant.'

'But Nik, it's, it's . . .'

His hand drifted to the hollow of my neck.

'It's what?' he asked, chocolate eyes assessing. 'It's not *me* you want, is it?' he asked with a grin in his voice.

'Yes it is. It is you I want. I want you behind the bar, ordering stock, filling fridges, cashing up, and going to the bank.'

He placed his hands around my waist and lifted me up.

'And you'll have me; just give me another couple of months,' he said, setting me on my feet.

'Months! You've got to be joking!' I shrieked, voice shaking.

He grabbed my wrist and twisted my arm behind my back. I stumbled towards him.

'You can run this place better than I can, and you know it. And I love you for it, and you know that too. I'll make it up to you, I promise, just see me through the summer, and I'll never ask you for another favour,' he exhaled a stiff smile. 'You know what's at stake.'

This was blackmail, there was no other word for it.

He kissed my forehead.

'Don't eat until I get back. I'll take you out for dinner,' he said.

And with that he was gone.

Chapter Twenty

I was back in Paris. I spread my arms with a blissful smile and lay down on the grass in the grounds of Malmaison, the April sunshine warm on my face. My group had filtered into the château, and so I had two hours to enjoy the scents and tranquillity of the gardens and read my biography on the Empress Josephine.

I had mixed feelings about escorting these Paris fly tours. The clients are in their forties, fifties at most, and fairly independent. They take themselves off on public transport in search of restaurants and monuments, clutching internet trip advisor printouts. I hardly see them, whereas the coach tour passengers, who are seniors, hang on my every word like I'm the charismatic leader of some tourist cult. They literally break a leg following me around. This younger crowd suit me perfectly at the moment. They don't really need me in a hands-on kind of way; they just need me as a means of getting from A to B. Sure I was missing my coach tour grannies, but I had to admit they wouldn't be getting their value for money from me; my mind just wasn't on the job. My mind was lost in lustful reflection, overflowing with thoughts of Rob.

Two elderly ladies lifted their voice in greeting above the drone of a lawnmower. I returned the gesture, gave the gardens a wistful look and opened my book. Josephine Bonaparte was an inspiration, she was! I flicked back a couple of chapters to refresh my memory. Josephine had moved into a convent on the insistence of her first husband, Alexandre. Fortunately she had the presence of mind to book into a convent-slash-spa, more of a hotel really, where she spent her days sat around gossiping in a comfortable salon, as opposed to a draughty cave of a place where everyone chanted Hail Marys morning, noon and night. She didn't let convent life get her down; she kept her chin up and her spirits high. She was smitten by Alexandre, and did want him, but she was a master at divorcing her head from her heart, always putting her own best interests first. I sighed. Obviously I had to try to divorce my head from my erogenous zones. It was here in black and white – if it worked for Josephine, it should work for me.

The guillotine finished Alexandre off, so we don't actually know if Josephine would have taken him back, or tried to live happily ever after . . . but knowing her now as I feel sure I do, I think she would have dumped him.

Credit where credit is due, Josephine bewitched and married Napoleon, even though Napoleon had his heart set on finding an heiress. Josephine led Napoleon to believe she was rich, which in fairness is an understandable purple lie to tell, because in those days it was fashionable to have a dowry. Nowadays, it's fashionable to be skinny, so it's no difference to me telling a bloke I'm a size eight when I'm really a twelve.

And she lied about her age; she told Napoleon she was twenty-nine when she was thirty-two. Think of the genius involved in keeping that lie going year after year. Did she have a party on her fortieth, I wondered to myself, admiringly.

And after she had married Napoleon she took lovers. She learned in the convent that infidelity was acceptable and even expected. (At least her time there hadn't been wasted!)

And she was a fanatical shopaholic, which in itself is an inspiration. I had to marvel at her cunning. I mean, how do you pass off a new crown as though you've had it for years, or bought it in the sale? It must have been tough! I had found it hard enough convincing Rob that Primark had a Karen Millen concession . . . A fair bit of Josephine's day was spent scuttling along the corridors of Versailles hiding in doorways from merchants she owed money to. Imagine Barclaycard employees stalking you around Oxford Street. I shook my head in admiration and empathy. There was no doubt about it: in the face of adversity, Josephine Bonaparte endured. She overcame all that life threw at her, and I fully intended to do the same. I closed my book with a thoughtful smack and got to my feet. I felt happy and carefree. As soon as I got home, I would arrange a girls' night out. I whipped my phone from my bag. I would text them all now. No time like the present.

Three nights later, Lexy, Lulu, Tina, Miranda and I went to the Pitcher & Flag in Clapham to celebrate my twenty-seventh birthday.

We swayed on our four-inch heels, as the acne-blighted waiter elbowed in to our circle to deposit two bottles of chilled champagne pre-ordered by Nikki. We could have sat down because there were plenty of empty seats, but Lulu preferred to stand at the bar to be jigged and squashed. So that's where we were, getting drinks spilt over our feet and having elbows jammed up against our ribs. Despite this, I felt the happiest I had in ages. I felt relaxed.

'What do you do for a living?' Tina asked Miranda.

'I'm a bids coordinator for an auction house.'

'What exactly does that involve?' Lexy asked Miranda politely.

'Oh! It's very easy and straightforward. I ensure all the accurate procedures, regulations and compliance laws are applied to the bidding processes, and make sure the proper software is correctly installed prior to every sale, so that our worldwide online bidders can take part. I manage the sale schedules and online catalogues and collect and collate all post-sale figures and statistical reports on the different aspects of the program that support the daily operation of each auction. You know the kind of snoresville stuff?'

Lexy's lips parted and her eyes glazed with uncertainty, she hadn't expected to have to concentrate, after all she was on a night out.

'Oh, sounds amazing,' Lexy told Miranda, smiling and holding her glass aloft.

Miranda ploughed on.

'Incident reporting, pre-sale and post-sale quantitative stats showing levels of interest based on registrants versus successful bidders, bla-de-blah-blah. And I present these figures to press and the media – nosy buggers and the scourge of my life,' she said, plucking the strawberry from the rim of her champagne flute and popping it in her mouth.

'Really?' Lexy said, funnelling her drink into her mouth.

'And I handle and approve all clients, liaising with credit control, and legal and risk. We don't want someone bidding a million quid for a painting if they don't have the dosh, do we?'

'No, no, of course not,' Lexy said, belching softly.

Tina and I exchanged surprised glances. I had just about understood all that, I was glad I was still sober. Lulu's expression was blank; she's not interested in career overviews or family sagas.

'Do you have a boyfriend?' Lulu asked Miranda conversationally, although in no real doubt as to the answer. Miranda has large brown eyes, hooded with long spiky lashes and perfectly arched dark eyebrows, which give her a permanent expression of amused surprise.

Miranda took a gulp from her glass, and tugged on a sheet of chestnut hair.

'Kind of,' Miranda said.

Tina lifted an interested brow, as did Lexy.

'I've just started seeing my boss, but the relationship isn't *exclusive* yet,' Miranda explained.

'What does *exclusive* mean?' Lexy asked.

'We haven't yet signed the unwritten agreement of sexual exclusivity,' Miranda explained.

Lexy looked bewildered. She had no idea what Miranda was talking about.

'They both still see other people,' Tina explained to Lexy tactfully.

'That's . . . *different*,' Lexy said with a wrinkled brow.

Miranda wiggled a finger between Lexy and me.

'So, you're sisters?'

Lexy brightened, gave a chummy giggle and reached for my hand. She pulled me to her side.

'Who d'you think is the oldest?' Lexy asked Miranda, beaming, and pressing her cheek to mine.

'You!' Came the reply, flat and correct.

Lexy dropped my hand, smiled artificially and absorbed herself in her drink.

She is the oldest.

'Do you have a sister?' Tina asked Miranda.

Miranda nodded.

'Yes, Bella, she's thirty, she's five years older than me.'

'That's quite a big age gap. Are you close?' Lexy wondered.

Lulu shifted her weight from one foot to the other, and checked her reflection in the mirror behind the bar.

'Yes I suppose we're quite close,' Miranda said brightly.

'What does your sister do for a living?' Lexy asked.

'She's a call girl,' Miranda said chirpily.

Lulu's eyes roving the bar honed in on Miranda, and her brows shot up, almost reaching her hairline.

'Does she make good money?' Lulu asked in an interested rush.

Tina tipped forward, her gossip antenna now on code red, and Lexy looked around worriedly to check for eavesdroppers.

Miranda gave a proud snort.

'She makes a bloody fortune and she deserves it. My sister Bella could suck-start a speed boat,' she said, her chest puffing with pride.

Lulu gasped, and clapped her hand to her mouth in wonder.

'Could she really?' Lulu asked reverentially. 'Would she teach me, d'you think?'

Lexy and Tina exchanged a look of embarrassed surprise. Personally I doubted the speed boat boast.

The night progressed with a captivating account of Bella's proficiency as a hooker. And Miranda telling us about the 'you're sleeping with my sister' discounts she used to get when she was growing up – half-price pizzas, free drinks in pubs and all sorts of other freebies. I was quite envious. I decided Lexy was an abysmal disappointment as a sister by comparison.

'Are you all right!?' Lexy asked me, pitting her voice against the rising hum of the crowd.

'Of course I'm all right, why?'

She sided closer, looking doubtful.

'Because you look absolutely plastered?' she confided in my ear.

I *was* absolutely plastered; mind you, she had a nerve saying that to me, she was no better. We were *all* plastered, especially

Tina, who had just blown her rape whistle in the barman's ear for another round of drinks.

'It's the only time I get to use it,' Tina said, tossing the whistle back in her handbag.

I was wilting. Suddenly the music seemed too loud and the lights over bright, and standing was an effort.

I hadn't seen Lulu or Miranda for ages.

I steadied myself against the bar, stretched on to my tiptoes and had a look around. They were inside the DJ's box, together with a couple of bouncers. Lulu, clearly annoyed, was whirling her arms. Miranda was wide-eyed and taken aback and trying to calm Lulu down. The door to the DJ's box burst open, and Miranda and Lulu exploded out from the booth, manhandled by two bouncers. Affronted and struggling fiercely, they were being marched out of the pub! Tina and Lexy followed my gaze. On impulse we abandoned our drinks, and lurched forward, breaking the crowd, knocking over a couple of chairs as we raced after them.

A yellow light fell from the awning of the bar in a corn circle on the pavement where we stood. I rubbed my arms for warmth.

'I can't believe we've been thrown out of that dump,' Lulu snapped, incensed. 'It's insulting. And for nothing!' She added with a watery hiccup. 'I have a good mind to demand to be let back in, just for the pleasure of walking back out!'

'You must've been thrown out for a reason,' Lexy pressed, piqued.

'We were staging a sit-in in the DJ's box because his music was crap. OK, perhaps Miranda singing, *I whip my hair back and forth, I whip my hair back and forth*, and doing the actions was mildly irritating . . . but hardly offensive,' Lulu said. 'Speaking of which, where is she – where is Miranda?'

We exchanged blank glances.

Tina squinted left and right down the street.

'There she is!' Lexy said triumphantly, pointing in illustration.

I caught my breath, so did Lulu and Tina.

Miranda, drunk and tottering perilously on her heels, was doing her best to wrestle a police dog's leash from its handler.

'I'll take him for a walk!' Miranda insisted, yanking on the lead. 'I will! I love Labradoodles! This is a Labradoodle isn't it? I love walking dogs. Give him to me!'

She was absolutely plastered.

The policeman, equally determined, but crucially distracted by his aerial view of Miranda's cleavage, was losing the fight.

Miranda's face was puce with effort, she was wearing herself out.

'It's − not − fair − expecting − a − dog − to − sit − outside − a − nightclub − all − night!'

She lost her hold on the leash, spun in a circle and lurched for the bus stop for support.

Her eyes met mine.

'Evie! It's a poochy Labradoodle,' Miranda shouted, enchanted.

'I think it's actually a German Shepherd,' I told her flatly.

She frowned at the dog thoughtfully.

'Has someone straightened his hair?' she asked.

A squad car, lights flashing, screeched to a halt and two policeman stepped hurriedly from the car. Backup obviously. Miranda looked startled. Lexy looked worried. Tina looked lustfully at one of the policemen. And Lulu looked pissed off.

'Oh my god, I so fantasise about police uniforms and handcuffs,' Tina admitted.

'She's a fucking nuisance with a drink in her, we'll either all get arrested or we'll get a lift home,' Lulu said, grudgingly marching forward to referee the situation.

We got a lift home. Miranda offered the police driver a tip. He politely refused.

At the flat we played Abba, and drank wine until three o'clock in the morning. We had a great night. It was the tonic I needed, a real pick-me-up-evening. I went to bed feeling fantastic, absolutely fan-bloody-tastic.

VENICE

Chapter Twenty-one

I had all sorts of problems the next morning. Like trying to raise my head from the pillow, open both eyes at the same time and swallow. Sitting up was achieved by flopping on to my tummy and using the bedpost as a climbing frame. It took me over an hour to get out of bed and into the shower.

I had to get to work, I had to. I managed it, but only just.

As I walked into the bar I adjusted my expression to one of stern professional dependability, which was a cheek because I was four hours late. But Nik is no slouch at reading body language or facial expressions. If I showed weakness, he'd pounce. Well if he pounced, so would I. My head was thumping; I haven't had a hangover like this for ages. Nik stood beside the cash register, legs apart, chin high, arms crossed. Like a Roman Emperor at the Colosseum ready to signal the thumbs down, and have me put to death.

He drew a deep breath and marched towards me.

On impulse I reversed.

'Where have you been!?' he bellowed. 'You knew I had a full day of appointments!'

My face flushed crimson, the bar was busy. Knives and forks hovered and conversation halted as everyone stared.

'I came across to the flat. The curtains were drawn and no one answered the door!'

I honestly hadn't heard him, not that I would have answered the door if I had.

Although he was already too close for my liking, he took a final step forward and loomed soberly above me. I so didn't need this.

Bloody hell, Nik is tall, or have I shrunk?

'I told you I had a lunchtime meeting with the planning officer!'

I tilted my chin for battle.

'Don't you dare challenge me!' I volleyed clenched fists on hips. 'All the hours I put in for you, if I'm late or don't show up on the odd occasion, it's no big deal!'

I could feel the blood travelling the length of my neck; we were almost nose to nose.

He tucked his shirt unnecessarily into his waistband, and exhaled noisily.

'Evie, I'm fuming!!'

Aware of our attentive audience I dropped my tone to a dramatic hiss.

'You knew that I was going out last night, and that I would've preferred the day off. You should have offered to cancel your appointments today and work here instead of treading the boards waiting for me to come in, and screaming at me when I get here.'

A minefield of thoughts skittered behind his dark piercing eyes. He was calculating his reply. As well he should. The chances of me turning on my heel and leaving him stranded were 50/50, depending on the next word that came out of his mouth.

He gave me an icy smile.

'I'll be back by six,' he said.

Now to the untrained ear 'I'll be back by six' means 'I'll be back by no later than six p.m.' But I knew better, in this case it was code for one of five things:

1. If I had time to do so, I would strangle you.
2. Sorry, you're absolutely right, I should've worked today because you've done enough.
3. The main thing is you're here now.
4. If you ever leave me in the lurch again I *will* strangle you; I'll make the time.
5. Happy Birthday. Did you enjoy the champagne I ordered for you?

He strode out of the bar and slammed the door without looking back, so hard that the glass rattled in the frame. I closed my eyes to the noise, as did most of the customers.

Lulu and Miranda were in the lounge studiously painting each other's toenails when I walked into the flat after my shift at the bar. Their heads swivelled towards me. I picked up the remote, jabbed on the television and dropped down into the armchair.

The only noise came from the television. Lulu and Miranda remained silent: I watched the television, they watched me.

'What is it?' I asked.

They exchanged confused glances.

'Why are you here?' Miranda asked, holding her nail varnish brush aloft.

'Why shouldn't I be here?'

Lulu gave me a long shrewd look.

'Why shouldn't you be here?' she asked, as if the answer was obvious. 'Why shouldn't you be here?' she repeated.

289

Miranda placed her feet carefully on the edge of the sofa, hugged her knees, and stared at me in earnest.

'This is a two bedroom flat on a main road in Tooting, with an interesting but dreary view of a bus stop,' Miranda pointed out factually. 'And you have an invitation to spend the evening in one of the largest mansions on Park Lane.'

'Even more confusing,' Lulu chipped in. 'Why work in a bar when you have a millionaire chasing you.'

'Chasing me?'

'Yes, chasing you! The call you took before we left for the pub last night from John, he invited you over for dinner tonight. Remember? You do remember speaking to him, don't you?'

'Of course I remember speaking to him, I'm not senile. I called him this afternoon and cancelled; I told him I couldn't make it. I'm exhausted.'

They exchanged a horrified stare.

'You told him you couldn't make it?' Lulu asked, and checked to see if Miranda remained as unbelieving as her. She did. 'Are you mad?'

'I've never met him, but I've heard all about him,' Miranda said. 'If I were you I wouldn't let that one go.'

'John and I are just friends,' I said tartly.

Miranda shook her head wisely.

'*We* are your friends,' she said meaningfully, as if stating a straightforward scientific fact. 'He is *not* your friend. He is a single millionaire.'

Lulu gave Miranda a spirited nod.

'He's handsome, and I mean seriously handsome,' Lulu said. 'He's absolutely minted and he has a good body for an old man. He's not a weedy stoaty head with glasses, which is usually the case with your average Park Lane resident; and he smells nice.'

I found a comb down the side of the chair; I pulled it meditatively through my hair and stared at the ceiling in consideration. I couldn't fault Lulu's observations. Miranda gave me a knowing smile and reabsorbed herself in toenail painting.

'Evie, just tell me straight so I can get on with my life. Do you think you'll ever get back with Rob?' Lulu asked.

This was the first time she'd brought up the 'R' subject in ages. I felt a rush of blood to my head. Miranda screwed the lid on the nail varnish, smiling reservedly. Lulu sat still, her eyes blinking expectantly like a pair of flickering headlamps. It was a minute before I answered.

I gave a brittle smile.

'I'd say not,' I said.

'That's not a no!'

'I don't think I can forgive him.'

'That's not to say you *won't* forgive him,' Lulu challenged.

I ploughed on.

'It would be difficult . . . '

'Difficult is not impossible,' she cut in.

'What do you want me to say?' I snapped, rattled.

'I want you to tell me it's finished, because mark my words, you don't know all there is to know about him . . . And you never will.'

Miranda raised her hands up.

'Why don't you get with that bloke John. He has better cars than the *X Factor* judges. This is a no brainer situation.'

Lulu nodded in agreement.

'The thing is Evie – John could make all of us happy,' Lulu said. 'You could have a wedding at Claridge's, an ivory silk Vera Wang dress with a ten foot train, and a six foot cake!'

'A wedding? What are you talking about?' I interrupted, frowning so hard my head ached.

She was on a roll, her eyes blazing with ideas.

'Celine Dion on the mike, ten bridesmaids also in Vera Wang.'

'A wedding list at Harrods, honeymoon on Necker Island, five-hundred guests. *Hello!* and *OK!* magazines fighting for piccie rights.'

'Alicia Keys on the keyboard, William and Kate in the front pew of the church.'

'A tiara on loan from Garrard. Hell, no, not on loan, the skinflint!' She bashed an adamant fist of the sofa. 'He would buy you one, because you'll wear it again.'

Miranda fidgeted excitedly, matching Lulu's fervour.

'And just imagine what his wedding gift for you might be,' Lulu added.

They both loved this thought so much that they sat dreamily for a minute, arms linked and heads touching, savouring whatever fairytale fantasies were running through their minds.

'Your own little jet,' Miranda suggested.

'A Sunseeker, named *My Wife Evie*,' Lulu guessed.

I sighed.

'Consider it,' Lulu said, 'for all our sakes.'

'Consider what? Consider marrying a man who hasn't asked me, who happens to be married already and is same age as my dad?'

'Yes!' they chorused.

'We're going out tonight, do you want to come?' Miranda asked.

Was she joking, after last night? That police dog nearly bit me, as I angled into the police car.

'No thanks, you two go. I'm happy to have an early night,' I told her.

*

No sooner had Miranda and Lulu left when Rob called. Normally when I see his name on my call display these days I don't pick up, but some internal alarm told me I had to speak to him. I wish to god I hadn't.

His call changed everything.

I felt hollow, bruised and dizzy. I think I was in shock. I sat hunched in my dressing gown, like a turtle in its shell, knees to my chest, rocking back and forth in the armchair. The fire in the lounge was roaring, but the heat didn't seem to be reaching me. I felt drained and numb; but at the same time every single nerve ending in my body was tingling. In one sense I had never felt more alive; in another, I had never felt less like living. A steady rhythmic low-level drone sounded in my ears.

Cassie was six weeks pregnant.

And yes, it's Rob's.

There was, of course, a reasonable explanation. Rob had been drunk, and lonely, and missing me like mad ... But the good news is that I needn't worry, because he then went on to tell me his news changed nothing.

'Changed nothing' he said. Just like that, while I was sitting there feeling physically sick at the thought of him having slept with someone else, even if she was his wife.

Rob quite rightly pointed out that technically we hadn't been 'together' at the time it happened – something he deemed highly pertinent to his argument. Ever the charming optimist, he had gone on to highlight the 'positive side of things' by assuring me that this situation did not in any way change his feelings towards me. Which I thought was very gallant of him.

As I stared into the crackling fire a fog shifted in front of my eyes, and a contraction of panic squeezed my chest. I felt faint. I bent forward, put my feet flat on the floor, and my head between my knees, and closed my eyes to the sound of my own heart breaking.

The decision I'd been torturing over had been made for me. Rob and I were finished.

I told him so and by the end of our call he was in no doubt whatsoever that I never wanted to hear from him again.

Chapter Twenty-two

It's been three months since Rob dropped that bombshell. I have been coping well. It helps that no one mentions him. Ever! In fact, if I refer to him accidentally or conversationally, eyes glaze over, heads turn away and voices drop to a level you'd need a hearing trumpet to pick up. I can understand that – because of that man, I had for a while transformed into a madwoman. I would storm into the lounge and accuse Miranda and Lulu of heinous crimes, such as *laughing*. They would be laughing, watching *Friends* or *Celebrity Juice* or something, but would quickly deny it the moment I walked in the room, quickly switching the channel to something much more suitable, like a programme on serial killers, or obesity, or terminal illness. They would sit side by side, bolt upright, grim-featured and stony silent. Appeased, I would join them on the sofa, my molten wrath cooling to a simmer.

At the bar, I would march between the tables, hands clasped behind my back, like a general inspecting his troops, up and down, again and again. My piercing gaze daring customers to ask me to do anything for them – no one ever did! And I'd buy things in shops just for the delight of taking them back, purposefully, without the receipt. I'd take great pleasure in causing an absolute uproar, to the extent company rules were flouted so that I'd be handed cash for goods I'd bought on credit.

Worst of all, and to my eternal shame, I told Lexy she looked fat in my purple dress. In my defence she has put on a little weight, and the dress did cling to all the wrong places, but I could've been more diplomatic. I had seen her smile buckle, heard her miserable sigh, and had tried my best to back track; but it was too late of course. The damage was done. She had whipped the dress over her head, grabbed the bottle of washing-up liquid, aimed at the kids' leftovers from lunch like an armed policeman, and commenced attack. 'It's the fish fingers,' she'd yelled, 'and the tiddly turtle burgers.'

Only two people gave me as good as they got. Nikki, who had dragged me out of the bar to tell me that if I didn't start behaving myself, and keep a civil tongue in my head, he would treat me like the naughty toddler I was turning into. And John, who had frog-marched me out of the Ritz, saying sulking didn't suit me, nor did bad manners, and until I stopped behaving like a spoilt little madam he wasn't taking me anywhere.

Eventually, I got round to calling Mum and Dad to tell them the wedding was off. Oddly they seemed pleased for me. 'You're too young to be getting married,' they'd said, adding, 'play the field, see the world.'

I cancelled my Paris trips, because apart from a car or a house, a holiday is often the most expensive thing you buy in the course of a year. In my present frame of mind, I knew I wouldn't be giving the clients value for money, and that wouldn't have been fair. Some people save all year for a break; they deserve a tour guide who cares. Tina had been disappointed, but she understood and changed the rota accordingly.

Basically, I sulked the entire summer away and now, it is time to get my life back on track.

Tina has scheduled me for a trip to Venice. I've accepted because I'll be *alone*, with no group in tow. A department of Insignia Tours operates a Mystery Guest Service, where a hotel pays for someone to evaluate their key areas. The hotel in Venice wants a mystery guest familiar with both the corporate market and the world traveller. In short, I'll be a spy, making sure the barman offers the same service at opening time as he does when he's exhausted five hours later. It's crucial that my identity remains secret. If Tina has reminded me of this once, she has reminded me ten times. I mean, what does she take me for? No mystery guest worth their salt would let their guard down. I'll be incognito, sleek and professional. I am looking forward to it. I'll be spending four nights in one of the most magnificent cities in Europe and I cannot wait. I'm going next week, and between now and then I have some apologies to make.

I cornered Miranda and Lulu when they came back from the bakers. I gestured towards the dining table for them to sit down. They exchanged wary glances. We sat at the table, facing each other in a triangle configuration.

'I'm sorry,' I said.

'For what?' they chorused.

'For being so bad tempered and impossible to live with, over the last couple of months.'

Lulu gave a mock yawn.

'Forget it,' she said.

Miranda flapped her hand dismissively.

'It's understandable.'

'I'm fine now,' I told them.

They exchanged a guarded glance.

I was determined to make amends.

'I really want to make it up to you. How about a night out?' I suggested brightly. 'My treat! I'm over Rob, I've moved on.'

'Eer, there really is no need,' Lulu insisted.

'My thoughts exactly,' Miranda chipped in.

I could see they wanted to believe me, but at the same time they were trying to assess the chance that, with drink inside me, I might relapse and turn into the Antichrist again. In fairness it was a reasonable enough concern.

'I think a girly bonding night would be fabulous,' I said. giving them an encouraging smile.

'I have to get up early as you know,' Lulu said.

'And I'm pretty busy over the next week or so,' Miranda said.

I gave a patient sigh.

'Is there anything else I can do?' I asked officiously.

Lulu shook her head good-naturedly.

They don't trust me.

'Anything?' Miranda said, her eyes piercing.

I blinked a yes. Hadn't I just said that?

'Can I borrow your Prada Saffiano-print tote bag for a week?' Miranda asked boldly.

Obviously by *anything* I meant anything *except my Prada Saffiano tote.*

I felt I'd fallen down a hole in the ground. I suffered loss of breath, my breathing became jerky. My eyes grew large. What was I supposed to say?

'Sure,' I managed, lips pursed tightly. 'If that's what you want.'

Miranda beamed.

Lulu's jaw tightened, her stare was laser like.

'Can I borrow the bag for two weeks after Miranda's week?'

I was positively frothing inside. My mouth went dry and my nostrils twitched with rage. I wrenched my hair over my shoulder, and twisted it into a tight tube – so much so that it pulled and hurt at the roots. *One week for Miranda, plus two weeks for Lulu.* Practically a whole month!

'Of course,' I said, standing up and slapping my hands on the table in conclusiveness. 'That's settled then, I best be off to work,' I told them, storming from the room.

Having learned the hard way, I decided I wasn't going to ask Nikki if there was anything I could do to make it up to him. He'd probably have me mopping floors, ironing shirts or cleaning toilets. Anyway, he hadn't put up with my moods, had he? I owed him nothing. I was here working on a Saturday – he should be making up to me. And as for Lexy, she's my sister, so she has to put up with me no matter what. I decided there was no need to make up with her, either, still I would let her keep the Armani jeans she borrowed.

I walked through the door of the bar with a heavy tread, in mourning for my Prada Saffiano tote. I felt sick at the thought of being parted from it. I'd be staying awake at night to make sure it got home safely.

Nikki raised his eyebrows in welcome.

'How are you my angel, my darling, the love of my life, my sweetheart?'

I turned to him with a deep breath, and eyed him suspiciously.

'Why are you so happy, are you on weed or something?' I asked.

'Of course not, don't take your jacket off, we're going out, I have something I want to show you, my mum will look after the place for an hour or so,' he said, sidestepping the bar and walking towards me.

'*You* are taking *me* out, during working hours?' I asked, incredulous.

He clutched my elbow.

'That's right,' he said, spinning me towards the door. 'Actually, the truth is, I need you to do something for me. A small favour,' he confessed, putting his arm around my shoulder.

No surprises there then.

Nikki's Saab, as always, was parked on a double yellow line outside the bar. He's the only person I know with an unconditional immunity agreement with every traffic warden in south-west London.

He opened the car door with a polished gesture.

'Where are we going?' I asked, sliding into the passenger seat.

'To Wimbledon to see my building, it's almost finished,' he said, closing the door with a sharp click.

The tarmac rolled like satin beneath the noble Swedish tyres as Nik pulled out into the line of slow moving traffic.

What had once been a crumbling ruin was now an elegant Victorian-style dwelling comprising four self-contained apartments, each boasting spacious high-ceilinged rooms with oak parquet flooring and huge sash windows with shutters.

On impulse I linked my arm through Nik's and pulled him to me, as we strolled slowly from one freshly painted corniced room to another.

'Nik, it's, it's just. It's,' I floundered, 'fantastic!' I took in a small gasp of admiration. He gave me a shy smile, and, as he met my eye, a patch of embarrassed pride spread across his handsome face. My heart melted at his modesty; he looked like a little boy. I held his arm tighter.

'Show me everything,' I said eagerly.

He pointed out the integrated sound system.

'You'll break it,' Nikki warned, leading me away from a cleverly designed panelled wall in the hallway, housing a docking station and an air conditioning control pad.

300

'Nik I love it, I absolutely love it.'

'What, the docking station?' he said, teasing me gently as we advanced down the hallway. He ushered me into the sunlit kitchen of the ground floor flat. It looked enormous. Unlike the other flats, which were fitted with a range of limed oak units, shiny granite tops and slate flooring, this kitchen was unfurnished and empty.

'I love everything, it's terrific, these apartments are huge, bigger than most houses, and bright and classy and . . .'

I was lost for words. I clapped my hand over my mouth.

'And what?' he asked.

There was a set of double patio doors. Outside, an archway of clematis-covered trellis opened to a pretty walled garden with a York stone paved patio and an emerald lawn with a centrepiece water feature. I turned to him.

'Nik, it's beautiful.'

He grinned with silent pride, reached out and took my hand.

'I have a key. Would you like to see the garden?' he asked, with a gleam of shy delight in his eyes.

I nodded.

'I was thinking about keeping this flat, renting out the top floor flat and selling the other two,' he said conversationally. 'I've purposely held back on installing the kitchen in this one, because the architect thinks I should dig out a cellar. What do you think?' he asked, turning the key in the lock of the freshly painted patio door.

'Definitely . . . Nik, it's fabulous, it's homely and beautiful, and . . . and perfect, and cellars are for wine, aren't they, so why not?'

He held out a steadying hand.

'Be careful, the steps and paving stones haven't been cemented,' he warned.

A scented breeze brushed my hair as I slipped my hand in his and stepped outside. We walked to the end of the garden, turned and looked up at the tall vanilla-coloured building reaching into a blue sky. Nikki, behind me, held my elbows and pulled me to him, resting his chin on the top of my head. A giant wisteria covered almost a third of the house, and the huge casement windows glistened like sheets of metal in the morning sun. It was so *striking*. I felt an unexpected rush of contentment.

I turned to him, blinking against blowing flakes from an orange blossom tree.

'You've done a brilliant job, you're so clever, it's as pretty outside as it is inside.'

He looked delightfully smug.

'I'm so pleased for you, and . . . and proud, and . . . ' I said my voice trailing away.

'Proud?'

I nodded.

'Yes, proud. This is an amazing achievement, Nik. Just think, this is all yours,' I said, eyes scanning the garden.

'I couldn't have done it without you,' he said.

'Without me?'

He gestured towards the house.

'If you hadn't kept the bar going, I wouldn't have had the time I needed to see to this,' he told me.

I nodded, he had a point.

'True.' I said. 'Very true.'

His mouth curved into a smile.

'I'll pay you back,' he told me, his voice low and serious.

I glowed at the prospect.

'In cash or kind?' I asked.

His shoulders lifted as he chuckled.

'In kind, preferably, if you're willing.'

He clutched the lapels of my jacket, raised me to tiptoes and gave me a loud kiss on the forehead.

'I'll take the cash,' I told him.

'You women are all the same,' he said, slowly setting me on my heels.

'What was the favour you wanted?' I asked.

He closed his eyes in thought.

'The favour? Ah yes! I want you to furnish the top floor apartment. I have an inventory list from the letting agent detailing everything I need to provide before I can rent it out. I haven't got a clue where to start; women have a better eye. Will you do it? God help me but I'll have to give you my credit card and pin number.'

'Will I go shopping with your credit card? Of course I will.'

He pointed a finger in warning.

'Behave with the card,' he said sternly.

I gave an affronted snort, as if I wouldn't behave with his card.

'You'll cover in the bar?' I asked. 'While I go shopping?'

'Actually, I was hoping you could go late night shopping, so that you could still work the lunchtime shift.'

He's insufferable.

'What?'

He darted a swift step back and caught my hand as it made its way towards his ear. I wrenched my wrist from his grasp and wheeled from him.

'The thing is Nik, I know you're not joking!' I snapped over my shoulder, wobbling perilously down the uncemented path.

'Evie!' He spread his arms wide. 'What's wrong with late night shopping?' he asked, striding in my wake.

VENICE

Chapter Twenty-three

I called John to ask if he was free for lunch. I told him it was my treat. For some reason he thought that hilarious. He roared with laughter for so long, it was on the tip of my tongue to tell him to bugger off, and that I had changed my mind. I still don't get the joke if I'm honest. I was meeting him at Inamo, a cool Pan Asian restaurant in Soho; the food there is fantastic but John had never heard of it, which frankly didn't surprise – after all, it's trendy, funky, stylish and ultramodern. Unlike John. You select your menu via a touch pad in the tabletop – the order goes straight through to the kitchen, so no need to stand on a chair semaphoring service from gossiping waiters.

I was early, so had a cocktail in the bar and flicked through *Heat*. The man himself was, as always, on time. He looked different to me. There was a shadow of stubble on his face, he wore an open collar without a tie, and the Savile Row suit had been replaced by chinos and a blazer. His eyes roved the bar, stopping when they found me. He smiled. Inexplicably I felt a rush of jittery nerves. As his tall broad frame moved towards me, it struck me that he looked somehow more comfortable dressed-down like this, more relaxed, less austere than usual. I swallowed a giggle, because in his honour I'd actually scrubbed up. I wore a high waisted red skirt with a matching box jacket, and a white frilly blouse that I found in Lulu's wardrobe. I had straightened my hair and tied it in a ponytail at the nape of my neck, and completed the look with a smattering of charcoal eyeshadow and red lipstick.

I slid off the bar stool and hugged him.

'Madam this is a very pleasant surprise, very pleasant indeed. But before I get myself comfortable, I hope you don't mind me asking if your *mood* has improved?'

He held my forearms and looked down at me speculatively.

'Yes, it has,' I said, emphasising the word 'yes'.

He raised an eyebrow, clearly unconvinced.

'It has,' I repeated.

I felt an embarrassed glow flooding my cheeks.

'Actually that's why I asked you to lunch, I wanted to . . . apologise,' I told him, inching on to the bar stool.

His eyes softened.

'Apology accepted, minx that you are.'

'You look different,' I told him, giving him an appraising up and down.

'I was working from home today, so hadn't suited and booted, as they say.' He lifted his hand and palmed my hair. 'And you, my lovely girl, look as beautiful as ever.'

He scanned the bar.

'Shall we go upstairs and eat? I'm starving. It's a little on the bright side in here, is it not?'

I sighed inwardly. It was not on the bright side at all! We made our way up to the restaurant. OK, this is simple. You choose what you want to eat and drink by using an interactive keypad on the table. It's *not* the control panel of a Boeing 747. It's simple. Two kids at an adjacent table were coping brilliantly. John, on the other hand, was not faring well at all. I'd ordered my meal and a glass of white wine; all John had managed to do so far was change the colour of our electronic tablecloth from pink to lemon to a floral design to a purple swirly pattern. He was getting more and more frustrated, I could tell by the way he was jabbing at the keypad much harder than necessary.

I tried for diplomacy.

'Be careful you don't order a taxi home,' I said helpfully.

His head was bent and busy, eyes travelling the screen.

'Why would I want to do that, when I have Alistair waiting outside?'

My finger hovered instructively over his keypad.

'You're not on the illustrated food and drinks menu; you've just pressed the little car icon, and the little car means—'

'I know what I'm doing,' he snapped.

I doubted it.

My glass of wine arrived.

'Can I help you?' I asked him, leaning forward in earnest.

'No, no you can't, thank you.'

I subsided into my chair, sipped my wine and watched him over the rim of my glass. The tablecloth changed colour again, to red and then back to the purple circles.

He harrumphed.

'What is the bloody point of the table changing colour?' he asked, without lifting his head from the keypad.

'The concept is that you set the mood; it's a good idea, don't you think?'

He harrumphed again.

My Alaskan King Crab and Vietnamese Spring Rolls arrived.

I eyed John warily. The local neighbourhood map flashed on his table surface. He still hadn't found the menu icon.

'Would you like to share?' I asked, placing my dishes between us.

'No thank you. I'll order my own,' he snapped without making eye contact.

I speared my King Crab, nibbled it thoughtfully, and contemplated the crown of John's bent head. A waiter placed a bottle of red wine and a bottle of Heineken on the table with overstated precision.

'Are you drinking red wine *and* beer?' I asked John.

'No of course I'm not.'

'It's just that you appear to have ordered both.'

His eyes flicked briefly from his key pad to the wine and beer.

'Have I? Well, I may as well drink both now they're here,' he said crisply.

'John, I'm sure you would much rather get down to the business of ordering lunch, it's just that at the moment you're touring Soho on the locality information section, I'm happy to help and . . .'

He slapped his palms on the edge of the table.

'Get around here now and show me how to work this dammed thing, before I starve!'

I bit my lip to stop myself laughing, stood, and edged around the table. I leaned over him and pulled up the illustrated food menu.

He slipped his arm round my waist.

'Ok, now just look at the pictures and decide what takes your fancy,' I told him. 'When you've decided, press SELECT – I'll do it for you, shall I? You can do it yourself the next time you come.'

His smile from where I stood was lopsided.

'Are you patronising me?'

I squeezed my arm round his shoulder.

'Yes, I think I am, but it's usually the other way around, so let me savour this while I have the chance.'

He turned his head and kissed my cheek.

'Right, well if you must be patronising be quick about it, I'm too hungry to let you humiliate me for long,' he said with mock displeasure.

He wanted Shangai Snapper, Thai Red Curry and Cinamon Chicken. Rather a lot, I thought.

'You have a state of the art study at home. How can you possibly have a problem operating an interactive menu?' I asked, my finger dancing over the keypad.

'I only use the phone in the study,' he confessed. 'And the conference call monitor.'

'No! I don't believe it, all those fabulous toys and you don't play with them!'

I slipped back into my seat.

'Do you use the gym and the swimming pool?'

'Yes, every day.'

'What about the jacuzzi?'

'What jacuzzi?'

'The one beside the pool.'

'Is that what it is?'

I took a greedy gulp of wine, draining the glass.

'You're kidding me.'

He took an equally greedy a gulp of beer.

'I'm not.'

I eyed the bottle of red wine.

'Shall we drink it?' I asked. 'Now that it's here.'

'Why not?' he said, lifting the bottle.

A roar of laughter went up from a table of city gents behind us.

'They're having a good time.'

'So am I,' John said.

'Me too.'

'What are you doing at the weekend?' he asked.

'I'm going to Venice.'

He gave me a curious smile, poured an inch of red wine and performed the ceremonious sniff and sip.

'Are you working?' he asked, sliding a glass in front of me.

I dipped my nose over the rim and inhaled, mirroring him. Not surprisingly it smelled like a glass of red wine.

I leaned forward confidentially; on impulse John did the same. Tina was most insistent that no one discover my identity. I hadn't even mentioned it to Nikki or Lulu, but I could trust John.

He eyed me expectantly.

I dropped my voice to a whisper.

'I'm going to be a mystery guest, and so I'm going alone,' I told him proudly. 'Do you know what a mystery guest is?' I asked politely for form's sake, although almost positive he wouldn't have a clue.

'Of course I know what a mystery guest is,' he said.

'You do?'

'Yes, I do.'

He's such a know-it-all; in fact he's actually a bit of a show-off sometimes, now that I thought of it.

He sat straight and tipped a torrent of wine in our glasses.

'How long will you be in Venice for?' he asked casually.

'I'll be there for four nights, from Friday.'

An infusion of spicy this and cinnamon that, made my mouth water as the Thai Red Curry and Cinnamon Chicken was placed with ceremony between us. I speared a piece of chicken from the dish and popped it in my mouth.

John looked at the food, his expression was blank at first, switching to pensive.

'What's wrong? This is what you ordered, isn't it?' I asked, twirling a strand of noodles around my fork.

Ignoring the food, he eyed his glass with a focused narrowed stare, as though seeing something other than just the wine inside.

He lifted his gaze to mine.

'I'll meet you there,' he said decisively. 'I'll fly to Venice on Sunday morning, and bring you back with me on Tuesday.' There was a smile in his voice, but a question as well, 'If that's all right with you?' he added.

It was a good job my mouth was empty, because when he said that my jaw dropped.

John, coming to Venice to meet me?

He gave me an interrogative glare.

Why not?

'Of course it's all right,' I said.

'That's settled then. I'll see you in Venice,' he said, smiling. 'Now tell me, what have you been up to since I last saw you?' he asked, flapping a napkin open on his lap.

Not surprisingly, John paid.

At home I read through the mystery guest briefing notes. The concept is that I highlight and evaluate potential areas of improvement on a business intelligence basis, starting from the initial point of contact – which, obviously, is making the hotel reservation. I went online to make a booking. I found the web-site and reservations facility simplistic and user-friendly; the whole process only took six minutes – I timed it! – so no real scope for improvement there. Then I rang the hotel to cancel my booking, hoping they would rant and rave, refuse a refund or at the very least not be able to trace my reservation. The charming receptionist took three minutes to process the cancellation, in fact she sounded delighted that I was cancelling, which irritated me slightly, because if you cancel it's for a reason – I could've been ill or something. I called back and rebooked, and the same receptionist was beside herself with joy that I'd changed my mind. So far I hadn't found any areas for improvement. I tried not to be too disappointed because I was hopeful I would find lots to complain about when I got there.

I quickly rang Tina to explain I had just wellied the debt of the third world on my debit card and asked her to transfer the money I had paid for the hotel in advance of me submitting my expense sheet. Not for the first time, I cursed Rob for confiscating my credit cards. I would replace my cards as soon as I had time; it would be an essential part of the healing process. If I couldn't have a fiancé and a wedding, I could at least have a Goldfish card.

Chapter Twenty-four

I emerged from the arrivals hall of Venice airport in to the daylight. There was a warm Adriatic breeze and the sky was a clear blue.

I trundled my suitcase past a sign telling me I was a five minute walk to the Vaporetto – Venice's water bus service. The thing is, I could have sworn I passed the ten minute marker about fifteen minutes ago. Just how long is this walkway? It's at times like these I really miss Rob – I don't have the biceps and triceps for humping luggage; he does.

I was really looking forward to embracing the public transport system; after all it represents the spirit of the city. The history and culture of Venice is based on the echo of the lagoon and the canals. Centuries ago, traders flocked to the city and they left behind them a signature of their own traditions, resulting in Venice's diverse beauty and vivacious hospitality – all of which is best seen and appreciated from the water. I for one was determined to experience the best that lagoon life had to offer, and to travel as the locals do. Apart from that, the water bus costs thirteen euros and a taxi costs ninety-five euros, which frankly I think is a rip-off! I refuse to pay ninety-five euros; I could fly home for that price!

I trundled on, eagerly.

At the end of the hooded walkway I rounded the bend, leaving the shelter and shadow of the terminal building. I halted, dropped the handle of my case, hugged myself and smiled at the view. A line of sleek polished speedboats with bright yellow TAXI signs bobbed and jostled in turquoise water alongside a broad wooden boardwalk. They looked so *welcoming*. Before I knew it, I was holding the hand of a handsome taxi captain, his Ray Bans reflecting the sun, taking tentative steps down into the leather upholstered cabin of my very own private speedboat. I'm here for four days – I can take the water bus anytime. It goes all round the houses; I could easily get confused and get off at the wrong stop, couldn't I? Clearly best to familiarise myself with my surroundings first, before I go venturing off and doing anything rash, like using public transport.

I casually propped my elbow on the side of the boat and reclined back into my seat; a gentle spray of water from the lagoon misted my face; I breathed the fresh Adriatic air; and all at once I felt a rush of exhilaration. It was heaven on earth, I thought, tilting my face to the sun. I couldn't help but think I would have been suited to a life at sea. I felt *at home* on the water, but at the same time I felt *intrepid*, in a noble sense – I was after all on my own.

I was going to enjoy this.

The captain throttled forward. As the boat bounced over a couple of waves and shot ahead, my neck snapped back. Gravity pulled my cheeks to my ears as we raced in the wake of a speeding police boat.

I wasn't so sure about *this*.

I clung on to my sun hat, and clamped a hand to my mouth, overcome with a rush of nausea. What is it with me and motion sickness? I travel for a living, this isn't fair!

313

The captain punched the air victoriously as he overtook the police boat. (Bloody hell. I was paying ninety-five euros for this joyride!) He did a loop-de-loop of honour, tipping our boat to the left; I nearly fell overboard. This driver is a lunatic, I thought as I threw myself across the seat and my hat and glasses fell off. I closed my eyes, breathed hard against the queasiness, and held on for dear life.

'My brother,' the captain explained, waving at the police boat. 'We race.'

I clawed my hat and glasses from the floor, sat up and gave a flaccid smile and burrowed in my bag for a Polo mint to settle my stomach. I flicked open my hand mirror; I looked dishevelled. The captain sank into his chair, leaned back, lifted his leg to the steering wheel and started guiding the boat with his foot. My life was at the mercy of someone driving a speedboat with their big toe! I couldn't watch. I palmed a handful of mints into my mouth and pulled my hat over my face to shut out the sight of the sloshing wake. It was bloody horrendous. That's the only word for it.

Venice is the most beautiful city in the whole world. OK, I know I always say that, but that was before I had been *here*. From now on everywhere else will come joint second. The cityscape is breathtaking. Orderly rows of vaulted, domed, vanilla and terracotta buildings of varying heights reach out to a cloudless sky; everything is connected by picturesque rose-and-butterscotch coloured bridges. Canals of various widths, shining like liquid silver, are awash with lavishly decorated gondolas all furnished with crushed velvet seats, rugs and ornaments. Everything is so bright and multicoloured and regal, and the city is alive with people; it seemed as if the entire population of Europe was here on a daytrip.

No cars, trucks or buses. I loved it. The captain turned from

314

the steering wheel and smiled at me, and teased his sunglasses as we cruised up the Grand Canal. In reply I beamed back. I felt much better now I had the city around me; the water was less choppy. It's amazing!

My smile buckled when I saw a coffin laid out on a boat bobbing along beside us. A coffin! I hoped it was empty. I suppose it stands to reason if the city is an archipelago of islands joined by a labyrinth of canals, with no roads to speak of, you're bound to float past the odd funeral procession. People do die here, I told myself, and there was nothing wrong with that at all; it was just the shock of seeing death so close, and amid so much life. I had never seen a funereal boat carrying a coffin side by side with a boat full of oranges before.

Finally, I stepped out of the water taxi on to the trellised jetty of the Grand Hotel, took a deep breath, and sighed with satisfaction. For a minute, I was speechless. The hotel was palatial; large picture windows, underscored with window boxes spilling clusters of heavy-headed red and white geraniums, sparkled in the midday sun. An ancient liveried footman nearly broke his back heaving my suitcase from the boat on to a gold tiered trolley while another elderly footman gestured for me to follow him into the hotel.

I wondered if there was a pensionable age in Venice.

I pushed my glasses to the top of my head and reminded myself that I was here for a reason. I couldn't get all doe-eyed at every little thing I encountered. I had a job to do. As my heels ricocheted on the marbled lobby floor, I switched roles – no more giddy tourist. It was time to mount my super-efficient mystery guest offensive. First things first: check-in!

I leaned against the reception desk admiring the domed, painted ceiling, rich velvet drapes and the glittering Murano glass chandeliers. It was stunning. Disappointingly, checking in to the hotel only took four minutes; three minutes later I was being waltzed through a lobby crammed with antique furniture and cabinets displaying jewellery and handbags to die for. No room for improvement with the arrivals and check-in procedure then, and I didn't even think they could improve on the merchandise. Still, it was early days.

My room was a-m-a-z-i-n-g. I had a lagoon view, not a wheelie bin or double-decker bus in sight. I gazed awestruck at the dancing water. It was magical and perfect and romantic. I opened the casement window and smiled at the sight of a young couple cuddling in a gondola, and giggled at the two men bickering on the boat delivering fresh linen to the hotel. I swivelled from the window and, at a slow admiring pace, marvelled at the rich red and gold fabrics of the bedroom interior.

It was perfect.

I flopped on to the bed, splayed in a starfish, and wished John was coming tonight, because suddenly I didn't want to be alone; I wanted someone to share Venice with. And perhaps John could help me find something constructive to write on my evaluation report. He can be very good at complaining.

I sat up.

Duty calls. I would check out the bar service – someone has to do it. I changed into a belted black minidress and a pair of heels; tousled my hair, touched up the kohl and folded a notepad into my handbag.

The barman in the opulent Bar Grand Canal, Ronaldo, according to his name badge, was absolutely delighted to meet me. He extended an arm edged with a gold trimmed cuff and pumped my hand eagerly. He looked very young and tender-skinned, slim and almost girlish, with long dark lashes and an eager smile.

I inched on to a bar stool, and forty-five seconds later had a gin and tonic in my hand. I palmed cashew nuts into my mouth, took a healthy gulp of my drink and flicked idly through a magazine that Ronaldo thoughtfully slid in front of me. I checked my phone; no messages. None at all. I considered playing Word Mole but I couldn't be bothered. What do you do when you're sitting at a bar on your own? I cast a discreet look around. Four obviously wealthy old gentlemen nodded a cordial welcome. I gave a polite wave in return and drained my glass. One raised brow later and my empty glass was swiftly refilled. I didn't even bother to count how many seconds it took. I have to admit I was becoming a little despondent. Being a mystery guest wasn't as easy as I'd first thought; apart from the fact that I couldn't find anything to evaluate objectively, I was absolutely bursting to blow my cover and tell Ronaldo that I was a mystery guest! Once the notion to confide in him was in my head, I became obsessed. The desire to share my secret was so intense; I put it down to loneliness. I felt isolated and friend-less. I had never stayed in a hotel on my own before, or been out for a drink on my own for that matter. Why would I? I breathed deep, edged off the bar stool and made my way to one of the comfortable barrel chairs in the corner, reasoning that if I kept my distance from Ronaldo I would keep my secret. I'd hardly yell it out from the other side of the room. I sank grace-fully into a seat, and checked my watch: fifty-two hours until John arrived. My face crumpled. Fifty-two hours on my own. I smiled over at Ronaldo, and thirty-six seconds later another gin and tonic was placed in front of me. Maybe I should just relax and forget all about the mystery guest thing. I'd concen-trate on that side of things tomorrow. Perhaps things will brighten up a bit then – like, tomorrow's barman could be a lazy good for nothing, and give me plenty of material for my notepad.

Now I thought about it, I wasn't overly enthused at the prospect of eating in the hotel restaurant on my own, but I had to appraise the in-house dining experience because it represented a whole page of my evaluation report. I picked up my glass, swirling my drink in an aid to thought, and considered ringing John to ask him to come earlier. I enjoy eating out and sightseeing with John; there are never any awkward silences. In fact I liked shopping with him too. He walks slowly, making a concerted effort to keep to the pace I set. In shops he finds a comfortable corner, shakes his newspaper open and contentedly waits, lifting his head intermittently to offer an opinion or give a curt nod of approval. John would come sooner, if he could, and if I asked him . . . No! I swiftly shook the thought from my head. I wouldn't ring him. I'll go shopping tomorrow, I'd rather go alone. I wouldn't want John to think that I expect him to spend money on me – and he would.

My attention drifted.

Two ladies, tall and elegant, clutching silk wraps around their slim shoulders and carrying an assortment of designer carrier bags, dropped into chairs at the table adjacent to mine. They crossed slender legs and signalled to Ronaldo, who appeared like a genie with two glasses of pink champagne. It's all right for them, I thought. They've got each other to talk to. I've got no one.

I signalled for my cheque; typically I didn't have long to wait.

I scanned the bill. A whoosh of blood pounded in my ears. My jaw dropped. I clutched the edge of the table, closed my eyes and tried to mentally tot up how I'd managed to drink sixty quid's worth of gin in less than an hour. *I can't afford it myself*, I thought, and whipped out my notepad.

Suggest a health warning on the price list! I wrote.

I'd had three or four drinks, I wasn't sure. So, I deduced, they're more than a tenner each; in fact they're fifteen quid a go. My hand flew to my mouth in realisation. I'd have to go on the wagon! There was no two ways about it. But what if I dehydrated? I avoided eye contact with Ronaldo in case he misread my look of horrified astonishment for thirst, and served me another drink and sent the pre-dinner drinks bill soaring off the Richter scale. I whizzed the strap of my bag up my arm, stood and smoothed my dress over my hips, and quickly signed the cheque and edged round the table. Sixty quid! I made my way across the bar.

I would have a bath, that's free, and would kill an hour or so. And then perhaps I would take a stroll along the canal, that's free as well. I may buy a ready-made meal for one in a deli, because dinner will likely cost as much as a pair of Louboutins. I'd rather starve and have the shoes. I had a sudden vision of me begging for coins with a Styrofoam cup, bedraggled and emaciated. I shivered at the apparition and decided as a matter of urgency to call Tina and confirm how much I was entitled to claim on expenses. Yes, that's what I would do, I'll simply explain to Tina that I can't afford to be here, I decided.

Sixty quid, I had just drunk sixty quid! Even the most hardened alcoholic would be hard pushed to match that at home in less than an hour, surely.

Walking through the lobby, I collided with a broad chest.

'Sorry, so sorry,' I said distractedly, to the owner of a solid wall of muscle.

'Hi Evie!'

I looked up towards the voice. My mouth opened to reply but no sound came out.

'Close your mouth Evie, you don't look at all ladylike.'

I was stunned! Two strong hands clutched my elbows and held me at arm's length, inspecting my face.

'What the bloody hell are you doing here?' I asked, in sucker-punched astonishment.

'What sort of welcome is that?'

'That's a sensible enough question. You here? Of all places, I mean—'

'I fancied a couple of days away, there's nothing too surprising about that.'

'No, but for us to bump into each other in Venice is a bit of a long shot, don't you think?' I asked, sweeping an arm theatrically around the lobby.

'No not really, why wouldn't I visit Venice? It is as good a place as any to get away from it all.'

'I'm not saying you wouldn't visit Venice, I'm just saying it's a surprise that you're visiting Venice, at the same time as me. Where are you staying? Not here?' I asked.

'Yes I'm staying here; it's quite nice, isn't it? Are you staying here?'

'Yes! I'm staying here!' I said, my eyes narrowing suspiciously.

'That is a coincidence, isn't it ... Can I buy you a drink?'

I eyed my bar receipt scrunched in a clenched fist.

'Yes, yes you can,' I said decisively. 'You can buy me a drink, have you brought your bank manager with you? Because you might need him.'

Nikki looped my arm in his.

'Is that so?'

'It is.'

Where's the bar?' he asked with a lazy smile.

'Behind me,' I told him.

'Shall we?' he asked, guiding me back through the lobby.

I was back in the comfortable barrel chair. I tried to call Tina while Nik ordered drinks but her line was busy – typical. I wanted to catch her before she left the office. I had to speak to her before I ate or drank another thing. My eyes scanned the price column of the wine list; it looked like the Wall Street ticker tape, with jumping figures and columns. The rattle of ice cubes in glasses and the swilling of drinks rolled on apace; the bar and terrace were now quite busy. This had got to be the calm before the storm. Any minute now everyone's going to realise what's going on here and stampede the door. Surely! This was aggravated robbery.

'One gin and tonic!' Nikki announced, placing our drinks on the table.

I gave a distracted nod, and felt a swoop of horror when I spotted the price of champagne. I wondered how much it would cost for me to get pissed, or indeed, how much it would cost for anyone to get pissed. The measures weren't even large. I could hardly taste the gin in my drink; it was too fizzy to be a double measure. I closed the price list; it was a depressing account of legal extortion.

A shadow fell across my face as Nikki sat down.

He relaxed back and lifted his right ankle to rest on his left knee.

'So ... what are you doing here?' he asked nonchalantly.

My heart gave a little leap, I couldn't tell him.

'*Me?*' I asked, drumming my fingers on my chest. 'What d'you mean, what am I doing here? What d'you think I'm doing here?'

'I don't know, that's why I asked; this doesn't look like standard accommodation for the kind of tour packages you usually escort,' he said, sliding his eyes a quick left and right.

I tried to sound indifferent.

'Right, well to be honest, I'd rather not say,' I told him.

'You'd rather not say! You'd rather not say what you're doing here? Are you some sort of special agent? Or are you working for the Russians?' he asked with a contemplative frown.

I felt a rush of indignation.

'Never mind me, what about you – what are you doing here? And who are you with?' I asked.

He spread his arms wide, and did a mock search of the bar.

'I'm not with anyone,' he said, his expression deadpan.

OK, I was definitely missing something.

'So, let me get this straight. You've come to Venice, on your own, for a couple of days, on a whim? And yet, this time yesterday, when we were working together in the bar, you didn't think to mention it? You didn't think to say, "By the way Evie, I'm going to Venice for the weekend?"' I challenged in a sardonic tone.

'That's right. But then you didn't mention it either, did you?' he pointed out.

'I told you I was going away for the weekend,' I said, giving him a big-eyed look.

I was distracted by a couple at the bar ordering a bottle of champagne; so people *do* buy it by the bottle.

'But you didn't say where you were going.' Nik said, invading my thoughts.

I gave him an even stare.

'You didn't ask me where I was going,' I told him factually.

'Likewise. You didn't ask me what I was doing at the weekend. Had you asked, I would've told you,' he said.

I sipped my drink; to be honest I was bored ~~of~~ with this conversation, what did it matter? At least I had company until John arrived. But then, who is he kidding? He's hiding something. He leaned forward, his hand drifted under my hairline; he drew me towards him and kissed my cheek.

'No more questions. I'm here and you're here, and surely that's all that matters.'

'Oh shut up Nik, what are you doing in Venice?'

322

'I told you, I'm having some time out.'

A girl marched towards the bar with a bill in her hand, she swung her handbag violently. I didn't blame her.

'Finish your drink, change out of those heels, we'll go for a walk and I'll buy you dinner,' Nik said, his voice quiet and controlled. 'Are you free for dinner? I'm assuming you're not otherwise engaged in some official capacity? Feel free to tell me if you are.'

Bloody hell, the girl signed her bill with a smile. I was gobsmacked.

'Evie!'

'What?'

He grabbed my chin between forefinger and thumb, and fielded my gaze.

'Evie, I said—'

'I know, I know what you said, fine, yes dinner.'

'Pay attention when I'm talking to you.'

'Not everything you have to say is riveting enough to warrant my undivided attention. And let go of my face, you're squeezing my cheeks!' I snapped, slapping his wrist.

I sipped my drink. He stood.

'I haven't checked in to my room yet, I'll need half an hour to shower and change.' He glanced at his watch. 'I'll meet you in the lobby at five o'clock,' he said.

He tipped forward, placed his hands on the armrests of my chair and bent his head. His dark eyes were no more than six inches from mine. On impulse I sank further into my seat.

'Nik, you're making me feel claustrophobic, you're crowding me.'

He broke away. 'Don't be late,' he said. And he walked out of the bar without looking back. I bloomed over the armchair. I felt quite exhausted, in fact I was knackered. Had I been drinking doubles? Am I suffering from some sort of syndrome whereby my insides are melting? I finished my drink and reached for my handbag, perhaps I needed a lie down.

I sat on the edge of the bed, phone pressed to my ear waiting for Tina to pick up, guzzling a glass of sparkling water. Likely the water cost about the same as a Joseph blouse.

Two nights in Venice with Nikki, how weird is that? I was assuming he was here for two nights, that's a weekend, Friday and Saturday. John arrives Sunday morning, so I suppose I should be pleased, at least I'll have someone to eat and drink with, and . . .

'Tina, hi, it's Evie! Oh my God I'm glad you answered,' I said in a rush.

'Don't tell me you're back with Rob?'

'No!'

'Pregnant?'

'No!'

'What's up then?'

'Er, nothing, not really, well, I suppose yes, something is up yes, but not life or death. As you know I don't have a group here in Venice, and so—'

'Get to the point, I don't mean to be rude but it's Friday. I don't want to be in this office a second longer than I have to, if you have something to say. Say it.'

I gnashed my teeth as she cracked a piece of chewing gum.

'Right, I was wondering—'

'Wondering what?'

She was getting on my nerves now. This is what happens when you work for a friend. I've heard her speak to other guides, often with what I'd call gracious serenity. To the point where she doesn't even sound like herself, the bitch!

'Give me a bloody chance!' I snapped. 'I want to know what the daily expense allowance is.'

'Same as always, forty euros.'

I gave a horrified gasp.

'It can't be! Tina, do you know how much fresh air costs in this hotel?' I asked, my voice jumping.

She tapped the keyboard of her computer, only half-listening.

'The same as fresh air costs here I suppose,' she said, giggling at her own wit.

My chest rose with indignation.

'Teen, I reckon I'll spend about a million dollars in four days.'

She gave a snort of laughter.

'I don't work on the mystery guest programme. Ellen who does is on holiday. You'll have to play it by ear and take it from me that it's forty euros until Ellen comes back on Monday and tells us differently.'

'Monday? Are you joking? I'll be bankrupt by then.'

She clicked her tongue.

'Evie, you're such a drama queen.'

'OK, perhaps that's a slight exaggeration because when John gets here—'

'John? You mean *John Jackson*?'

I heard her spit out her gum.

'*John Jackson* is spending two days with *you* at the Grand? Evie, what are you up to?' She asked, her voice rising.

I felt a dart of frustration.

Her voice dropped to a confidential whisper.

'The guy is God in here. You're playing with fire. This will all end in tears, I can just see it. What are you thinking? You can trust me, you know you can. What's the score with you two?'

'I'm not up to anything, he invited himself,' I told her firmly.

'He *did*? John Jackson invited *himself*? Evie, hang on the line a minute.' she told me in hushed tones.

'Tina, wait—'

She clicked off, I seethed and listened to Barbra Streisand for what seemed like light years.

'Evie, the MD, Griffo the Grump, wants to talk to you, this is *waaaaaay* over my head, I had to tell him.'

'Tell him what?'

'I'm putting you through,' she said, and cut off.

I could feel my nerves stiffening. Tina really was making a disproportionate amount of fuss over nothing.

An authoritative voice burst down the line.

'Hello Evie, Grenville Griffiths here, I don't believe we've met.'

Grenville? What sort of name is that? He probably prefers Grump.

I gave the phone a guarded smile.

'I believe Mr Jackson will be joining you in Venice. I'm surprised, although pleased, because try as we might, we have not been successful in persuading Mr Jackson to attend any of our hospitality functions. We would like the opportunity to thank him for his continued business but he appears reluctant to allow us to do so, or to accept any invitation extended to him.'

'Really?'

'It seems an opportunity has arisen, am I right?' he asked cryptically.

'Er well, I'm not sure that I follow, I haven't invited him anywhere as such—'

'But you are . . . *entertaining* him.'

What sort of a euphemism was that? My nostrils twitched in annoyance. Entertaining indeed! The cheeky—

'Evie, if Mr Jackson is your guest, then spare no expense. Whatever he wants, he gets, is that clear? And Evie that goes for you too. I appreciate you being in a position to do something for me, that I haven't managed to do myself.'

Spare no expense! I liked Griffo. My face broke into a smile. I twirled a long strand of hair round my finger pensively.

'I can assure you, I'll do my utmost to look after Mr Jackson, although he's not easy to please,' I said primly.

'I can imagine. Thank you in advance,' Griffo the *Great* said. 'My pleasure!'

'Would you like me to transfer you to Tina?' he asked.

'No thank you, Tina was anxious to be off,' I told him. 'She gets like that on Fridays.'

'Is that so?' he said, with a sigh. 'Enjoy Venezia.'

He ended the call by saying something in Italian, which I didn't catch, not that I would have understood it, unless he'd said pizza pizza pizza!

The main thing is the pressure is off, I can afford to live. Expenses or not, John would never allow me to sign a bar tab, he would think it embarrassing. But I'll tell him what Griffo said, it was very kind of him to offer.

Chapter Twenty-five

Nikki and I made our way back to the hotel after a very pleasant candlelit dinner. The moon was full and bright and moved me to look at it. We walked slowly, footsteps in time along the bevelled paving flanking the Grand Canal. Nikki led me up and over the steps of a cobbled bridge, mindful of a group of elderly ladies.

'It's a beautiful city,' he said, his voice husky and relaxed.

'It is.'

'World's most beautiful, apart from London,' he added, jerking his head at the shifting glassy lagoon.

He rubbed his nose with a forefinger then stretched his arm over my shoulder and pulled me close. A lazy smile curved on his lips.

'I love it, just love it,' I said, waving an admiring hand at the elegant floodlit Renaissance façades on our right. 'I'm glad you're here, I didn't enjoy being on my own, but I can't believe you left Pepi and Costas in charge of the bar for a whole weekend,' I said.

'They need to learn, and I can't be there all the time, nor do I want to, and I can't expect you to always be on hand.'

'D'you think they'll fight?'

He looked at me sideways.

'I reckon they might even kill each other,' he said, deadpan.
I giggled.

'I think you're right,' I told him.

He gave a casual shrug. The moonlight threw a shard of light
across his head, silhouetting his black hair, giving it a dark blue
hue.

'I'm not sure I care,' he said. 'It would save me a job, if they
finished each other off,' he added, with a humourless laugh.

'You don't mean that,' I said, craning up at him.

He kissed my forehead without breaking his step.

'No, you're right, I don't, it's just that sometimes the weight
of the responsibility is too heavy. I know it's my bar, but they
could help more by fighting less.'

I studied my feet, privately trying to recall the last fight or
argument in the bar that Nikki himself hadn't been in the
middle of. I couldn't think of one.

'Oh! I know exactly what they're like,' I said diplomatically.

He palmed my hair.

'I know I don't have to tell you, I owe you big time. I couldn't
have got through the last couple of months without you,' he said
in earnest.

'If you mean running and building your business for you and
working every hour God sends, then please, think nothing of it,'
I said with a gracious wave.

He sighed and mumbled something low and grumbly.

'Do you have plans for tomorrow?' he asked.

'I thought I'd go shopping.'

'OK, fine, we'll go shopping.'

I halted. Nik, go shopping with me?

'What?'

He gave me a slow confirming nod.

'I was planning going shopping alone, men usually . . .'

He raised the flat of his hand.

'Don't compare me to other men! Take me shopping first, before you decide if I'm a nuisance or not,' he said, his tone firm and reasonable.

I gave him a look for look.

'OK, you're on, but you better behave or I'll send you home,' I said, waving a finger in warning.

His shirt sleeves fluttered in the warm evening breeze.

'Oh you will, will you?'

He took my hand, and guided me round a dip in the pavement.

'Yes I will.'

'I'll have to behave then, won't I?' he said, with an edge of laughter in his voice.

'You will, yes.'

Outside the hotel I stopped for a minute to look over the glittering silver shadows flickering across the lagoon, highlighting the occasional drifting gondola. It was so serene and calming, with the sound of the water gently lapping the wooden trellised jetty.

Nikki gave me a warm glance.

'Beautiful,' he said for the second time.

'It is,' I agreed.

'Do you want a drink in the bar before going to bed?' he asked.

'I'm not sure I do,' I told him, a little awkwardly. 'But if you want one . . .'

He shook his head, and steered me towards the revolving door of the hotel.

'No, I don't want another drink either, to bed then!'

I felt a rush of guilt.

330

'Nik, if you want a drink I'm happy to come with you to the bar.'

'No, no! Honestly I'm not bothered,' he said, as we walked through the opulently lit, chandeliered lobby.

'If you're sure.'

'I am,' he said, lurching towards the elevator door as it was about to close.

'I'll walk you to your room,' he offered gallantly.

'You don't have to do that,' I told him.

'Of course I do,' he said.

We stepped into the elevator behind a pink-haired octogenarian, escorted by a dutiful young boy of about fourteen. I watched as the boy took the old lady's handbag and placed her veiny hand on his forearm.

'I have a lagoon view,' I confided to Nikki quietly in the lift. 'It's gorgeous.'

'Lucky you,' he said, uninterested.

He closed his eyes, folded his arms and relaxed back against the wall of the elevator.

The door whispered closed.

I smiled at the old lady, who smiled back. There was a pleasant silence. I dropped my gaze to my bag to burrow for my room key, I couldn't find it. The young boy reached in his pocket and found his key straight away. I excavated a Polo mint from a crevice, popped it in my mouth and continued the search for my key.

Nikki next to me suddenly straightened.

'Careful Nik,' I snapped. 'You dug your elbow in my rib then.'

'Sorry, sweetheart. Sorry!' He said swiftly. 'Can I see it?' he asked, in urgent enquiry.

'Can you see what?'

'Your lagoon view.'

I met his gaze straight on.

'You want to see my lagoon view?'

'Yes!' he said with a raised brow. 'I'd really like that.'

I was taken aback.

'Can you wait until tomorrow? It's late; you won't see much in the dark. And Nik, we've only just walked a marathon along the bloody lagoon. You must have seen enough of it for one night. I know I have.'

He took a step forward, his face impassive.

'No, I want to see it now, from a different perspective,' he said, lowering his dark head to mine.

'A different perspective?' I challenged. 'Nik a lagoon is a lagoon no matter how many angles you look at it.'

'I'd like to see . . . an aerial view,' he said with a ratifying nod.

'An aerial view?'

'Yes!'

'I'm only on the third floor Nik, it's not much of an aerial view from three floors up,' I told him. 'But if you must.'

'I must!'

In the room, I threw my bag on to the dressing table, hopped out of one shoe at a time, and walked over to the window, and with a theatrical sweep pulled back the drapes.

'Ta-da-ta-da,' I sung, then announced 'a lagoon view,' before whirling to face Nikki.

A smiling sauntering Nik, hands jammed deep in his pockets, crossed the room. He took my arm, and turned me to the window, folded his arms around me, and back bowed, pressed his lips into my hair. I felt the vibration of a heavy sigh as he pressed my back against his chest.

Outside the inky water shifted, sliced by a lone late night Vaporetto.

We stood in admiring silence.

'That's the Basilica of Santa Maria della Salute,' I told him. 'Amazing, isn't it?'

'Yes, it is,' he agreed.

'Are you at the other side of the hotel, what view do you have?' I asked.

'Mmmm, I have the same view as you,' Nikki said flatly, his voice warm on my cheek.

It took a couple of microseconds to absorb this news.

'What did you just say?' I asked.

He gave me a noisy kiss in my ear.

'I said . . . it's the same as the view from my window.'

I lifted my chin and craned my neck to look at him.

He took a deep contented breath, and clamped his arms tighter round me.

'If *my* view is exactly the same as *your* view, then if you don't mind me asking, why insist on seeing the lagoon from here?'

He laughed a deep throaty sound. I tried to wriggle free; I couldn't budge him, not by so much as an inch. He held me tight with no visible effort.

'No not *exactly* the same,' he conceded thoughtfully, as I squirmed and twisted like a mad thing. 'My room is four doors down, so I suppose I have a slightly better view of the church. Still your view is every bit as nice as mine,' he agreed graciously.

He clamped my struggling forearms to my chest.

'If you have your own lagoon view, why make such a stonking big deal about seeing mine?' I was bloody exhausted; his arms were like the vice of a trap. 'AND WILL YOU LET GO OF ME!'

'I decided that perhaps I would quite like a night cap after all,' he said conversationally. 'And your room is every bit as good as the bar, and well . . .'

'LET ME GO!'

Laughing, he spread his arms wide. I stumbled forward, and wheeled to face him, swept my hair from my eyes, and took a backward step.

'What are you playing at, squeezing the life out of me like that?'

A lazy smile curved his lips.

'Hardly!'

He caught my arm and pulled me to him, grabbed my wrists and pinned them to my sides, and took a couple of steps forward, forcing me to reverse against the wall. He loomed above me, dark eyes piercing mine.

'Although squeezing you sounds like quite a good idea,' he said, his already wide smile widening. 'In fact the more I roll the thought around in my mind, the better I like it.'

He looked different. He looked . . . catlike, the smile was still there, but the humour was missing, he looked serious, and . . . *mad.*

I slid a glance at my trapped wrists.

'Nik, have you gone crazy?' A thought speared my mind. 'Have you . . . taken something?'

'No Evie, I haven't gone crazy, and you know better than to ask me if I've taken anything.'

There was a charged stillness, as our eyes locked.

I had an urge to step backwards but couldn't on two counts. First, there was nowhere to go; I was already flush to the wall. And second, because strong yet gentle thumbs were massaging my hip bones, causing a spreading heat in my groin, and a jellified weakness in my legs.

My breath caught in my throat as he lowered his head and pressed his lips to mine.

His lips, on my lips?

His kiss felt soft and warm and oddly familiar. I closed my eyes and opened my mouth to him, and knew without looking that his eyes were closed too. His lips moved from my mouth to my cheeks and ears and travelled behind my neck to my hairline.

My back arched, pressing my chest against his.

He pressed his thumbs deeper into my skin, tracing the outline of my knickers, and stared at me through hooded eyes.

'Do you like that, Evie?' he asked, with a sidelong look at his busy hands.

I did. I did like it. But I couldn't form a reply. I was gripped by the same kind of nervous exhilaration you suffer from the top of a roller coaster seconds before the big plunge. Fear mingled with breathless anticipation. Speaking was totally out of the question.

He gave me a long appraising stare, and then brushed his lips against mine for the second time. I felt a pang of yearning so strong I had to swallow to find air.

'Look Nik ...' I managed, and then broke off, as his kiss deepened.

I tried for a rational thought. This was Nikki! But with my bravado shattered and my libido on code red, all I could do was kiss him again, as if I were on autopilot.

He took both my wrists in one hand and moved my arms above my head.

'If you asked me to stop do you think I would?' he asked, teasing the front zip of my dress.

Blood flared in my cheeks, as I eyed my slowly descending zipper.

'Nik, this will change everything.'

He nodded slowly.

'I'm banking on it,' he said, brows creasing sharply.

The dancing rhythm of the pulse in his throat seemed to match the pounding of the beat of my heart. And I knew that as composed as he tried to appear on the outside, he was nervous on the inside.

The air was thick with tension.

This was Nikki, for god's sake, me and Nikki. And I was standing dress undone, and my bra and knickers exposed.

'So do you, Evie? Do you think if you asked me to stop, that I would?' he repeated, a fingertip trailing my cleavage.

'Yes, you would, you would stop,' I said in a whisper. 'If I asked you.'

He gave a chivalrous nod. Lowered his head and nibbled the hollow of my neck and along my collarbone. And then bit my shoulder, hard. I pulled back, startled.

'Would you like me to stop?' he asked, tracing a slow finger in an aimless circle around my belly button.

I met his gaze.

'Would you, Evie?' he asked, his hips brushing mine. 'Would you like me to stop?'

'No,' I told him breathlessly.

His thumb was worming inside my knickers.

'No, Evie? No what? Say it; tell me that you don't want me to stop.'

'I don't want you to stop,' I said in a rush.

He smiled.

'Good.'

He released my hands from above my head, spired his fingers through mine and led me to the bed. He slipped my dress over my shoulders and smiled as it fell to the floor in a pond of black linen.

When I woke the following morning I had a disorientating flash-thought that the bulk and weight behind me was Rob. But

336

I was naked and in bed with Nikki, who was also naked. I was mortified; this was Nikki, my neighbour, friend and boss. I squeezed my eyes shut and swallowed a lump of shame, accepting with sickening clarity that this being in bed and naked business was a pretty solid and permanent arrangement until I did something about it, but what? This was *my* room, so I could hardly sneak out of bed, get dressed and tiptoe into oblivion, which is par for the course in an awkward social situation such as this.

Nikki was lying on his side, his chest pressed fiercely against my back and with a strong toned arm curved around my tummy. I was pretending to be asleep, mainly because I couldn't bear the thought of him knowing I was awake. I really hadn't planned what happened last night; in fact, a part of me was trying to convince myself that nothing had happened at all. But it did happen . . . Twice! And as if that wasn't embarrassing enough, the second time – I asked for it! I woke him up and asked for it. And now, given the choice, I'd rather snap out of a trance to find myself naked and curled up in a Selfridge's window display on a Saturday afternoon, than lying here beside Nik. He was awake; I was positive, because I could feel his mickey twitching on my back. I know that mickeys can twitch in their sleep, but this one was far too busy to be sleeping.

I'm not saying I didn't enjoy last night, because I did, I enjoyed it very much. But that could've been as a consequence of the fact my loins were on super high alert due to the amount of time that's elapsed since they've seen action. I made a sleepy mewing sound. I closed my eyes. The longer he thought I was asleep the better. I had to rally my thoughts. I couldn't face him, not yet.

'Evie?' It was a question.

I felt a swoop of panic. My eyes pinged open and slid the length of my chest, a rope of tendons in his forearms flexed as he pulled me into him. I had to breathe out, or I'd burst, but obviously I had to exhale slowly to maintain this lifeless comatose pretence. I felt as though I was underwater. He mustn't know I'm awake!

'I know you're awake!'

I clenched my fists around the sheet.

'Evie, I've been listening to you breathing for most of the night, I can tell the difference. I know you've been awake for over half an hour.'

I rolled my eyes; my heart was going like a bongo drum, with a bit of luck it may wear itself out and stop altogether. This was *so* embarrassing. I could hear a noise like the sea roaring in my ears. He rubbed his chin into my hair, and then angled his head to press his lips against my forehead.

'Evie, what happened last night was inevitable.'

My eyes grew wide, and my jaw dropped. Was he joking? Inevitable? What happened last night was *unbelievable*, not bloody *inevitable*!

He put a hand on my shoulder and lightly pressed me on to my back. His eyes held mine with a force that had my tummy doing a rumba. A smile lit his face.

'It was bound to happen,' he said, rubbing his knuckles against my mouth.

This was news to me. I tried to twist my lips into a smile, and almost succeeded when he quickly pulled the sheet off me, and whipped it behind his back.

'Give that to me,' I shrieked, lurching across him.

He dropped the sheet on the floor, rolled towards me, pressed me into the mattress and moved to lie above me, resting on his elbows. A slow hand stroked my hair.

338

'Evie, *we* enjoyed last night,' he said with a smirk in his voice. 'I challenge you to deny it.'

I tried to frame a response, but I couldn't think of one. A flush of embarrassment in the hollow of my cheeks spread over my face. Taking my silence as a reply, he lowered himself slightly so that every centimetre of our naked bodies touched, causing a heaviness to blaze in my chest. He bent his head and flicked his tongue over my nipple, and then gave it a soft bite. I inhaled a squeak. I couldn't believe I was watching Nikki with *his* mouth around *my* nipple.

'In fact I distinctly remember you waking me up for round two,' he murmured to *my* nipple. 'Greedy girl.'

I found my voice.

'I did no such thing!!' I lied defensively.

He lifted his head, and raised himself a little.

'You did.'

'I – did – not!'

Still resting on his elbows, he waved a forgiving hand.

'Think nothing of it, I wasn't really asleep anyway, and I had nothing better to do.'

'Nothing better to do?' I echoed, affronted.

'That's right,' he said with casual matter-of-factness.

'Well, I do have something better to do,' I told him. 'So if you wouldn't mind getting off me, I'll be . . . on my way.'

'On your way? And where exactly are you planning going, since this is *your room*?'

My eyes slid a quick left and right for inspiration, but saw none.

'I'm going . . . out!' I said.

'Out?'

I nodded, not trusting my face or tone. He smiled, eyes half-shut, and slowly pressed his hips into mine.

'You're not going out. Not just yet. You're not going anywhere,' he mumbled through a kiss.

His thumbs brushed my earlobes. My mind was trying to engage with reality: *I am here with Nikki, naked, skin to skin. He's tickling my ears, and pressing his very excited willie against my groin. My hands are clawed into the mattress, my spinal cord is on fire and my mouth is hanging open.* I quickly snapped it shut. He looked at me intently enough to make my eyes glide from his.

'Let's play doctors and nurses,' he suggested.

'What?'

'Don't you know how to play that?' he asked in mock impatience.

I took a deep breath, which arched my spine and elevated my chest, pushing me into him. He lowered his head and kissed me; I felt his wide smile against my cheek.

'We'll start with an internal examination, shall we?' he said, his voice thick through the folds of my hair. 'Now if you could just open your legs a little, you can then lie back and leave the rest to me.'

This made me laugh, because it sounded funny and silly, and laughter is a great aphrodisiac. And now that he mentioned it, I did know how to play doctors and nurses. I gave in graciously, because I realised . . . I wanted to. I wanted to more than anything, because Nikki nibbling my ear melted my insides.

But afterwards as I sat up in bed with the sheet pulled into a toga around me, the burning mortification returned with a vengeance.

'Shall I order breakfast?' Nikki asked, walking in comfortable nudity back from the bathroom.

'Yes,' I said avoiding the sight of his jigging willie. His jigging *very well formed* willie.

'What would you like to eat?'

340

'Erm . . . toast,' I said.

'What else?'

'Just toast . . . and coffee.'

I wasn't usually shy about being naked, so why my fingers were clenched around the sheet – so tight that my knuckles were almost white – I did not know.

He stood beside the bed. I lifted my gaze to his. His eyes scanned mine, reading my thoughts. There was a heavy beat of silence; he gave an exasperated sigh, and climbed slowly into bed. He put his arms around me and hugged me close. And the strangest thing happened; I dropped the sheet, circled his neck and buried my face in his shoulder. It wasn't the fact that I was cuddling him so forcefully that I thought strange, it was that I realised while my mind wasn't overly comfortable with this new level of intimacy between us, my body was. Without the intrusion of awareness, it seemed the most natural thing in the world to be here and in bed with him.

His arms tightened around me.

'I know what you're thinking,' he said.

'What am I thinking, clever clogs?'

'You're thinking, "What's going on here? How did this happen? And what happens next?"' he said.

He wrapped a fist around my hair and gave it a gentle pull.

'That's more or less spot on,' I admitted. 'And are you thinking the same?'

He cleared his throat.

'No!'

'What are you thinking?' I asked.

'I'm thinking about breakfast, because I'm starving. We'll eat, have a bath, and spend the rest of the day in bed getting to know each other better.'

'We know each other pretty well as it is.'

'Oh no we don't, there's so much about me you still have to learn,' he said.

I nibbled his collarbone.

'Is that so? Now that you mention it, there are a couple of things I'd like to tell *you* about *me*.'

He gave me a sidelong glance.

'I insist you don't tell me anything just yet. I'd rather you gave me the chance to find out for myself,' he said.

That sounded good to me.

'You're on.' I told him, forgetting all about our proposed shopping trip.

Chapter Twenty-six

I sat up in bed and hugged my knees.

'I'll be gone for two hours tops,' Nikki said, hands fastening the buckle of his belt.

'Where are you going for two hours?'

He pulled his collar from his neck, letting in air.

'First of all I need to check out of my room,' he told me.

'Why do you need to do that?'

'Why do you think, there's no point in us having a room each?' I don't intend to sleep alone for the next three nights ... Not after last night.'

An apricot blush, faint but obvious, soaked my face. I cleared my throat.

'Three nights? I assumed you'd be flying home tomorrow,' I said.

He gave me a puzzled frown.

'Why would I come all this way for two nights?'

'Why did you come all this way at all?' I fired back. 'You still haven't told me.'

His reply was a knowing wink.

'Are you warm, sweetheart, it's stuffy in here, shall I open the window?'

I nodded distractedly, as he angled around the bed.

A gentle breeze and the animated sound of lagoon life spilled into the room.

'Checking out will take you fifteen minutes, not two hours,' I told him, pitting my voice against the sound of a motor boat engine grinding to a halt.

He lifted his jacket from the back of the chair.

'And then, I'm going to the gym, I need a workout,' he said firmly.

The gym? We'd been shagging a triathlon, what's wrong with him?

He crossed to the bed and sat beside me, took my hand and pressed my palm to his cheek.

He smiled.

'What's wrong, my beloved, can't you bear the thought of being parted from me?' he asked with a smirk.

'Hardly.'

He straightened.

'Be ready to go out for dinner when I get back. I'll be starving by then,' he said, striding towards the door.

I rolled my eyes, Nikki's body has a built-in detonator, triggered by a starvation trip switch which ignites every four hours. Both his room service orders had been delivered on a gurney. He ate a banquet for breakfast and a buffet for lunch.

He checked his watch.

'Evie! Seven o'clock, no later!' he said, and was gone.

The room was still and quiet. I hugged myself and had a mental post–mortem on last night's events.

'I'm sleeping with Nikki,' I said aloud, my voice sounding peculiar, even to my own ears. 'Shall I call Lulu and tell her?' I asked the ceiling, and immediately erased the thought from my mind; Lulu would think I'd gone mad. I rested my forehead on my knees and let my shoulders slump. 'What am I doing? He's a bad-tempered, bossy, big, big ... horny bastard,' I admitted, nodding in reminiscent contemplation.

Nikki had known I was in Venice, I was sure of it. The only explanation was that he overheard one of my calls to Tina. I'd rung her from the bar a couple of times. But then, most of my private calls I make from the ladies' toilet, because Nikki freaks out if I stop toiling and sweating for anything over thirty seconds.

The fact is that while I'm absolutely stunned at the turn of events here, Nikki wasn't in the slightest bit surprised. I pulled back the sheet and walked to the bathroom at a pensive pace. I would challenge Nik the minute he gets back. I turned on the bath taps. Actually, I would challenge him the second he gets back, I decided.

I was sitting at the dressing table straightening my hair when I heard the swish of a key card in the door. *Nikki's key card for my room.*

Nikki looked immaculate in a navy suit and a pale pink shirt with a button down collar. Radiating happiness, he dropped a holdall and a suit carrier beside the door, and crossed the room purposefully. It was all very 1950s movie-ish. All very 'Honey, I'm home!' My tummy did a flippy thing when he pressed his palms on my shoulders and bent his head to kiss my cheek.

Our eyes met in the mirror.

'Cut the crap Nik! What are you doing in Venice, and how did you know I was here, in this hotel?' I asked brusquely. 'Because you *did* know I was here, didn't you?'

'I've booked a boat trip for tomorrow – we're going to Murano, Torcella and Burano. We have to be at Ponte della Paglia no later than noon.'

He hunkered down beside me, put an arm around my shoulder and gave me a hug.

345

'That'll be nice, won't it?' he said.

I slid him a glance and rolled my eyes for patience.

'Nik,' I began, but my trail of thought drifted, something else pierced the margin of my mind.

Tomorrow . . . I lifted a wing of hair with my brush. *What was happening tomorrow?*

Nikki sank into the winged armchair next to the dressing table with a contented sigh.

My memory clicked. I felt a whoosh of panic. John arrived tomorrow. I dropped the straighteners and hairbrush on the dressing table with a clatter, and turned abruptly to Nikki.

'We can't go on a boat trip tomorrow, John is arriving,' I told him urgently. 'I have to be here, to meet him.'

He relaxed deeper into the chair, and tapped the armrests.

'We can't go,' I insisted.

'Leave a message to tell John when you'll be back,' Nik suggested casually. 'No real need to hang around waiting for him, is there?'

'I can't do that,' I told him, my voice lifting. 'John is coming to Venice to spend a couple of days with me. I can't be *out* when he arrives. Don't be ridiculous, that's the height of bad manners.'

Something moved behind his eyes.

'Yes you can.'

'No I can't,' I snapped, picking up my mascara wand.

'Why not?'

'Well, I . . . you, you don't know what he's like.'

'What's he like?'

'Actually he's very much like you when you don't get your own way.'

He leaned forward and lifted my chin with a finger.

'And what exactly do you mean by that?'

'You're hostile,' I told him.

He gave me a sinister smile.

'I'm not!'

'Nik, I've arranged to meet John, and—'

He cut me off.

'OK, I'll call the boat company and add another person on to our booking. If John arrives in time he can come with us. He would be fine with that, surely?'

'Come with us?' I echoed, doubtfully.

Nik stood and walked towards the window, hands clasped behind his back. He wheeled and gave me a straight look, one eyebrow raised.

'Are you trying to tell me something? Would you rather be alone with him?' he asked. 'Is that it?'

As if?

I turned to the mirror and spluttered a *tsk* sound as I flapped mascara on to my lashes.

'Don't be ridiculous! Of course not. It's just—'

'Just what?'

All of my breath went out in one long sigh.

'I don't know, I can't explain it, I can't see John in a threesome somehow.'

'That's good because he's not being offered the opportunity,' Nik said starchily.

'Oh shut up Nik, you know what I mean; you have friends you keep in separate pockets for no reason you can put your finger on. John is a private person, that's all. He's older, and quite intense, not what you'd call a laugh, but I enjoy being with him, and—'

'Find out what time he arrives, if you want to be here in the hotel waiting for him, then we will be,' he said matter-of-factly. 'It's not worth arguing over, it's only a bloody boat trip. If we can't make it, then so be it.'

I screwed the lid on my mascara and tossed my lipstick in my handbag. Nik lifted my jacket from the back of the chair and draped it over my shoulders.

We stood facing each other.

'What are you doing in Venice?' I asked crisply.

He held me tight against him.

'I'm sorting out some business I should have taken care of a long long time ago,' he said, his voice meditative.

'Is that so?'

'It is.'

He pressed his mouth over mine.

'I have a problem,' he mumbled through his kiss.

'What's that?'

'I'm starving.'

I circled my arms around his waist.

'We'll eat and your problem will be solved.'

'It's not food I'm hungry for ... well it is, but not ... only food.'

I nibbled his neck.

'I'm wearing my nice tight red dress, I've done my hair and my make-up is perfect, if you ravish me I'll have to get ready all over again.'

'No you won't.'

'I will.'

He lifted me effortlessly on to the dressing table.

'If you sit up straight your hair will be fine, it's all the thrashing of your head on the pillow in wild abandonment that messes your hair,' he said, pushing me back against the mirror.

'I don't thrash my head in wild abandonment,' I told him, sharply.

'You do!'

'I don't!'

The breath of his laughter brushed my neck, as he wriggled my dress over my hips.

'And if you hold back on gnawing and sucking my shoulder, as though I'm a melting ice lolly, your lipstick should stay on,' he told me helpfully.

'I don't gnaw and suck you as though you're a melting ice lolly.'

'You do! And if you don't rub your face in my—'

'Ok Nik, I get the picture, just get on with it,' I said working the buttons of his shirt.

And as he crushed his lips against my teeth, and tore my dress off, I thrashed my head in wild abandonment, and gnawed and sucked. I couldn't help it. He is delicious.

I cast a casual eye around the terrace of the Grand Canal Bar. Geraniums tumbled like rambling ivy over the trellised decking into the lapping lagoon, where a line of gleaming jet-coloured gondola bobbed in the scented air.

Nikki placed a glass of wine and a lager on the table, and took the seat next to mine.

'Nik, have you seen the price list?' I asked, clutching the cocktails menu.

'Yes.'

I leaned forward conspiratorially.

'It's extortion, isn't it?'

'No, not really,' he said, holding his lager mid-air. 'You think it's expensive because you're not accustomed to buying your own drinks. With that in mind, any drink you have to pay for you think is extortionate.'

I scrunched my brows, piqued.

'Of course I buy my own drinks,' I punctuated, insistently.

'No you don't.'

'I do!'

He licked a line of froth from his top lip.

'Well I've known you for two years, and I've never seen you buy a drink,' he said brightly, as if this was something I should be delighted to discover, and justly proud of.

'I must have done,' I told him forcefully. 'Lots of times,' I felt compelled to add.

'No, you haven't,' he said, smiling at the view. 'Never.'

'I have!'

'No, you haven't. I would have remembered, it would've been one of those occasions I would've committed to memory for its rarity.'

I shot to my feet.

'Are you calling me mean and tight and thrifty?' I snapped. 'Do you want a drink?' I asked, eyes wide and challenging. 'Do you? Because—'

'No, I don't want a drink! Sit down! I wouldn't let you buy me a drink. I have more money than you, why would I want you to pay for my drinks?'

I dropped into my seat.

A coat-tailed waiter placed a bowl of cashew nuts on the table. Nikki thanked him, palmed a quarter of the bowl into his mouth and straightened his cuffs needlessly.

'I'm on expenses so I suppose it makes sense I take advantage, if I'm ever going to buy you a drink it will be here.' I said.

'Why are you on expenses? I thought you didn't have a group, you certainly haven't done any work today that I'm aware of,' he said with a distant shrug.

I felt a shimmer of nerve-stiffening guilt. He was right, I hadn't done any work at all.

His look sharpened.

'Well?' he challenged.

350

I sipped my wine, and decided I could trust him. I slid my eyes around the terrace in fear of eavesdroppers.

'Are you looking for someone?' he asked.

Satisfied we weren't being overheard, I quickly gave him a run down on the responsibilities and tribulations of a mystery guest.

He sat back, arms crossed, lips curving into a smile.

'Evie, in ancient Egypt when the men went to war, the lucky guy with the biggest three piece was left behind to impregnate as many women as he could, to boost the population of the race,' he said in a wise tone. 'Did you know that?'

I nodded and smiled politely, although I hadn't known that. Why would I know that?

'I've always thought that was the best job in the world, but I've got to say, your job comes a *very close second.*'

I gave him a frosty glare.

'It's not as easy as you think. I can't think of a single thing to write on the evaluation report.'

'I can,' he said.

I eyed him sceptically.

'You can? What?'

'The running machines in the gym face a brick wall, they should face the lagoon, that would be much better, don't you think?'

I gave a brisk nod.

'Absolutely,' I agreed.

'I personally don't need a fitness instructor, but a couple of people in the gym did. I had to show them how to operate the machines, there should be a member of staff in there at all times.'

My eyes brightened.

'Of course there should,' I said forcefully.

'And when I checked out of my room earlier, I asked to

transfer my extras account to your room, and offered my credit card as security. I thought it would be easier to pay for our stay in one transaction when we left on Tuesday, but the receptionist wouldn't allow it. I couldn't be bothered to argue, but it would have been more convenient to have paid just once.'

I felt an irrational lifting of spirits; the hotel wasn't perfect after all, far from it.

'Well of course it would have been,' I told him.

He cast an admiring glance around the terrace.

'The setting couldn't be more perfect for a bar, could it?' he said.

'No, I love the view,' I agreed.

'We'll have dinner in the hotel, that way we can kill three birds with one stone. Satisfy my hunger, check out the restaurant for your report and be closer to our bed than we would be if we went out.'

That sounded good to me. He stood and offered me his arm.

The restaurant was amazing with panelled walls, lavish furnishings and the Venetian trademark enormous chandeliers. Each course was delivered with an air of sombre ceremony.

'The service was excellent,' Nikki complimented, at the end of the meal. 'It's all about attitude of body.'

I eyed him over the rim of my wine glass.

'What do you mean?'

'You're in the service industry; you know how hard it is to be pleasant to a customer who is a right pain in the arse,' he said.

He gave me a long hard look.

'I changed my order three times; you messed around changing yours twice, and you spilled a glass of water over the waiter's sleeve, and credit where credit is due, the guy wasn't fazed at all,' he said with a smile of reverence. 'He passed our tests, hands down.'

A couple at an adjoining table were talking in low voices. Nikki's gaze shifted towards them.

'They haven't stopped complaining, I'd have lost patience with them by now,' he said.

Nikki was brilliant at this mystery guest business, likely because he gripes so much on a day to day basis himself; he can quickly identify that trait in others. And when he's not busy whining and bellyaching, he's rushed off his feet looking for things to whine and bellyache about.

'And as for you,' he said, waving a fork in counsel. 'You would *definitely* have lost patience; you are far less tolerant with customers in the bar than I am,' he said in a stern voice. He gave the offending couple another quick glance. 'But our waiter seems oblivious to their nitpicking.'

'Excuse me, but did I hear you say *I* was less tolerant than *you*?' I asked, stunned.

The bloody nerve of him.

'I did.'

I leaned across the table on crossed arms.

'You are the least patient, most bad-tempered, intolerant, bossy big bastard I have ever met,' I told him.

He grinned.

'And you are a spoiled little brat, who, without a shadow of a doubt, would be a spoiled big brat, if I wasn't an impatient, bad-tempered, intolerant, bossy big bastard.'

I harrumphed.

He threw his napkin on the table and stood.

'I don't fancy dessert or coffee. Do you want to go for a walk before bed? We haven't been across the door of the hotel all day,' he asked.

I gave a casual shrug. He put his hand under my elbow, and helped me to standing.

A welcome breeze from the lagoon brushed my face, as we stepped outside. We paced slowly side by side, not touching. I stole a glance at Nik, his face was hidden in the shadows with the moon behind him. A beam of light fell on the cobbled pavement in front of us, Nik pulled me to him, as a laughing crowd of revellers spilled from a bar.

'London seems a million miles away,' he said softly.

I stared fixedly at a uniform line of sleeping gondolas bobbing in the dark shifting water.

'It does,' I agreed.

'I'm in no rush to go home. Are you, Evie?'

'No, no I'm not.'

'And now that I think of it, I'm in no mood for a walk; let's go back to the hotel,' he said.

Outside the rain fell in heavy drops, splashing noisily against the bedroom window. I lay with my head in the hollow of Nik's shoulder, the quilt tucked around us, and watched his lazy smile shift as my palm travelled the line of his belly and the slope of his hip. He brushed his lips against mine, and let out a sigh. I snaked my fingers through the soft black hair on his chest. I wanted him, again! I touched him quickly, and softly, my fingers light and flirty. Suddenly he grabbed my wrist, so tight that my hand went instantly numb, and jerked me on top of him; spilling my hair over his shoulders and face. And then with measured deliberation rolled me on to my back and moved to cover my body with his.

When Nik cried out, although I felt an overwhelming tenderness towards him, I felt an element of power as well, and I liked it, I liked it a lot.

He gathered me in his arms and held me against a chest as solid as granite.

'Nik, what are you saying when you whisper to me in Greek?' I asked. 'When you, well, when you—'

'It's best you don't know,' he said, stroking my arm lightly. 'Not yet anyway.'

He teased me on to my side and curled himself around me. 'Go to sleep sweetheart,' he sighed. 'I'm drained.'

Chapter Twenty-seven

I pushed back the curtains and squinted over the glittering lagoon, it was another beautiful morning.

'Shall I order breakfast?' Nikki asked.

He was sitting at the dressing table, scrutinising the room service menu in search of anything he may have missed and not previously eaten.

I tucked the folds of my toga towel tighter under my arms.

'Yes I suppose so,' I said.

'What would you like?'

'Anything, I'll share whatever you order.'

'No you won't, you'll order your own.'

He really is a greedy gremlin.

'I'll have toast, coffee and fruit,' I said, almost savagely.

I know Nikki is a big bloke and he burns it off in the gym, but still, he studies the menu at every meal as though contemplating a mathematical equation. Frankly, I find it irritating. I can't believe I haven't noticed his obsession with food before. But now that I think on it, he often stands in the kitchen before lunch or dinner eating a steak sandwich.

'Toast and coffee. Are you sure you don't want an omelette? I don't want you digging into mine.'

356

Digging into his, as if. I'd be taking my life in my hands.

He exhumed his head from the menu. A ray of morning sun danced on his face, giving his dark brown eyes a chestnut tinge.

'I won't touch your omelette,' I assured him.

He beamed.

'Are we going on the boat trip? he asked, standing.

'I left a message for John to ask what time he would be arriving, but he hasn't got back to me.'

He stopped en route to the bedside phone to take my earlobe between his teeth. 'Call him again while I order breakfast,' he said, giving my backside a playful slap.

I stood quite still. I loathed the thought of John's disapproval. I would have to tell him about Nik and me. And disapprove he would. He would tell me I should have given myself time to get over one relationship before involving myself in another. And he would be right. Not that I'm in a *relationship* with Nikki as such, but it's certainly a complicated romantic entanglement that I didn't have the last time I was bemoaning my love life to John. And if I was honest, I was embarrassed. I know John has had four wives and a string of girlfriends. But in his esteemed opinion what's alright for a man is not alright for a woman. He may take the view that my behaviour was nothing short of *wanton*. A man my own age with that outlook would annoy the hell out of me, but John's commanding presence, and his prevailing character, dictates respectful acceptance of his views and opinions no matter what they are. Well I thought so anyway. I cared a lot what he thought of me. In short, I was bloody dreading him arriving in Venice.

A vision of me babbling a random flood of incoherent bollocks to John, telling him everyone sleeps with their neighbours these days, flashed through my mind. This was swiftly followed

357

by the irrational hope that another volcanic cloud would emerge from somewhere unpronounceable in Iceland and ground all European flights, leaving John and his jet stranded in London.

I took my phone from my bag. There was a text in my inbox, from the man himself no less. A coil of tension bounced inside me. I felt quite sick.

Call me!

Call me! he says ... a euphemism for *are you shagging your boss?* if ever I've seen one.

A draught from the window sent the curtain billowing and made me shiver. I reluctantly scrolled for John's number. He picked up on the second ring.

'Evie, I am so sorry but something has cropped up, I won't be able make it to Venice,' he said apologetically.

I nodded at the phone. A wispy smile spread across my face. I felt floaty and light-headed, like I'd won something.

'Oh! Well, thanks very much for letting me know at such short notice!' I replied crisply. 'I had been expecting you any minute!'

'I'll make it up to you. I'll take you somewhere special in rec-ompense. We'll go to Vienna or Monte Carlo, or anywhere ... your choice.'

'What do you have to do that's better than spending two days in Venice with me?'

He chuckled.

'My darling girl, I have nothing to do that's better than spending two days in Venice with you. But something demand-ing my immediate attention keeps me in London. I sincerely hope you'll forgive me.'

'Of course,' I said genially.

'You are so gracious. Have you cancelled your return flight ticket? I did say I would bring you back with me. I can arrange to have you flown home.'

'No, I have a return ticket.'

'And how are you finding Venice?'

'I love it.'

'I knew you would. I'll show you Venice properly, as soon as I have a spare couple of days.'

I smiled at the phone. He is so kind and thoughtful, and . . . grown up.

'Did you hear me?' he asked.

'Yes! And I'd love to come back here with you.'

'And so you shall,' John said.

'I'll do my best to soldier on without you,' I told him.

'I'm sure you will,' he said with a hint of laughter in his voice.

When he rang off, I stared at my phone in bemused silence. I know I'd been dreading John arriving, but now that he wasn't coming, I was strangely disappointed. Nikki planted a tender kiss on my shoulder, and took the phone from my hand.

'John's not coming,' I told him.

'I gathered as much.'

'Did you order breakfast?'

'Of course, it will be here in twenty minutes. So get in bed and on your back.'

I hesitated.

'I'm not sure I can be bothered,' I told him haughtily.

His lips curved at my tone.

'Is this your way of telling me that I'll have to do all the work again?' he asked.

'Again?' I echoed, rattled. 'I work pretty hard myself.'

He gave me a lopsided grin, and looked at me with

unblinking eyes, which made my lips tingle. He gripped my forearms and tackled me to the bed. There was a thud and a curse as his head made contact with the headboard.

Half an hour later an impatient room service waiter rapped on the bedroom door.

Now that I no longer had to worry about facing John, I was relaxed and looking forward to our half-day boat trip. First stop was the island of Murano, renowned for its glass manufacturing. And then we would visit Burano, famous for lace-making and for the island's colourfully painted fishermen's houses. The last stop was Torcello, the first centre of civilisation in the estuary. I was quite excited.

But waiting for the water bus, I was overcome with nausea. I tugged fiercely on Nikki's arm; he looked down at me.

'What is it?' he asked.

'I'm sea sick,' I confessed, grimly.

'Sea sick? Don't be ridiculous, we're not even on a boat, we're standing at the bus stop. You can't possibly be sea sick. And this is a lagoon, not the Atlantic.'

I looked wildly around the bus stop, which was like a floating, pitching train carriage.

'I've got to get out of here,' I muttered.

He stood tall, arms crossed, and glared down his nose at me. I clamped my hand over my mouth. A muscle in his jaw twitched suspiciously.

'Nik, don't laugh.'

'Evie, you *cannot* be sea sick, we are not. On. A boat! And we are not. At. Sea!'

I closed my eyes, and fought down an inner tidal wave.

'Nik, please, I, I can't—'

He grabbed hold of my arm and led me towards the lolling,

swaying throng of people forming a crocodile line to board the newly arrived water bus.

'How are we supposed to get from A to B if you won't get on a boat, there's no other way to travel. Has it slipped your attention that the entire city is surrounded by water?' he asked. 'Because it was the first thing I noticed when I got here.'

I stumbled beside him, keeping my eyes tightly closed, trying to stabilise my rolling stomach.

'Sit down,' he said, pressing my shoulders so that I landed with a thud in a seat by the window.

OK this is ridiculous, he's right. I won't see the city if I don't use the boats, it's that simple. Nik sat beside me, smiling randomly at a row of passengers sitting opposite. I cuddled his arm, bent my head and laid my cheek on his chest. He craned his neck to look at me.

'Evie!'

I swallowed hard.

'Evie!'

'What,' I bleated.

He lifted my chin.

'Oh,' he said, peering closely. 'You do look pale.'

'Nik, I feel like crying,' I confessed.

He ran a hand through his hair, making it stick up at the top, and flexed his broad shoulders, pulling his shirt from his waistband.

'I'm trying,' I said.

'I thought, well, I thought you were ... exaggerating,' he broke off uncomfortably. 'Rest your head on my lap,' he said, teasing me gently off his arm. 'Your sense of balance is in your ears, if you lay flat you'll feel better.'

'I need to anchor my stomach.'

'This will help,' he told me pressing my ear to his thigh.

And it did help. At least I didn't vomit. But at one point I wished the boat would sink and that a helicopter would be sent to rescue us, which, OK, was rather extreme considering we were only on a half-day excursion, and no more than fifteen minutes from land at any one time.

It was the longest half-hour of my life.

'I'm not getting back on this boat,' I assured Nik, as I followed the line of people queuing to disembark at Murano. 'And Nik, look at the height of the waves crashing against the breaker; I can't believe we're expected to take our lives in our hands and walk on water to get back on terra firma.'

'Evie, they're not *waves*, it's a light ripple of wake, lapping against the pier.'

'Call it what you like, I'm braving it once and once only.'

'Well sweetheart, I think you may have to reconsider, because as this is an island surrounded by water, I think you'll find you have no choice but to get back on this boat, unless of course, you decide to spend the rest of your life here.'

I overtook him.

I loved the glass-making display in the glass factory. I watched with the keenness of a hawk hunting a rabbit, and do you know what? I still don't have a clue how glass is made. It's a miracle. A twisted hot sticky globule at the end of a long iron pole was taken out of a blazing furnace, and before my eyes it was crafted into a beautiful seahorse.

There was a hearty round of applause from the enthralled audience at the end of the demonstration.

'I'd love to go on a glass-making course,' I told Nikki, in a rush of enthusiasm.

'Would you now?'

'Yes, I would,' I said, as we followed the slow moving group out of the factory and into the shop, which was an amazing Aladdin's cave of glittering glass.

'I want that chandelier,' I said, pointing to a beautiful crystal chandelier in tranquil blue, with long slim candle bulbs. 'It's stunning.'

Nikki nodded at the chandelier thoughtfully.

'It's also eight hundred quid, and you have a chandelier, and there's no room for another one in your lounge.'

'But it's fantastic,' I said.

He folded his arms and relaxed against the wall.

'You don't need it, and you can't afford it.'

'What's it got to do with you?' I snapped.

'Everything! It has everything to do with me, because when you're in debt you're unbearable to work with.'

'I'm not.'

'You are, you sulk.'

'I don't.'

He gave a dubious shrug.

I sighed.

'Do you know what, Nik? I can't be bothered to argue with you, because I'm too busy worrying about getting back on the boat. But I do not sulk.'

He gave a objective shrug.

Actually he was right, I couldn't afford the chandelier, and I do get grumpy when I'm in debt, but I'd rather have root canal treatment than admit that to him. I rubbed my temple as we walked out the shop. I really wasn't looking forward to getting back on the boat. My entire body clenched at the thought of it. We had been land lubbers for forty minutes now, and I felt so much better.

Nikki gave me a tight smile.

'I feel sick at the thought of getting back on the boat.'

His smile melted.

'We could miss the other two islands on the tour and take a water bus straight back to Venice,' he suggested.

'Would you mind?' I asked.

He put his arm around my shoulder.

'Of course not, so long as you rest your face in my crotch all the way back, I quite liked it.'

'Don't be rude!' I told him.

As feared the journey back to Venice was horrendous.

My face cooled and my pulse normalised as we walked alongside the Grand Canal on our way back to the hotel.

'It's only three o'clock; would you like to go shopping?' Nikki asked.

'You want to go shopping?' I questioned sceptically.

'Not really but you do, don't you? And I said I would go with you,' he reminded me. 'We'll go to Calle Vallaresso.'

'Calle Vallaresso? What's that?'

'The Venetian equivalent to Bond Street.'

'I'm not my usual spirited self, I might miss a bargain. I feel drained to be honest. Let's do something more relaxing,' I suggested.

'Like what?'

My eyes shifted behind him to the imposing caramel façade of the Danieli Hotel.

He followed my line of vision.

'I read on Travel Finder that you can't visit Venice without having a glass of champagne in the Danieli.' I told him.

He gave me his arm.

'Is that so? Well then, that's exactly what we'll do.'

The Danieli is awesome. With precious antique rugs, hand-carved pink marble columns, gilted ceilings and a wealth of antiques, and that was just the lobby. I sank into a silk covered chair in the bar, which was seriously plush, glamorous and . . . deadly quiet.

'Nik,' I whispered. 'I love it, do you?'

'You don't have to whisper, and yes I love it.'

'The flowers are gorgeous, and look at the chandeliers,' I said, pointing ceilingwards. 'They're enormous.'

'Yes they are impressive,' he agreed, following my gaze. He picked up the wine list. 'We might as well have a bottle of champagne now that we're comfortable,' he said.

'Yes, we might as well,' I agreed.

We drank two bottles, which were delicious, and were back at the hotel and in bed by seven o'clock.

'Evie, we're knackered, there's no point going out, we'll eat in.' Nik said, reaching for the bedside phone.

I was pissed. The room was spinning. I curved an arm on the pillow above my head. Nik ordered room service, with what I can only describe as animated excitement. He's a food obsessive, there's no doubt about it. He banged down the receiver.

He looked down at me.

'I'm pissed,' I confessed, the back of my hand pressed to my forehead. 'I don't want to eat, I want to sleep.'

I shut my eyes to the spinning ceiling.

'I know you're pissed, I can see that, but you'll have to stay awake long enough to eat something, and tomorrow we'll take your evaluation report seriously ... and we'll make it to the shops.'

His hand smoothed my hair.

'Whatever,' I agreed, half-dozing.

'Evie, wake up!'

I grabbed the pillow and put it over my head to drown him out.

'Leave me, let me sleep.'

He got out of bed, pulled back the sheet, tossed my pillow on the floor, and lifted me in his arms as though I weighed nothing at all. I blinked into his neck.

'A shower will wake you up,' he said inspirationally, striding towards the bathroom.

'Nik, I don't want a shower. Think positive, if I pass out, you can eat all the food yourself. You would like that, wouldn't you?'

He shifted me into a firmer position.

'That would be nice, but then you'll wake up hungry in the middle of the night and you'll be hungover all day tomorrow.'

'I won't!'

'You will.'

'I won't!'

'You're a bear's head when you're hungover.'

'I'm not!'

'You are.'

'Evie, I've known you for a long time; I've lived with you through a lot of hangovers. You are *not* spoiling tomorrow because you won't get out of bed.'

'Nik ... don't ...'

He set me to my feet in the shower, and with an earnest smile, pressed me against the wall.

'Evie, this will sort you out,' he told me with a wise nod, and then turned on the cold tap.

'Aaaaaaagggggg!'

Ice-cold water splattered my face. The shock of it froze my lungs.

'Evie, this is for your own good.'

I disagreed.

'You are a wicked spiteful bastard Nikki!' I shrieked, puddles discharging around my feet. 'I hate you!'

'You don't.'

'I do!' I spluttered.

'You don't.'

'I'll catch pneumonia!'

'You won't.'

'I will!'

'You won't . . . Evie, I'm doing this because I care about you,' he said stepping into the shower with me.

The following morning we made it to the shops. Nikki halted in front of Gucci, dug his hands in his pockets and rocked on his heels.

'Would you like to go inside?' he asked with bright eyes.

I pushed my sunglasses to the top of my head, and shook my head good-naturedly.

'I don't want anything in there.'

His brows lifted.

'Nothing?' he asked.

He pulled me to him.

'You don't want anything in Gucci? Are you by any chance slightly hungover, and can't be bothered to try anything on?' he asked, rather too observantly for my liking.

'No!' I shot back.

'Liar.'

I tried to wriggle from his cuddle.

'Nik, according to you, I'm mean with money, I gnaw and suck at you, I'm impatient, and I'm a spoiled little brat. I sulk when I'm in debt, I'm a bear's head when I'm hungover, I'm prone to exaggerate and now I'm a liar. In your opinion do I have *any* favourable characteristics at all?' I asked, incredulous.

He tightened his already tight hold and gave me an evaluating look.

'Those *are* your favourable characteristics,' he said flatly.

'Is that so? Dare I ask what my vices are, if those are my virtues?'

His eyes narrowed in thought.

'You don't have any vices at all,' he said. 'Not that I've noticed anyway. In my opinion, you're perfect.'

His lips curved into a smile.

'Perfect?' I asked, smiling myself.

He bent his head and pressed his mouth over mine.

'The business I should have attended to a long time ago was to tell you that,' he said. 'You *are* perfect.'

He lifted my arms and placed them around his neck.

'And here, among the crowds of shoppers in Calle Vallaresso is the time and place to tell me?'

'It is,' he said, with a definitive nod.

He lifted a lock of my hair to his lips and kissed it.

'It most definitely is.'

We went into a rock chick boutique. Nikki bought me three jelly watches in purple, orange and pink. They were huge and gorgeous, and only ten euros each. I felt a disproportionate sense of jubilation at finding a bargain in Venice, no easy task I can tell you.

'How were you able to pick out the colours I would go for?' I asked him, as we waited to pay.

'Because you wear purple, orange and pink bras under your white shirt in the bar, and you always wear a splash of the same colour, either a band in your hair, nail varnish, or a ring.'

'And you noticed?'

'Of course I noticed.'

The attractive sales assistant with a soft pout and long dark hair eyed Nikki shamelessly as he fixed the pink watch on my wrist. Oblivious to her admiration he cupped my face and kissed me.

'I notice everything,' he told me.

We stopped at a pavement café for a drink in St Mark's

Square. A smart-looking waiter in a white tuxedo swooped towards us. Nik leaned back in his chair, spread his legs wide, pushed his sunglasses on to his forehead and ordered two lattes. We sat facing the square. I swivelled in my seat; there was so much to see and admire, the ornately decorated arches, Romanesque carvings, beautiful statues and of course the amazing clock tower. The piazza was heaving. There must be a thousand al fresco places, perhaps more. A crocodile of patient tourists curved the Basilica of San Marco which, drenched in the sun's rays, radiated shades of vanilla and peach. It was breathtaking.

I slumped forward, elbows on the linen covered table in a state of satisfied bliss, and eyed a slow moving line of Japanese schoolgirls, all with glossy black hair, dutifully following a tour guide waving a white flag.

'Fantastic isn't it?' I said. 'Do you know what makes this place stand out over and above anywhere else?' I asked Nik.

'No, what?'

'Voices!'

'Voices?'

'Yes, voices as opposed to the screech of brakes and the roar of cars and buses.'

I waved my hand randomly.

'Listen to buzz of the crowd, and listen to the . . . the music.' I closed my eyes and swooned to the sound. 'Nik, without the intrusion of traffic the background music sounds *live*. I can literally feel the violin strumming my heart strings,' I told him, palm pressed to my chest. 'I feel quite emotional; the notes are drifting in the air colliding with my senses. You would *really* think there was an orchestra right here in the café,' I told him. 'Wouldn't you?'

'There is,' he said flatly. 'There's an orchestra behind you.'

I opened my eyes.

'What!'

I bounced around in my chair. And sure enough in front of the café entrance, on an elevated platform draped with scalloped black velvet, was a five piece orchestra.

'Nik, I *love* Venice.'

He tipped forward and kissed me. An orchestra. Right here in the café. My mouth was aching from all the smiling. Nik relaxed in his chair with a contented sigh and flicked through the menu.

'If you love it, we'll come back. Four days isn't enough.'

I weighed up what he had just said. 'We'll come back.' I gave him a guarded glance. He was absorbed in the carte du jour, concentrating fiercely. Any minute now he'll leap into action, signal for the waiter and order everything he can pronounce. My heart missed a fraction of a beat at the thought of going home. Surprisingly I quite liked having Nik to myself. In fact, I loved having him to myself.

'Shall I order a little of everything?' he asked. 'And we can share.'

If he was offering to share, that meant he was indeed ordering everything.

'Fine,' I said.

After lunch, we went back to the hotel and studied the brief on the mystery guest evaluation criteria. We decided Nikki would go back to the gym, and then to reception to test the patience of the duty manager by making a couple of silly demands and to try and make a reservation during the Venice carnival when he knew the hotel would be sold out. I was going to look over the facilities at the conference centre, and visit the gift shop, and then to make a nuisance of myself at the concierge desk. We reasoned splitting up would help match the mainstream guest demographic against the services provided. Our aim was to provide a comprehensive overview of our customer experience, and to focus on areas where we saw room for improvement. We would then regroup, after collecting our data, and tailor an analytic report based on our findings. We were on a mission. Mission Mystery Guest.

But we had a shag first!

In the evening, Nikki took me to a restaurant near the Rialto Bridge, in Calle della Madonna. Burning torches heralded the entrance to a large bustling trattoria alive with music and tables crammed with animated diners. Enormous vases of flowers were placed randomly, and smart waiters wearing black ties and long jackets with tails zigzagged deftly between the tables, trays of drinks held high.

The head waiter escorted us to an alcove table, and with a twiddle of his stiff winged collar and a swish of his tailcoat, disappeared.

Nik placed his hand over mine, and eyed me with appreciation.

'You look beautiful, have I told you?'

I rolled my eyes.

'About ten times,' I said.

'But you do, I love your hair loose, you always wear it tied back in the bar. '

'Nik,' I began with a sigh. 'What happens when we get home?'

'What do you mean?'

'With us? What happens with us? And what do we tell everyone?'

'Nothing, we don't tell anyone anything.'

'But—'

He pressed his finger to my lips.
'No buts, we'll take it slowly, a day at a time.'
And that sounded just perfect to me.

VENICE

Chapter Twenty-eight

We were in my flat. Nikki was *not* taking things slowly. He wanted to stay the night, but I wasn't convinced it was a good idea. Lulu would be home soon, I'd have to tell her about Nik and me. I couldn't just let her walk in on us.

He gave me a curious look.

'I don't get it? So what if Lulu walks in on us?' Nik asked, spreading his arms wide.

The contents of my suitcases were splayed over my bed. I was unpacking.

'Nik, just let me explain my – I mean, *our* situation to her, she—'

'Explain what? What are you going to say?'

'What do you think I'm going to say? I'm going to tell her about us.'

He gave an incredulous snort.

'Don't you think if she comes home to find me in bed with you, she may be bright enough to work it out for herself?'

'Well yes, she would, and that is the whole point, I'd rather forewarn her.'

'Forewarn her? We're not talking about an impending earthquake or a natural disaster of some sort; don't you think you're being a little melodramatic?'

'No, it's simply a matter of courtesy, you obviously don't understand.'

I gathered a bundle of clean knickers from my case, tossed them in the bottom drawer of my dresser and kicked the drawer closed.

He moved behind me and began massaging my shoulders.

'I have a compromise,' he said, nibbling my ear.

'What's that?'

'We sleep at my place tonight. And you speak with Lulu tomorrow, that way I don't have to spend the night in a lonely bed without you.'

He turned me to him, put his arms around me and unzipped my dress from neck to waist. I smiled as a chill from the open window licked my back. He ran his knuckles slowly up and down my spine, and pushed his hips into mine.

'Surely you have no objection to that?' he said.

I didn't, far from it.

'OK, we'll stay at your place.' I agreed primly.

After all that, Lulu told me when I called her that she was sleeping at Vic's. Which to be honest was a relief. So we stayed at mine. We were in bed before *News at Ten*.

Restless, I pulled away from him, raised myself on one elbow and watched him sleep, heavily and dreamily. I finger-tipped a moonbeam moving across his face. Instinctively he rolled towards my touch, gathered me to him, turned me and pulled me against his chest and pressed his chin into my hair. And it felt wonderful, blissfully wonderful. I was glad Nikki had stayed, so glad. I didn't want to be in a lonely bed either.

'Go to sleep,' he said softly.

I wriggled my bum into the curve of him and fell asleep, soundly.

There was an almighty thud as the bedroom door flew open and light drenched the room. I squeezed my eyes shut and buried my face in Nikki's chest.

Lulu's voice exploded.

'Evie! Me and Vic have had a fight, he is so selfish. Move over, I'll tell you all about it. Can I sleep with you?'

There was a rustle of quilt.

'No! You *cannot* sleep with her. What time d'you call this?' Nikki thunderous voice boomed. 'Get to bed.'

A ripple of goosebumps stood on the back of my neck. I sat up against the headboard, pulled the quilt around me, and watched the colour drain from Lulu's face. Her eyes grew wide and her lips parted. She gripped the chest of drawers for support and stared.

'You . . . ' she managed, pointing a finger at me in accusation. 'And . . . him.'

Her brown eyes were huge, the biggest I've ever seen them, and wild and shining. She opened her mouth but no sound came out.

'I can explain,' I said, a hand held up in surrender.

'I fucking doubt it,' she snapped, finding her voice, 'you've got Nikki in your bed. Are you naked?' she spluttered. 'Is he naked? Are there any more of the neighbours in there? Why not?'

The quilt fell across Nik's lap as he bolted upright. He ran an irritated hand through his hair.

'Let's have all the neighbours round. Are you mad?' she ranted.

'More to the point,' Nik bellowed, 'are you *smoking*?'

Lulu's haunted eyes darted to the telltale Marlboro billowing between her fingers.

She inhaled sharply, and eyed the cigarette in disgusted bewilderment.

375

'No . . . No, I'm not smoking!' she denied swiftly.

'Well it looks like you are to me, because you have a cigarette in your hand,' Nik challenged.

'I'm holding it . . . for someone. It's not mine,' she shot back.

'Who! Who are you holding it for? I don't see anyone here in the room except us,' Nik counter-attacked.

Her eyeballs were practically rotating in panic.

'Erm, it was, it was . . . the cab driver's cigarette, he asked me to hold it, and, and . . . he forgot to take it back,' she lied in a flash of deceitful genius. 'I don't smoke, everyone knows that,' she said, with the shadow of a proud smile.

I put my head in my hands and cringed in embarrassment.

She tucked a lock of hair behind her ear and scanned the room for somewhere to stub out the cigarette.

'You're a liar, put that cigarette out, and get to bed,' Nik said. 'It's two o'clock in the morning.'

She waved her ciggie.

'This is all wrong,' she said with a shaky voice. 'You two, doing . . . doing what you're doing . . . it's practically incest.'

Nik jerked his head towards the bedroom door.

'Bed!'

Eyes wide, she looked like a rabbit caught in the headlights of a car.

'Now!'

He made as though to pull back the quilt and get out of bed. She stumbled backward, whirled around and shot out the room, slamming the door behind her.

'How dare you talk to me like that!' she shouted bravely, from the other end of the hall.

Nik gave me a coy smile, and shook his head wearily.

'She is an almighty pain in the arse, but it's hard not to love her. Nevertheless she would try the patience of a saint.'

He pointed a finger in warning.

'You knew, didn't you?'

'Knew what?' I asked, although in no doubt about what he was referring to.

'You knew that she still smoked.'

I considered denying it.

'Don't deny it!'

I pressed my lips together.

'And to think we've had to listen to her day in and day out on the radio, blowing her own bloody trumpet, the lying scheming little baggage,' he said.

My phone buzzed, it was a text.

'Who is texting you at two o'clock in the morning?' Nik asked as I reached to the bedside table for my phone.

'Lulu,' I said, seeing her name on my display.

He's a raving nutter!!!!

Nik read the message over my shoulder and chuckled. He pulled back the quilt and got out of bed to turn the light off.

'A nutter am I? I can't believe it; I can't believe she still smokes. No wonder your face was burning when I pointed out that billboard on the drive from the airport, with her face blazoned all over it. What was the caption? LULU: MENTOR TO MILLIONS, or some such rubbish.'

He squeezed my shoulder gently as he got back into bed. There was a flash of neon blue in the gloom as my phone buzzed again.

He won't tell will he?

He pulled the quilt across his lap, took my phone from my hand, and sucked his teeth in mock indecision as he read.

He drew in a deep breath.

'I'll tell!' he bellowed, loud enough for her to hear. 'If you don't behave yourself!'

She didn't text again.

Despite having been wakened at two o'clock Nikki got up at six-thirty to go to the gym. I made two mugs of hot chocolate, edged into Lulu's room and placed the drinks on her dressing table. She slept on her back, mouth slightly opened, snoring softly, blonde hair fanning the pillow, with her Zorro sleep mask over her eyes. I crawled into bed beside her.

'Lulu.'

'What?' she asked, roused by my voice.

'About last night—'

'I've been thinking about it, about you being with Nikki. It's a brilliant idea,' she said.

'It is?'

She pushed her mask on to her forehead and sat up on her elbows.

'Yes, it is! It will stop you from turning into a crazed manic-depressive. It will also keep you from sticking to that other fanny magnet you just got rid of. Because I doubt we've heard the last of him. And well, Nik has fancied you for ages, and I like him.'

'Fancied me for ages?'

She gave a knowing sigh.

'Evie, please don't tell me you hadn't noticed,' she said in a measured tone.

'Why didn't you tell me?' I asked.

'Tell you? Why should I have needed to tell you? It was obvious. He gave you a job despite the fact that when you started you were the most useless waitress breathing. He nursed you like an old woman when you had your accident last year. He walks you home at night if you work after eight o'clock. He trusts you with his business, and he won't let me slag you off no matter what you've done,' she said, with a haughty grin.

I reached across her for my hot chocolate, digesting her words. Now that she mentioned it Nik will often walk me across the road if I work at night. It really hadn't been something I even noticed before.

Her body tensed, she clutched her chest.

'Evie! He saw me!' she began in a rush. 'Nikki saw my fag. I let my guard down. Can you believe it? I'm so used to us having the place to ourselves, that I lit a fag outside my bedroom perimeter. You could have had anyone in your bed,' she pressed a palm to her forehead. 'You could have had one of the producers from my show. What was I thinking?'

She flopped back against the pillow, and shot me a haunted look.

'Nik won't tell anyone he saw me smoking, will he?'

'No, no, he won't, don't worry,' I assured her.

'Are you sure?'

'Yes. Positive.'

'Evie, you don't think . . . he might, well . . . ' she trailed off.

'He might what?'

'Blackmail me.'

'Blackmail you? Why would he do that?'

'I would if I were him,' she admitted, deadpan. 'He could and I'd have to pay up, wouldn't I?'

'But you don't have any money,' I reminded her.

'You're right, I don't . . . So what shall I do?'

'Lulu, don't you think life would be easier if you were to . . . *stop smoking*,' I hedged.

She chewed her inner jaw.

379

'It would, but, it's hard, and I can't, I've tried. You know I've tried. I hallucinate and dream about fags. I cry. And my car breaks down. All sorts of nightmares happen. My life falls to pieces. I fall to pieces.'

'But you've done incredibly well, despite . . . *everything*.'

'I have?'

'Yes, you have. You only smoke in this bedroom,' I said waving a hand demonstratively. 'You never smoke at work, or when we're out. That's a fantastic achievement.'

There was a glint of pride in her eyes as she lifted her hot chocolate.

'You're right, I've done brilliantly. In fact, I've practically taken all my own best advice.'

'You have. So, I suggest you stop buying cigarettes, and see how you get on, because if you don't buy them, then you can't smoke them,' I told her.

She goggled at me, understanding distilling inside her.

'You're right,' she said with sudden passion. 'You're absolutely right.'

I licked the froth from my hot chocolate, and gave her an encouraging smile.

'I'll have a fag now, because obviously I need to finish this packet, but after that, I won't buy any more,' she said, with a definitive nod. 'Or perhaps what I'll do is buy packets of ten, as opposed to packets of twenty, for a couple of weeks.'

'Great idea,' I said encouragingly. 'As we're awake early shall we go out for breakfast?'

'Why not?' she said.

I walked into the bar at ten o'clock. It was an hour before we were due to open. The bar was empty except for Nikki who was sitting at a table littered with credit card receipts.

He looked at me with weary eyes, rolling his pen end over end.

'No one has bothered to do the banking since I left on Friday,' he said.

'Can I help with it?' I asked, shrugging out of my jacket.

'I'm almost finished.'

I edged in beside him; he put a strong hand between my shoulder blades, leaned forward and kissed me.

'Did you speak to Lulu?' he asked.

'Yes, she's fine. In fact, she's delighted, she's really happy for us,' I told him.

'Good, so she should be, I know I am,' he said stroking my cheek.

He gave me a warm smile. I'd had something on my mind all morning; I didn't quite know how to broach the subject without causing offence. I stretched linked hands in contemplation.

'Nik, I'm not sure I'm ready—'

'Ready for what?' he asked, short circuiting my voice.

'To, well, to,' this was a tough one, 'to receive your mother's good wishes,' I admitted in a rush. 'Because she's been quite keen for us, to—'

He held up the flat of his hand.

'Evie! My sentiments exactly, I tell her nothing, absolutely nothing. And if you know what's good for you, you'll do the same . . . for now anyway.'

I exhaled a smile.

'We'll tell her . . . later,' I said, fears allayed.

'Agreed!'

I inched towards him, took the pen from his hand and placed it on the table, and pressed my forehead against his. I felt a flood of warmth in my chest.

'Nik, I had a fabulous time in Venice.'

'So did I.'

He lifted my hand from the table and pressed my palm on his thigh.

'I see you're wearing your pink watch,' he said, thumb circling my wrist. 'And a pink bra to match,' he added, trailing his finger inside my blouse.

He pushed back the table, lifted me across his lap and positioned my legs to straddle his hips. I looked him full in the face; his eyes were dark glittering triangles. He pulled my shirt free from my waistband and ran his hands roughly the length of my back, causing a bubble of heat to burst in my tummy. I unbuttoned his shirt, raked my nails over his chest, and quickly pushed his shirt over his shoulders.

I didn't know which was the louder, the pounding of blood in my ears or the beating of his heart against my chest. He clamped strong fingers around my wrist and forced my hand between his legs; drew a deep breath, and closed his eyes to my touch. I was as horny as a fiend, frenzied with desire. So was he! I curved my free arm behind his neck and held him in a head lock, and rubbed my cheek against his hair. He gripped my bum and thrust me to him in a series of sharp jerky movements.

'Now! I want it now!' I demanded. 'Let's go to your office upstairs, you have the only key, no one will come in. Take me there!' I said, in a rushed desperate voice.

I shook my hair from my eyes and pressed his face into my cleavage.

He gave a deep growl. I had to have him! Right now this minute! It was the growl that did it, I love it when he growls . . .

Gooseflesh pricked my neck as his hot breath spread across my breasts.

'Take me to Valhalla!' I yelled to the ceiling, like an Apache who had just got hold of a cowboy with a good head of hair.

Valhalla! What the hell was I saying?

He breathed deeply in, and slowly out. His eyes flickered with pleasure as I groped inside his waistband, curving and straightening my palm. I quivered at the thought of having an impromptu daytime ride in the office upstairs.

A shadow fell across Nik's face. His eyes drifted behind me. I fielded his gaze, the shadow on his face didn't move. I tilted my head, and realised in a flash of horrified awareness that the shadow hadn't moved, because . . . the shadow wasn't mine. I swivelled. Lined like a firing squad ready to take aim, stood Maria, Pepi, Costas, Uncle Spiros and the little buffet chef, also called Spiros, and the wines and spirits delivery driver.

I caught Nik's agonised expression; his lips were pressed tight and the colour had drained from his face. He gave a tormented sigh. But it wasn't so much the look on his face that bothered me, it was his near naked torso and seriously tented crotch that concerned me more.

'Put me down,' I said to him, rallying decorum.

He pressed my ear to his mouth.

'If you move off my lap, I'll kill you,' he warned in a dramatic whisper.

My eyes travelled to his groin. I could see his point. I slid a glance over my shoulder. The line-up stood wide-eyed and motionless. As Nik angled his shoulders into his shirt and set his hands to the buttons, he snapped something sharp and meaningful in Greek. His words had an immediate effect. Pepi and Costas bolted, taking the wines and spirits delivery driver with them, and the scraping of flip-flops on the tiled floor followed the departure of Buffet Spiros. Nik fastened the top two buttons of my blouse that I hadn't realised were undone, smoothed my hair from my face, and placed his hands on my waist, lifting me from his lap.

Uncle Spiros, brows drawn, gave me a heavy look, more evaluating than judgemental, and then turned squarely on Nikki. A blistering argument erupted between them. Nikki's voice was like a whip, matched lash for lash by his uncle who was not uncharacteristically furious. Spiros stood fists on hips; he gestured commandingly towards the kitchen door. Nik, enraged, stormed after him.

That left Maria and me. She stood in front of me. Her eyes were glazed, swimming with love and dreams, her lips quivered, her nostrils twitched, and her L'Oreal tinted beehive shook with emotion. She looked like a Moonie, like some crazed cult follower who spends all day chanting and banging on a tambourine. We eyed each other, time froze, and the space around us seemed to shrivel, to close in on us. Her mouth worked wordlessly. It was like being in a silent movie. I took an impulsive step back, I knew what was coming next. Suddenly, I was in her arms, lights jigged in front of my eyes, as she set about cutting off my air supply. She reached up, buried her fingers in my hair and pulled my face to hers and kissed me, tears splashed her chubby cheeks, tracking her two inch thick foundation. She cupped my face.

'You tell Nikki, I have the day off, I'm very very busy,' she said with urgency. 'Understand?'

I nodded. And was about to ask her why she needed the day off when she whirled, grabbed her bag from the counter and shot out the door.

There was a ceasefire in the bar, with no fights, none at all, not even an argument. Pepi and Costas didn't call me names, steal my orders, or skive to the betting shop when Nik went to the bank. They were cordial, polite in a formal way, it was most unlike them. And when I told Nik that his mum had taken the day off, he didn't explode. He stared at me for a moment and then nodded at my words, it was all quite strange. Uncle Spiros's steely gaze followed me with a look I'd never seen in his dark eyes before; it was as if he had something to say but didn't quite know how to go about saying it. I drew a trembling breath, and found I had to rally my own courage every time I clattered through the kitchen door. My nerves were shot to bits.

'Does Spiros think I'm, I'm . . . *loose* or something?' I asked Nik, my voice sounding higher than I'd liked.

Nikki's face went white; he pressed his fists on the bar and looked at me appalled. He leaned forward and placed a reassuring kiss on my forehead.

'No! Of course not, whatever makes you ask that?'

'He hasn't spoken to me all day,' I told him.

'Oh! Well, he hasn't spoken to me or anyone else either, so I wouldn't worry too much about that,' Nik said dismissively.

'What did he say to you when you were arguing?' I asked.

'I'm not telling you,' he said.

'Why not?'

He ran his hand through his hair.

'Because it was unjustified, he's out of order, and I expect an apology.'

'What was unjustified?'

He moved abruptly to the fridge, took out a bottle of white wine, twisted the corkscrew in the cork and popped it open with practised ease.

'What. Was. Unjustified!' I punctuated, rattled.

He closed his eyes briefly and sighed.

'We'll talk about it later,' he said.

Just after three o'clock Maria arrived with seven friends, all clones of herself. She insisted on sitting at one of my tables, despite the fact that Pepi had a table for eight available, and I only had a table for five.

I smiled in welcome, and waited patiently as eight large tweed covered bottoms bloomed with difficulty over five chairs. All eight stared at me reverentially.

I stood, pen poised over my order pad.

'What can I get you?' I asked Maria.

'Nothing!' she said, smiling over-brightly.

My eyes scanned the chubby heavily made up faces around the table, all nodded in agreement. I turned my head to Nik, behind the bar. He crooked his finger. 'Come here,' he mouthed.

I walked over to the bar, he leaned towards me.

'Tell them we need the table and ask them to leave if they don't want anything,' he said, deadpan.

Was he mad?

'Ask your mother and her friends to leave, are you joking?' I hissed, horrified. 'I'd rather be shot.'

'No! I'm not joking. And they're not her friends, they are my aunties.'

'You have seven aunties?'

'No! I have thirteen aunties; well, thirteen living in London, there are a few more in Greece.'

I cast a backward glance at Maria. She brushed a tear from her cheek and gave me a watery grin; she looked on me as though I were the only person in the bar. She wheeled her arms and rallied the seven aunties to smile at me. They did.

There was sudden gust of air and the clatter of the door against the wall.

'Ah! Speak of the devil. Here come the rest of them now,' Nik said, with a sidelong glance towards a barrage of chiffon neckscarves, pastel-coloured tweed jackets, chignon hairdos, and a mushroom cloud of windpipe strangling perfume.

'Why are they here?' I asked him. 'Is it a special occasion?'

'Yes it is! My mother is showing you off,' he said flatly, squinting at Maria.

'Showing me off?' I asked bewildered, and my face prickling with embarrassment.

He nodded sadly.

'Humour her,' he said, vertical lines showing as he frowned. 'She'll tire of it eventually . . . or I'll fire her if you like,' he added casually.

Costas sided with me.

'They want fifteen coffees and chocolate shortcake,' Costas told Nik, nodding at the aunties, who were busy scraping chairs noisily along the floor and generally rearranging all the furniture in the bar to accommodate their inflated party. 'And they want Evie to join them,' Costas added nonchalantly.

Nik gave me a nod of encouragement.

'Off you go then, sweetheart. Have a tea break,' he said.

I sank into the chair next to Maria; my senses seemed to be operating on some sort of unique super sensitive frequency. I was acutely aware of the sound of the traffic outside, the hiss of the cappuccino machine, the background music, a mobile phone vibrating on the table, and the hum of the air-conditioning unit overhead. But I had *no* idea whatsoever what any of the aunties were talking about. None! And by that I mean absolutely nada, because all fourteen were talking at the same time. I wondered if perhaps they were 'gifted' in some way. Could this ability to converse en masse be a seventh sense that I had never heard of? Or was I, unbeknown to myself, suffering from some sort of disorder where I could only hold one conversation at a time? I was out of my depth here. Totally.

Maria patted my arm, her searching brown eyes beamed at me.

'I have a little *geeft* for you,' she said, her voice throbbing with emotion.

My face blazed.

The table conversation halted, the aunties eyed Maria and me with bated breath.

Maria tugged her bag from the back of her seat, thumped it ceremoniously on the table, and foraged inside violently. The aunties tipped forward, overwhelmed with interest. Maria paused in her search, building tension. Thirteen mouths hung loose, reverential and attentive. Maria's eyes roved the table. She was elated, this was *her moment!* She excavated a small black velvet jewellery box. There was a collective gasp, beehives and chignons quivered. Maria put the box on the table and hugged herself. Thirteen backsides rose from their seats as the aunties bowed forward in anticipation. Maria opened the box to an energetic round of applause. It was a cameo ring and a matching brooch. Curiosity satisfied. Thirteen big backsides bloomed back into their seats.

A grin crept across Maria's face.

'Do you like it?' she asked, dreamily.

'I do,' I heard myself say.

She scooped my hair to the side and slid a large diamanté fish with an aquamarine eye in my fringe. Where had that come from – up her sleeve?

'I knew it!' she said. 'I knew the feesh would match your eyes.'

My eyes lifted and caught a sparkle; it was a life-size fish.

I looked at the velvet box. I wasn't ungrateful, I was just . . .

388

surprised. The cameo ring was very nice, if a little big. But the brooch was the size of an ostrich egg. What was I supposed to do with it? Nik and I had only been sleeping together for five nights, six days. I was undeserving of family heirlooms. This was all a tad overwhelming. Nikki would have to help me out. He'd have to.

Nik was relaxed against the bar, arms folded, eyelids half-closed against the glare of the late afternoon sun. He gestured towards the diamanté fish in my hair and gave me the thumbs up. Isn't he hilarious? I jammed my hands in between my thighs and raised my chin as Maria fastened the top button of my blouse and pinned on the cameo. What must I look like? The brooch was so big that I couldn't lower my chin.

It was almost six o'clock before the aunties finally filed slowly out the door, and I was able to take off the brooch and slide the fish out of my hair. I was exhausted, we'd had a smiley photo-shoot and everything.

Nik and I had dinner in an Italian restaurant three doors down from Bar Thea. The stream of wine being poured in my glass was positively musical.

'What was all the shouting about between you and Spiros?' I asked him.

His face clouded.

'Oh! It was just him being him. You've heard it all before. Did you email in your mystery guest evaluation?' he asked, changing the subject.

'I did.'

'And?'

'Fine, yes, Tina said it was well-received.'

He reached across the table and palmed my cheek.

'Good, maybe we'll get to do it again sometime.'

'Nik, your mum—'

'Evie, I'm an only child, not by design I can assure you. What can I say? She is what she is. Humour her.'

He put his hand on the table over mine.

'She'll wear herself out eventually.'

I doubted it.

Chapter Twenty-nine

Nik and I now have a key for each other's flat. In the past month we've only spent five nights apart. Four nights when I escorted a weekend break to Barcelona, which I loved. And one night when I had dinner with John in London, and stayed at his house because I had an eight-thirty meeting at Insignia Tours' office the following day and it's is only a five minute cab ride from Park Lane. I had started to tell John about Nikki, but John had seemed preoccupied and distant – twice I'd had to repeat myself and drag him back into our conversation. Likely he had some trillion pound deal on his mind, and my love life wasn't overly important or interesting. In the end I gave him a basic overview and pretty much nothing else.

Lexy's reaction to my news was much more enthusiastic. She has always liked Nikki, now she *loves* him because Nik doesn't mind if she dumps the kids in the bar at lunchtime and takes herself off shopping. The kids are in their element at the bar, because Nik gives them ice cream for dinner and can lift them above his head with one hand. He also lets them deliver cakes to customers and pays them a salary to do it. Becky actually suggested Nik fire Pepi and give her his job. Which I think shows promise for professional success later on in life because she's only four years old and obviously already ambitious.

Costas and Pepi soon grew accustomed to the idea of Nik and me being an item. They no longer treat me with reverential respect. They've reverted to the couple of lazy bastards I knew and loved, skiving to the bookies, chatting up girls and generally working as hard as they can at not working at all. But I wouldn't dream of telling Nikki, not on pain of death, because I live in constant fear of Costas or Pepi reporting to Maria with feigned alarm, that I looked unwell, or tired, or heaven forbid . . . thin, because this triggers all sorts of repercussions. Maria accuses Nikki of not looking after me; plies me with vitamins and force feeds me meals I don't want. I'm in no doubt whatsoever that Maria would like nothing better than for me to be struck by some tropical disease, or the latest global epidemic, just for the pleasure of looking after me. The overwhelming impulse to shoot her comes and goes. Reasons against shooting her being:

1. I would go to prison.
2. She means well.
3. I don't have a gun.
4. I don't know where or how to apply for a gun licence.
5. I have no idea how to dispose of a body.
6. I would be a murderer and my family would be mortified.
7. Nikki has promised to ask his dad to put forward a motion for a conclave of the aunties, to see if anything can be done to help me.

I was hopeful; I had to be. I had to think positive. I now have fourteen brooches, am a member of Maria's book club, and she's threatening to sign us both up for an eight week course on illustrated pottery-making.

But all said and done, Nik and I are getting along fine. In fact, things couldn't be better.

I sat on Lulu's bed, legs crossed. I wasn't convinced that she needed the blackout curtains she was hanging, especially as she buys cigarettes in packets of ten with a view to buying none at all over the course of the next few weeks.

She took a step back to admire her handiwork.

'You never know, someone with a telescopic camera lens might film me having a fag, and I could end up on YouTube. I'm not taking any chances,' she said, with a glow of pride as she pleated folds into the curtains.

I doubted it.

My phone vibrated in my pocket, I eyed the call display, and felt a swoop of surprise. It was a text from Rob. My face blazed. Rob! I hadn't heard from him in weeks or no . . . months.

Lulu swivelled to face me.

'I know black curtains are dowdy but needs must,' she said.

A feeling of irrational guilt spread in my chest. I didn't dare look at Lulu, and didn't want to speak; for fear of my voice echoing my thoughts. It was only a text, why should I feel guilty for having received it? But I did! I stared at my phone as if it were radioactive.

Her eyes met mine questioningly.

There was a heavy silence.

The room was still.

'What? What is it?' she asked.

'Nothing. It's nothing!' I said, too quickly.

Suspicion flitted across her face, she pointed an accusatory finger.

'Do you know something I don't?'

'No!'

She slow marched towards me.

'You're . . . cagey!' she said.

'I'm not.'

'You are! You're hiding something.'

'I don't have anything to hide.'

'You receive a text yet you don't read it. Your face is burn-ing . . . And you're lying!'

'My face is not burning and I am not lying.'

She buried her head in her hands.

'Evie! Tell me . . . Tell me you're not cheating on Nik? You won't pull it off, trust me, I know. Some guys will overlook the odd indiscretion. Nik *will not*! Some guys will swallow anything you tell them. Nik is no fool, he can practically read minds. And, he's big, with a temper, and lives across the street. Evie, we would have to move! He would—'

'I'm not cheating on Nik.'

Her anger was rising.

'What is it then? What are you up to?' she snapped.

I jammed my phone in my pocket. She dived towards me. 'Let me see your phone!' she shrieked.

I tried to lurch away from her; she grabbed me by both arms.

With the advantage of surprise she straddled me, pressed me into the mattress and gripped my waist with her thighs.

'ITSNOTHINGITSNOTHING!' I yelled.

'GIVEMEYOURPHONE!'

I grabbed both her hands and held them tight between my own, and with a Herculean effort managed to flip her on to her back and straddle her in turn.

'GETOFFME!' she screamed. 'GETOFFME.'

Her spine buckled and curved. We tottered on the edge of the bed and then landed with a thud on the floor in a tangle of arms and legs.

'IF IT'S NOTHING THEN LET ME SEE YOUR PHONE!'

'NO!!'

'YOU'RE HIDING SOMETHING!'

'IAMNOT! HIDINGANYTHING!'

'LIAR!'

The bedroom door crashed against the wall.

'What the hell is going on?' Nikki shouted, striding purposefully into the room.

Lulu froze, the colour sapped from her cheeks. She was stunned. So was I. We hadn't heard Nik come home; he would have shouted out, he always does. We hadn't heard a thing. Lulu squared her shoulders, and placed a balancing hand on my elbow. We helped each other to standing. She smoothed my hair from my face, while I straightened her blouse.

'Explain!' Nik snapped, eyes shifting between us.

'It was nothing,' Lulu said.

'Nothing?' he challenged.

'Nothing at all,' I blurted.

Nik's eyes burned with cynicism. Feet planted wide, he held out a hand to me. I took it, and followed him down the hallway. He closed our bedroom door, sat me down on the bed, sat beside me and pressed his palm on my thigh.

His eyes searched mine.

'Do you want to tell me about it?' he asked, softly.

'It really is nothing. Rob texted me,' I told him. 'That's all . . . and Lulu was trying to get my phone off me.'

He spired his hands and leaned forward, resting elbows on knees. His eyes shifted sideways, narrowed reprovingly.

'Does he text you often?' he asked.

'No, I haven't heard from him in months.'

'What does he want?'

'I don't know, I haven't read the text.'

He sat up and turned to me, brows drawn.

I stood and took my phone from my pocket.

Evie, let's have a drink, it's been so long. Surely we can still be friends. Rob. X

I tilted my phone to let Nik read the message.

'Do you want to meet him for a drink?' he asked.

'No . . . No, I don't.'

'Are you sure?'

'Yes, I'm sure.'

His arms circled my waist, he pulled me against him and laid his head in the folds of my blouse. For a minute he didn't speak.

'When was the last time you thought of him?' he asked, at last.

I ran my hands through his hair, pressing my fingers hard to massage the solid bone behind his ears.

'I thought of him in Venice.'

'You thought of him, when you were in Venice with me?'

'No, I thought of him when I arrived in Venice and had to drag my own bag to the water taxi.'

I felt the rumble of his laugh vibrate against my chest.

'Did you think of him at all after that?'

'No I didn't, because you carried my bag on the way home.'

He pulled me down on to his lap.

'Is that all we men mean to you?' he asked, burrowing his nose in the hollow of my neck.

I pressed my hand on his chest, and traced the outline of his nipple with my thumb.

'It's all that particular man means to me.'

There was a raggedness in his breathing, a mixture of laughter and relief.

'Truly? That's how you feel . . . in truth?' he asked.

'Yes, yes, it is! In truth, that's . . .'

The bedroom door burst open.

'That's brilliant!' Lulu proclaimed, her eyes shining. She threw her hands up. 'At last, I knew it would happen, it was just a matter of time, and—'

Nikki held my elbow, he inched me from his lap, stood and slow marched towards Lulu.

'Were you listening outside our door?' he challenged.

She had the nerve to look insulted.

'No, of course not, what do you take me for? I just . . . happened to be passing and so I thought I'd—'

'Out!' he bellowed.

She tugged her cardigan around her, shoulders pulsing with indignation.

'I'm leaving. I know when I'm not wanted,' she snapped.

'You don't, that's your problem,' he told her. 'You have no idea when you're not wanted.'

'I feel left out; you two are shutting me out of secrets, keeping things from me.'

'We keep nothing from you that you need to know,' Nik said.

'Shall I order a Chinese takeaway?' she asked, changing the subject completely.

'Yes,' Nik told her, taking his wallet from his pocket. 'You do that.'

Later in bed, I lay in the curve of his shoulder, my palm on his chest. He pressed his hand over mine, turned on his side and rolled to face me. His finger whispered from my eyebrow to chin.

'What's wrong?' I asked him.

397

'Are you happy, Evie?'

'Of course I am, are you?'

'I've never been happier in my life.'

He pulled me to him with a sigh.

'Go to sleep,' he said, with a smile. 'We're going shopping for the flat tomorrow. I expect it'll be a long day.'

Nikki and I had been shopping in Kingston for six hours, no time at all considering we had a whole flat to furnish. I could easily take six hours just to buy a pair of shoes and a matching handbag.

I contemplated the majestic glass atrium of the Bentall Centre as the escalator glided slowly to the second level. To be honest, I wasn't enjoying this shopping trip one single bit. Nik hadn't stopped complaining. My head was pounding. I stepped off the escalator, finger-tipping my temple, and cast a look over my shoulder. Nik's face was miserable, his hands were jammed in his pockets and he was a good three paces behind me. If I'd told him to keep up once, I'd told him ten times. If it wasn't for the fact that he was driving and had the car keys, I'd give him the slip, and make my own way home. He'd shown little to no interest in anything we looked at. When I asked him which he preferred between a faux leather four seater pillow back sofa and a mink and mocha velvet corner unit couch, he said, 'yes'! Now what exactly was that supposed to mean? And when I asked his preference between an oak dining table with ladder-back chairs and a smoked glass table with black leather high-back chairs, he said, 'they looked the same to him'. Now! Even with the worst eyesight in the whole wide world, you could *not* mistake an oak ladder-back chair for a black leather high-back, nor a smoked glass table for an oak table. I darted another glance at him. He was flagging back, easily now a good five paces behind me. I felt like killing him. The infuriating thing was, this shopping trip was for *his* benefit and *his* alone. I personally had nothing to gain by furnishing *his* flat with a view to renting it out. I was here as a favour to him. I wasn't the one who had to kit out a kitchen with everything from an egg whisk to a full dinner service.

I whizzed the strap of my bag up my arm. My heart thumped with fury when I thought how bloody ungrateful he was. I wheeled to him and gestured towards Boots. I needed headache tablets. Didn't that just say it all? He was making me ill. I wouldn't dream of starting an argument in the middle of a shopping centre. I drew a deep breath.

I whirled round.

'You,' I shrieked, 'are getting on my bloody nerves!' I jabbed an accusing finger in his chest. 'You want your flat furnished, don't you? That's why we're here, isn't it? So show willing! And keep up with me. I feel as though I've been dragging a Henry Hoover behind me for the last six hours!'

He grabbed my jabbing finger and squeezed it . . . hard.

'But we haven't actually bought anything for the flat yet, have we?' he said, dripping venom. 'Everything we've bought so far has been for you!'

OK, I was absolutely flabbergasted that he took that view. Because although we hadn't actually bought anything for the flat, I had a whole line of green ticks on the list of items the letting agent advised Nikki to provide before advertising for tenants. A green tick meant I had decided on a possible purchase – *possible* being the key word. A green tick with a 'B' meant the item was in Bentalls, and a green tick with a 'JL' meant the item was in John Lewis. I had explained this to him. I wasn't repeating myself.

I slapped his hand off my finger, and turned on my heel. He matched me stride for stride.

'You've bought a dressing gown, scented candles, a duvet cover with matching pillowcases and a set of bath towels, a pair of gloves and three hair bands! And I'm carrying the lot!'

My throat tightened. I decided to ignore him. I needed all those things, I can't remember the last time I've spent money on soft furnishings, and it made sense to buy them while we were here. And I saved a fortune because the Cream Company was relocating and everything had been marked down by seventy-five per cent. And as for who carried the bags, what did that matter?

'You spent half an hour trying on shoes, and then decided to wait for the sales. And you bought a raincoat, and a ton of make-up!' he ranted.

Also fifty per cent off, I reasoned inwardly.

I pushed my way through the door of Boots, my heels sounding on the tiled floor. I wasn't getting any pleasure out of this shopping trip. I wasn't experiencing the rush of adrenalin you get when you buy something you've coveted for ages, or the euphoric little tummy tickles you feel when you've grabbed a bargain. I felt, frustrated, unfulfilled, and hollow, and I felt . . . pissed, because we'd had lunch in TGIF's. I ordered a bottle of wine thinking Nik would share, but he didn't fancy any wine, and so I had to drink the whole bottle myself, which I could have done without! And here I was, doing *his* shopping, when what I really wanted to do was sit down and take the weight off my feet.

'What are we buying in here?' he asked.

'Anadin, I have a headache brought on by your constant complaining.'

'Brought on by the vat of white wine swilling around inside you would be closer to the truth,' he accused.

I snatched a packet of Anadin from the shelf and headed for

the checkout. Nik stepped up behind me. He pulled a fiver from his wallet, handed it to the young cashier and without waiting for his change, clutched my elbow and strode from the shop. We were obviously in a desperate hurry.

'We're going home,' he said flatly.

'We can't. Not yet. I told you. I have some Bs on my list that I'm considering changing to JLs. One last look in each shop should help me decide.'

'Evie, we are going home and ordering a takeaway. I will watch the football. And you can buy whatever you want from your Bs and JLs list online, wine glass beside you. Now you can come quietly or . . . not so quietly. But you *are* coming home.'

I wouldn't admit it to him, but his plans for the evening didn't sound too bad. He held out his hand, and grudgingly, I took it. And my feet were killing me. It was the idea of the wine glass beside me that made me follow him.

But the evening didn't go according to plan. In fact it was one of the worst nights of my entire life.

Nikki and I had to work in the bar because Nik's dad and uncle wanted to go to a darts tournament. We could hardly say no, because in fairness it's rare that we work in the evening. But working was the last thing I felt like doing, due to the after effects of a lunchtime bottle of wine, fatigue, aching feet and grieving over the shoes I hadn't bought earlier, because they would've gone with everything. By nine o'clock I had reduced myself to a state of acute restless misery. I couldn't wait to get home.

It was past midnight.

A hen party of eight girls had taken over the back section; they were the last customers in the bar. The girls were drunk, tossing back wings of highlighted hair, hiking hemlines up and pulling necklines down. A leggy blonde angled Nikki against the wall whenever she got the chance. Monopolising him with her silicone implants to the shrieking delight of the other girls. That in itself wasn't what irked, although the spectacle did nothing to improve my mood, it was the fact that Nikki seemed to be enjoying it that annoyed me more.

The leggy blonde whispered something in Nik's ear, he replied. I stood behind the bar, watchful, twisting a tea towel in a glass. She craned around his shoulder, glanced at me with piqued inquisitiveness, and slipped a card in his back pocket. Nik patted his pocket in assurance and gave her his card. His card!

'So you'll try to make it?' I heard her ask him, as she laced her arms around his neck and swung against him like a clock pendulum.

'Sure,' he said.

Uncle Spiros, sitting at the bar, looked at me over the top of his newspaper, and then shot a disapproving look at Nikki. He placed a vice-like grip on my wrist.

'Ees nothing,' he said.

I gave a dismissive shrug, and crushed the towel into the glass.

'I know,' I replied, trying for calm.

One of the girls stumbled past me en route to the toilets. Tall and swaying, she clutched a black wrap around orangy shoulders. I tipped over the bar, eyes following her. She really was quite carrot-skinned, I thought.

'Evie, I see you tomorrow?' Spiros said, tucking his folded newspaper in the pocket of his chef's whites. He lifted the collar of his jacket, snorted judgementally at the table of girls and walked slowly to the door without looking back.

Nikki strode towards me, shoulders set for business. He gave a loud clap.

'Eight sambucas . . . And don't put them on the tab, I've offered them on the house,' he said, fingers drumming the bar.

'That was *very* kind of you,' I told him with a lofty sniff.

On the house? Why the hell not? I reached for the shot glasses, lips set in a seam.

The *orange* girl trailed a finger along Nikki's backside in passing. A V-shape frown appeared on his forehead as he beamed back at her. He gave me a dry smile when he caught my stare.

'Go to bed if you want, I'll follow you as soon as the girls pay their bill, there's no point both of us staying here. You have your key, go upstairs, I won't be long,' he urged.

I raised my brows in artificial gratitude. A lithesome brunette squealed with delight, seized a bottle from the ice bucket, and sloshed a flood of wine into her glass. Nikki laughed as he watched her.

'At least someone's enjoying themselves,' he said.

He reached for the keys hanging on a hook at the side of the till and, head bent to the task of searching for the right key, slow walked to the front door. I filled the shot glasses. Leggy blonde flipped open her phone, and eyes shifting between Nik's card and her crimson fingernails, she typed out a text with the exaggerated concentration of the pleasantly plastered. Nikki's phone beeped. My head swivelled towards him. He took his phone from his pocket, smiled at the message, and flipped it closed.

My face burned. It hadn't taken her long to get in touch. I watched her drain her glass and get to her feet. Grinning she gestured to Nikki to come over to her table, which he did, leaving me with an unpleasant taste in the back of my throat. He dropped into a chair beside her, crossed one leg over the other, and relaxed back, a strong arm draped casually across her seat.

'Wannahavadrinkwifus?' she asked.

'Why not?' he said.

She dropped her cleavage in front of him, and put a glass in his hand.

I'd seen enough.

Blood rushed the length of my neck to my ears. Suddenly, the smell of the cheese trolley was overwhelming, the traffic outside roared, and the heat from the overhead light on the bar felt like a nuclear blaze. I pinched the bridge of my nose and drew in a deep breath, and watched him. What was he playing at? I wouldn't cause a scene, I decided, mustering pride. I'd look an idiot. I'd sort him out later, too right I would. But not now, not in front of that lot. I hurriedly tugged my jacket on, picked up my bag and burrowed for my keys. I was going home, to my flat, not his. I edged round the bar, and weaved smartly through the tables. I'd seen enough. On tiptoe, I unlocked the front door, and left. I was absolutely steaming.

I tossed and turned in bed in a state of confused rage. Why would Nik behave like that in front me? I just couldn't shake the image of that girl draped over him from my head. Eyes opened or closed the vision was as vivid. Only now in the margin of my mind, the girl was sober and wearing a bikini. Why does my imagination always embellish situations that are already bad enough? My mind torments me.

It was almost one-thirty when the doorbell rang. I put my head under the pillow to drown the noise. I knew it was Nik. He could stay on the doorstep all night. I heard Lulu thunder down the hallway.

I quickly kicked off the quilt and leaped from bed. We collided outside my bedroom.

'Don't answer the door!' I said urgently, my hand clamped on her arm.

'Why not?' she asked, tightening the belt on her dressing gown.

'Because . . . It's Nik!'

'Why doesn't he use his key?' She asked, pitching her voice against the sound of the doorbell.

'He can't use his key, because I left my key on the inside,' I shouted.

She threw her hands up at the noise.

'Is his finger glued to the bell? Why did you leave your key on the inside?'

The noise was deafening.

'Because . . . I hate him!'

'Oh, fuck off, and open the door before he bursts our ear drums, or rips the door off the hinges, you know what he's like. And I'm trying to watch *Gone With The Wind*.'

'No! I mean it, leave him out there.'

A smile spread across her face, and her eyes sparkled with devilment.

'Yes, we could leave him, couldn't we? Because then I can have a fag, and now that you're awake you can watch the film with me. I can't sleep.'

The ringing stopped. Nik's footsteps sounded in the communal lobby, his heavy tread was unmistakeable. Lulu and I stared at each other, the smile slid from her face.

'Thanks Miranda,' we heard Nik say, from behind the door.

'That nosy traitor upstairs has let him in,' Lulu said in a frenzied whisper.

Miranda's voice drifted from the lobby.

'Oh! That's all right; I can't believe they left the key on the inside, how irresponsible,' she said, as if she hadn't caused enough trouble already.

A nanosecond later the door bounced against the wall.

'It's the honey monster, it's home!' Lulu said, big eyed. Gathering the tail of her dressing gown, she rushed down the hallway, hair billowing.

Nikki filled the doorway, clenched fists on his hips. I backed into my bedroom.

'Right! What's all this about!?' he asked, throwing my keys on the bed.

An icy spear twisted in my chest, which was wrong somehow because I should have been fuming not anxious, and . . . jumpy.

'I don't want you to stay here; go back to your own place,' I said, in a shrill tone.

Three giant steps and he loomed above me.

'Why?'

'Because I don't particularly want you around me, that's why,' I told him.

He frowned.

'And why wouldn't you want me around you?'

'You have the gall to ask that?'

He nodded absorbedly.

'I do, yes,' he retorted crisply.

'What were you playing at?' I snapped.

'What are you talking about?'

'What am I talking about? I'm talking about you giving out your card, letting that blonde drape herself over you. I'm talking about you buying those girls drinks although they'd clearly had enough to drink already.'

'I was keeping customers happy, no more than that.'

'Is that what you call it?'

'Yes, yes it is, that's exactly what I call it,' he said.

'Leggy blonde is welcome to you.'

He tilted his head in enquiry.

'Welcome to me, is she?'

I took a step back, which only encouraged him to start towards me.

'Oh! So you know who leggy blonde is?'

'Yes, I do, and she means nothing to me, except that she's booked a party of thirty for next weekend.'

'Make sure you're free!'

A pulse beat at the base of his throat, a sign he was struggling to keep his temper in check.

'Make sure I'm free? Free for what exactly?'

'Oh Nik, go home, I can't be bothered to argue with you. In fact I can't be bothered with you full stop.'

He glared at me.

'Is that so?

I squared my shoulders.

'Everyone has a different level of tolerance. I can't tolerate infidelity—'

At my words, a hurricane gathered in his eyes.

'What!'

'I can't tolerate—'

He pressed his knuckles hard against his hips.

'I heard what you said, I just can't believe that you said it!' he roared.

'It's true!'

'I know it's true! But it's unwarranted to say it to me; you're making a big fuss over nothing.'

'So if I were to give a guy my number, and smile like an idiot at my phone when he texted me . . .'

He blanched.

I pressed my advantage.

'Leave! Leave if you think there was nothing wrong with the way you behaved tonight. In fact leave anyway. I'd rather be alone.'

'You would, would you?'

I raised my chin.

'Yes! Yes, I would!'

'Be on your own then!' he bellowed.

For a moment his furious dark eyes held mine, before he abruptly turned and, without looking back, slammed the door as he left; it sounded like a clap of thunder.

For a drumbeat I was frozen to the spot like a statue, before sliding down the length of the chest of drawers to land on the bedroom floor with a thud.

Lulu appeared in the doorway, fag aloft.

'Don't get me wrong Evie, I love Nik, I love him to death, but you have to admit, he's a raving lunatic. But for all his bellowing and stomping he wouldn't hurt a fly, you know that, don't you? It's all hot air.'

I nodded. I did know that.

VENICE

Chapter Thirty

I glanced at my watch on the bedside cabinet; it was almost three o'clock. I'd missed lunch – a bonus, saved calories – still I suppose I should be thinking of getting out of bed.

It's been four days since Nik and I argued. I haven't seen or heard from him, or been to the bar. I hadn't planned to boycott work, it just happened. I'd woken up, couldn't face Nik, and went back to sleep. And Nik hadn't stormed through the door to drag me out of bed. So I hadn't bothered to get up. After a whole twenty-four hours of no contact, I decided he could stick his job.

Not going in to work had made things worse, because now it was obvious to everyone that all wasn't well. In an act of solidarity, Maria has also fallen out with Nikki, and has taken to her bed, suffering from a very impressive illness that she diagnosed herself. Basically the symptoms are an inability to go to work, clean her house, cook, iron, speak to her son or drive. All she can manage to do is to eat like a horse, drink like a fish and send texts until her thumbs must be ready to drop off. She texted me to say she won't be going back to work in the bar until I do. I admit this prompted an uplifting of spirits in a morbidly pleasing way. Because it's nice to be missed, and believe me, Maria and I will be positively pined after. Nik will be friggin' demented.

OK, if I were to be objective, I would admit that flirting was hardly the crime of the century. Still my face burned at the memory of Nik with that girl. What if I had behaved like that with another man? I felt clammy with panic just thinking how Nik would've reacted. He would've exploded! Actually, he had exploded, and I hadn't done anything wrong at all.

What happened in Venice had sneaked up on me. I hadn't expected it. I'm not saying I didn't enjoy it. I did, very much. And I'm not saying I haven't equally enjoyed the last couple of months. But perhaps therein lays the problem: 'couple of months'. The emotional maximum when men start pursuing a replacement, ignoring texts, not returning calls, and cancelling dates. Perhaps Nik was starting to feel the pull of old habits. It certainly looked like it. Perhaps the nights spooning on the sofa watching *Supernanny* or *Strictly Come Dancing* were boring him? To be honest I was getting pissed off with *Strictly* myself. Perhaps the obligation of being one half of a whole was beginning to grate on his nerves. For Nik, the weight of domestic intimacy may well have transgressed to conjugal monotony. It happens.

I lay with my arm curved on the pillow above my head and contemplated the ceiling.

All said and done, Nikki is the one in the wrong. If he hadn't behaved so badly, there would have been nothing to argue about. It's as simple and as factual as that. And he hasn't been in touch for *ninety-six hours*. What's going on? Is he in denial? Hell will freeze before I'll call him. Anyway, far better to end our relationship now, while I'm in control of my emotions, than for the pull I feel for him to strengthen to the point where I end up a snivelling wreck when the happy bubble bursts. Obviously Nik is faring well, the selfish bastard! Because as I said *ninety-six hours* have passed without a single word from him; his emotions are clearly well under control.

I pushed back the quilt, got out of bed, and pulled on my dressing gown. I checked my phone, as I walked slowly down the hallway. No missed calls. No texts. I looked to see if I had network, I did. I took the landline handset off the kitchen wall and called my mobile. My mobile rang, so obviously there was no technical reason why I had no missed calls or texts. When I checked my phone five minutes ago, I had four texts from Maria; clearly no one had tried to get in touch since then, fine, absolutely fine.

I made a coffee and started towards the lounge. Bar Thea is only across the street, but it's at the end of the block on the other side of the road, next door to Tooting Broadway station. So I can't see the bar from the lounge window. I'd have to go outside and hang over the garden gate, which I would never do, because all I would see would be 'the door to the bar'. So, there was no point. But then, I thought, I would be able to see who was going in and out of the door, wouldn't I? I sank into the sofa. Why would I want to do that?

I twirled a long lock of hair, and blew into my coffee.

I was bored.

The summer season was over and there wasn't very much happening in autumn. As a miserable upshot, Insignia Tours didn't need me. I had no work to go to, no plans, no arrangements. I had *absolutely* nothing to do. OK that's not strictly true, it would be closer to the truth to say that I had nothing to do that I felt like doing. I could visit Lexy, but the twins would expect Nikki to be with me. I shook the idea from my head. No, I wouldn't go to my sister's. Definitely not.

I surveyed the lounge.

Glasses, a wine bottle end over end in an ice bucket and an

411

array of old magazines littered the coffee table, and the radiator was strewn with a kaleidoscope of bras and knickers. I could clean the flat, I thought, but what was the point. I cleaned it last week.

My phone vibrated in my dressing gown pocket. Ahhhh! I drew a deep breath. This would be Nik. About time too! Feeling shaky and hot-faced, I burrowed in my pocket. Took his time, I thought, with a triumphant smile. I stared at the caller display; it wasn't Nik, it was John. My mind did a rollercoaster dip. *Not Nik?*

John's voice burst down the line.

'Evie, my darling girl, how are you?'

Despite myself I felt surprisingly uplifted, hearing from John always made me smile.

'I'm fine.'

'That's a rather flat tone for you, are you all right?'

'Yes ... well no, actually I'm not all right. I've had an argument with Nikki,' I confessed miserably.

'Have you now? I'm sure it's nothing serious,' he said brightly.

I could hear the rhythmic plod of a finger on a keyboard and the echo of a telephone in the background. He was calling from his office.

'It was, it was serious,' I insisted.

'What have you been doing with yourself?'

Had I not just told him?

'What happened was ... Nik and I were—'

'We haven't had dinner together for a couple of weeks, what are you doing tomorrow night?'

'Nothing, at the moment I'm available for the rest of my life,' I bleated in a rush, and pushed on. 'Nik and I—'

He laughed a deep throaty chuckle.

'We need to get together, there's something I'd like to discuss with you. It's a . . . proposition of sorts,' he said, lengthening his words.

Now I'm interested.

'What do you mean? A proposition?'

'I'll explain when we meet, it's rather detailed. Are you free tomorrow evening?'

I exhaled a sigh.

'I'm free any and every evening. Were you *not* listening? I want to tell you about Nik and, and—'

'Not now, tell me tomorrow. I have someone waiting to see me. I'll send Alistair to collect you, be ready at seven o'clock. No, in fact,' he interrupted himself reflectively, 'make it six o'clock.' There was a thoughtful silence. The one finger plod on the keyboard stopped, replaced by the crackle of paper.

'Evie, I'm flicking through my diary, I have nothing pencilled in for the next couple of days.'

I drank deep from my coffee cup, he wasn't interested in the slightest about my argument with Nik. I put my cup on the table with a thud, spilling most of my coffee.

'I'll take you to Venice,' he said assertively, piercing my thoughts.

'You'll what?'

'Take you to Venice,' he repeated.

My ears pricked.

'Just like that?' I asked, with a click of my fingers. 'You'll take *me* to Venice?'

'Why not? I promised, didn't I? You are free and I find myself with time on my hands,' he said. 'You suggested I work less and relax more, I'm merely taking your esteemed advice. So, what do you think?'

I reached for my cup.

What did I think?

413

'Fantastic idea! I'd *love* to go back to Venice.'

'That's settled. Alistair will collect you at six as planned. We'll have dinner together tomorrow evening, and fly to Venice the following morning. We'll come back when we've grown weary of each other's company. How does that sound?'

My heart thumped hard, Venice the day after tomorrow, just like that. My world expanded from the shrinking boring confines of my lounge to the dizzy heights of cosmopolitan Venezia. I did a dressing gown waltz, coffee cup in hand. And Nik could get lost, I've brooded long enough. Ninety-six hours! Who the hell did he think he was, anyway?

'Evie!' John prompted.

'Yes, yes . . . Oh yes, definitely,' I smiled at my reflection in the mirror, wheeled, and drifted across to the window. 'I'll be ready at six. Venice! Fabulous! I can't wait,' I said, adrenalin speeding through me. 'Oh! John, could Alistair possibly collect me at lunchtime, I'd like to have a swim and a dip in the jacuzzi, if that's all right with you? And then I'll just hang out until you come home,' I asked, smiling at a buzz of people swarming on to the 220 bus.

'Of course you can darling, I'll text you Alistair's number, and I'll make sure he's free all day. Call him when you're ready.'

I felt instantly better. I had something wonderful to look forward to. It's not as though moping around the flat would make Nikki call me. I may as well mope around Venice. And get me, 'Could Alistair possibly collect me at lunchtime?' Who do I think I am? I've never had a chauffeur in my life. Who has? And not only was I totally comfortable with having someone 'collect me', I was rescheduling him to accommodate my needs, I could get used to that. I was looking forward to an invigorating spa experience at John's house. I love his jacuzzi. And I would get in shape for my trip, I would swim twenty lengths or so. I would push myself. It would be worth it because I would feel great afterwards.

The jacuzzi was like a frothing volcano, the thermostat must have been stuck on a million degrees. I lasted two minutes, before high legging it over the edge and slithering to the tiled floor like a fat slug in an exhausted heap. I had a swim; it was horrendous. My lungs burned and my arms ached after three lengths. Why do people swim? I didn't want to risk cramp or drowning so I gave up swimming and spent an hour or so bobbing in the pool on an inflated sofa, mindful of my half-bottle of champagne, crystal flute and bowl of chilli Sensations. I felt rested, and cleansed. I felt I'd achieved something.

I remembered pyjamas but had forgotten to bring a dressing gown, so John's housekeeper who looks like Nanny McPhee loaned me a bath robe. Not one of the lovely thick white monogrammed towelling robes I saw hanging in the atrium the last time I visited. Apparently, they were being laundered. (All four of them?) Nanny McPhee loaned me a lemon flannel granny gown, made of corded candlewick with a rolled polo neck, frilled cuffs and deep square pockets. I looked like a knitted toilet roll dolly. I don't want to speak out of turn, but I suspect that for whatever reason, she purposely set out to frumpy-me-up. She had a half-day; she was going to visit her brother, I wasn't overly sorry to wave her off. As soon as she left, I swapped the dressing gown for one of John's crew neck sweaters that I found in the laundry.

I leaned on the wrought iron railing of the roof terrace, face tilted to the autumn sunshine. Damp clean hair fluttering, crystal flute in hand, I marvelled at the buzz of the afternoon Park Lane traffic and the contrasting tranquillity of Hyde Park. I balanced my glass in the crook of my arm and hugged myself. It was kind of surreal to stand looking down on a bustling cityscape with the contrasting serenity of palm trees and a swimming pool behind me.

By six o'clock there was still no sign of John. I didn't mind; I was at the helm in Nanny McPhee's immaculate kitchen, cooking dinner. I had her *Chefs of the World* cookbook opened and propped against the tiled wall. My mission was Spaghetti Bolognese. I needed to keep my mind occupied; because thoughts of Nikki were simmering in my head, making me feel queasy and love sick, or I suppose I could've been queasy and pissed, because I was now on my second half-bottle. Glass in hand, I sautéed onions, garlic and tomatoes, and was doing a brilliant job in my own estimation. I found cooking curative and therapeutic, and wondered why I hadn't taken it up before. It was a matter of common sense, and aptitude, and it seemed I had both. In fact, the more champagne I drank the more common sense and aptitude I was able to apply.

I opened the fridge door with a flourish and took out the mince. Cunningly I'd already checked that Nanny Mac had all of the ingredients in stock that I needed. In truth, she had the ingredients in stock for just about every recipe in her cookbook. My phone buzzed, announcing a text. My heart gave a leap. I walked quickly towards the work island. This would be Nik! Surely! My tummy dipped in disappointment. It was another text from Maria.

Will you come to Nikki's birthday party tomorrow night?
You know I invite everybody. Please come, we don't speak
to him still. Xxxx

I exhaled a sigh, and pulled at a loose thread in my jumper. Unexpectedly, a tear rolled down my cheek. I quickly wiped it

416

away but it was swiftly replaced by another. As I looked around the large shiny kitchen I felt hollow, and lonely and inexplicably nervous.

How would that work? Maria and me at Nik's birthday party, but not talking to him? With all the upset of the past week I'd completely forgotten Nik would be twenty-nine tomorrow. Maria had invited the world and his wife to the bar for a surprise party, which wasn't a surprise at all. Nik told me he knew all about it.

I edged on to one of the high kitchen stools. I missed Nik, I missed him a lot. I wanted him. But he didn't appear to want me. I wiped my flushed face with a dish towel. He didn't care. That unwelcome thought kick started an argument between Nik and me in my head. I took a huge shuddery breath and a swift sip of champagne, I won the argument; Nik had little to nothing to say in his own defence.

I slid off the stool, and rescued the sizzling onions.

I was going to Venice. That would be much more exciting than a crappy party in a bar in Tooting Broadway. But I wouldn't tell Maria just yet, because she would bombard me with pleas and tears. And I would feel bad. I would text Maria tomorrow before I boarded John's plane. And I would leave my phone in John's car. Without my phone, I could concentrate on having a good time. And not be constantly policing my message inbox. Yes, that's what I'd do.

Nikki could go to hell.

I set the table in the kitchen with the posh crystal and china from the cabinet in the dining room, lit candles, and even figured out how to work the computerised sound system. The ambience was perfectico. I was a closet culinary genius; who would've thought it? All I'd needed to bring it out in me was a cookbook, a couple of hours to myself, the best part of a bottle of champagne inside me and a kitchen worth a couple of hundred grand to play around in.

Just after seven o'clock, wearing an immaculately cut black coat over an elegant metal grey suit, John arrived home. He pulled off his tie as he strode into the kitchen.

'Look at you, pyjamas, my jumper and my socks? I expected you to be dressed, and ready to go out,' he said.

He caught my hands between his and drew me to him, and scanned the kitchen.

'Are we having guests?' he asked, eyes crinkled in amusement.

'I had time on my hands, and so I cooked.'

On impulse I hugged him. He smelled of the cold evening air, spicy soap, and fine wool.

'I'm honoured. Pour me a drink, while I change out of this suit. I'll have a brandy. Do you know where the brandy's kept?'

'I do, I've been snooping around for close on four hours. I know where everything is kept.'

His broad chest vibrated as he chuckled.

'Do you indeed?

I broke away from him.

'Go get changed,' I said, gesturing towards the door. 'I'll dish up.'

While John ate everything on his plate I toyed with my meal, hiding most of my spaghetti under a blanket of lettuce. The conversation limped along at a steady pace. This was due to the fact that John suffocated any sentence I started with a heavy sigh, and made an upbeat effort to interject joviality. When he finished eating he dropped his cutlery, put his napkin on the table and slunk further into his seat.

His face was wreathed in smiles.

'That,' he said, 'was wonderful,' and exhaled a smile. 'And as you cooked, there's the added advantage of not receiving a bill for it.'

I sat straight, elbows on the table.

'As if that that matters to you.'

He smiled at the glow from the table candle.

'Perhaps not, still, it was very nice.'

I caught his silent stare as I busied myself spaghetti hiding.

'Let's move into the lounge,' he said assertively, his charcoal eyes serious. 'I can see you have something to tell me, and I have something important that I want to discuss with you.'

He got to his feet.

'Shall we load the dishwasher?' I asked.

'Don't be ridiculous, Marion would be most put out.'

I scrunched my face.

'Who is Marion?'

'My housekeeper of course, what on earth have you been calling her all day?'

'Err, well, nothing really, we didn't chat much, I'd forgotten her name until you mentioned it.'

I could hardly confess I'd nicknamed her Nanny MacPhee.

John relaxed into a graceful winged armchair in front of the fire and I sat at his feet on the fireside rug. He leaned forward, elbows on his knees, took my chin in his hand and turned my face towards him.

'OK, me first,' he said.

I gave a brisk nod, crossed my legs, and folded my arms. He dropped back into his seat, brandy globe in hand.

'I've spent a considerable amount of time with my accountants in the past month. They tell me I spend over two million pounds a year on management events.' He gave a slow nod. 'That's a fair amount. My leisure marketing budget is twenty-five per cent up on two years ago.'

419

I hid a frown, and eyed him wisely. Did I need to know this?

He ploughed on.

'Now that most of our conference specifications are in place and the formulas work, it will only be the venues that are likely to change.'

'Right,' I said stiffly. 'That makes sense.'

'My finance director estimates bringing leisure marketing in-house will save approximately four hundred thousand a year, this being the twenty per cent margin an events management organisation would generally work on.'

'That's a lot of money,' I said in a level tone.

He abandoned his drink to a side table and palmed the arm-rests.

'It is. And so that's exactly what I've decided to do.'

'Great idea!' I said, shifting about a little on the floor.

'And I want you to head it up.'

My jaw dropped. Was he joking?

'Me?' I gave an incredulous snort. 'But I don't know anything about management events.'

'You have a degree in media, don't you? And while media is not events management, your degree is proof that you have the discipline of learning. And you know everything there is to know about operating events if not organising them,' he said with a confident smile.

I gave him a wary look. He leaned forward, charcoal eyes held mine. His expression shifted to serious and intent.

'Evie, you can do it! You're a *bright* girl!'

I got to my feet and moved to sit on the arm of the sofa.

'I'm pulling my business from Insignia Tours and bringing it in-house.'

'I don't disagree with that, although being their key client a few of the girls at Insignia will likely lose their jobs. '

'Bring the girls with you. Hire whoever you need. I don't expect you to do this alone. Evie, this transition makes perfect sense. You can escort the events you organise, pretty much as you do at the moment. With the added advantage of utilising the years of studying you underwent to achieve your degree. And of course financially you will be better off.'

'How will I be financially better off?'

He stood, plucked his glass from the table, and slowly walked to the fireplace.

'I'll give you a quarter profit share of any new business you secure from outside my organisation.'

I was stunned.

'But what's in it for you? Why should you give so much to me?'

He rolled his brandy globe in an aid to thought.

'What's in it for me? Well, I'll save four hundred thousand in the first year. So that's an immediate plus. And another benefit is that you and I can have lunch together more often,' he said, 'because I've set aside a hundred square feet of my office for this venture.'

My mind ripped through the pros and cons. This was a fabulous opportunity, absolutely amazing, but . . . it was also a proper grown-up job. I was happy touring, gallivanting around Europe without a care in the world. But being a tour guide didn't offer financial stability, the work was sporadic, while mortgages were permanent. And it appeared I no longer had my job in the bar, which had been tantamount to economic survival. Things had changed. I needed a regular steady income. He was offering me a full-time well-paid job, and to be my own boss, with the advantage of still being able to travel. I gave myself an inward shake. I had missed out this year, by working for Nikki and brooding over Rob. I'd hardly been anywhere. I would put that right next year.

A flame from the fire lit his face.

'Think about it,' he said solemnly. 'Sleep on it,' he added.

I would have business cards made, I thought. And I'd have a dressing table in the office, discreetly hidden behind a screen of course. And a sofa, and . . .

'A friend of mine will be visiting shortly,' he said in a guarded tone. 'A lady friend, she left her phone here this morning; she'll be calling to pick it up,' he added, expressionless.

Left her phone here? How did some random woman's phone come to be *left behind*? I wondered. Of course it was absolutely none of my business! I wouldn't ask! Of course I wouldn't!

'Did she leave her phone here this morning because she stayed the night?' I blurted. 'With you, she stayed the night with you? Not in one of the spare rooms? *She actually stayed the night with you?*'

'She did indeed,' he replied boldly.

He moved to the armchair, sat and spread his hands on his thighs matter-of-factly. I laughed. I couldn't hold it in. I laughed so hard I slid from the arm of the sofa into the comfortable cushion.

'Do you mind telling me what is so amusing?' he asked sharply, and he was about to say something else when his phone rang. He answered it instantly, pressing the phone to his ear with a coy smile. He said one word, 'OK.'

'She'll be here in five minutes,' he told me.

That shut me up. I sprang to my feet. My hands flew to my face.

'Look at me. No make-up, wearing pyjamas and your socks and jumper. But more to the point look at you,' I said pointedly.

He sat straight.

'What's wrong with me?'

I held up my hand.

'I'll be back in a minute,' I said.

I ran into the kitchen, grabbed my make-up bag and flew back to the lounge. I fell to my knees in front of his chair, and tipped the contents of my make-up bag on the rug.

'You need to shave, but I like you unshaven, but you have a grey moustache and too much grey in your eyebrows, let me touch them up, make them darker. You'll look fabulous.'

I whipped out my mascara wand and scrambled towards him.

'Don't be ridiculous.'

'Let me brush a little black on your grey bits, just a sweep above your lip and along each brow, nothing major. Lots of movie stars do it,' I told him informatively.

'I'm *not* a movie star.'

'I know but still you want to look your best. Don't you?'

I took a step back to admire my handiwork, then leaned forward and gave his brows a final whisper.

'You look dashing, so dark and handsome, and . . . mysterious in an Arabian Knights kind of way.'

'Oh! Shut up Evie.'

'You are handsome, very handsome!'

The doorbell rang. My tonsils and my tummy switched places. John grinned. I dropped to the floor and gathered my make-up, tucked the bag behind a cushion, and perched ceremoniously on the edge of the armchair.

'Are you going to answer the door?' I asked.

'Of course I am,' he said, standing slowly.

My eyes followed him out of the lounge.

I stole a sideways glance at the intimate murmur of warm voices coming from the hallway. John had his hand on the shoulder of a slim elegant blonde; she smiled up at him as he guided her gently into the lounge. She wore a black chiffony skirt and black and white Chanel jacket.

'Evie, I'd like to introduce you to Estelene.'

I blushed hotly, and stood to greet her. On recognition, my jaw slackened. John caught the surprise on my face. I gulped and managed to transform an unbelieving harrumph into a tickly cough, which I buried in my fist. John dropped a step behind Estelene, and gave me a warning glare. At his warning, my lips inched into a smile. I stepped forward, and kissed her cheek.

'Evie, it's a pleasure to meet you,' Estelene said in regal tones, needlessly smoothing carefully styled hair.

'Likewise,' I managed, starstruck.

'Evie was in the process of making hot chocolate, weren't you Evie?' John said firmly, and with an authoritive nod.

'Yes, yes, I was,' I replied, sidestepping them. 'I'll just go, and, and . . . Do that now.'

I crashed around the kitchen, what was John playing at? Estelene is a member of the Royal Family. She's a duchess, and a married duchess to boot. With a duke in tow! She was featured in *Hello!* magazine last week, with her husband and two boys. Wait until I tell Lulu, and Lexy, and . . . and, I was about to add Nik, but I won't be telling Nik anything, will I? I sighed, and took my phone from my pocket, nada! Not a whisper, no messages at all. One thing I'll say in Rob's defence, when he coveted my good graces he made a fanatical effort to do just that. Nik didn't give a toss. I know I'd said I missed Nikki, but I was quickly changing my mind.

I placed three cups and a pot of chocolate on a tray and headed back into the lounge. A duchess? Bloody hell, a married duchess!

As I picked my way around the sofa to the coffee table, I concentrated like mad on not dropping the tray. Estelene raised her chin and gave me a brilliant smile. My lips parted, my eyes grew wide, and my heart raced with horror. The cups rattled as I lost

424

my footing, I rebalanced the tray and forced myself to look at John. I wished I hadn't. Not surprisingly his face was white with rage, and his grey eyes had turned to pieces of steel flint. I felt a shimmer of terror. I would be blamed for this, I knew it; I would have to *rescue* the situation. They'd had a snog, that much was obvious. John's jaw twitched with fury. I shivered as an icy trickle travelled the length of my spine. I would have to *do something — somehow*? Their faces were frozen; hers wreathed in smiles, his enraged. I could see how it happened, and although I knew I would get the blame, it wasn't really my fault. The thing was, Estelene, Duchess of Devon, was sporting a wide black moustache and two thick black eyebrows. I hadn't thought when I skimmed over John's grey stubble that the mascara would rub off. Well, who would've thought it? I placed the tray on the table with measured precision. The Duchess of Devon stared dreamily at John, she looked ridiculous. John glowered at me. I mentally died, John's broad chest lifted as he inhaled testily.

'The chocolate smells delicious, doesn't it?' Estelene said, flashing a smile that widened her moustache. She leaned towards John and stroked his hair.

His lips twitched as though he was about to speak, but he seemed at a loss for both air and words. I could understand that. I felt the same.

I clapped my hands in an act of decisiveness, and took the only sensible course of action under the present circumstances.

'I think I'll have an early night,' I announced. 'I'm tired and we have an early start in the morning, don't we John?'

Estelene nodded sagely, and toasted her cup primly.

'Please don't let us keep you.'

Well, there you go! She had just more or less implied that I was the third wheel and asked me to leave. I tipped forward and kissed both on the cheek. John's eye glinted sideways, shining

425

with madness. I pivoted on my sock, and headed towards the door, cup cradled protectively.

An hour later, John barrelled through my bedroom door. I wasn't entirely surprised. I dropped the television remote and crabbed back against the headboard, the bigger the distance between us, the better for me, I was sure.

'I'm sorry. Of course I am. How was I supposed to know the mascara would rub off? I've never camouflaged grey stubble before. I won't do it again,' I blurted in a rush.

He loomed above me.

'You're right, you won't!'

I stared at him for a moment; his face was no more than four inches from mine. His lips curved.

I felt a whoosh of relief.

'Are you trying to be mad, but not quite pulling it off?' I asked.

His eyes sparkled.

'Yes, I suppose so.'

'What did you do? I've been dying to know.'

'I told her. I could hardly allow her to leave the house looking like Max Wall, could I?'

'I'm sorry . . . what did she say?'

'That I have a loyal little ally in you.'

'You have.'

'I know.'

He sat next to me on the bed, hunched his shoulders and pulled me to him. I felt cosy and safe and a bit sleepy.

'Evie, I need to be sure of your discretion, this is not my secret, its Estelene's. I hope I can trust you.'

I put on an affronted expression.

'Of course you can trust me,' I shot back, loyally. 'I'll take it to the grave.'

There was a dignified hush. I felt a spear of scary guilt.

The thing was I'd already told Lulu and Lexy by text, but in my defence, how was I supposed to know it was such an earth-shattering secret? I mean, she just breezed in here as bold as brass, no dark glasses, no disguise. What was I supposed to think? I would tell Lulu and Lexy to keep it to themselves, there's no reason why the secret can't be taken to three graves.

I was suddenly very tired.

'Well, you have an opinion I'm sure,' he said. 'I might as well hear it.'

'You're having *an affair* with a married woman, and—'

'I do wish you wouldn't call it that.'

I lifted hooded eyes.

'What is it then, if it's not an affair?'

'It's a meaningful relationship.'

'OK, you're having a meaningful relationship with a married woman,' I said flatly.

'Hopefully she won't be married for much longer.'

'That would be handy,' I said sarcastically, as a thought pierced my mind. 'Are you still married?' I asked.

'No! No I'm not.'

'That's a step in the right direction.'

'Are you judging me?'

'No. Not really.'

'Are you judging her?'

'No.'

'But doesn't this contradict your principles?'

'I don't know why, but whatever you do is fine with me. I feel like you're all grown up, and that you know what you're doing.'

He rested his chin on the crown of my head.

'And I want you to be happy,' I told him, palming his fore-arm.

427

'And I want you to be happy,' he said planting a kiss in my hair, 'and so, I've cancelled our flight to Venice.'

There was a confused pause. I felt a sweep of disappointment. I tilted my head to look up at him.

'Why would cancelling our flight to Venice make me happy?'

'Because I think you should go to Nikki's birthday party tomorrow night, so that's exactly what we're going to do,' he announced.

Chapter Thirty-one

I stormed into the lounge, John hot on my heels.

'Evie! Your behaviour is disgraceful! I'm appalled!'

Maria and her two sisters had stormed John's office that afternoon, and brainwashed him. And how did Maria know where to find John? Lulu! And how did Maria gain immediate and undisputed access to John's inner sanctum? By telling John's commissionaire that she had some very bad news for me, and that she wanted John's advice on how to deal with it.

John was one hundred per cent on Nikki's side, despite the fact that I'd told him everything that had happened. And lest there be any confusion as to my views and feelings on the matter, I told him at *point blank range and at the top of my voice.* Our argument had raged from my bedroom, along the landing, down the stairs, through the hallway and into the lounge.

I raised the flat of my hand.

'I am NOT going to Nik's party!'

'You are!'

I rounded on him.

'I am not!'

'Oh but you are!' John said, voice ragged but controlled.

My head was pounding. I was running out of steam. My jaw

trembled, and I could feel tears pressing. I wasn't winning this argument at all. John, eyes narrowed, walked towards me, head slightly bowed, there was a tight ripple in his throat as he gave a frustrated sigh. He put his arm tight around my shoulder and shepherded me to the sofa. I slumped down miserably.

'I haven't heard a word from Nik in five days – five bloody days. And, were you listening? This situation is his fault. *It's his fault*,' I repeated. 'He should be making up with me. He should be the one making calls and apologising!'

The lounge was dark, save for the shafts of light streaming into the room from the hallway, and an amber glow from the fire. John squeezed my knee, stood and walked over to the drinks cabinet. I lifted my chin to the comforting rush of liquid being poured in a glass. He handed me a generous measure of something golden.

'Amaretto, for a change. Now, when you've calmed down, you'll listen to me. And you'll stop acting the little madam, it's not becoming of you.'

My mind drifted to my drink.

Instead of sitting beside me, he pulled over a footstool and sat facing me.

He eyed me critically, set his drink on a tripod table beside the sofa, and sat, elbows on knees, hands clasped.

I finger-tipped the rim of my glass.

'Now! This is nonsense! Absolute nonsense!' he raised quizzical brows. 'Had you known Nikki to sit with customers and buy them drinks on the house before? Surely that's something he would do on a regular basis and as a matter of course?'

I shifted in my seat.

'Yes, I suppose, but—'

'And would Nikki buying drinks for customers irritate or upset you?' he asked in a quiet voice.

'No, no, it wouldn't,' I admitted, 'but it's not the same—'

'The acts themselves were *exactly* the same. It was your perception of the situation that was different.'

He exhaled a weary breath.

'Your attentiveness was heightened by the fact that you now have an intimate relationship with him. What you saw was innocent enough, what you perceived of it was something completely different.'

He paused thoughtfully.

'Evie. If a man is considering playing the field, believe me, he will not do so on his own doorstep and in full view of his beautiful girlfriend. You witnessed something that jarred your self-esteem, and as a result of that, you magnified the gravity of it in the periphery of your mind beyond all reason. My darling . . . you were *jealous*,' he said with grim assurance.

'I'm not a jealous person,' I defended.

'No you're not, you're not jealous by nature, but that doesn't mean to say that you can't suffer from an attack of the green-eyed monster just like everyone else. Nikki is a great lad. I like him, I like him a lot. He works hard, he has drive and vision, and he adores you. He must have called me five or six times when we were in Amsterdam. The boy wanted to fly out to Holland to take you home, his calls were heartfelt. I had looked forward to meeting him,' he said in a quiet voice. 'And when I did meet him, I could see immediately that his feelings for you were far stronger than you realised.'

He beamed in recollection.

'Yes, he's the boy for you. I'm sure of it. That's why I sent him to Venice.'

I sat straight.

'*You* . . . sent Nik to Venice?'

He nodded.

431

'I did, yes.'

'Why? Why did you do that?'

He gave me a wide smile.

'When you and I had lunch at that dreadful restaurant in Soho, you were in good spirits. No sulking, no extended silences and above all else, no tears. It was time for Nikki to make his move before you thrashed on and met someone else. I called him and told him so. He didn't need telling twice.'

I rubbed a finger on my chin fondly.

'So . . . did Nikki know that you had no intention of joining us in Venice?

'Of course he knew. I told him to make the most of it. And to make sure that by the time you came home you had no designs whatsoever on that old flame of yours, the married chap.'

'You can use his name . . . it's Rob!'

'Is it?' he said with a dismissive shrug, and pushed on. 'And so you see, I have a vested interest in this relationship working, as I put in a fair amount of groundwork to get it going in the first place.'

He moved to sit on the sofa next to me.

'Come here.'

I inched towards him; he closed his arms around me.

'I'll admit Nikki may have been a bit reckless in giving the girl his card. You should have a few stiff words with him about that. But I think you should drop the rest of the charges against him. It's his job to foster a friendship with his customers. Likely the boy is still trying to work out where he went wrong, and wondering what ignited your wrath. And as far as him not calling you is concerned, has it not occurred to you that his conviction and strength of character could be his appeal? And that a man with a weaker resolve than your own may not have the staying power to hold on to you?'

I looked at his solemn face.

'We'll go to the party, if you want to leave early, then we'll leave, but ... *we're going*, and that's not negotiable!'

I chewed my bottom lip, digesting his words.

'Tomorrow, I'll take you to visit my office. I'd like to show you around. And then we'll have lunch.'

Had I been jealous?

'I want you to think over what I've said. And, Evie, if you and Nik ever have another lovers' tiff, call me. Give me time to leave London, or at least hide from his mother.'

I dropped my chin to my chest and giggled.

'Nikki's mother and his two aunts make a formidable trio, for the first time in forty years I felt intimidated. One of his aunts actually accused me of abducting you. That detonated a bilingual explosion such as I've never witnessed in my life. When that died down, and they said what they had come to say, it took myself, two security guards and Alistair to coax the three of them out of the building and into Alistair's car.'

He gave a thankful sigh, crossed one leg over the other and pulled me close, resting his chin on my head.

'Where did Alistair take them?' I asked.

'I booked them a table for dinner with my compliments at the Ritz, they were delighted. It was my PA's idea, I'm thinking of giving her a salary increase for the genius of the suggestion. And I told Alistair to wait and take them home,' he glanced at his watch. 'That was six hours ago, and as far as I'm aware Alistair hasn't returned.'

He reached for his drink.

'I got a cab home today, for the first time in fifteen years.'

'I thought you had more than one driver?'

'I do, but they're not available at forty seconds' notice. As soon as Alistair closed the door on them, I hailed a taxi and took off in the opposite direction.'

433

His head was silhouetted by the light from the hallway behind him. I smiled at his expression. His lips were set in a line, as though he'd sucked on a lemon or had been set a particularly unpleasant task.

'John . . . Are we going to the party because you promised Maria that we would?'

'Yes, yes we are,' he admitted.

'Was all that rubbish about me being jealous just a smoke-screen?'

'No, you were jealous. We are going to the party. And I have promised that we'll be there! Now, finish your drink and let's get to bed, it's been a long day.'

In bed, I called Lexy and Lulu, they told me they were going to Nik's party. Maria had extracted promises of attendance on pain of death. Perhaps John was right? Perhaps I had been jealous and unreasonable. I punched the pillow into a balloon. I'd sleep on it. I put my phone on the bedside table and pulled the quilt over my shoulders. If nothing else I should go to the party to ask Nik why he hadn't called me. I also told Lexy and Lulu not to tell anyone about John and Estelene. Typically Lulu had already mentioned it to Miranda – honestly, Lulu can't keep anything to herself – but she managed to get to Miranda before Miranda told anyone. So all is well, John's secret is safe and under wraps. It will be going to four graves, I'd see to it personally. I turned out the light. OK, so I wasn't going to Venice; strangely I wasn't too disappointed. I thought that odd.

John's office was nothing like I imagined. In my mind's eye I had pictured a tall imposing white Regency mansion, with polished marble floors and walls adorned with priceless works of art. And a sweeping Georgian staircase leading to an assortment of high ceilinged rooms crammed with antique desks, business-suited men and Miss Moneypenny lookalikes.

The reality couldn't have been more different.

When John pushed his way, me following dutifully, through the large glass doors, I felt a churning of excitement. The huge open plan honeycomb shaped building, dominated by an imposing stainless steel water feature buzzed with life, with people milling around on each of the four levels. Three smartly dressed young girls, super-charged with charm and chatting into headsets, stood behind a semi-circular glass reception desk. I gave them my friendliest smile, as John piloted me through the lobby. Two florists slow-stepped around an explosion of birds of paradise in an enormous granite flowerpot beside the elevators, their jaws dropped on their hinges when their eyes rested on John.

I linked my arm into John's.

'Why are they surprised to see you?' I whispered, jerking my head at the florists. 'This is your building.'

'I never use the main entrance. I have my own elevator leading from the underground car park straight to my office, but I thought you'd like a tour.'

'Oh!'

We travelled up in the lift wordlessly. How lucky was he? *His own building!* The elevator door opened on the third floor. John signalled right. I followed, past a row of limed oak doors. Their functions – Meeting Room 1, Meeting Room 2 and Video Conferencing – were displayed on gold plaques. John opened the fourth door without knocking, held his arm in an arch and ushered me inside.

He gave me a warm smile.

'I'm thinking of sticking you in here,' he said, his eyes crinkling with humour.

I stepped inside.

It was a magnificent spacious rectangular room, with fabulous floor-to-ceiling tinted windows, and a view of the city stretching the length of the Thames. My heels sounded on the wooden floor as I crossed the room to stand by the window. I felt a fizz of excitement, as I looked down at the river, with sparks of light glinting from its shifting granite surface.

'Well?' he asked. Although close behind me, his voice sounded echoey and far away.

'I feel like I want to cry. It's . . . stunning.'

'Don't be silly.'

'This is a lot for you to do for me, it's a lot for you to give to me, when you could find someone more experienced and better qualified.'

I turned to face him.

He pressed his palms lightly on my shoulder.

'There's something between us, isn't there, John? It's like; I don't know how to explain it,' I said, trailing off.

'There is, there is something between us, and it needs no explanation,' he said. 'We've been fortunate to get to know each other very well, circumstances as they were.'

He was thinking of Dublin.

'Let me give you this,' he said, scanning the room. 'But of course I need you to be certain it's what you want.'

I smiled sideways at the river view. He held both my hands in his.

'So think very carefully. But what I really want to know at this precise moment is, are you hungry?' he asked, slanting his eyes in question. 'Because I am.'

'Yes, I'm starving. And John, this is what I want. I would love to work here, and for you.'

There was a drawn silence, a frozen moment, when his eyes held mine.

'Good, a wise decision, which I'm sure will benefit both of us,' he said with firm certainty.

VENICE

Chapter Thirty-two

I craned my neck and peered out the car window at the sky; a huge gunmetal cloud shifted and darkened, forming a black pelmet over Park Lane and Hyde Park. A clap of thunder reverberated over London, followed immediately by a deluge of large splurging raindrops. I slumped silently into the seat, flinching as the sky blazed and cracked with lightning.

John, beside me, gave me a sideways glance. He crossed one long leg over the other and placed his hand absently over mine.

'It's only a little storm, lightning won't hurt you,' he said, flicking nonchalantly through a batch of spreadsheets.

'It can do,' I said numbly.

He shook his head dismissively.

'It's highly unlikely when speeding through central London in the back of a car.'

The rumbles of thunder rolled on. I didn't really mind, the storm was a welcome diversion to the jumble of thoughts going through my head. I was excited at the thought of seeing Nik, terrified at the thought of seeing him, furious, animated, overwhelmed, nervous and excited. In short I had psyched myself up to a state of near hysteria.

I engrossed myself in pleating the hem of my dress. I'd have to calm down. I took a deep breath, and shifted in my seat as the car hissed through a lake of rain rounding Sloane Square. Looking out at the boutiques on the King's Road had a restorative effect, I felt a little better, in fact, I felt much better. I was almost calm . . .

'Evie, will you stop squeezing my hand, you'll cut off my circulation,' John snapped.

'What?'

'My fingers are white. What's wrong with you?'

I turned on him; he wore a charcoal suit, with a white polo shirt, and as always, looked debonair, commanding and impeccable.

'What's wrong with me? You really need to ask that? I'll tell you what's wrong with me since you want to know, I'm—'

He raised the palm of his hand, cutting me off.

'I've changed my mind; I don't want to know what's wrong with you. My uncanny sixth sense has tipped me off. There's no need for you to fill me in. Anyone would think the way you're behaving that I was selling you into slavery. We're going to a party, for god's sake.' He dropped his file on the floor. 'Pour a couple of gins.'

I inched towards the drinks cabinet. John was right. What was I worried about? I should be the one in the driving seat. I dropped ice cubes into two glasses. Nikki was the one with the apology to make. And OK, here I was at his beck and call, speeding towards his birthday party, but in fairness, I had been press-ganged into it. I wouldn't have been here if left to my own devices. I exhaled a sigh, and sloshed a generous measure of gin in both glasses. I was glad the rain had stopped, and that I wouldn't get drenched between the car and Bar Thea, because I had made a Herculean effort to look my best. I'd show him! I smiled at my black Empire dress; it was an old dress, but it was Nik's favourite, and underneath I wore black silk knickers, with lace-trimmed stockings, a suspender belt and a matching bra. When we had returned to the house after lunch, John asked me to amuse myself while he chaired a conference call, so I asked Alistair to drive me to Selfridges. I could get used to having a chauffeur. No parking tickets, no public transport. A girl on the MAC counter gave me a free makeover and glued on false eyelashes, and used her influence to wangle a last minute appointment with the in-store hairdresser. That was free as well because the hairdresser was a trainee. She trimmed my fringe and washed a rich chocolate rinse through my hair; it was much darker than my usual shade but I liked it. I scrutinised my reflection in the window. The girl from MAC had been a bit heavy handed on the kohl, and I wasn't sure about the wartime red lipstick. I tweaked my bronze choker and closed my eyes to a whoosh of nausea at the thought of going to Nikki's party.

'Are you going to hand me that drink or not?' John asked, sounding impatient. 'It will have evaporated by the time you give it to me,' he said, brows arched in an expression of frank irritation.

I handed him a glass. There was nothing for me to be nervous about. If Nik wasn't the one for me, then so be it.

I composed myself.

'I can't believe *you* weren't brave enough to stand up to three middle-aged women,' I said, pondering the turn of events that brought us here.

His eyes sharpened, his look was intent. 'I can't make up my mind who you remind me of most – Cleopatra with all that dark eye make-up or the wicked little snake she kept in a basket.'

Snake indeed. I was just about to fire back a reply when I

realised in sudden panic that we had pulled up outside Bar Thea. My heart swooped. I drained my glass, and clutched my bag to my chest. I could always ignore Nik, he would hate that.

Alistair opened the door with a professional flourish, an umbrella held high in the event that it rained in the twenty seconds it would take me to step from the car to the bar entrance. I placed a high-heeled court shoe on the pavement, and raised my eyes to John who glanced down at me, the firm line of his mouth relaxed in a smile. He held out his arm. I flicked a glance at the party-ballooned entrance of the bar, and looped my hand into the crook of his elbow.

'Evie, you look beautiful, absolutely beautiful,' John said, folding his hand over my knuckles. 'Are you all right?'

'Of course I am,' I told him, calm and confident. And surprisingly, I was all right, now that I was here.

A draught of Chanel No. 5 floated towards us as John guided me through the door, hand resting lightly in the small of my back. The bar was packed; Nikki's family had certainly answered the piper's call, I thought idly. I gave the room a sweeping glance, everyone was chatting and laughing above the music drifting low through the overhead speakers. I acknowledged a clutch of regular customers with a wave, and gave a chin raising smile to a couple of Nikki's diamond bejewelled, big-haired aunties. Their animated gossip died to a curious hush when their eyes shifted from my face to John's.

'Evie! You're here, at last!' Lulu said, sailing towards me, looking suntanned and streaky around the neck and cleavage.

She wore a short black leather skirt, and a figure-hugging black wraparound cashmere sweater. Not uncharacteristically, she held a drink in each hand.

'Lexy and Graeme are stuck in traffic, and Miranda got

drenched on her way home from work, so they're not here yet,' she said, eyes darting between John and me.

She placed her drinks on the bar, and threw her head in a spin.

'Alice! Duncan!' she shouted randomly.

'They're here somewhere,' she told me, with an earnest nod.

Duncan's broad chest divided the crowd as he walked towards us. He lowered his head to kiss me.

'My God yer the double of Cleopatra,' Duncan said. 'Only yer prettier.'

John behind me made a 'tish' sound.

'Nik's here, I saw him a minute ago,' Lulu said in a rush, eyes roving the throng. 'Have you ever seen so many kitschy diamonds in one place in your entire life, do you think the aunties are jewel thieves? And will you cop yourself on to the state of this place,' she said, waving an arm around the bar, which was festooned with streamers, balloons and birthday banners.

Alice edged from behind Duncan; her smile broadened when her eyes fell on John. Arms outstretched and with a red Mulberry dangling off her wrist she deftly inched a semi circle around me, and proffered her cheek to John for a kiss.

I scanned the bar wildly. I couldn't see Nik. Where was he? *Where?*

'John! What a lovely surprise! I didn't know Evie was bringing you!' Alice said, twisting a strand of shiny black hair.

She turned and held my hands in hers.

'Evie. We always leave it too long; you look fabulous, so nice of Nikki's mother to track us down. She's a little detective, isn't she?'

I felt a sharp pain in my chest. Nikki was standing at the far side of the bar, dressed all in navy. He stood shoulders back, legs apart, watchful. My mind disintegrated.

Alice prattled on.

'So, I asked Duncan, the green dress or the black? And he said "fine" . . . Fine! What was that supposed to mean?'

I felt a rush of terror. Nik's unblinking eyes held mine. A nervous smile tugged at my lips. Nikki looked . . . *stiff*, not at all like his relaxed self.

He gave me a curt nod.

Lulu barrelled in between Alice and me.

'Let's get a drink, the drinks are free! Did you know that, Evie? Brilliant, isn't it?' Lulu enthused, beside herself with joy. 'Evie, did you know that the booze was free all night?' She raised steadfast brows. 'That doesn't mean to say that I'll take the piss and pig out. I might be a lot of things, but I'm not greedy,' she insisted forcefully. She tipped forward to field my gaze. 'Evie, are you stoned? You look weird, you look . . . spaced out, and kind of in pain. Are you constipated? I'll get you a gin, shall I?' she said, grabbing Alice by the sleeve and leading her towards the bar.

John stood behind me; he pressed his palms on my shoulders. My arms wrapped themselves around my chest.

'Go and speak to him,' John said, his voice warm in my ear.

I couldn't move. I was soldered to the spot. Nikki looked *wild* around the eyes. His expression was frozen and blank, neither a smile not a frown. I couldn't read his mood.

I shrugged my shoulders into John's hands.

'Go on,' John said, giving me a gentle push forward. 'Go to him.'

Although Nik's jaw was tight and his face shadowed with emotion, his stance relaxed. He let out a resigned sigh, dug his hands in his pockets and walked slowly towards me.

Urged by a prod in the back from John, I stumbled forward, a storm of nerves fermenting in my stomach.

Nik took a closing step, drew a deep breath and let it out heavily.

'All right, Evie?' he asked, frowning slightly.

'I'm fine,' I said with edgy politeness.

He looked down at me, not changing his expression.

'You're fine, are you? Well I'm not.'

He reached out and brushed a finger up and down my cheek. My breath caught in my throat, and I slow blinked at his touch.

He ran a hand the length of my arm.

'I've missed you,' he said, eyes shining like polished onyx.

This was more like it. A bit of grovelling, this was what I'd been waiting to hear. I knew all along that he'd come to heel. I raised a defiant chin.

'If you missed me, you should have called me,' I told him bluntly. 'I thought you were bright enough to work that out.'

Ignoring my sarcasm, he lifted my hair from my neck.

It felt . . . good. Instinctively I circled my head into his hands.

'You caused the argument,' he said, eyebrows arched. '*You* should have called *me*.'

My neck whipped straight back. I tried to give an indignant laugh, but it came out as a snorty grunt. I smacked his hand from my hair, and took a backward step.

'Me!' I challenged, giving him a prod in the chest. 'You have the nerve to say that I started the argument? You – you were the one *whoring* right in front of my face!' I snapped with barely restrained fury.

His brows met in astonishment. He opened his mouth to say something but was interrupted when Lulu came steaming excitedly in between us. He caught her elbow, turned her around, and much to her surprise, sent her back where she'd come from.

'Don't you do that to her, she—'

He stepped quickly forward, tangled his fingers in my hair and

444

pulled me to him with an urgent jerkiness, put his mouth over mine and kissed me hard. My body and my mind were obviously operating on totally different frequencies. Because while my mind was silently screaming 'the nerve of him', unbeknown to me, my hands had slipped to his backside and were grinding his hips into mine. My thoughts were in free fall. He broke away from me, took a step back and lifted my chin.

'We need to talk,' he breathed, dark eyes searching mine. 'Outside!'

'Too right we do,' I said, smoothing my hair into place.

My fault? He thinks the argument was my fault?

He took my hand and led me through the restaurant and out the fire exit.

The air was cold and damp. I shivered, rubbed my hands briskly on my forearms and looked to the dark shifting clouds. Nik took off his jacket in awkward slow motion, and draped it over my shoulders. His eyes dropped to my neck where my pulse was pumping double time. He exhaled deeply before speaking.

'OK, we were both to blame,' he said.

'Why didn't you call me?' I asked.

'Why didn't you call me?' he shot back.

I pulled the folds of his jacket around me in a dramatic unnecessary tug.

'I asked you first,' I blurted.

He stared down at me, shoulders slumped in exasperation.

'I didn't call you immediately after our argument because for the life of me I couldn't see where you were coming from. I was furious; I thought you'd caused a big stink over nothing. I didn't want to call you because I thought it would be best to wait until you calmed down, saw sense and well — I assumed you would just stroll through the door for work the next day and the whole

445

stupid episode would be forgotten. But . . . you didn't come in to work. Which annoyed me more than the argument, I felt like crossing the street and dragging you out of your bed, because I knew that's exactly where you would be. And then – my mother decided to go on strike, and that annoyed me more than you not coming to work, because she had bugger all reason to get involved. Not only that, she revved my dad up, and I ended up falling out with him too.' He jammed his hands in his pockets and gave a weary sigh in recollection. 'I had a bloody war on my hands over nothing.'

I struggled to stifle a smirk.

'By the end of day two, I was knackered because I was three staff members down. And as if that wasn't bad enough – I had a blazing row with my Uncle Spiros. He said I didn't know how to treat a woman, and that I didn't deserve you. And that it was no surprise to him that I'd blown it, the surprise was that I hadn't blown it sooner.'

Instinctively I gave an agreeable nod, this made perfect sense to me. This was my point exactly. I know Spiros is a raving mad, machete-waving lunatic chef, but I've often suspected an intellectual telepathy between us.

I folded my arms purposefully, and gave an attentive smile.

'Spiros had said all this before, the day he caught us . . . kissing in the bar, and I'd shot him down. But this time, I thought, perhaps he had a point, perhaps he was right,' he said, looking shy and caught-out.

'And so, I replayed everything in my head, and I found myself admitting that OK, fair enough, perhaps I was *slightly* out of order.'

'Slightly?' I ventured.

'Yes! slightly!' He gave a melodramatic sigh. 'Evie, it's been a *long time* since I've had to consider someone else's feelings, it

446

takes practice,' he said with a weighty nod. 'But you're not totally blameless. We could have sat and discussed things quietly, you could've told me how you felt and I would've listened.'

'Why did you give that girl your mobile number?'

He looked slightly bewildered.

'I didn't,' he said.

'It's on your card, isn't it?'

There was a frozen pause. His eyes grew wide in understanding.

'Evie it's an out of hours number, that's all. Is that it? Is that what all this rubbish has been about?' he asked, in a surprised voice.

'Yes, that's it, but not – not all of it,' I said guardedly, dropping my gaze from his.

He cupped my face, with warm hands.

'What then? What else?' he asked softly.

To my horror, two hot fat tears slid down my cheeks.

'Evie, tell me, what is it? You're a lot of things, but you're not unreasonable, what's going through your head?' he asked, eyes brimming with concern.

'Rob,' I breathed.

He eyed me levelly.

'What about him?' he said, his voice suddenly tight and ragged. 'I thought we'd tied up that loose end.'

'I trusted him . . . I trusted him *completely*.'

'That's the way it should be, you trust someone until they prove you wrong.'

I gave a helpless gesture.

'Oh! I see! I get it! You're thinking that you don't want to get caught out again,' he said, his gaze penetrating and direct. 'You're comparing me to him, for no other reason than a silly notion you've got floating in your head. Despite the fact that I have nothing to hide and that you know everything there is to know about me. Evie . . . You *can* trust me.'

And with those words came a rush of understanding, although I hadn't even realised it myself. Nik was right, that's what all this had been about. I gave a slow nod. I was finding it hard to give one hundred per cent, just in case, in case anything went wrong, and my trust was betrayed and my feelings hurt all over again. He pulled me to him. I pressed my cheek to his chest, and closed my eyes, comforted by the rhythmic beat of his heart.

'Evie, I've missed you so much in the past five days that I've felt physically sick.'

'Why didn't you call me then?' I asked.

'I thought I'd teach you a lesson.'

I took a step back.

'You what?'

'You are a drama queen—'

'A drama queen?' I shot back, rattled.

'And I can't possibly allow you to get your own way all the time. There can only be one head of the household, after all.'

I gave a lofty sniff, and wiped my nose with my fist.

'Oh! Is that so? And which household would that be?'

'Wimbledon,' he said bluntly, 'I thought . . . I mean, I think, we should live there . . . together.'

It took me thirty seconds to consider and process this possibility, and to decide that I liked the idea. I liked it a lot. A flame of excitement ignited inside me. I loved the flat in Wimbledon, and looking at Nik's handsome earnest face, I knew that I loved him too.

He grinned.

'Another reason I didn't call you was because I knew you would be here tonight.'

'Is that right? And how could you be so sure?'

'Because . . . I asked my mum to make sure you were,' he said. 'She was like a missile on a course, determined to hit the target; I knew she would pull it off, I knew you would be here.'

I didn't doubt it.

He spread his arms wide.

'Evie, if I can barely manage five days without you, I think it's time I did something about it. Move in with me, as soon as the cellar and kitchen are finished.'

He pressed a finger to my lips, grinned and closed the step between us.

'Evie, I've never said this to a woman before, so I might be a little . . . rusty.'

His face was a cross between hesitancy and satisfaction. He took a deep breath.

'I love you,' he said.

'You what?' I asked, although I'd heard him loud and clear. I just wanted to hear it again.

He rolled his eyes.

'I love you,' he repeated.

I tilted my head in question.

'Did you just say . . . you loved me?' I asked.

'I did,' he said, finger-tipping my eyebrow.

'Good, that's what I thought you said, because . . . I love you too.'

'You what?

'I love you.'

He grinned idiotically.

'Oh! You do, do you?' he said.

I circled his neck, and drew my head back to look up at him.

'I know I love you because you annoy me so much; if I didn't love you, I wouldn't care enough to be annoyed. And I think of you every waking minute, and you smell nice, and feel nice, and you make me laugh, and you're clever, and ... you can be the head of the household when I'm out,' I told him. 'But when I'm home, I'd like it to be me.'

'We'll see about that, maybe we could have a head of the household rota,' he suggested. 'We'll take it in turns.'

'Mmmm.'

His hands cupped my backside and drew me to him.

'Actually, I have a better plan,' he said, 'it's kind of a ... master plan.'

'You do?'

'Yes! I do!'

'What is it? Am I part of your master plan?'

'You are, very much so.'

'Tell me.'

There was a sheepish expression on his face.

'I would have preferred a more romantic setting,' he said, frowning at the hissing overhead air conditioning unit. 'But I'm suddenly impatient,' he said, casting me a lopsided smile.

'I'm impatient too; will you ever get to the point? Tell me about this plan.'

He kissed me, and reached for his inside jacket pocket, taking the time to flick his thumb over my nipple while he was about it.

He held a little silk box. My breath caught in my throat and my eyes blurred.

'Evie, will you marry me?' he asked, popping the box open.

I stared, speechless, at a beautiful platinum mounted oval shaped diamond.

'I want to spend the rest of my life with you,' he said. 'I know what you're thinking. You're thinking this is too quick, too sudden, but it isn't quick or sudden, not for me. I've known I wanted this for a long time, but I wanted to wait until I thought you were ready. I needed to know you'd got Rob out of your system completely. And you have. So will you, Evie, will you marry me?'

The tender look in his eyes sent the blood rushing through my veins. I gave a slow wordless nod.

'You have to say, "Yes, I'd love to marry you" before I slip the ring on your finger.'

'Yes, I'd love to marry you,' I said, a little breathless, and feeling light-headed with happiness.

He reached for my trembling left hand, and gently wriggled the diamond ring to the base of my finger. I looked at it in over-joyed amazement.

'A good fit,' he said.

He held my hand for a moment, and then folded my knuckles and pressed them to his chest.

'I love you Evie, you mean the world to me,' he said, his voice thick.

'Oh Nik, I love you too.'

He curled his arms around me.

'Let's go upstairs,' he suggested hoarsely, 'to my flat, because . . . I want to show you something,' he said.

I could feel the imprint of what he wanted to show me press-ing against my groin.

'No Nik, it's your birthday party, we should be there,' I told him in a determined voice.

'We will, we'll go . . . later,' he said.

'No! I know what you're like, you get to the point where you don't care and we won't get to the party at all,' I pointed out.

He backed me against the wall.

'An hour,' he said, 'no one will notice.'

'Fifteen minutes,' I bartered.

A look of amazement flashed in his eyes.

'Fifteen minutes! Don't be ridiculous! When have I ever completed the job in fifteen minutes?' he said, edging a hand inside my bra.

'Admittedly you haven't, but I thought maybe you could fast track, kind of like a lunchtime cosmetic surgery procedure.'

His other hand, travelling my leg, found my suspender belt.

'What the hell are you wearing?' he asked, his eyes wide and lustful.

'The full monty,' I admitted.

He grabbed my thigh and lifted it against his hip.

'Evie, you have a choice – here against the fire exit, or in my bed upstairs! No time limit imposed.'

Put like that, and on account of how much it had rained earlier, I opted for the bed upstairs.

I was mortified; it was over an hour and a half before we rejoined the party. As we edged through the door, the bar fell silent. Everyone stood in a smiley semi-circle, as though posing for a building society photo shoot. Blood pinged to my face. They knew, they all knew what Nik and I had been doing, it was obvious. Why had I let him talk me into it? There was an expectant hush. Maria wearing a swishy peach dress broke through the crowd and came slapping towards us, wreathed in smiles, her big hair bobbing.

'Where have you been, my beautiful birthday boy?' she asked, her eyes ranging between Nik and me.

Nik clasped my hand and lifted my arm, as if I'd just won the World Lightweight Boxing Championships.

'Evie and I are engaged to be married,' he announced proudly.

Maria skidded to a halt. The colour drained from her face

and her wide dark eyes dilated. She swayed. My heart leaped into my mouth. I knew what was going to happen, but was too far to reach her. She swooned and slumped to the floor in an undignified peach balloon of chiffon. But she was obviously too excited to faint for long, because a drumbeat later her eyes pinged open. She lay on her back, her upward gaze reverential.

She massaged her chest with a trembling hand, as Nik and his dad levered her to sitting.

'My wedding,' Maria mumbled importantly, scrambling on to all fours. 'Get me my Filofax,' she said, eyes unblinking and darting.

I scanned the bar; I wanted to speak with John.

'Congratulations my darling girl.'

I wheeled.

John spread his arms, I circled his waist.

'I have an engagement present for you,' he said.

'You do?'

He held me at arm's length, and gave a smug smile. His gaze drifted behind me.

'Good lad,' John said, reaching across me to pump Nik's hand. 'Are you packed and ready to go?' John asked Nik.

'I am,' Nik said.

'Evie's suitcase is in my car.'

'Mine is behind the bar,' Nik told John.

'What's going on?' I asked, my head bobbing between them. John eyed his watch.

'You better get going,' John told Nik. 'I'll call the crew and tell them you're on your way to the airport.'

'Going where?' I asked.

'Venice of course,' John said. 'My engagement present.'

Nik put his arm around my shoulder.

'You remember what a great time we had in Venice, Evie?' Nik asked, raised brows above a splitting smile.

I certainly did.

'I thought you might like to do it again,' Nik said, dropping a kiss on my forehead.

He took me by the hand.

'Shall we go?' he asked.

And for once I was speechless.

'Evie! Evie!' Lulu yelled, running in our wake. 'Again? You're engaged again? That's twice this year! Do you have some sort of syndrome? Is this a compulsive disorder or something? Where are you going? When will you be back? Can I come?'

I gave her a backward glance.

'Ignore her,' Nik said.

And I did. Everything except the thought of being with Nik and what happened in Venice emptied from my head. And we were doing it all again. I couldn't wait.

Epilogue

Six Weeks Later

Lulu has been offered a permanent position at the radio station, and hasn't had a cigarette for four-hundred-and-two hours. I'm proud of her. On the downside she no longer does the ironing on a Thursday night.

Tina has agreed to leave Insignia Tours to work with me on John's new venture. Skinflint that she is, she won't resign until she receives her Christmas bonus. John said this is fine, as he's committed to events operated by Insignia Tours for the next six months.

Lexy emailed me her CV. She said if she can look after twin girls, then she can look after corporate groups. The thing is her CV is riddled with lies and I told her so, only to be sharply informed that she copied all the lies from *my* CV.

Mum and Dad are home, but only for a month. They're going to Kenya to build a school. Frankly, I have mixed feelings about this, because Mum has never so much as fitted a curtain pole. Still, I'm sure they know what they're doing.

Rob is living with Cassie. I know this because Cassie wrote

me a letter. She more or less thanked me for dumping Rob. I wrote back to tell her it was my pleasure. A wife in the background is a fabulous contraceptive.

The builders working on the Wimbledon flat don't seem to be making much progress. So out of curiosity I've installed a hidden camera. I'm not spying on them; of course I'm not, I just want to determine what actually constitutes a tea break. Nikki said if the builders find the camera he'll make sure they know I installed it. Which is a bit of a cheek, as I've caught him several times, beer in hand, bent over my laptop, watching the tape.

Maria (big sigh) . . . She *will* change! I'm sure of it! She can't possibly maintain this level of interest in everything I do. She will tire of texting and phoning me sometimes upward of twenty times a day. She will stop ordering clothes for me from her catalogue, and taking photographs of me, she will, of course she will. But the thing is, Nik told me not to hold my breath, because Maria has been stalking him for twenty-nine years. I find myself fantasising about Maria deserting the family. I enjoy this fantasy so much that I have several versions of it. These fantasies have become a lifeline, often sending me to sleep at night.

OK, the first fantasy is quite boring. Basically it's that Maria joins the Red Cross and goes to work in one of these really faraway places where it's a seven-day mule ride to the nearest airport and no direct flights to London. So she doesn't come home to visit very often.

The second fantasy has more of an air of finality to it. Nik's dad wakes to find a letter from Maria explaining she's met someone else and that she's gone to live in South America and that she's never coming back.

But as I said, I'm sure she'll change. And as an amazing fortunate coincidence Josephine Bonaparte had serious mother-in-law problems, and so I'm hoping Josephine's biography will offer me some advice on how to deal with Maria, pre-supposing that my fantasies are never realised.

And as for Nikki, my *fiancé*. Why didn't I recognise the blatantly obvious fact that I was truly madly deeply in love with my good friend? And that he felt exactly the same way about me. I must have been blind. With Nik it's *real* love, a love born from friendship, familiarity and above all else *trust*. We know everything there is to know about each other. Although he doesn't know I accidently reversed into the bus stop in his car, but the dent is only the size of a beer mat, so not worth mentioning or arguing over.

Nikki Joanou is the love of my life, my *raison d'être*. An invisible cord draws me to him, heart and soul. This randy handsome Adonis is my destiny, of that I am absolutely positive. I simply cannot get enough of him. Every nerve ending in my body tingles and jives when he puts his arms around me (like he's doing right now). When he kisses me, a cascading torrent of excitement erupts and percolates in my chest. My obsession with him is both physical and psychosomatic. I'm driven by and demented with lust. My fiancé, Nikki Joanou, doesn't have a normal willie like any other bloke I've ever known. Nikki Joanou has a bloody magic wand . . .

You've heard it all before, I know, but I mean it this time.

VENICE

Evie's Helpful Travel Facts

✤ Beware of the delicious rum punch in Barbados. What happens is that you hear yourself say 'this is delicious, it's so fruity and refreshing and tasty,' – and it is – but then oddly your vision blurs, your lips go numb, and your head spins, and you slip into unconsciousness, and wake up with sunstroke. Also, from a logistical viewpoint, it isn't possible to hide a pitcher of margarita under your arm to take home when the bar closes in the evening, no matter how wide your sleeves are. And anyway, the bars reopen before you've sobered up and got out of bed so it's no big deal.

✤ A tip for looking good on the beach is to sunbathe next to someone who is much fatter than you. The advantage of staying in an all-inclusive resort with a 24/7 buffet is that this is relatively easy to do, because there are loads of enormous people around. I find this very uplifting and cheering, and much more effective than torturing over which cut of bikini makes you look slimmest.

✤ In Marrakech do not mess around with the jars of lip gloss in the market, unless you find a colour you absolutely love, because it stains your fingers and your lips for about three and a half months. The eyeliner comes in pallet form; under no circumstances should you allow the girl on the stall to put it on you, unless you don't mind looking like Jack Sparrow.

✥ In Moroccan restaurants the staff will never admit that they don't understand what you are saying. So that when you order a diet Coke, you may be given a pot of tea. My advice is to just drink the tea. Because trying to reinforce your diet Coke order is exhausting and pointless, because you'll end up with a plate of cakes, a chicken casserole, a pipe, and a waiter who is convinced you fancy him.

✥ In Dublin, if you don't have enough money for both a take-away *and* a taxi back to your hotel, you should order a pizza in person and ask if you can be delivered to your hotel on the motorbike together with the pizza. In most cities this would be considered a piss-take. But the Irish are nothing if not accommodating. When I asked to be delivered to my hotel with my slim crust meat feast, the bloke in the shop was delighted to oblige. And of course I saved the cab fare (perhaps I should start offering financial services advice).

✥ In Dublin be careful who you ask for directions. Inexplicably some Irish people think it's better to get you hopelessly lost than to admit that they don't know where your hotel is. Directions are given with such friendly conviction that you truly believe that they know what they're talking about. You're halfway out of the city and stumbling along some random dirt track, tearful and knackered, before you've tumbled them for the liar they are.

✥ In Amsterdam you are more likely to be mowed down and killed by a bicycle than anywhere else in the world. I almost was, twice! Be careful!

✥ Before travelling to Venice you should stock up on travel-sickness pills and condoms, especially if you are single. I didn't see one bad-looking water taxi driver, they were all gorgeous (not that I was perving or anything). And Lulu says there is no such thing as an Italian man with a small willie, so if you find one you like, grab him! Obviously the more water taxis you jump on, the larger the spectrum of selection.

VENICE

The Alternative Travel Quiz

1. Which Venetian painter at the age of ninety and after completing over 100 brilliant paintings is famous for saying, 'I'm finally beginning to learn how to paint?'
   a) Titian
   b) Michelangelo
   c) Zuccato

2. Which Venetian citizen admitted in his autobiography to having had over 122 affairs?
   a) Casanova
   b) Pavarotti
   c) Gino d'Acampo

3. What is the name of the most famous Italian explorer, born in the Republic of Venice?
   a) Gina Lollobrigida
   b) Marco Polo
   c) Theresa Viglione

4. On average how many tourists a day visit the city of Venice?
   a) 25,000
   b) 50,000
   c) 6,000

5. When the San Marco bell tower measuring 275 feet once collapsed, who was the only unfortunate victim?
   a) The local tax inspector
   b) My sister–in–law
   c) The bell tower's caretaker's cat

6. What drastic measures does legend suggest that the Chief Magistrate (the Doge of Venice) took to ensure the magnificent San Marco Clock Tower was never replicated?
   a) Burned the Artisans' technical drawings
   b) Made the Artisans blind
   c) Denied European architects access to Piazza San Marco

7. What is it forbidden to do in any part of Venice?
   a) Ride a bike
   b) Ride a man
   c) Ride a horse

8. Which of the following blockbuster movies was filmed in Venice?
   a) *The Italian Job*, starring Charlize Theron and Mark Wahlberg
   b) *Only You*, starring Marisa Tomei and Robert Downey Junior
   c) *The Tourist*, staring Angelina Jolie and Johnny Depp

9. Which famous wine region lies north of Venice?
   a) Prosecco
   b) Champagne
   c) Aquitaine

10. What was considered to be one of the main benefits of wearing a mask during the Venice Carnival (a tradition dating back to the middle ages)?
    a) To camouflage blemished skin
    b) To conceal one's identity
    c) To act as a sunscreen

Answers

1 (a)* Now I find this truly inspiring because I have always been embarrassed by the fact that I failed three driving tests. And that after six golf lessons I still cannot make contact with the ball. By the age of ninety I'm certain I will be a crack golfer and I will have a maximum no claims insurance bonus (well, almost . . . sort of).

2 (a) OK, however many affairs a guy admits to, you have to double it to come anywhere near close to the truth; everyone knows that. So by my reckoning Casanova had a quarter of a million affairs. (Big gulp of admiration/disgust.) Errr . . . was there an STI clinic in Renaissance Venice?

3 (b) Frankly, I'm surprised that most famous explorers are men, because women have a much better sense of direction. Men will not admit to being lost, whereas women are happy to ask for directions. If I was 'exploring' the Arctic or anywhere like that, there's no way I would go without downloading the satnav application on my iPhone.

4 (b) A staggering truth and doesn't surprise me in the slightest.

5 (c) Which is a pity because I quite like cats.

6 (b) OK, this is seriously out of order. Where the hell was the clock tower HR department when all this was going on?

7 (a) Hear, hear! In fact I can't help but think London would be a better place without all these show-offy cyclists whizzing around, showing the rest of us up for taxi-hopping.

8   Trick question to see if you're still awake and paying attention. The answer is 'all three'. How irritating am I?

9 (a) I made up this question inspired by the bottle of Prosecco in my gym bag. God bless the lush rolling hills of Conegliano and Valdobbiadene.

10 (b) This was an amazing concept. The idea was to break down all social barriers. Princes could flirt with barmaids and Dukes could cavort with house servants – even nuns were known to go out on the pull. Now let's be honest, girls: have there been times when you've woken up next to someone who would have looked so much more appealing if they'd been wearing a mask?

*Historians are not exactly certain when Titian was born – he may have been in his eighties when he died. Gordon Brown and David Cameron actually had a fall out about it (ridiculous).